ALSO BY NANCY BILYEAU

The Chalice

The Crown

THE
TAPESTRY

NANCY BILYEAU

TOUCHSTONE

NEW YORK   LONDON   TORONTO   SYDNEY   NEW DELHI

Touchstone
An Imprint of Simon & Schuster, Inc.
1230 Avenue of the Americas
New York, NY 10020

First Touchstone hardcover edition March 2015

TOUCHSTONE and colophon are registered trademarks of Simon & Schuster, Inc.

For information about special discounts for bulk purchases, please contact Simon & Schuster Special Sales at 1-866-506-1949 or business@simonandschuster.com.

The Simon & Schuster Speakers Bureau can bring authors to your live event. For more information or to book an event contact the Simon & Schuster Speakers Bureau at 1-866-248-3049 or visit our website at www.simonspeakers.com.

Interior design by Akasha Archer

Manufactured in the United States of America

10   9   8   7   6   5   4   3   2   1

Library of Congress Cataloging-in-Publication Data
  Bilyeau, Nancy.
    The tapestry : a novel / Nancy Bilyeau.—First Touchstone hardcover edition.
    pages ;   cm
  "Touchstone fiction original hardcover."
  "A Touchstone book."
  1. Great Britain—History—Tudors, 1485–1603—Fiction. I. Title.
  PS3602.I49T37 2015
  813'.6—dc23
                                                    2014032751

ISBN 978-1-4767-5637-0
ISBN 978-1-4767-5639-4 (ebook)

In memory of the nuns and friars and monks
of Tudor England

THE
TAPESTRY

1

I was once told that whenever I felt suspicious of someone's intent, no matter how faintly, I should trust that instinct, but since the man who issued this advice had himself tried to kill me, and nearly succeeded, it was difficult to know how much weight to give his words.

I felt this distrust in a place where all others seemed at ease, as I followed a page through the tall, gleaming rooms of the Palace of Whitehall, filled with the most prosperous subjects of King Henry VIII. To anyone else, it would seem the safest place in all of England.

But not to me. Never to me.

Only eight days earlier I'd received the summons, calling me back to London, the city where I had seen much cruelty and death. I read it in my small house on the High Street of Dartford, where I had come to serve as a novice at its priory of Dominican sisters and hoped and prayed to prove my worthiness to take vows and become a Bride of Christ. But, two years ago, by the king's command, our exquisite priory was torn down, and I was cast out with the others.

"This missive is from the king's council, Sister Joanna," said Gregory, pushing it into my hands as if it were a loaf pulled fresh from the oven that was singeing his fingertips. Gregory was a clerk in the town. He married the vintner's daughter just after Candlemas Day, and his face soon thickened, like a hunting dog turns fat and sleek when brought into the house at season's end. But Gregory, no matter his station now, once served as porter to our priory and continued to take an interest in my welfare. He still called me Sister. When a letter came to town bearing the royal seal, Gregory insisted on delivering it to me.

I thanked him and closed the door on the bright noise of the High Street. My fingers heavy with dread, I found a knife to break the beeswax seal. It was light brown, with these words circling the figure of a man on horseback, holding sword and shield: "Henry the Eighth, by the grace of God, of England and France and Ireland King, Defender of the Faith, and on Earth, of the English and Irish Church, Supreme Head."

I smoothed the sheet of thick, creamy vellum onto my table. "Touching on the matter of the commission of tapestry, Mistress Joanna Stafford, daughter of Sir Richard Stafford, is hereby summoned to the Palace of Whitehall, in the third week of April in the Year of Our Lord 1540, to wait upon the Keeper of the Great Wardrobe of His Majesty, King Henry the Eighth, and receive the King's command."

I was dismayed but could not say I was surprised. I knew full well that the king took an interest in my tapestries. Bishop Stephen Gardiner had told me, with his usual gleam of bland menace, that King Henry was pleased with *The Rise of the Phoenix*, the first tapestry I wove on my own after leaving the priory. I sold it to Anne of Cleves, who came to our kingdom to become the fourth wife of Henry VIII, and she made a gift of it to him. Said Bishop Gardiner, "His Majesty dislikes everything about his new queen, with one exception: the present of the phoenix tapestry."

A week after Bishop Gardiner told me that, the first letter from the king's court appeared. Unsigned and unsealed, it was a simple request for my presence at court to speak of tapestries.

If I were of a more sanguine humor, I might find comedy in this. Henry VIII wished to commission a tapestry from a woman who'd treasonably opposed him, not once but twice. The king now lived because of what I did—or, rather, what I failed to do. Yet he would never know any of this history, never realize how tightly our fates were intertwined. No, to Henry VIII, I was but a distant cousin with an intriguing talent for weaving.

And the truth was, I *did* have another tapestry planned. I'd ordered a drawing from Brussels of *The Sorrow of Niobe* but had not yet stretched it on the loom. I did not wish to sell this one to the royal couple. For that and other reasons, I failed to respond to the first royal summons. Beset by a troubled marriage and rumors of foreign invasion, His Majesty King Henry VIII would forget about me, surely?

It seemed he would not.

Not only was the second summons worded more forcefully, it was signed. As I stared at the precise strokes of ink slanting across the vellum, my throat tightened. Henry VIII did not write the command himself, of course. One of his secretaries composed the words. But the paper was signed by a different hand. The script was precise and clear, with each curved letter slanted to precisely the same height: *Thomas Cromwell, Lord Privy Seal.* The king's chief minister, the man whom we, the faithful of God's Holy Church, hated and feared above all other men, even the king.

I was in need of advice.

The summons carried a legal import, but I could not bring this matter to the constable of Dartford. Geoffrey Scovill was recently bereaved and still suffering. Three months ago, I stood with him beside the grave of his wife, Beatrice; weeks later, I attempted to offer further condolences, but was met with cold silence. I could not blame him, considering my role in his circumstances. He came to Dartford because of me. I knew that he'd wished to marry, and at times Geoffrey evoked strong feelings in me—equal parts longing and shame—but we often quarreled and clashed. It was Edmund Sommerville, a one-time friar in the Dominican Order, sensitive, erudite and kind, whom I chose to marry. Geoffrey then wed Beatrice, my friend and fellow novice, who had loved him from the first moment she saw him. Now Edmund was gone and Beatrice was with God. Constable Scovill and I were both alone, and lonely, but we did not turn to each other.

What should I do about the royal summons? I prayed for hours that day and far into the night, touching no food or drink. If only that feeling of certainty would fill me, the grace of God's undoubted wisdom. But it didn't come; I was unworthy. When morning came, I hurried up the High Street to Holy Trinity Church. There, the way forward could be revealed.

I always took a seat near the chantry chapel. Like a hand that by force of habit drifts to the ridge of a scar, my gaze lingered on the back chantry wall once beautified by a mural of Saint George. More than a year ago, the painting was whitewashed over, at the same time that the candles were snuffed and the altar stripped, but if I squinted a bit, I could still detect the outline of the saint on horseback, sword raised to fight the dragon.

Father William Mote, he who must disseminate the New Learning, preached a dry, cautious sermon that day. Ever since Parliament passed the Act of Six Articles, England no longer followed Martin Luther's lead away from the Catholic Church. Yet, to my disappointment, there seemed no hope of returning to obedience to Rome, either. We now took some unfathomable middle path. From priests and landowners to humblest tinkers and carpenters, no one in Dartford could discern where we headed as a kingdom. But we did know that any mistake in religious practice, no matter how small, could bring savage royal punishment: a chopped hand was the best consequence.

Father William's voice rose at the end of his sermon. "Not enough of you have opened the Great Bible kept at this very altar by instruction of Lord Privy Seal Thomas Cromwell and Archbishop of Canterbury Thomas Cranmer." He pounded on the platform, his fist nearly striking the massive book resting atop it. This, at least, he was sure of. "You dishonor God, the creator of all things, if you do not shun evil and ignorance and idolatry for the profound wisdom of Scripture, written here for you in English."

There were a few sighs, a few shrugs. The people of Dartford were a timid lot, willing to obey the king, but only a handful had been taught to read. Many could write their own names and add sums. Long stories of Scripture were beyond them.

"Christ deliver us," whispered a woman to my left.

It was Sister Eleanor, unable to suppress her disgust over Father William's outburst. When the king's men closed our priory, six of the sisters, unwilling to forsake their vocation, formed a community in a house outside town. Sister Eleanor did not officiate over them as prioress—we no longer had a prioress—but she was the oldest of the sisters.

After Mass, I beckoned to her in the back of church. Startled, Sister Eleanor took a moment to follow me. She was uncomfortable in my presence, and always had been. My disposition was too riotous for her severe spirit. But it was that severity I now required.

Outside the church, it was raining, and we pressed against the wall so that its slanted roof would protect us. I slipped her the summons.

Sister Eleanor read it in seconds and made the sign of the cross.

"The king would commission you?" she asked.

"It seems so, Sister."

"But your tapestries are a God-given talent," she said. "To adorn the walls of the apostate king with one of your gifts . . . it is not to be borne."

"To refuse to serve King Henry would bring criticism," I pointed out. "Men of the court could follow. Even soldiers."

Sister Eleanor clasped my hands. Her fingertips, callused from the labor of the nuns' farm, dug grooves into mine, but I did not flinch. "Leave your house in town and come to us, Sister Joanna," she urged. "You know you should live among us again—we are only safe if we are together."

"I would not carry such risk to your house, Sister."

Sister Eleanor said, "You would show yourself to no one, as if you were still enclosed. The king and his men would not know where you were." Still gripping my hands, Sister Eleanor stepped back, heedless of the rain spattering her capped head. "But should they find you, we will be at your side. God in His Mercy will protect us. We will *not* submit."

I gently pulled my hands from hers, murmuring, "I thank you for your valuable counsel, Sister. Christ and the Virgin be with you."

Before I'd reached the other side of the High Street, leaping over the spreading puddles, my decision was made. I could never expose the sisters of Dartford to danger. Such hot, eager anger in Sister Eleanor's eyes—it sprang up because she had never witnessed firsthand the wrath of the king. I had.

To face royal condemnation alone—could I do that? Certainly. I had done it before. But *would* I? No. For there was a pressing reason to conform to the royal will. Arthur. I wanted to once again raise the orphaned son of my cousin Margaret Bulmer.

I'd written letter after letter to Margaret's brother, the head of our family, Lord Henry Stafford, asking that Arthur, now eight, be returned to me in Dartford. I'd sent the boy north to Stafford Castle before leaving England. Now, despite the fact that he was a difficult child to raise, I missed Arthur greatly. His ready laughter, his determined step, I ached for them in my silent house. As much as it was possible to plan in a time of chaos, I planned to lead a quiet life: weave tapestries, honor friends, submit to God's will. It would be an honorable existence; after all, I was the daughter of Sir Richard Stafford and Isabella Montagna. Living without honor was unthinkable. But there would be no more dangerous quests or conspiracies. My fervent hope was never again to hear the word *prophecy*, nor to find myself among spies, seers, and necromancers. That was the world of fear, of darkness. I wanted only light.

In devoting myself to another person, to Arthur, if I could bring that about, I would be truly blessed. I wanted to serve Arthur, too, in a way that only I, the guardian of the secrets of his parentage, could. It was so important that he learn how precious his mother was, learn of her kindness and her courage. I feared that as Arthur grew older, the horror of her death—burned to death for treason in Smithfield before the mob—would overshadow all.

At first, Cousin Henry refused to return him—stating again that he had never understood why my father placed Arthur with me, an unmarried woman of no prospects, rather than with Henry's own large family—but of late I'd detected a softening. And he let slip in one letter that Arthur missed me. If I were the holder of a royal commission in tapestries, the head of my own budding enterprise, my cousin might relent. He hated trade, but he hated failure more.

"Your storm and fury"—that is how Beatrice once described my nature. But, for the sake of that small boy, I would quiet my storms. Now that I'd been forced to accept the triumph of King Henry and Thomas Cromwell, there would be no cause for anger. I'd travel to Whitehall, see no one but the wardrobe master who managed the king's tapestries, and slip back home.

Thus I resolved to go on this journey. How could I know that it was not a journey but a dance? I was taking the first step forward on a vast dance floor, and on the other side, a partner would emerge from the darkest shadows to meet me—a partner who hungered for nothing more than for my death.

2

Moments after I made up my mind to go to court, a knock sounded at the door. It was my onetime novice mistress, Sister Agatha, now Mistress Gwinn, married to the most prosperous farmer in town and a devoted gossip.

"Why would you have occasion to speak to Sister Eleanor?" she asked, her eyes bright with interest.

I decided to tell her of my decision to go to Whitehall. Unlike Sister Eleanor, Agatha was delighted. She had been at my side when Anne of Cleve's page came to Dartford to purchase the phoenix tapestry. She applauded then—and did now.

But her excitement brought complication. Agatha insisted that she and her husband, Master Oliver Gwinn, escort me to Whitehall, along with some menservants. My protests were brushed aside. "You cannot ride to London, a solitary woman—that is unheard of," she exclaimed. I'd done so before, the first time when still a novice professed at Dartford priory. I left without permission, determined to stand by the side of Margaret as she faced her execution at Smithfield, and I was arrested there. Months later I was sent back to the nuns, and my novice mistress was among those who chastised me. Perhaps Agatha had forgotten. All of our lives had changed greatly in the last three years.

We departed for London at dawn, the mist disappearing before we'd ridden past Dartford's apple orchards. It promised to be a day of unbroken sun. "So propitious for our journey, so propitious," said

Agatha, riding alongside her husband. Master Oliver Gwinn raised her plump hand to his lips and kissed it.

It was fortunate, indeed, that the Gwinns received permission from the court to remain married. Like a smattering of other nuns, she had taken a husband after the priories were brought down. But then came those new laws of faith. One of the acts of the Six Articles forbade any person who had taken vows of chastity in a religious order from ever marrying. The penalty was death by hanging.

Would that have been our fate, Edmund's and mine, if we had married last year? A former friar and a former novice, who came within moments of joining before God. But we were stopped as the news reached Dartford of the act of Six Articles. Hurled into a limbo created by a king.

The night before I set out for Whitehall, Edmund appeared in my dream. It seemed to be during our earliest time, bound together once more, charged by Bishop Stephen Gardiner with a dangerous quest, trusting and not trusting. Now the details of the dream had broken apart like ice on a warming river, and I was relieved at its dissolution. Seeing Edmund in my dream had brought back the pain I so much wanted to overcome.

We rode by grasslands and patches of woods and then a tame field opened up between the trees. A team of two oxen pulled a plow that clawed into the soil, turning it over for planting. A young man strode behind the plow, as was common, but he was not alone. A red-haired woman walked with him, a baby balanced in a cloth slung and tied around her. She laughed at something and their child caught the sound of it and echoed in a half laugh, half cry. A little hand escaped from the cloth to wave at the parents, wildly.

I shifted in the saddle to fix my gaze on the road to London.

We stopped for dinner earlier than I would have, if the time had been my choosing. In fact, I would have waited until we reached Southwark and the home of Master Gwinn's cousin. Our plan was to stay there, rest, and then to ride the rest of the way tomorrow for presentation at Whitehall first thing in the morning. But Agatha and her husband, devoted eaters, insisted on a picnic and a place was found. Servants unwrapped sliced leg of mutton, capon pasty, and manchet bread to put before us.

"You've grown too thin," said Agatha, scolding, as she pushed a slice of bread into my hand.

I forced myself to nibble food as I listened to the Gwinns' amiable chatter. Agatha had never been to London before; most of her adult life was spent in our strict Dominican order. She peppered her husband with questions, which, between bites, he answered time and again with "Soon enough you will see." The sun was warm on my limbs as I sat on their blanket beside a tall tree of unfurling leaves. I would always be apart, I knew that. I was twenty-nine years old. Never for me the march beside a husband in new soil, or brushing crumbs of pasty from his beard, as Agatha did now. But I could have these peaceful moments of friendship. It would be enough.

My serenity was ripped away when Master Gwinn, draining his tankard of ale, said to his wife, "It will not be a simple matter to find another constable of Scovill's ability."

"Geoffrey Scovill is leaving?" I asked, my stomach a knot.

"Yes, by end of summer."

"But why?"

Master Gwinn said, "No reason or destination given, only that he will move on. It is for the best, perhaps, for there's grumbling about a constable who is rarely seen in the town."

I leaped to my feet, indignant. "Have they no decency, these men who grumble? Don't they know of his dead wife, his stillborn child?"

Master Gwinn looked up at me, shading his eyes from the sun with his grease-stained hand. "We all of us honor the constable's loss, and especially those who have buried wives." Agatha patted his arm. "But Scovill may be able to perform his duties better in a new town, away from memories."

I was seized by a powerful desire to jump onto my horse and ride to Dartford, to comfort Geoffrey, make amends, *something*. But the urge passed. I could do Constable Scovill no greater service than to stay away from him.

When the Gwinns had finally finished every crumb of dinner, we set out again, the sun nearing its highest point. Soon we reached Southwark, the sprawling borough on the other side of the Thames from the City of London. The roads thickened with others on horseback, with wagons, with young apprentices on foot. We passed a few shops and a great many taverns.

It was in front of one tavern, at a sharp corner of the road, that I first felt something. I turned, quickly, to see . . . what? Who? The inn's shutters were thrown open and shiny-faced men leaned out of the windows, enjoying the spring day while they gulped their ale. Nothing looked amiss.

I nudged my horse to catch up to the Gwinns. But before my mare had plodded five minutes more up the road, I swiveled again. There was no mistaking the feeling this time: someone watched me, someone followed. But when I turned, no one met my eyes. Every man and woman seemed bent on their own ordinary business.

Was it because we neared London that I felt apprehension? My usual dread of the capital city and the king's court was laced with fresh turmoil over the departure of Geoffrey Scovill. But as much as I tried to assure myself that must be it, I sensed something else. Something threatening.

The string of shops and taverns had given way to a foul-looking marsh and, beyond that, the top of London Bridge, stretching across the Thames in the distance. I'd thought myself well prepared, but as London loomed, a sour dread clutched my stomach. Between that and my jangled nerves over being watched, I felt rather dizzy. I tried to breathe deeply, to steady myself, but it only served to suck in deeper the odor from a nearby tanning pit.

When I first heard it, the rumbling was a welcome distraction. It resembled thunder—but that was impossible. It was a bright, cloudless afternoon. Tightening my hands on the reins, I slowed my horse to peer up into the sky and then all around us. The Gwinns heard it, too; Master Gwinn pointed at a long, high brick wall south of the marsh. Handsome brick towers rose beyond it. Perhaps this was someone's fine manor house. A faint cloud of dust hovered just above the wall—it seemed somehow connected to the rumbling.

"Shall we have a look?" asked Master Gwinn, his face crinkled with curiosity. Agatha agreed at once. Their lives in Dartford were predictable, prescribed. They were happily caught up in the strange sights and sounds of our journey.

Turning points are not always evident to us when they appear. How different everything might have been for me if I had not nodded in agreement and then ridden with my friends to discover what was on the other side of that wall. But I perceived no harm in it. No harm at all.

We fell in behind a group of men scrambling through an opening in the wall. We had entered a large, square courtyard. But despite the fact that this was a handsome property, worthy of careful tending, all was in disarray. A mountain of rubble stood in the middle of the courtyard. Planks of wood stretched across another part of it. Men shouted to one another. I heard the bellow of animals.

"Secure the ropes, ye bastards!" screamed a man. "And clear the path if ye want to live."

The dust settled, and I could make out a long row of oxen. These were not like the farm stock I'd seen in a field earlier this day, but massive animals, chained to one another. Three of the walls of the courtyard stood, but the fourth had collapsed, and not by some failure of construction. These men must have torn it down. At the opposite side of the courtyard a stone structure abutting the main house was half collapsed. The workers now fastened ropes round the base of a tower that still stood at the base of that structure, a tall one with a cross atop it. As the workers pushed one another out of the way to clear a path between the oxen and tower, I realized, with a sickening rush, that the stone structure—tower and all—that man and beast struggled to demolish was a church. Why did no one protect it? I peered at the windows of the magnificent main house and realized they were empty of glass. This place had been stripped and abandoned.

Master Oliver Gwinn, who had bent down to speak to someone standing amid the rubble, turned to his wife and me, his face grim.

"Bermondsey Abbey," he said.

I knew of Bermondsey Abbey, as did every nun, monk, and friar. It was a revered Cluniac house, where once even queens lived in retirement, such as Elizabeth Woodville and Catherine of Valois. The abbey's monks had obviously been ejected, the house's precious belongings hauled to the royal treasury. Now the walls themselves must come down. It was happening from one end of England to the other, the destruction of the monasteries. My own beloved Dartford house was demolished down to the last brick. The king then ordered the raising of a grand manor house on the same land.

But I had not witnessed my priory's annihilation; all the nuns and friars stayed away, consumed with grief. It would have been like witnessing a murder.

The man atop the wagon whipped the oxen, hard. The animals strained forward, and a thick chain grew taut and trembled. But the tower on the other end of the chain did not move.

"Come down," screamed the ox driver, standing to whip yet more. *"Down."*

There was a snap, followed by a groan, and a centuries' old tower crumbled. Almost nothing remained now of the church of Bermondsey Abbey. Here was the will of Henry VIII and of Thomas Cromwell—they destroyed what was good and holy, and God did nothing to punish them.

A new cry rose a moment later, as dust settled again. A pale female head peered above the ravaged base of the tower. For a terrible instant I thought it was a woman who had been trapped inside the structure. But then I realized what it was: a statue of a saint.

"No, Joanna, don't," said Agatha. But I was already going forward, steering my horse around the people and piles of broken rock to get closer.

She was beautiful—a pure, marble woman clutching a book to her bosom. It seemed a miracle that she survived the wreckage. Perhaps it was a sign?

A snickering raced around the knot of men who'd also drawn closer. Something was about to happen.

"No." It was half groan and half gasp. No one paid heed.

A young man ran past me, holding something. The others stood aside to clear the way for him. He charged toward the statue, raising the object, which I realized was a large hammer.

With a grunt, he slammed his hammer into the saint's face. Where there had once been eyes and nose was a savage, gaping hole.

"Death to all Papists!" he shouted.

3

The toppling of the abbey church set forth a vicious glee among the people of Southwark, like a torrent of bright blood after a scab is ripped away.

The destruction had quite another effect on me.

A devouring rage dampened my senses. The laughter of the crowd faded. The odors I always choked on in Southwark and London—privy buckets, rotting food, ale, and burning lye—receded. The faces of those surrounding me blurred, with one exception: Agatha stared back at me, her hand clamped over her nose and mouth, as if her face had been mutilated and not that of the marble girl of the tower.

A crowd of men swarmed to the tower. When the young man swung back his hammer to strike the statue again, another grabbed it from him. Laughing, the two of them fought over the weapon. A heavyset man pushed his way to the front of the crowd, pulled out a long knife, and raised it in an exaggerated arc, aiming for the girl's marble breast. He turned and leered to the crowd. Hoots of laughter sounded.

How I wanted to stop them. Words of condemnation—angry and accusatory—burned my tongue. I dug my nails into my palms to force myself to stay silent. The old Joanna Stafford would have plunged into the fray. But I had sworn to govern myself with more caution. I must not call attention to our party. What would a crowd of at least fifty tough and coarsened men who hated Rome do to two women who'd once served in a Dominican priory, defended only by a farmer in middle years and two country servants?

"Cease this at once," shouted a voice. I touched my lips, unsure if I'd been the one to say it, but it was a man who'd given the order. And he was obeyed. The ruffian lowered his knife from the statue.

I turned in the saddle to see. The man who stepped forward wore a plain, dark doublet and hose; he was hatless, and gray streaks lightened his hair, which must have once been as black as mine. He carried a bound book under his left arm. As he approached the tower, the mob fell back, sullen-faced. A few of them made a great show of resuming their tasks on the site.

Master Gwinn leaned down again to make inquiry and then told us, "That man is an agent of the Court of Augmentations."

"A court?" Agatha asked, bewildered.

"Not now. We must leave—we have no place here," said Oliver Gwinn with unusual curtness.

My fingers tightened on the reins. I knew what the court was and what this man represented. Thomas Cromwell had created it to administer the revenues of the monasteries. "Court of Augmentations." Such fine words to describe *theft*, to justify taking all the holy objects within the abbey churches, the chalices and plate and books and illuminated manuscripts, along with all the land. Which toady of the king's would receive Bermondsey as a reward for his loyalty?

Master Gwinn paused to wipe his face with a cloth as soon as we were clear of the fallen abbey, sagging in his saddle with relief.

We were safe now, but I was not glad of it. I was ashamed. Cromwell's agent hadn't stopped the mob from defiling the woman's statue because it was the right thing to do but in order to preserve a valuable piece of pillage. A passage of Scripture flooded my thoughts, about the apostle Peter's anguish after Jesus was taken. "I do not know that man," Peter swore to those who pointed at him in the courtyard of Gethsemane, and then, when he realized he had denied Jesus Christ out of fear and weakness, just as had been predicted, he wept. Hot salty tears pricked my own eyes. I brushed them back with a furious hand.

"Stop," I called out. I was so loud Agatha jumped in her saddle. Everyone halted.

"I will go to Whitehall today—or not at all," I said.

"Mistress Joanna, my cousin's house is not far from here," said Master Gwinn. "We are expected. We'll stay there tonight and escort you to the palace tomorrow morning, as planned."

"No. Today or not at all."

Agatha nudged her horse to get closer. "Joanna, I know how disturbed you are, and I share your sentiment. But we need to rest, all of us. You cannot go to a king's palace in those clothes." She pointed at my garments—a plain, dark gray riding kirtle and bodice, layered with the dirt of the road. In the travel satchel carried by a Gwinn servant were my finest clothes, appropriate for the occasion.

I said in a rush, "It does not matter what I wear, and after what we've witnessed, I could not bear to don finery to go before the royal household. With all my soul, I do not wish to proceed at all." Arthur's round face appeared in my mind. "But there are sound reasons to continue. If you would be so good as to point the way to London Bridge, I can manage the route to Whitehall alone. You can ride to your cousin's house to rest, or return to Dartford, whatever you wish."

After a hushed conversation, the Gwinns, obviously reluctant, said they would accompany me to Whitehall this afternoon.

"But what if no one will see you today?" Agatha asked.

"Then I leave Whitehall having carried out my duty, which was to wait upon the keeper of the wardrobe. The summons didn't say how long I had to wait. An hour or two will do. If he will not see me, so be it."

Master Gwinn opened his mouth to say something more, but Agatha shook her head. She knew how little likelihood there was of my altering course.

Riding faster now—or as fast as we could up crowded streets—we made our way to London Bridge. As the horses plodded through that square tunnel stretching across the Thames, it happened. The sensation returned. While I was near blind with rage in Southwark, I had no awareness of being observed. But now that my anger had banked, I felt eyes burning into the back of my head once more. I didn't bother to turn, for I knew that I'd see nothing, learn nothing.

There was no other explanation for this. While my horse plodded across London Bridge, I concluded that my mind was twisted by Jacquard Rolin, the imperial spy who trained me as part of the conspiracy, demeaned me, and, finally, attacked me. Because the third part of the prophecy could only be revealed in Ghent, the birthplace of the Emperor Charles, Jacquard took me there. *When the raven climbs the rope, the dog must soar like a hawk in the time of the bear.* That was the full prophecy. After the hanging of the "raven," the mystic nun Sister Elizabeth Barton, it was up to me, the Dominican, the order associated with the dog, to act swiftly in the time "of the bear." And the objective was . . . to kill the king. When I had recoiled, Jacquard demanded, "Are you so stupid that you did not perceive that from the beginning this was the conspiracy to build the perfect assassin?" But no matter what King Henry had done to my family and friends, to my chosen way of life, I could not commit murder. I spent four harrowing months in Europe, most of it imprisoned in Ghent. After I escaped from Jacquard—when he nearly killed me—I managed to make my way back to England.

In the peace of Dartford these last months, I'd never felt threatened, never been contacted again by those men of the shadows. None of these self-protective instincts Jacquard nurtured in me had stirred. But now, traveling to the most dangerous city in England, they were awakened.

I reached up to press between my fingers the slender chain holding a crucifix, hidden beneath my bodice. When I returned home, I would seek guidance in prayer for how to return to true peace, the obedience and humility and wisdom of the Dominican Order that I would always revere.

Our horses reached the other side of the bridge. Judging by the position of the sun, there was ample time for this mission. I'd been told king's officials performed business until nightfall. That was hours away. We rode past the churches and taverns, the goldsmiths and grocers, the haberdashers and brewers, the salters and sadlers. And we wove around the Londoners who'd emerged from their narrow homes to embrace April—perhaps the first genuinely warm day of the Year of Our Lord 1540—with their pale, dirty faces turned upward to the cleansing rays of the sun.

With the Thames now on our left, we rode on the Strand and then the King's Street to the massive complex of buildings rising in the distance before us. We left the city of London for the liberties of Westminster, where the seat of government lay, whether it was the king's grand palace, Parliament's vast hall, or the church's soaring abbey.

I had not been inside palace or abbey. Last summer I came close. An anonymous woman, I'd watched as thousands of men marched before the king and council in the Great London Muster, proving their readiness to defend the realm. I remembered the men striding past a platform in front of a massive gatehouse.

Today I approached the same gatehouse not from a park but from a street that grew so crowded that we had to dismount. The street continued under the gatehouse archway, beyond to the abbey and Parliament. Entrance to the palace itself on the left appeared to be through a large door in the side of the gatehouse.

Now I faced a new problem. Perhaps one hundred men, many of them clutching papers, jostled to move forward in the mass of humanity trying to gain admittance to that door. Master Gwinn, a bear of a man, pushed his way forward, creating a path for me and his wife. As we shuffled forward in his wake, one name was repeated, to the right and left, forward and behind: *Cromwell, Cromwell, Cromwell, Cromwell.* Once again I saw that precise script on my royal summons and shuddered. He had signed the document, but I was not here to see the Lord Privy Seal, I told myself. My humble business would involve only the wardrobe master.

But would it be possible to see anyone today? The desperate peti-tioners formed a near-impenetrable wall before the gatehouse. Even with the efforts of the stalwart Master Gwinn, I might not succeed.

A part of me did not want to succeed. From a distance, the gate-house was majestic, and I assumed that on drawing nearer, it would diminish in grandeur, as official buildings often do. But the effect was the opposite—now that I was yards from it, the palace gatehouse dazzled. The entire building was made of stone carved and painted in a white-and-black checkered pattern. The raised squares gleamed, as if they had been not merely washed but polished. Two rounded towers stretched three stories high. Between the towers sparkled tall windows. The busts of four crowned heads stared sightless into the distance, representing members of the pitiless Tudor family. Fleurs-de-lis graced the stones, along with carvings of lions and dragons, greyhounds even. I couldn't begin to guess how costly it must have been to fashion such a building, resembling a game board more than a gatehouse.

I took a step backward as I strained to look all the way to the top of the octagonal turrets. To my surprise, two distant human heads peeked over the wall. From lofty heights, the people of the king's court surveyed us. With a start, I realized that people peered at us from behind the thick glass of windows as well. Perhaps it amused them, to survey the grubby pack from within their lavish stronghold.

The crowd shifted before me, and an opening yawned. Master Gwinn surged forward. Now we were in front and could finally be seen by the man in charge, tall and wide-bellied, planted in front of the gatehouse door.

With an oath, he waved off a gray-haired clerk, jabbering his pleas for entry. When the clerk edged toward the side of the archway, as if to scramble into Whitehall uninvited, a soldier surged forward, waving his picket. The clerk shrank back into the crowd.

"In the name of the king, state your business here, sirrah," called out the tall man. It took me a few seconds to realize that he ad-dressed Master Gwinn, who in answer turned toward me.

I took a deep breath and stepped forward, declaring, "I am summoned to appear before the master of the king's wardrobe."

"The master of the king's wardrobe—*you*?" he said scornfully, his eyes scanning my shabby garments.

Without another word, I handed him my summons. His eyebrows knotted in skepticism until his gaze reached the bottom. "Signed by Cromwell," he said.

"Correct," I said crisply.

"But even so, I must send word to—"

"I shall be honored to escort the lady," said another voice.

A smiling young man with a neatly trimmed brown beard emerged from the doorway of a turret tower opposite the entrance. He wore the uniform of a royal page: a red doublet with a large Tudor red-and-white rose on the left side.

The page bowed to me with courtesy that seemed extravagant, considering my uncertain status. The man in charge of entry to the palace shrugged. Evidently all that needed to be done was produce a paper bearing the name *Cromwell* for doors to be flung open. It all felt a little strange, but what did I know of palace procedures?

I turned to say good-bye to the Gwinns. We had worked it out that one servant would wait a short distance up the King Street with two horses, and when my business was finished, I would find my way back to him. He'd take me to Southwark and my waiting friends.

A hand grabbed my arm, so tightly I gasped. Agatha dragged me away from earshot of the men, of husband, gatehouse official and royal page, giving me a shake, just as she used to when she was novice mistress and I needed correction.

"You don't have to do this," she said. "All the things you've always said about London, about *this*"—she pointed at the palace with her wobbly chin—"I see now you were right. We've come to an evil place."

Agatha had been so quiet as we waited for entry, I thought her awed by Whitehall. Now I saw that it disturbed her. It was gratifying that now, finally, she saw the court through jaundiced eyes. But there was no turning back.

I hugged her, whispering, "All will be well."

"How can it be? How can good flourish here?"

"Did not Thomas Aquinas say, 'Good can exist without evil, whereas evil cannot exist without good'?" I said.

Agatha shook her head. "You are clever, Joanna, and you are learned, but I do not think that will be enough to keep you safe inside these walls."

With a final squeeze of her shoulder, I turned to follow the page into the gaping door of the gatehouse.

"God be with you and protect you," Agatha called after me, her voice shrill.

As much as I wanted to, I did not turn around.

4

With a graceful beckon, the page led me past a long, wooden gallery overlooking a garden and orchard. We took a walkway direct to the tallest of the white stone buildings. He walked quickly; I had to scramble to keep up. There was no question of walking side by side. I would trail him all the way to the keeper of the wardrobe.

When I stepped over the threshold, it was the first time I'd entered a royal home since the terrible day in 1527 when I arrived to carry out my duties to Henry VIII's first queen, Catherine of Aragon. Whitehall was grander than my memory of Greenwich. The page led me to a hall that seemed to stretch forever.

The hall, like the courtyard, was filled with men, though these were calm. High above their heads stretched a ceiling possessing as much meticulous grandeur as the gatehouse. The same black-and-white checks, the judicious sprinkling of fleurs-de-lis. Mullioned windows were set high in the walls. It struck me that this was a very modern palace. I strained to remember what I knew of Whitehall—it was the London home of the archbishops of York until Henry VIII's first minister, Cardinal Thomas Wolsey, took ownership and spent a fortune expanding it. After the king turned against Wolsey, he took Whitehall. Just as, years earlier, he had my uncle the Duke of Buckingham executed on trumped-up charges of treason and then took all his properties. That was what Henry VIII did—he took.

It seemed that my destination was not within this hall but beyond it. As I hurried after the page, I passed groups of men talking

in low murmurs. Everyone seemed well acquainted. My whole life I'd
felt an outsider, but here the feeling was most pronounced.

My fervent hope was that I not encounter the Duke of Norfolk,
Bishop Stephen Gardiner, or any of the other men whom I had an-
tagonized in the last three years. So far there seemed little chance of
that. The men of the king's court I passed all looked very prosperous
and respectable, but they were not attired in the sables, silks, and furs,
the robes and chains of office that denoted the highest ranks.

It would have been a source of great pleasure to see the Lady
Mary, the king's eldest daughter. We became friends two years ago
when she learned I was among those who'd nursed her beloved
mother, Queen Catherine, during the last weeks of her life. But I
knew from the Lady Mary's last letter that the advent of spring had
sent her from court lodgings to Hunsdon House, her favorite establishment in the country.

There was only one other person whom I would have liked to
see—my young friend Catherine Howard, one of the queen's maids
of honor. But that could require seeing the queen herself, Anne of
Cleves, and I did not want to do that. The prophecy called for the
murder of King Henry before he could father a second son by the
German princess, for that son would have set the world on fire. In
place of killing Henry VIII, I gave him just enough of the drink
from the chalice to sicken him and render him unable to be a husband to his bride. I did what I had to do, but Anne of Cleves did not
deserve it. When I met her on the ship from Calais, she was kind
and dignified—and generous. She paid a great deal for *The Rise of the
Phoenix*, and this added to my guilt and confusion.

All emotions receded as I caught sight of the king's own tapestries. Behind the clusters of men, they covered the walls, one after
another: arresting, glittering tapestries. I had never seen any this huge.
They looked to be twenty feet wide. At Dartford Priory, we created far
smaller ones. These must have been made in Brussels, the center of all
tapestry production in Europe, making use of long looms and many
workers. To create a story from a biblical source or mythology or
history—a war, a tournament, a wedding—showing this many human

figures, ten and more, would demand a team of eight weavers working at least a year. And the faces of the figures shown in the tapestries—they were so symmetrical. What control to create visages so lovely. There was more, too. I was accustomed to tapestries fastened to the wall; after all, their more practical aspect was to warm houses during the cold months. But these tapestries hung a few inches away from the wall, hanging from narrow poles. They moved ever so slightly, becoming live, colorful sagas rather than flat woven pictures.

Even with all the troubles of the day—and the looming troubles of what was to come—I could not restrain myself from making my way to the wall to get a closer look. I wanted to figure out the story being told and assess its craftsmanship. Now that I was inches away, I could appreciate the meticulous line of the weave. I grasped the edge and, to my surprise, a whiff of grease and smoke puffed into my nose. I also spotted some dulling of the colors here and there. The tapestry was dirty.

"This way, mistress—this way," said the page, who had circled back to find me.

"Forgive me, but I weave tapestries, that is why I am summoned today," I said, reluctantly moving away from the wall.

"This way," the page repeated yet again with the same vacuous smile pasted on his face. I supposed that he took no interest in the people he escorted around the palaces. Something about him seemed odd. I found I did not want to follow him. Yet I suppressed my first twinge of suspicion. After all, I had little knowledge of the ways of royal pages.

A shallow set of stairs led to a landing crowded with servants carrying crates. While we waited to get around them, I peered out the window. It was dizzying how close I stood to the Thames; its waters seemed to lap the palace wall.

Minutes later, I found myself walking down another long gallery. Tapestries covered these walls, too. I wondered how many the king possessed and whether they traveled with him from palace to palace or if some were permanently affixed. With such a vast and magnificent collection, why would he commission anything from my humble home loom?

And then I was outside, blinking in the sun. The page had led me out a door that opened the way to a larger nascent garden and empty sporting yards: tennis, which King Henry helped popularize; bowling; cockfighting.

"Where is the keeper of the wardrobe?" I called out to the red jacket bobbing a short distance in front.

Without answering, he pointed at a building only one story tall, on the other side of the bowling yard. I hurried to catch up to him, which was not easy.

"Are you sure you know the way?" I asked. "This doesn't seem right."

"You've been to Whitehall before?" he asked, very polite.

"No."

The page's smile deepened. In the sun I could see he was not as young as I'd first thought. There were tiny crinkles around his brown eyes. Beneath his beard, I detected a weak chin.

"I know the palace and all its buildings very well, I assure you," he said, with another of his bows.

We resumed our walk, past a neat orchard, but it still didn't feel right.

"Trust your instincts always"— that is what Jacquard Rolin said. He had been a liar and schemer and murderer. A breaker of all holy commandments. But he was clever, too, fiendishly so . . . "Very well, Jacquard, what would you do?" I muttered to myself, exasperated.

Be ready, Joanna Stafford. I could hear his Low Countries accent in the master spy's hiss. A chill shivered up my arms in the sunny courtyard of the king.

We finally reached the far building. It had fewer people in it, just three men near the entrance, talking together as they shared a look at a ledger. A maidservant scrubbing in the corner. Passageways stretched in two directions from the front.

"Come, mistress, it's this way," said the page, moving toward the one on the left.

At the end of the passageway was a door. The page walked to it, then turned to beckon to me again. I took two steps and stopped.

"Mistress Joanna Stafford?" he called out. "This is where you will meet the wardrobe master."

"In this small room, so far from the king?" I asked. We were alone in the passageway.

The page's smile widened into a laugh, as if I'd said something amusing. "That is his preference, yes."

I walked to the door, all the time wishing I could think of an excuse to turn around and get away from him, fast. In the end, my sense of impropriety silenced the warning bells that exploded in my head. The page opened the door and I moved around him to enter. I took a deep breath, preparing my greeting.

Suddenly I was sailing through the air, propelled by a powerful shove. The room was dark and cluttered. No one awaited me or anyone else here. I slammed into a rough table with my hip and cried out in pain.

The door shut behind us.

"What are you—" Before I could finish the sentence, a hand clamped over my mouth. With the other hand, the page grabbed my right arm and twisted it so sharply that my stomach turned over from the pain. He was a head taller than me, and quite strong. He started to drag me to the far corner of the room. I knew with utter certainty that I did *not* want go there.

I bit his hand. It was not the slobbering of a desperate victim. No, I tore at this man's hand with savagery; I wanted to reach bone. Now it was his turn to cry out, a squealing grunt. His grip on both my mouth and my arm loosened.

I sprang toward the door, shouting, "Help—help!" I had reached it, my fingers on the doorknob, when the page grabbed me by the shoulder and spun me around.

I had seconds to survive. With the side of my right hand, I chopped through the bottom of his beard to land a sharp blow to his windpipe, a move Jacquard had taught me.

His eyes popping in shock, he staggered away, choking.

I yanked open the door. There was no one on the passageway. He could still emerge and drag me back in. I started to run, but the pain in my hip was such that I half limped. "Help!" I cried again.

"What has happened?" said a young man's voice from the direction of the door. "What's wrong, mistress?"

Tears of relief filled my eyes as my savior approached. He was tall and dark-haired and, in my semidelirious state, seemed possessed of a singularly beautiful face, like an angel sent by Christ to deliver me.

"A page attacked me," I said, turning to point. "Down there."

The young man bounded past me, toward the door.

"Don't," I cried. "You must get help first. He's very strong."

Ignoring my warning, he hurtled into the room. Seconds later, I heard the words: "There's no one here."

I couldn't believe it. But as soon as I joined him, I could see for myself that the page was gone. There was a far door on the other side of the room. The page must have decided to flee rather than chase me down.

"Are those drops of blood on the floor?" exclaimed the young man. "Are you wounded?"

"No, it's his blood," I said. "I bit his hand. Quite hard."

The young man looked at me, his lip curling with distaste as I tucked the loosened strands of black hair back into my hood. "What were you doing with one of His Majesty's pages?" he said. "Was this some kind of assignation?"

"It was *not*. He said he was leading me to the master of the king's wardrobe. I have a summons. I am expected this week."

He snorted. "The wardrobe master in *this* part of the palace? This is for equipment. I was seeing to the work on a new jousting lance when I heard you. Very well, what was his name?"

"He never said."

The young man sighed. "You're telling me that a royal page led a woman he didn't know to a room in Whitehall for a bit of frolic? Do you know how carefully trained these pages are? I should know, for I served as a page in His Majesty's service myself."

"He didn't want a frolic," I said. "He wanted to hurt me." My voice caught. "I think he wanted to kill me."

"Kill a woman he didn't even know?" His voice again rose in disbelief.

"He knew who I was," I said. "He used my name in this hallway, moments ago."

Something gnawed at me, some source of confusion, but before I could sort it out, the young man found my summons, on the floor of the room where I was attacked, and read it. "This summons is signed by Cromwell," he said, turning somber. "You are Joanna Stafford, the daughter of Sir Richard Stafford—you are related to the third Duke of Buckingham?"

"My uncle."

"Ah, so the Earl of Surrey is your cousin," he exclaimed.

"Correct," I said, rather surprised my family connections were this widely known. My cousin, Elizabeth Stafford, married the Duke of Norfolk, and their eldest son was indeed the Earl of Surrey, a poet and soldier and someone who had acted as a friend to me.

"I apologize for disbelieving anything you said," he said. His eyes traveled up and down my clothing. "In my defense, you're hardly dressed for court."

I sighed. "I am aware of that."

"I don't have much time—I must make my way to Westminster Hall—but I will take you to the sergeant-in-arms to make report. He will launch a thorough inquiry, believe me. The palace will be turned upside-down. He will find this criminal. And the matter will be addressed by the lord steward, perhaps even the chamberlain himself. The king will be made aware. This is one of his most particular rules, that there be no violence within the boundaries of the court."

"No, I don't want that," I said. "I don't want that sort of attention." I had no idea where such an inquiry would lead, and I kept too many dangerous secrets to risk it.

The young man said, "You can't just proceed to the keeper of the wardrobe now, after this. The page—he could be searching for you. That would be the first place he'd look. Or do you think he was too deranged by violence to seek you out?"

I said slowly, "His actions were deranged, but in words he did not seem so. No, he seemed very . . . calm."

"All the worse, if he is able to conceal his vile nature behind a gentle manner," he declared. "We must find this page, and be sure he is punished."

I rubbed my temples, trying to think.

"Do you just want to go home?" he asked, gently.

My attacker knew who I was, so he could easily find me in Dartford, where I lived, defenseless. How could I press suit to my cousin, Lord Henry Stafford, for the return of Arthur, when violence hovered?

"I want to find out who this page is," I said, "but not through an official inquiry. " My head cleared. "You know the court well. I know it not at all. Will you help me learn this man's identity?"

"Mistress Stafford, you are a cousin to the Earl of Surrey, a man I'm proud to call a friend, and so of course I will help you in any way I can," he said, straightening. "My name is Thomas Culpepper."

"I thank you, Master Culpepper," I said. "What course of action should we pursue to learn this page's name?"

He caught my eye, held it, and then laughed. "I don't know yet," he said with disarming honesty. Just as under close scrutiny I'd realized the page was older than I first thought, Thomas Culpepper was younger. I would have put his age at about twenty-five. Even when laughing, his face was eerily perfect. With such symmetry of features, he resembled one of the king's tapestry figures more than an earthly man.

"Until we form some sort of plan, you'll have to come with me, since I can't leave you alone and unprotected," he said. "I must attend this special convening at Westminster."

"What sort of convening?" I asked, apprehensive.

"Just yesterday, the king called for his council, the nobles, and the commons to appear at Westminster Hall this afternoon. He intends to make Thomas Cromwell the Earl of Essex."

5

Master Culpepper was in a hurry to witness the elevation of Thomas Cromwell, but I was not.

"You would not see the actual ceremony," he said. "There will be no women present, certainly. I know Westminster Hall well, and there is a small room you can wait in, undisturbed. When the ceremony finishes, I will reclaim you."

"I do *not* want to be seen by any member of the king's council."

Glancing again at my filthy kirtle, Culpepper said, "I can't blame you for that."

I was content for him to believe that it was fashion which motivated me to steer clear of such men as Bishop Gardiner and the Duke of Norfolk.

"If you can guarantee concealment, I will accompany you," I said. "But are you certain that afterward we will be able learn the name of this page?"

With great confidence, Culpepper assured me he would find a way. And so I followed him down the walkway past the gardens of Whitehall, toward Westminster Hall, struggling to keep up, since my hip and my shoulder throbbed.

But what troubled me more was Master Culpepper's popularity. While no one had spoken to the page who led me across the grounds to the room of my attack, every single person we passed on this walkway called out a salutation, or made a quick bow. Who *was* my young protector? I had come to harm by not exercising all caution. That practice must change.

"A moment, sir?" I called out. "I must speak to you."

He swiveled around. "Could it be later, Mistress Stafford? The Great Hall is not directly connected to the residence, and I fear we have not much time."

"No," I said, stopping. "It must be now."

Concern outweighed impatience, and Culpepper drew me off the walkway, to a path to the garden, presently chained.

"I can see you are a respected courtier, but I must know your exact position here before I accept any further assistance," I said, despising my awkward little speech.

Master Culpepper took no offense, though. Drawing himself up with pride, he said, "I have the great fortune to be a gentleman of the privy chamber to His Majesty." He scrutinized my face and then chuckled. "The minute most people discover that, I am buried in petitions and requests for favors, grants, if not marriage proposals. You look as if I'd just declared I were a rag-and-bone man."

As always, my face betrayed my feelings. I was indeed dismayed that a man who waited personally on the king, entrusted to dress him and sleep in his bedchamber at night, knew anything about me.

More somberly, Culpepper said, "You fear the king? Is it because you are a Stafford, and your uncle the Duke of Buckingham was executed for treason? I know that your family is not in favor, that the fortune is gone. That is perhaps why your dress is humble, why no family members accompany you, nor even a servant—why, indeed, you find yourself seeking a commission to weave?" I drew back, surprised. It was a more perceptive analysis than I'd given him credit for.

Culpepper's voice softened. "I know what it is like to be worried about losing everything, Mistress Stafford. The king favors me, yes, but what is here today may vanish in a fortnight. And I would then be no better than my brother, whose hand is always out for coins and advantages. What must sustain us is . . . true friendship. I told you God's truth when I said that a relation of the Earl of Surrey would be awarded my every courtesy. If Surrey were at Whitehall, I would take you to him. But, in his absence, I shall help you however I can."

These were heartfelt words, and, looking into his clear brown eyes, I knew, without a doubt, that Thomas Culpepper would not harm me. I also knew that he deserved a measure of honesty in return. It was a gamble, but I took the plunge.

"My Stafford birth puts me out of favor," I said, "but also, I was once a novice at the Dominican Order of sisters in Dartford, now dissolved. That is, I assume, another mark against me, sir."

Culpepper showed no disapproval but nodded. "If you were pledged to a priory, I can see why the elevation of Cromwell would disturb you."

To that I was silent. Criticism of Cromwell was highly dangerous. He was a man alert to threat and aggressive to protect himself. When, over a year ago, he'd seen me at the tragic execution of Henry Courtenay and Baron Montagu on Tower Hill, he'd made it his business to learn more about me, which inaugurated a frightening period of surveillance.

"I wager that half the nobles will watch today's proceeding with anger in their heart," continued Culpepper. "But no man could ever be of more value to the king than Thomas Cromwell."

There was an edge to his voice, and I wondered if this gentleman of the privy chamber shared such anger. But I was careful to betray none of my own hatred of Cromwell.

Culpepper led me into the palace, up some stairs and then, to my surprise, we were outside and atop the gatehouse, walking across it to a manicured walkway that paralleled the street where petitioners still swarmed. It would not do for the courtiers to walk on the same street as the unfavored to the Great Hall and the abbey.

My heartbeat quickened when a man wearing a red doublet swerved in front of us on the walkway. Before I could say a word, Culpepper grabbed him by the arm. But the man who whirled around to face us was . . . barely a man. A red-haired page of perhaps sixteen gaped at us.

"Never mind, lad, be about your business," Culpepper said, and we continued to Westminster Hall, walking so quickly that it was but a beat short of running.

The instant we reached it, I spotted a doublet that plunged me into a different sort of panic. In front of the main entrance to Westminster Hall milled groups of men, and among them were at least three wearing black doublets sporting golden lions, meaning they were retainers of the House of Howard. The Earl of Surrey was my friend, but his father, Thomas Howard, the third Duke of Norfolk, was my sworn enemy.

As I nervously scanned the crowd for a slight but vigorous man with graying hair, I remembered my last encounter with the duke, on Tower Hill, the same horrific day I came to the notice of Cromwell. To break free of Norfolk's control, I had threatened him with a letter revealing his role in a sordid attempt to procure my cousin Margaret Bulmer for the king's bed. I could still see his reaction so clearly: his lower lip trembling as he glared at me, his obvious desire to tear me limb from limb, thwarted only by the presence of so many potential witnesses surrounding us.

"This is not over," the Duke of Norfolk had whispered, his black eyes murderous, before leaving me behind on Tower Hill.

It was a desperate gamble, to threaten the duke like that, and with a letter that did not even exist. His despicable procuring was real; he was known for his shoving of young women into the king's bed. But I had no written proof of what he'd done to Margaret. It was the only thing I could think of, the only weapon that a powerless woman could wield against the senior nobleman of the kingdom. But now, should I come before the duke, I shuddered to contemplate his reaction.

It was just another reason why coming to Whitehall today was an astoundingly risky decision.

Culpepper, fortunately, led me to the far end of Westminster Hall, away from the crowd. We hurried to a narrow door, easy for someone like me to miss, but plainly my new friend was an expert of the court and all of its buildings.

Inside was a narrow passage sparsely occupied. At the far end, I could hear the low rumble of many men's voices. That must be the large hall where the commons and lords convened. As Culpepper had promised, the room in question was discreet. Inside was a dusty chair by the narrow slit of a window and, on the other side, far from the light, a plain bench.

"What is the room for?" I asked as I stepped inside.

Culpepper shrugged. "A place to rest from the proceedings? Contemplation?" He pivoted. "I *must* hurry now, it's to begin any moment."

And with that he was gone.

I chose to wait on the bench. It was quiet here, giving me the first opportunity to collect my thoughts since I left Dartford at dawn. I was exhausted, and thirsty, too. So much had transpired, and there was so much yet to come.

In this dim little room, recalling what happened since I set foot in Whitehall, it all became absurd. Why would a page wish to hurt me, a woman of a fallen family carrying a commission for tapestries? For there was no question that he knew who I was, he used my name in that passageway, when trying to convince me, against my judgment, to follow him. Had he used my name earlier? I thought back to the beginning, when I stood before the gatehouse, when I handed my summons to the official, when the page stepped forward to escort me, when I said good-bye to Agatha. And then it hit me, a realization so frightening that the breath rushed out of my body.

Neither I nor anyone had ever said my name aloud at the gatehouse or in the palace. And the page never read the summons.

Impossible, I whispered into the dusty quiet. For this would mean that he was prepared for my arrival, he was waiting for me. There was a plot to hurt me—perhaps to kill me—and the page was the instrument. He was not a deranged creature but an assassin.

This was not a matter for chivalrous Thomas Culpepper, nor for any of my innocent friends. I should get as far away from the court as possible. The only question was where. *Where?*

As I sat there, convulsed with fear, the door opened, and a man walked into the room. The ceremony must already be over.

But this was not gentleman of the privy chamber Thomas Culpepper.

He was thicker and older than Culpepper. He did not speak nor turn toward me, and as he moved toward the window, I saw at once that he did not know anyone else was within. He thought the room empty and did not detect my presence in the shadowy far end.

I should declare myself—I opened my mouth—when something about his profile made the words falter in my throat. Had I seen this man before?

Before I could place him in my memory, the man turned from the window and buried his face in his hands, his shoulders hunched.

"No," he groaned. "No." Was this illness? Or grief? Had he suffered some loss? It was quite wrong of me to bear witness to such a private moment. This man was in distress.

I must have shifted on the bench—made a noise—for the man turned to face me, his hands dropping from his face. We stared at each other, both of us shocked by the face beheld across the room.

The man in the room with me was Thomas Cromwell.

6

"J oanna Stafford," Thomas Cromwell said, as if he could not him- self believe it. "Why are you here?"

I could not speak, could not move.

He bore down on me and I flinched, as if preparing for a blow, the sort of vicious smack I'd suffered more than once from the Duke of Norfolk. But the king's chief minister did not strike me. He took the summons from my hand and read it.

"Of course," he said, his voice very quiet. "Gardiner uses the king's passion for tapestry to set his spy on me."

That helped me find my voice.

"I am no spy, my lord," I sputtered. "The Bishop of Winchester had nothing to do with my coming to court. It is your signature on the summons."

"Why come *here*?" he countered. "This summons directed you to the keeper of the wardrobe, not to Westminster Hall. This is where Parliament convenes. It's a stupid mistake, and we both know you are not a stupid female."

His calm words were laced with anger. It was not my being in this room that infuriated him but the fact that I had witnessed his distress, his fear. He was the second-most-important man of the kingdom. I knew that Cromwell and Gardiner were enemies, but he couldn't truly believe that the wily bishop would ask me to fol- low him *here*—in the building that housed Parliament? If I were to disclose the truth, it would end his suspicion. But I did not want to tell him why I'd come to Westminster Hall. If I did that, then I must also disclose the attack on me, and how could I trust this distressing business to Thomas Cromwell? It wasn't just that. I had to protect Culpepper—I owed him that much, at least.

Cromwell took a step backward, nodding. "No answers for me, of course. But I shall have my answers, Mistress Stafford. Come."

I rose, but I was so full of fear that my legs wobbled. To steady myself, I touched the chain round my neck.

Cromwell opened the door with a mirthless smile. "I expect that is a crucifix you fondle, Mistress Stafford. Before nightfall, we shall know for sure—and all of your other Papist secrets."

He was a man whose eyes missed nothing, whose mind worked faster than any other's. How long would it be before he knew every single thing about me?

In the passageway outside the room stood five men, all startled at the sight of me. "This lady shall accompany me," Cromwell said by way of explanation. The men immediately fell in behind us, as the Lord Privy Seal escorted me down the hall.

A way out of this suddenly occurred to me, and I said, "My Lord Cromwell, how could I be accused of spying on you if you entered that room after me?"

Cromwell said smoothly, "That is not yet an established fact, mistress, who was present in the room first."

So he intended to alter the facts. It would be my word against his, and who would believe Joanna Stafford? As I walked down the passageway, my thoughts circled around Agatha Gwinn. How distraught she would be. My onetime novice mistress had sensed danger for me beyond the palace gatehouse, and she had been right.

I expected that some sort of small room, sterile and windowless, would be my destination, the sort of place where Thomas Cromwell got answers to his questions, whether the targets be the lovers of Anne Boleyn or the friends of Henry Courtenay. But instead I was ushered into what was quite simply the largest hall I had ever stood in.

There were rows of men lined up in front of both walls, two groups facing each other, the sun slanting through tall, narrow windows. Above us was an interlacing of carved wooden kings. Undoubtedly, I beheld the assembled lords and commons. To my shock, I stood before Parliament itself. They were assembled for Cromwell's elevation, which I realized now had not yet taken place.

"My lord Bishop of Winchester," said Cromwell, not by any means shouting but loud enough so that all conversations going on in the hall ceased.

"Yes, my lord Cromwell?"

My heart sank at the sound of Stephen Gardiner's voice. A hand closed around my forearm, and Cromwell pulled me toward the voice. There the bishop stood, in the center of the front row of the lords of Parliament, next to his chief ally, Thomas Howard, Duke of Norfolk.

Impossible to say which of these two men looked more horrified. Gardiner's lips pressed together and red patches flared in his cheeks. Norfolk squinted at me and then, recognition breaking, he took a step forward. His strangled curse could be heard above the startled hush of the assembled men.

My face blazed hot as the attention of everyone in Westminster Hall turned toward me. Out of the corner of my eye I saw a young lord push aside another so that he could get a better look.

But for Cromwell, there was only one other man in the room. He said to Gardiner, "I have discovered one of your disciples, Mistress Joanna Stafford, and in a most interesting place. She bears a summons to come before the keeper of the wardrobe, yet I found her here, in Westminster Hall."

"She is not my disciple," said the bishop calmly.

"No?"

I turned to look at Cromwell. That satisfied smile reappeared, which had twisted his face when he accused me of wearing a crucifix. It did not warm his features; nothing could lighten the grayish hue that could only be caused by working punishing long hours indoors, day after day.

"But you are well acquainted with this Stafford woman," said Cromwell. "I think we can trace it to the Tower of London, in the autumn of 1537. That is when she came under your protection."

Norfolk flinched—after all, he was the one who first interrogated me in the Tower, who alerted Gardiner—but the bishop reined in all emotion. I knew how hard that would have to be for him.

Gardiner said, "She is not under my protection. She means nothing to me. You may question her all you like."

A high voice rang out across Westminster Hall: "My Lord Cromwell, who have you brought to our proceeding?"

It was the king.

Every single person in the hall had been so transfixed by Cromwell and Gardiner's confrontation—with myself as the hapless cause—that Henry VIII had entered the hall unnoticed. He made his way toward us, his gait stiff and nearly limping. A gold doublet covered with gems stretched over his enormous girth. I was dumbfounded by the sheer size of the king. It took a moment for me to recognize the young man walking behind, to his left. It was Thomas Culpepper, his eyes wide.

I sank into a curtsy, but it was a bad one, for my legs were trembling.

Cromwell said, "I thought you still in consultation with your physicians, Your Majesty."

Henry VIII made a dismissive gesture with his ringed right hand. "We await your explanation," he said, turning his assessing gaze on me. Those blue eyes—I remembered them from the day I was presented to him, a shy sixteen-year-old girl. Now they were sunk between bloated cheeks and graying brows. "This lady is known to me, she is of the Stafford family. But just why she has chosen to attend Parliament, a most unusual decision, no one has seen fit to tell."

Cromwell hesitated. No one will ever know how long he would have needed to gather his clever lawyer thoughts and deliver his reasons for my presence, because the next voice heard was mine.

"Your Majesty, I am Joanna Stafford and I am at fault." I curtsied before him, better this time, my spine straight. After coming back up, my eyes fixed on the stone floor, I continued: "I received a summons to court and I came today, but did not know where to go to find the wardrobe master. Lord Privy Seal Cromwell came upon me, lost, and kindly brought me to these good lords of your kingdom, that they might join together to form a plan."

A thick silence filled the hall for what seemed like hours, but might have been five seconds.

The king said, his voice lilting, "Ah, Cromwell, we always knew you capable of sympathy for a lady's plight, though others have deemed you indifferent to the fair sex. Would you have thought this possible, Norfolk?"

The duke called out, "Not until today, Your Grace."

Laughter filled Westminster Hall, so loud it echoed against the stone walls and pillars. I finally looked up. The reaction to what Norfolk said exceeded the joke. Norfolk himself laughed the hardest. It was ghastly, the way his lips curled to expose long yellow teeth. Only three men did not shout with laughter: Cromwell and Gardiner, who arranged their faces into benevolence but were still seized by their hatred of each other, and Culpepper, who could not take his eyes off my face.

"We shall attend to the business of the day," said King Henry. "But first, we must address our kinswoman."

Kinswoman? It was true, of course, my grandmother and the king's grandmother were sisters, but the Tudors never bore any affection for the Staffords. As the king stepped toward me, he smiled, most benevolent, and a pungent odor encircled me, of musk and lavender and rose water and something else, too, something less appealing.

"We are most pleased that Mistress Stafford shows her loyalty and willingness to serve the Crown by making her way here, in humble haste," the king declared. "We shall grant her a personal audience on her commission."

And then, half limping, the king of England made his way the length of Westminster Hall, walking alongside Thomas Cromwell, the chief minister he would now make Earl of Essex.

7

I've never seen a woman accomplish anything like that in my life,"
said Master Thomas Culpepper. "And, now that I think on it, I've
never seen a man accomplish such a feat either."

I had not remained in Westminster to witness the elevation of
Cromwell. After the king spoke favorably to me, it was Culpepper
who surged forward to escort "Mistress Stafford, the king's kin" to
Whitehall, keeping up the pretense I had begun that we did not
know each other.

"We need not dwell on what happened in there," I said.

"You don't think the entire court will dwell on it soon enough?"
Culpepper asked. After thanking me for the story I concocted for
coming to Westminster, a story that had removed him completely, he
could not stop rejoicing in my "cleverness."

I rubbed my forehead as I returned to Whitehall with Thomas
Culpepper. Two men cut their way in front of us, leading a string of
white greyhounds, their pink noses sniffing with derision. The dogs
were headed for the open park, away from the palace. How I longed
to join them.

Just a few hours ago, I had been part of the throng of the obscure, milling in front of the Whitehall gatehouse. Now the most
powerful men of the land were more aware of my existence than ever
before. And, according to Culpepper, my words to the king, born of
desperation, would award me fame throughout the court. Fame was
the last thing I sought for a myriad reasons, among them that now I
would be an easier target for an assailant to find.

As if he'd read my thoughts, Culpepper's smile faded. "I shall make all my inquiries with discretion," he promised me. "This business shall be dealt with straight away. There is a lord who serves the chamberlain, the master of pages, I shall begin by inquiring of him which of His Majesty's pages fit the description of the man who attacked you."

"I beg of you, exercise every caution," I said. "He is a most dangerous man."

"Mistress, I can manage an errant page, I assure you."

I did not tell him of the suspicion that formed within me while I was in that small room of Westminster: that the page waited for me to arrive, in order to lure me to a carefully selected room, where he would attack, perhaps even kill me. But now, as I walked on this path with Culpepper, the late-afternoon sun slanting on the radiant stone walls of the palace, such a conspiracy began to seem too fantastical. How could a royal page be recruited to harm me? Someone must have said my name aloud at the gatehouse without my hearing; was not the area noisy and chaotic? The attack was one of depravity, nothing more.

Nor did I tell Culpepper the whole truth about Thomas Cromwell. The only person who knew that he'd withdrawn into that room to give way to his own fear and distress was me. My instinct was to keep it that way.

With the assurance of a man who knows his master well, Culpepper told me that Henry VIII desired a court built on chivalry. "You've done Cromwell a great service today, to prompt the king to think that he wanted *only* to be of service to a lost lady," he said.

I must pin my hope on Cromwell's wanting to retain that gracious image of himself. Perhaps then he would not move against me after all.

"My problem is what to do with you for the next hour," continued Culpepper as we stood at the entranceway to the palace. "The king says he shall have an audience with you, and he may wish it before nightfall—or it could be tomorrow. When I attend on him later, I will find out. But in the interim, you cannot be left among the men. A lady belongs with other ladies, but there is only one place at Whitehall where they can be found. I don't suppose you are acquainted with the Queen of England? Nothing about you would surprise me, Mistress Stafford."

Don't be so sure of that, I thought.

Aloud, I said, "I am friends with one of the queen's maids of honor, and if she is not too occupied serving Her Majesty, I think she would be willing to take me in for a short time."

"Excellent," cried Thomas Culpepper. "I should be able to come up with some plausible reason for prying her loose to keep you company. Which maid is it?"

"Mistress Catherine Howard."

I had seen Culpepper exhibit many moods—amused and angry, sincere and skeptical—but I had never yet witnessed the dismay that was his reaction to hearing the name of my young friend.

"What is the matter?" I asked.

Instead of answering my question, he had one of his own: "When did you last see Mistress Howard?" he asked.

"At the end of December, but very briefly," I said, taken aback. "We were together at Howard House for a number of months earlier, in 1538. But why do you ask?" A frightening thought occurred. "Is Catherine not well?"

"She is well."

Culpepper had definitely turned melancholic. He turned from me, as if he needed to wrestle with a great dilemma unobserved. Two young men brushed by, greeting Culpepper, but he waved them off. I simply could not imagine what caused him such consternation.

"I shall take you to Mistress Catherine Howard," he said finally. "Perhaps it will do some good."

What good? I asked Culpepper not once but twice as we hurried through the palace. He refused to explain. Instead he peppered me with questions about the page. How tall? What color hair and eyes? What shape of beard? What manner of speech?

I answered his inquiries as best I could, forcing myself to remember every physical detail. The trouble was, the page wasn't distinctive-looking. He would blend into any crowd.

Culpepper led me to a quiet corridor situated on the main floor, facing the Thames. It didn't seem likely, but Queen Anne's rooms must be nearby. I remembered the design of Queen Catherine of Aragon's rooms at Greenwich: a large receiving chamber led to a smaller, more private room, and then, even more inaccessible, was the bedchamber. Did Henry VIII's fourth queen keep a household humbler than his first?

I bumped into Thomas Culpepper, for he had come to a halt outside a wooden door. A lanky young man of about sixteen sat on a stool next to the door, his ankles crossed. He looked up at us quizzically.

"These are the queen's apartments?" I wondered.

"No," said Culpepper. "This is Catherine Howard's chamber."

"But why is she not lodged with the other maids and ladies of the queen?"

Thomas Culpepper pointed at the young man, who was listening to us closely. I realized he wore a doublet with Howard insignia. "His name is Richard. He will announce you. I cannot stay."

Before I could respond, Culpepper had hurried back the way we'd come.

Richard rose to his feet, asked my name, and then rapped on the door. It opened a crack, a young face of a girl peeped out—not Catherine—and I was announced.

"Joanna!"

The door flew all the way open and there she was. Catherine Howard embraced me, all perfumed hair and fine white teeth and velvet-clad arms as she cried my name over and over with delight.

"You look wonderful, Catherine," I said. "More lovely than ever."

And she did. Catherine had grown plumper since I last saw her, but it suited her. The girl's pink-and-white skin glowed. Her green-flecked eyes were set off by her plush green gown. Our embrace had been so close, it knocked off her French hood, and her auburn curls spilled down her shoulders, which sloped like a child's, even though she was near eighteen years old.

She held me at arm's length and said, "I've missed you, but oh, Joanna, your kirtle. So *filthy*. What a fright. Will you never learn to care about your clothes?"

"You always cared enough for the both of us," I retorted, but not angry in the slightest. It was impossible to be angry with Catherine.

These rooms, Catherine's rooms, were well appointed. There was even a small tapestry on the wall opposite the window. I thought the dozen or so maids of honor crammed together, in quarters adjoining the queen's. But it had been thirteen years since I served Queen Catherine of Aragon at the palace of Greenwich.

The younger girl in the room said, "Mistress Howard, I must attend to your hood." She moved forward with pins in her hands.

Now, *this* was odd. Catherine had her own maid? But *she* was supposed to be the maid. I didn't want to ask intimate questions of her in front of the other girl, though, who was busy tidying Catherine's hair.

I told her why I'd come to Whitehall, a simpler and more benign version of the day's harrowing events. She reacted with equanimity, as was her nature, and proceeded to share tidbits of family news. My cousin Elizabeth, the Duchess of Norfolk, was once again completely estranged from her husband and quarreling with all of her children as well. The young wife of the Earl of Surrey had given birth to a second child. And, Catherine said, her own father, Edmund Howard, the duke's younger brother, had died not long ago.

"I'm so very sorry," I said. "I shall pray for his soul."

"Thank you, Joanna," she said calmly, tilting her head so that her maid could finish the work on her hair. I couldn't blame her for exhibiting little grief. Everyone at Howard House knew that her father was a debtor and a wastrel, and that after her mother died he did nothing to raise his many children, but foisted them on his relations. Such a man could suffer a long passage through Purgatory. Prayers were urgently needed, and not just mine. The Feast of the Ascension was less than a month away; I would try to persuade Father William Mote to say a mass of requiem for the deceased Edmund Howard on that day.

Catherine, her hair finally finished, said, "The Duke of Norfolk says I am to think of him as not an uncle but a father. That is why he had me moved to these apartments—I know you must be wondering why I don't lodge with the other maids of honor. He arranged it all and secured me a maid and a manservant. He wants the best for me."

I had had a great many shocks at Whitehall that day, and now this incredible statement took pride of place among them. The Duke of Norfolk had never shown much interest in Catherine and certainly nothing approaching paternal affection. She was the only Howard niece of the right age and appearance for royal service, and so he'd petitioned the king to place Catherine with his new queen. But Norfolk had often called her "fool" and "simpleton." And now he considered her a daughter, had even moved her to private quarters at Whitehall? The Duke of Norfolk I'd seen in Westminster was as harsh a man as ever; I couldn't believe she was talking about the same person.

"Sarah, will you fetch some wine and cakes for me and my friend?" Catherine said, smiling, to her little maid.

The minute the girl had left, I said, "Tell me, Catherine, about the queen."

"The queen?" My friend looked puzzled.

"Is she kind to you?"

Catherine shrugged. "I suppose. I can't understand much of what she says, she still uses an interpreter when speaking to anyone besides her German attendants. They surround her."

"But do you enjoy serving Queen Anne?" I persisted. "I have been told she and the king see little of each other. How does she spend her days?"

My friend grabbed me by both arms and said, "Let's speak no more of the queen. I must know what happened with Edmund."

I never spoke of Edmund Sommerville. My friends in Dartford

knew of my wish and rarely brought up his name. Perhaps that is
why Catherine's bluntness left me stunned.

"It didn't happen," I stammered. "The wedding never took
place—because of the Act of Six Articles, and our vows of chastity.
Surrey rode down from London, he came to the church just when
we were . . ." I couldn't finish the sentence.

Once again, Catherine embraced me. "Surrey finally told me
what happened. I'm so sorry, Joanna. But now what will you do?
Couldn't you find Edmund?"

I stiffened. "Why would I want to find him?"

"To marry him. The two of you are meant to be married."

"But I just told you, it would be illegal for us to marry. And I
don't know where he is, no one does. Not even his sister has had a
letter for months. He left England, Catherine. He left his family, his
friends, everyone. He left *me*."

My throat closed. Tears filled my eyes. I couldn't believe it—I'd
fought off an attack, bluffed my way through Westminster Hall,
lied to the king of England, and stood my ground against Thomas
Cromwell. Yet this exchange with Catherine Howard reduced me to
weeping?

"Joanna, please listen," she said, her lips quivering. "I was there
when Edmund came to Howard House. I saw the way he looked
at you. He loves you. And you could be married in Europe. Or even
here. It would be of no difficulty for you, Joanna, I asked a priest.
Only the vows of a full-fledged nun would forbid it, and you were
only a novice."

I flinched. Catherine could not know how much it hurt, every
day, that Dartford Priory was suppressed before I could commit myself to God. I was never able to shear my hair, put on a ring, assume
a new name. I never took the veil. Afterward, when I finally accepted
that I could not pursue my vocation in England and resolved to
marry, that ended in failure as well.

Catherine continued, "It would be more of a matter of dispute
for Edmund, but exceptions are made. You must try. I know you—

the proudest woman on God's earth. I fear that you are so wounded, you won't—"

"Stop," I cried. "Catherine, you don't understand."

A sharp rapping ended this painful conversation. I wiped the tears from my cheeks while Catherine saw to the door.

Culpepper had returned—no surprise to that. But he wasn't alone. A stout woman stood behind him, her arms heaped with dresses.

"Mistress Joanna Stafford, I come from the king," he said, with all formality. "He has ordered that these garments be made ready for you. Tomorrow, he shall dine with Queen Anne, and it is the king's pleasure that you join them."

8

Catherine Howard always slept with a window open. We were so different in temperament, in interests, but that was a preference we had shared at Howard House, even in the icy cold.

This was a cloudless night, and so the moon's bath of light swam through the bedchamber. I was too troubled by the day's events—and too apprehensive about what lay ahead—to find rest. But she slept soundly, one of her arms thrown over her head. She was a different person when she slept. Some cynical, calculating adults look like innocent children when their eyes are closed, but Catherine was more childlike when awake. Now that pleasing vitality she had, which sparkled her eyes and dimpled her cheeks, was absent. In the moonlight, in profile, she was older, serious, even a touch sad. And, most of all, with her long straight nose, she was a Howard.

Our friendship was formed almost two years ago, when we were thrown together in the Howards' establishment. I was kept in Howard House in Southwark, against my will, by the Duke of Norfolk, who had decided that since his wife was a Stafford, he could decide my life and put an end to my independence. Catherine was sent to Southwark from her stepgrandmother's house in Horsham to learn how to serve a queen. Two penniless daughters of unimportant younger sons of large families. A silent sympathy quivered between us. Who else could better understand what it was like to be viewed with barely concealed irritation by the heads of our respective families? The sighs of impatience when we outgrew our clothes, required an apothecary, held an empty plate at a banquet.

If we'd been the daughters of first sons—such as Mary Howard, Duchess of Richmond, or my cousin Elizabeth Stafford, Duchess of Norfolk—there would have been marriage by the age of sixteen and wealth and servants and vast homes to run. Failing that, we were still expected to secure noble marriages, but the path was fraught with uncertainty. The best position to be in to find a husband was royal service—maid of honor to a queen or a queen's daughter. My mother had trained me for years for such a position, but I'd lasted a single day. I was infinitely better suited for the cloister than for the court.

Now it was Catherine's turn. I always felt that she could be me . . . but without the benefit of being raised by my particular parents, a vigilant mother and an honorable father. She was raised carelessly, begrudgingly, until her prettiness vaulted her from the ranks of lesser relations to court service. Despite her disadvantages, Catherine was much more agreeable than I, so compliant a girl that I'd warned her at Howard House about the dangers to her virtue from immoral men, while she giggled behind her hands.

But Catherine could be stubborn, too, as she was earlier—insisting that I share her room during my brief stay at court. She made her case for it while Culpepper listened silently.

"I have friends who brought me here from Dartford, they are waiting for word from me this minute," I protested.

"But the commission from the king, you do not know when he will wish to discuss it with you," Catherine pointed out. "It might not take place at the dinner tomorrow. Are your friends prepared to wait for days, perhaps a week?"

This was indeed a problem. How *frustrating*. If only I knew what King Henry wanted from me, and when and how I should prepare myself, I could make arrangements and notify Agatha and John Gwinn. However, monarchs did not share their plans. It was laughable to suggest that he'd care if a party of commoners from Dartford were inconvenienced by his whim.

There was also the matter of the threat to my life. How could I wander the galleries and chambers of Whitehall with the page in the same palace, possibly tracking me?

As if reading my mind, Culpepper made an excuse to speak to me privately about the next day's dinner. Once we were in the passageway and out of earshot of Catherine, he said, "I wish I could make report to you of the page having been identified and taken into custody, but alas, that's not the case."

"Why not?" My heart started its quick, tight beat.

"I took your description to the master of pages and he says not one man who was unaccounted for during the time matches your description. There aren't many pages with beards—many of them are not much more than boys—so it didn't take him long to ask a few questions. The master of pages said it's impossible."

"Whether or not it's impossible, it happened," I said. "This man exists. And what's to prevent him from trying to hurt me again?"

Culpepper took a step closer to me, his voice dropping even lower. "Until we have an answer, *this* is the safest place for you, with Mistress Howard. She has a maidservant with her, and Richard stands guard outside."

I wasn't sure. "The page possesses cunning and strength."

Culpepper said reassuringly, "As long as you stay close to me or to her, you are safe." His lips tightened. "No man would dare disturb Catherine Howard."

Something about the way he said that struck me as odd. Yet I had to admit that his proposal made sense. As much as I disliked the idea of sleeping in the palace of Whitehall, it was better than riding back and forth from the Gwinns' in Southwark, exposing myself— and my friends—to danger.

This was an intolerable situation. I *had* to find out who the page was and what guided his violence. Perhaps the problem was that Culpepper had not seen him with his own eyes, and so he shared a secondhand description with the master of pages.

"Is there some way that I could see the royal pages, one by one?" I asked.

"Not without having to explain why. That means you'd have to say you were the person who was attacked. Up to now, I've kept your name out of it."

I said slowly, "But isn't there some sort of inspection that could be arranged, when they must assemble, perhaps walk in a single line? And then I could observe the pages, but be myself unobserved. There must be rooms or chambers that lend themselves to that here. A tall curtain? A door partly ajar?"

Culpepper burst out laughing.

"Is this a matter for amusement?' I asked. "I don't see how."

"You are just so *clever*," Culpepper said. "Yes, that is a most excellent idea, Mistress Stafford. I will arrange it tomorrow. It's too late for today—the sun's setting and everyone will be seeing about their suppers."

When we stepped back into Catherine's room, she and her maid, Sarah, were perched on the embroidered chairs, gleefully examining the dresses sent by the king. While waiting for me, they'd been nibbling the cakes Catherine sent for. A smudge of sugar clung to her lower lip.

"This would appear an admirable place for you to reside until the King's Majesty makes his pleasure known, Mistress Stafford," said Culpepper with a farewell bow.

Catherine glanced up. "I am so pleased that Master Culpepper approves," she said, her voice hard.

The two of them, Catherine and Culpepper, locked eyes.

"Enjoy your cake, Mistress Howard," he said finally, and was gone.

I had never heard Catherine speak like that to another. Nothing he had done or said warranted her reaction. With his angelic features and quick grace, he seemed like the last man worthy of spite.

"What is wrong?" I asked.

But she shrugged with a little laugh and did not answer. Perhaps this was court banter, the sort of man-and-woman byplay I'd never learned—never wanted to learn. I thought no more of her odd reaction to Culpepper, for there was much to do. I wrote a message to the servant of Master Gwinn, the poor man doubtless still standing in the King Street outside Whitehall all these hours later. There was another message, to Agatha Gwinn, emphasizing that I'd found safe harbor with a friend and that, once my business at court was concluded, I'd write to Dartford. I hoped it would assuage her fears.

Catherine insisted I change into one of the dresses sent by the king, so that my own "lamentable" garments could be cleaned and mended. It was distasteful to accept gifts from King Henry. But I couldn't see a way to refuse, so I donned the kirtle and bodice of the least ostentatious one, a dark blue damask with a tight waist and billowing sleeves.

"My, oh my, you are so slim, Joanna," Catherine said. "This fits perfectly, which means the lady it was made for was astoundingly slim. I wonder who that could have been."

"Are these dresses borrowed?" I asked. "I must thank that person, and be sure she knows they will be returned."

"Don't be silly. No one lends dresses like these, certainly not by way of the king. His Majesty has come into possession of them; it would be best not to inquire."

How nonchalantly she said it. Catherine was untroubled by the turpitude of the court. That troubled *me*.

But my mounting concerns for Catherine were once again pushed aside. She dragged me with her to supper with the Howards. Just as Catherine did not serve Queen Anne alongside the other maids of honor, she didn't eat with them. The Howards had lodgings at court. She explained as we went how they served a late supper there for the whole family. The duke himself rarely joined them, for he needed to attend the king until late into the night.

As I listened to Catherine along the way, I could not help noticing how much attention we drew. Every man we passed stared at us, eyes flicking back and forth. Perhaps it was because we were dissimilar, like two opposing chess pieces, white and black. My diminutive friend was so fair, while I, taller and thinner, resembled my Spanish mother in coloring: black hair, brown eyes flecked with green, and olive skin.

We were the only women in the private dining chamber, Cath-

erine and I. There were five Howard cousins at the table, one of
whom I remembered from my time with this fractious clan. I met
Catherine's brother, Charles, as handsome as she was pretty. My
presence at the dinner was accepted without curiosity. I was grateful
that, at the age of twenty-nine, I was too old to provoke the interest
of young courtiers.

We were halfway through our meal when the dogs came.

Two huge hounds bounded in, one grizzled with age and one
younger. These were not aloof white greyhounds but dark, noisome
beasts with long, red panting tongues. My appetite vanished. It wasn't
the presence of the dogs that disturbed me as much as what they fore-
told. For in strode Thomas Howard, third Duke of Norfolk, followed
by a trio of family retainers. Under the table Catherine squeezed my
hand, though whether in comfort or warning I did not know.

Catherine's brother, Charles, fled from the seat at the head of the
table and Norfolk hurtled into it. There was a flurry in the corner as
servants piled food on a plate and filled a tankard to the brim with
ale. My hope was that if I didn't move or speak, he wouldn't notice
me. Catherine sat nearer to him; perhaps he'd not look past her.

The plate heaped high was put before him. The duke swept it off
the table, and said, "God's wounds."

"What is the matter, Your Grace?" asked one brave nephew.

The duke glared at him for a full moment. The rest of us held
our breath, not daring to speak. The only sound was that of his dogs
devouring the food thrown on the floor.

"The matter is that last month a fool fell off his horse and died,"
Norfolk snarled. "Henry Bouchier broke his damn neck and who does
the king give his earldom to? Not one of his relations, and Bouchier
was descended from Edward III, connected by blood to most every
peer in the realm. No, he gives the earldom of Essex to *Cromwell*."

Norfolk drained his tankard of ale and then slammed it back on
the table.

"A brewer's boy from Putney is made earl—he is an earl," said
Norfolk, the word choking him. "And now Cromwell is in council
with the king, him alone, no one else, for hours. They finally sent out

Culpepper to tell us to leave. He's never ranked higher in the king's esteem than now. My God, how happy that bastard must be."

I thought of the man who buried his face in his hands at Westminster, who groaned "No" with such dread. Thomas Cromwell was not a happy man, I was sure of that.

The duke continued: "And tomorrow, His Majesty dines with the queen. Just the two of them." He paused, those furious black eyes settling on me. "And you, Joanna Stafford."

He hadn't seemed to notice me when he swept into the room, nor did he show any surprise at all to see me now. My stomach turned over as I realized that not only had he been told I would dine with the king and queen tomorrow but also that I supped with his clan tonight. Cromwell, Gardiner, Norfolk—they had spies everywhere, watching and whispering and running along these corridors and courtyards.

"Why did he choose you?" demanded Norfolk.

"The invitation came to me through Master Thomas Culpepper, but without a reason, Your Grace," I said, trying to answer him without provoking.

Norfolk leaned across the table, pointing at me. The others at the table shrank back, but I did not. Neither did Catherine, to my surprise.

"You will remember that you are a member of one of the old families—a *Stafford*," he said.

"I never forget it," I said.

"No?" His glare suddenly transformed into a filthy smirk. "I can think of a few times you've forgotten."

All the men in the room studied me with fresh interest. No longer able to stop myself, I opened my mouth to make an angry retort, but Catherine spoke first.

"I am so pleased that Joanna can stay with me for a few days." Her tone was calm and cheerful

I expected the duke to react to the news, but at this, too, he showed no surprise. So he knew all. Who was it who informed him— the maid who served Catherine or the young man outside the door?

"How did this come about?" he asked.

"Joanna has friends staying in Southwark, but no idea how long she will need to remain at court, so it seemed the best course. It's a treat for me, Uncle. Joanna was such a friend to me at Howard House, teaching me a dozen embroidery stitches, helping me prepare for court. And you know how I hate to be alone. I'm used to sleeping in a chamber with lots of girls, as I did at the dowager duchess's in Horsham."

I was astounded. Catherine was chattering as if the man in the room were a trusted, gentle friend, not the vicious Duke of Norfolk. Surely he would make a mockery of every word she said.

"If it pleases you, Catherine, then it is well done," he said. Just for a second his gaze raked over me, not with his usual contempt but almost as if he were worried about something. He had certainly never looked at me that way before. It unsettled me more than one of his bursts of rage might have.

A man's cry was heard outside the door. Someone opened the door to better hear.

Bang, bang, bang. It was the sound of a stick pounded on the floor of the corridor just outside our dining chamber.

"Be it known that today His Majesty King Henry the Eighth hath created Thomas Cromwell the Earl of Essex, Vice Regent and High Chamberlain of England, Keeper of the Privy Seal, Chancellor of the Exchequer, and Justice of the Forest beyond the Trent," declared the royal crier.

The duke of Norfolk stared at the table, his face flushed dark. I expected him to throw something, scream curses, lash out at whomever was closest. But instead he looked up, the wrinkles of his face carved deep, his focus on one person: his niece, Catherine Howard.

The way that the two of them stared at each other, it was as if no one else existed in the room. Neither spoke a word.

"Shut the door," muttered the duke, and he reached down to stroke the head of his younger dog.

9

When the thirty-six pages of His Majesty King Henry VIII stood in the line arranged by Thomas Culpepper, they stretched from one end of a Whitehall chamber to the other. I stood in a narrow gallery running across the upper half of the chamber. As I looked down at this restless parade of red Tudor doublets, I felt both frightened and resolute. And faintly ridiculous. At the last moment, Culpepper thrust a black mask into my hand and urged me to hold it in front of my face. The mask was carved into an expression of a lady's petulant sorrow, the corners of her mouth turned downward.

"I could not persuade the master of pages to order them all here without telling him that a lady had made complaint," he admitted. "But I would not give him your name."

"So they *all* know of the crime?" I said, horrified.

"The pages know nothing," Culpepper said firmly. "They were told only of a need for inspection. And so long as you keep the mask in front of your face, the master of pages won't know who you are."

Oh, but he wanted to know. That said master, a man of stout belly and long whiskers, stood at the end of the chamber, calling out orders to the pages. Yet every moment or so, he'd crane his neck in the most unnatural way, to scrutinize me. I stood but fifteen feet or so above him in the gallery, clutching my mask with one hand and pressing against a cold, smooth column with the other.

Stop looking up here, I silently pleaded.

It was high morning; a forceful yellow light streamed through the mullioned windows on the other side of the chamber. This was why Culpepper had arranged for the "inspection" to be held here, and not one of the larger halls of the palace. The master of pages could say that this room afforded the strongest possible light to inspect their official wardrobe, supposedly. Most important, I'd get a good look at each of their faces.

But it was an out-of-the-ordinary undertaking and this placed even greater strain on secrecy. A few curious courtiers gathered in the doorway to a connecting chamber, watching. I tried to angle myself so that I was out of their sight, shielded by a pillar running ceiling to floor.

At last—it began. Each of the pages strode forward, to be scrutinized head to toe while Culpepper, nodding, stood to the side. Each time a new man made it to the front of the line, my breath quickened. Because the mask was pressed against my face, my exhalations banked at the top of the gaping frown meant for my mouth. And so my nervous breaths, which I could not suppress, made the oddest noises, like wordless whispers.

It took no time at all to know that none of them was the man who'd attacked me. Culpepper was right, most of the pages were quite young, and beardless. There was one man who for a fleeting second fitted the description. But his beard was darkest brown, not the dull sandy color I recalled. And the page had round, merry cheeks above the beard. The physiognomy of this face was all wrong. Five pages later, I spotted a second bearded man, but his hair was so closely trimmed that I could see an Adam's apple throbbing in his throat during inspection. He rocked from side to side, an ungainly youth. Neither of these was the man who'd turned to look at me, over and over, and said, with that flat smile, "This way, mistress."

The crowd of curious men in the doorway was growing. I could tell by the way Culpepper bounced on his heels that he, too, was unhappy with the attention we drew. Fortunately, we were down to the last three pages.

The final trio of young men were inspected and moved toward the windows. Not one of them wore a beard or in any way resembled my attacker.

He was not among this group assembled today.

What could I possibly say to Culpepper now? Would he doubt my story—indeed, I was beginning to doubt it myself. Yesterday's assault had been so unprovoked, so bizarre, and now it seemed the man who had twisted my arm and hurled me across that room did not officially exist.

Thomas Culpepper hurried up the stairs and across the gallery to my side.

"Which one?" he said in a low voice.

"None of them," I said, turning away to face the wall so I could drop the ludicrous mask.

Culpepper sighed, not with impatience but genuine frustration. "I don't understand," he said. "None are missing. Thirty-six pages serve His Majesty's court at Whitehall."

The murmur of young men talking to one another below was pierced by a louder voice, an older person's: "The sleeves are filthy, sir, filthy—and do I see a missing *button*?"

We both glanced down. The master of pages was continuing to berate the tall young man, the one with a bobbing Adam's apple. He was even more distressed now, waving his arms as he defended himself. I heard the word *missing* in the middle of a stream of excuses.

I stiffened as it all fell into place.

"Thomas," I said hoarsely, "I know what must have happened."

"Hold up your mask again," he pleaded. And then: "Tell me, Mistress Stafford, I beg you, for I am damn perplexed."

"The man who met me at the gatehouse and led me through Whitehall to that room, he was not a page," I said, the words tumbling out from behind my mask. "He stole that page's doublet, that's why he is wearing one today that is dirty and torn during inspection, he had no choice. The other man, the one who harmed me, wore it and pretended to be in service. They are about the same height and weight."

Culpepper stared at me. "But for a man to do that, to select a royal uniform and steal it, to take such an audacious risk, he is *most* intent. Dangerous. First, I must confirm if that page's doublet is missing."

He wheeled in the other direction and was gone. I'd never seen a man move so fast—and yet with such assuredness—as Thomas Culpepper.

Within the minute, Culpepper was in earnest conversation with the master of pages and the nervous page. I could tell from the way they nodded at one another that it was true—his more appropriate doublet was missing.

I fought down the waves of panic rising in my throat, as if to gag me. Culpepper did not realize how true his words were—the man was intent. It was no longer any use trying to deny that a plot existed to hurt me, whether to injure or kill, I could not be sure. Perhaps he had intended to knock me senseless and spirit me away from Whitehall. But why? Who was at the heart of the plot?

Once again, the hostile visages of Bishop Gardiner and the Duke of Norfolk appeared. I knew they both loathed me. They'd appeared shocked to see me at Thomas Cromwell's side in Westminster Hall. But two men who'd survived the coups and conspiracies of Henry VIII's court for so long were perfectly capable of dissembling. Gardiner was the one who knew the king planned to summon me to court. What he knew, Thomas Howard, third Duke of Norfolk, knew. If they sought to make me suffer, a more straightforward imprisonment would suit better than this secretive assault. But what did I know about their means and methods?

I heard a soft step on the landing and turned, holding up the mask to my face. For the first time I was grateful for it, for it would help me hide my distress from Culpepper as I struggled to decide what to do next.

But it was not my friend on the other end of the landing. The man who walked toward me was clad entirely in black, including the mask he held in front of his own face. The visage was that of a laughing man. He must have been among the spectators below, and having spotted me, now planned to draw me out.

I took one step backward, and then another, careening into the pillar. If I kept going, the stranger would corner me. Down on the main floor, Culpepper still conversed with the master of pages. No harm could be inflicted on me in clear view of Master Culpepper and all of these people, I told myself.

Yet I felt most uneasy, for everything about the man creeping toward me looked wrong. In a court crammed with gentlemen wearing rich, varied colors—blue like the sea off of Dover, gold like newly minted coins—his black doublet and breeches seemed not just unfashionable but disturbing. He gripped a mask meant for play, but he was no lad to frolic so. Now that he drew closer, I could see that the hair above the mask was salted with gray strands. The pair of brown eyes staring at me through the slanted holes of the mask glittered with amusement.

"Do I know you, sir?" I said, my voice more defiant than I would have wished.

He halted, standing a few feet from me. "No, we have not met." His voice was low and smooth, almost caressing. "But I have seen you before. And today I have heard of you again. Mistress Joanna Stafford. The dark beauty who has come to court under such intriguing circumstances."

How I loathed flirtation, the empty and heartless banter that such men employed. It was time to banish this miscreant.

"I am not at liberty to converse with you, sir," I said. "And so I shall ask you, on your honor, to withdraw."

He drew up and was very still for a moment. I'd thought my reproof would extinguish the flicker of amusement from his eyes. But not so. It was as if my words were kindling, and those unsettling eyes now gleamed. With a dramatic flourish, he pulled down his mask, as if what were revealed would impress me. Yet I beheld someone most ugly. His skin, of sallow hue, sagged underneath the eyes. He had a thin nose and a chin dented by a long, pale scar, the aftermath of some vicious blow.

"My honor," he repeated. "But Mistress Stafford, what if I have no honor?"

10

Before I could respond to the man's declaration, Thomas Culpepper bounded toward us. "Sir Walter," he said, somewhat breathless for he'd hurried up the stairs. "So good to see you. I did not know you'd returned to court."

"I arrived last night, just in time to hear all of the news," said the black-clad knight, turning that sardonic gleam on me once more but then executing the deepest of bows. "Sir Walter Hungerford, at your service, my lady."

How surprised I was that Culpepper held good opinion of this man, and a little disappointed. They were such opposites as they stood before me, one handsome and well intentioned, the other unappealing in body and spirit.

"I must wait upon our newly ennobled Earl of Essex," Hungerford said. "I have news to warm his heart, of two Somerset traitors hanged under my authority as sheriff of Wiltshire."

Culpepper shook his head at him. "We should not speak of such things in front of Mistress Stafford."

Sir Walter proceeded to beg forgiveness in a tone that struck me as so patently false that I was sure he mocked me.

Irritated beyond measure, I said, "You do not need to conceal matters of the realm from me, my lord. What were the crimes that you ensured were punished?"

Sir Walter said, "The first traitor was one John Croche, who had been heard to boast that he had money enough, and he knew the king's needs so well, that he could buy all the lands that he has, even so far as to buy and also sell the crown of England."

It sounded like nothing more than drunken boasts, but such was the fearful climate of the kingdom that those words could lead to a noose.

Culpepper said, "And what of the second criminal?"

"Ah," said Sir Walter, "he was a vicar who uttered a prophecy that spoke of danger to our king. High treason."

Prophecy.

My knees weakening, I reached those few inches for the wall to steady myself, bowing my head so neither man would notice.

When the raven climbs the rope, the dog must soar like a hawk. Look to the time of the bear to weaken the bull. Here I stood in a gallery of the Palace of Whitehall, but those words, the words I could never forget, howled from deep within my very soul. I had learned it in pieces over eleven years of my life from three seers, first from the "Maid of Kent," Sister Elizabeth Barton; second from the fearsome necromancer Orobas; and finally from the French mystic Michèle de Nostredame.

What if that prophecy had spread—what if it were being repeated in churches and shops and alehouses throughout the land? I could not be sure that my role in it would remain hidden.

"Are you unwell, Mistress Stafford?" asked Thomas Culpepper, his forehead crinkled with worry as he noticed my state. "You have lost your color. I was right—we should not discuss such grim occurrences in your presence."

"No," I said firmly. "I am quite well." I glanced over at Hungerford, and to my dismay he was studying me closely.

"What was the substance of the priest's prophecy, Sir Walter?" asked Culpepper.

Never taking his eyes off me, Hungerford said, "John Dobson, the vicar, told his parishioners that the king would soon be driven out of his realm because 'He who bore the eagle would rule, the dun cow would restore the Church and the Crumb must fall.'"

Just as I had done my best to hide my fear, I now struggled to conceal my relief. There was some similarity, but the predictions were not the same. The prophecy that had devoured my life remained a secret one, at least to Sir Walter Hungerford. I felt the dark world of seers and necromancers recede.

Culpepper scoffed, "The priest's words sound like nothing but gibberish."

Sir Walter said, "Ah, not so, my young friend. In prophecy, all has a deeper meaning. 'He who bore the eagle' is the Emperor Charles, the 'dun cow' is the Pope, and of course 'the Crumb' is our very own Thomas Cromwell, royal minister." He cocked his head, and said, "And what do you think of *that*, Mistress Stafford?"

"I think that it fulfills the charge of treason," I said steadily. "Such evil words must be dealt with."

To my amazement, Sir Walter Hungerford smiled. "So you believe in evil, mistress?"

"All Christians believe in evil," I said.

He nodded. "Of course, of course. But still, I must tell you that in my private library at Farleigh Hungerford Castle, I have spent many hours with certain books that say acceptance of evil means that one cannot then accept the existence of God. For if God were omnipotent and wholly good, how could He permit evil to exist?"

"That is not what Thomas Aquinas writes," I countered.

He laughed in delight. "A woman who debates theology? I have long wished for—"

"Look who else has returned to court!" shouted Culpepper, interrupting with great excitement.

Following his pointed finger, I saw through the doorway of the chamber the unmistakable figure of my cousin Henry Howard, the Earl of Surrey: tall and red-haired, wearing a cape lined with fur.

Culpepper started toward the stairs to greet him, but Surrey spotted him first, and beckoned for us to stay where we were.

My feelings were mixed about this arrival. Thomas Culpepper had said from the beginning that he felt called upon to help me because of his loyalty to the Earl of Surrey. But my cousin was not a discreet nor a thoughtful man, and I feared that were he to learn of the attack on me, his testy family honor would prompt him to wild words and deeds that would worsen my predicament. Moreover, I suspected his father, the Duke of Norfolk, of being a part of the plot to harm me. Any time that Surrey was pushed to choose between his father and some other person, his father always triumphed.

As my cousin strode up the stairs, Sir Walter Hungerford moved forward on the gallery, making sure he would be first to greet him. He, too, must be devoted to Surrey, who without a doubt cut a dashing figure, being equal parts soldier and poet. His being the heir to the premier dukedom of the kingdom never hurt him, either.

I whispered to Culpepper, "Say nothing to my cousin concerning the page."

He looked at me, doubtful, but in the next instant Surrey was among us, greeting Hungerford and Culpepper with pleasure and myself with surprise. "I thought you happy in Dartford, Joanna, raising little Arthur Bulmer," he said.

"I'm here because I'm trying to get Arthur back," I said, and explained to him my tapestry commission, but suspected that he only half listened. Not from indifference to my circumstances—for whatever reason, Surrey was fonder of me than any other Stafford relation—but because he was troubled. His eyes glistened with emotion, and a nerve danced along his left cheek.

Soon enough Surrey burst out with the cause.

"The Howards suffer such a blow, it will be hard to surmount," he said. "My father, when he hears of it—I do not know what he will do."

Surrey explained that his father had sent him to the family estates in East Anglia. The Howards owned many hundreds of acres of land in that part of the kingdom, but this spring the duke was reluctant to leave the king's court "even for a single day." Still, business needed to be attended to, so the eldest son was dispatched. One pressing matter was the conversion of the Priory of Saint Mary's, for centuries a home of Cluniac monks near the Howard family seat. The king's Dissolution meant all abbeys must be closed throughout the land. But Saint Mary's contained the tombs of the dukes of Norfolk dating back to the first one, in 1250. The Howards successfully petitioned the king that the Cluniac priory be converted to a church of secular canons with the tombs left intact.

"My father has led the royal armies in Scotland and the north of England, he is most highly valued, so the king agreed to Saint Mary's being spared," said Surrey. "But two weeks ago I received a letter from Cromwell himself. Permission from the king for an exemption has been withdrawn. The priory must be dismantled and abandoned. Which means that all of our most illustrious ancestors must be . . . must be . . ." Surrey choked on his anguish and then blurted, "They must be *dug up*. Removed from consecrated ground and buried elsewhere. It is infamous."

Surrey slammed his fist against the stone column we huddled around. "How could the king sanction this insult?" he said. "Why does he disdain the nobility of his kingdom for the base new men?"

Culpepper said in a voice not far above whisper, "It is not the king. I *know* him, I am with him day and night. This is Cromwell's influence. If he were to be removed . . ."

"But how?" demanded Surrey. "His preeminence with the king cannot be altered. And now he is made an earl, equal to my own rank, God help us."

Cromwell's newly bestowed noble rank was painful salt to the wound for the Howards, both the Duke of Norfolk and his heir. In fact, Cromwell's lowly origins obsessed my cousin, who was only half Howard. His mother was a Stafford, and we Staffords were more royal than the Howards and, to our peril, more royal than the Tudors, some whispered. It was the reason my uncle the Duke of Buckingham was brought down. Yet I could not share Surrey's obsession. It was Cromwell's deeds that horrified me, not his bloodline.

"Everything has been tried to overthrow Cromwell," Surrey said. "It is impossible."

Sir Walter Hungerford said, "Not everything has been tried, and you know that."

Just as those strange words left his mouth, the bright light drained from the chamber as if poured from a cup. The sun must have risen to that point in the sky where it no longer slanted into the row of east-facing windows of this chamber. It was just the four of us now, since the pages and their master had left to resume their duties. Where before there was light and noise, now existed a dim silence charged with some tension I did not understand.

Thomas Culpepper shook himself, as if emerging from an unwholesome dream, and said he must escort me back to the rooms of Catherine Howard. The other two also sped away, Surrey to find his father and Hungerford to wait upon Cromwell, a man he served but hated, too. The disloyalties of the courtiers made my head spin.

It took less than a moment for Culpepper's attention to return to me, and I argued with him for most of our walk through the palace. He wanted to sound the alarm and call for a search of Whitehall. But I insisted we not pursue that course. I was certain that the man who'd impersonated a royal page would not attack other victims. No, Joanna Stafford was his sole target. I must discover who directed this conspiracy, but it would have to be a mission taken on alone. As much as I appreciated the earnest assistance of Master Thomas Culpepper, his proximity to the king had always concerned me. Now that I perceived his ties to unpleasant courtiers such as Sir Walter Hungerford, I knew I could not put my full trust in him.

At that moment, I realized that I had never fully trusted and confided in any man, not even Edmund Sommerville, whom I'd wanted to marry. In the case of Edmund, I'd hidden things from him to keep him safe from harm. But I'd hidden them just the same.

"Your safety cannot be assured at Whitehall while this man is at liberty," protested Culpepper.

"Once I have completed my audience with the king, I will leave court and no longer be at risk," I said.

"You must never be alone," said Culpepper. "Promise me that. At night Richard, the servant of the Howards, stands watch over those rooms. And during the day, it would be difficult to be alone even should you wish it, in a palace of eight hundred people. But still, I must hear you promise: *Never* alone."

I did so, willingly, and then said, "It would be helpful if you could learn when His Highness wishes to speak to me about my tapestries. If it is not at the dinner today, then I pray it will be soon."

Culpepper chuckled. "Do you think King Henry the Eighth is a tailor whom you could make an appointment with? We all of us serve at his pleasure, Mistress Stafford. All I can do to help is relay that His Majesty is an impatient man. He will not want to wait too long to speak with you on tapestries. In fact, I expect that seeing you in a couple of hours at his table will prompt some sort of action."

A couple of hours? I was consumed with dread and yet again I wondered why I should be singled out for this distinction.

To calm myself, I needed to pray and think in a quiet place. But after I'd reached her rooms, Catherine was more adamant than ever. "It will soothe you to walk through the garden—it's quite peaceful now, when they are planting."

"Peaceful" was not the word I'd have chosen to describe the vast walled garden of Whitehall, where sculpted hedges and a grid of marble statues of exotic beasts stretched before me. The pattern's intricacies dazzled, but I could not call it a maze. Those who walked were meant to admire; getting lost would serve no purpose at all.

Here and there, the royal gardeners knelt before the soil with tools meant for tilling. All was being made ready for the flowers and herbs. Catherine nudged me and said, "Look, Joanna, a girl is employed. How interesting."

Sure enough, a girl who looked to be not older than fifteen years of age knelt at the end of a line of men, busy tugging at a burst of light green.

"Do you enjoy your labors?" Catherine asked her.

The girl peered at the men of the line. But they did not appear to care whether she spoke to us.

"I do, mistress, I do—to be allowed into the gardens of Whitehall, 'tis a dream," she said.

"And what flower do you plant?" said Catherine, still interested.

The girl shook her head violently. "I don't plant, oh no. Would not be fitting for me to touch the primroses. I'm a weeder, mistress."

Catherine begged her to explain. Sidling closer to us, the girl whispered, "None of the men will stoop to pulling at the weeds, so they employ women like me, with small hands that have some strength." She proudly held up her toughened hands, stained with soil.

"I have small hands, too!" exclaimed Catherine, and she held one up, palm to palm, with the girl's. Indeed, they were of the exact same size. "Perhaps I could be a weeder," she said, laughing.

I glanced at the girl, worried that Catherine, dressed in fine clothes, offended her. But one look at my friend and anyone could tell she was the opposite of malicious. The girl laughed with her, until a stern look from the head gardener sent her back onto her knees, pulling at an errant plant.

We continued our stroll. But as we paused by the barren flower beds, I noticed Catherine shivering.

"You've not dressed warmly enough for this outing," I pointed out. "I've seen enough of the garden. Let's return."

"I'm not cold," Catherine insisted, although her long velvet sleeves jangled up and down as she rubbed her arms.

Only a moment later, the reason became clear for Catherine's patronage of the garden. First the sound of leather boots on stone and then two men appeared from behind a tall hedge: Stephen Gardiner, Bishop of Winchester, and the Duke of Norfolk.

I turned to Catherine. "Why did you deceive me?" I asked, hurt.

"I didn't," she said, but Catherine Howard was always a poor liar. Her cheeks reddened, a telltale sign.

Bishop Gardiner called out, "I am glad to come upon you here, Mistress Stafford. I would converse with you on a matter of some importance, if you would be so good as to join me on the path."

He beckoned toward a large raised sundial in the center of the garden. His tone was all politeness now, but his request carried the whiff of command. And I could not refuse him. No matter what had transpired between us, he was still a bishop and I was still a novice who had been trained to obey the leaders of the church.

We walked side by side, but he did not speak again for a time. Glancing back, I saw the Duke of Norfolk talking intently to Catherine. Perhaps he was telling her of the outrage perpetrated on the tombs of the Howards.

The bishop finally broke the silence with a question: "Have you been given any indication of why His Majesty has asked you to dine with him?"

"None," I said.

"He called you 'kinswoman' in Westminster Hall, but King Henry has never been fond of the Stafford family," mused the bishop. "He detests all monks and nuns and friars. Yet he must know that you were pledged to the Dominican Order for more than a year. He may well remember that you were ordered to the Tower of London because of interfering with the course of justice in your cousin's burning."

I should have been braced for it. Hadn't I learned, time and again, that the Bishop of Winchester had a talent for censure mixed with praise, for keeping his opponents forever off balance? But the callousness with which he spoke of Margaret's terrible death nonetheless brought hot tears to my eyes, and angry words to my lips.

"Perhaps the king plans to exact some punishment of me today, saving you the time and effort of devising your next plot," I said.

The bishop stopped short to stare at me. "Do you honestly feel that I mean you harm?" he asked. "Yes, I disowned you yesterday at Westminster Hall in front of Cromwell, but you could scarcely expect otherwise. I was the one who saw you released from the Tower of London three years ago, who protected and watched over you ever since, even though you've refused to serve me again. But no matter what you say or do, you will always be my Sister Joanna."

I was astounded to hear his side of our long and tormented association. There seemed no possible response, so I began to walk toward the sundial again and he matched my steps.

Gardiner went on, "I hope that you do not speak to His Majesty as you do to me, in which case you may very well provoke his anger, something which you must take all possible steps to avoid."

"I don't want to make him angry," I said honestly.

The bishop tapped his long, bony fingers together, a gesture I knew meant he was working out some problem in his agile lawyer brain. "King Henry never does anything without having a secret purpose to it and usually two purposes ahead," he said. "But what his purpose is in drawing you closer, I simply cannot fathom."

We reached the fountain, encircled by brown hedges beginning to bud. It was empty of water, not even a silt-thickened puddle at the bottom. It had been a dry spring. I glanced back, but the Duke of Norfolk and his niece had disappeared.

The bishop resumed his musings. "This must have something to do with his relations with Queen Anne. We'd thought him quite disaffected from her, but Cromwell's being made Earl of Essex, and now this formal dinner with her, they bode ill for our cause."

"I don't understand what Cromwell has to do with the marriage," I said.

"Don't you? This marriage, this alliance with the Protestant powers of Germany, was all Cromwell's doing. How could he have predicted that the king would take such a dislike to Anne of Cleves the first moment he laid eyes on her?"

I turned away from Gardiner. They all thought it a whim, a vagary of human desire, which made King Henry recoil from his fourth wife. But I knew the true reason why the marriage failed at the start. The king blamed Anne of Cleves for his being unable to perform as a husband. He would never know he was poisoned when he sipped from the chalice.

Gardiner said, "We have done all we can to make sure the king continues to detest her. And soon he may not need her. The king only married her because France and Spain had made a treaty and threatened invasion. But now that treaty is broken; our kingdom doesn't need Cleves any longer to survive. And if she falls, she takes Cromwell with her."

I felt chilled to the marrow, remembering the hopeful young countenance of the princess in the boat that crossed the channel, bringing her to her new home.

Gardiner frowned as he studied me. My emotions, the mixture of guilt and pity for Anne of Cleves, must have shown. "Do you not still support the True Faith, Joanna?" he asked.

"With my life, Bishop," I said.

Gardiner, still frowning, reached out and snapped an errant brown branch from the side of the hedge. But he did not toss it aside.

"Do you know a Doctor Robert Barnes?" he asked, now pulling a green bud off the branch so that no new life remained.

I shook my head, wary of this new direction.

"Ah, if only you would trouble yourself to follow the affairs of the kingdom, Joanna, you would be truly formidable. But that is something you don't do. A part of you always craves the cloister, to hide from the ugliness of the world. It's understandable; yes, it's understandable. But the time for hiding is over." Still gripping the branch, he peered across the garden, at the glowing walls of Whitehall Palace.

"Doctor Barnes began as an Augustinian friar, at my very own Cambridge University. But he ran afoul of the Cardinal Wolsey and was seriously questioned. I spoke for him then. I defended him and said he was worthy and capable of reform. But as soon as he was able, Doctor Barnes made a mockery of us all. He left England, journeyed to Germany, and became a faithful friend to Martin Luther. His views were so extreme that since Doctor Barnes's return, a passionate and committed Lutheran, King Henry had him imprisoned not once, but *twice*. Even apart from his heresies, he was a rash and intemperate person. Yet this very same man preached the Easter sermon at Saint Paul's this year, going out of his way to personally denigrate me. He was made to apologize by the king himself for it, and then he insulted me a *second* time. You may well wonder: How is that possible? I am the Bishop of Winchester."

Throughout Bishop Gardiner's strange rant about the heretical Doctor Barnes, I'd watched those large white hands running up and down the branch, tearing at bits of bark. With every few words, a piece of bark would fly from the branch and drift to the ground. To claw at it so must have caused him pain, but he showed no sign.

"Bishop, forgive me, I don't understand these matters," I said. And I didn't. The rapidly changing fortunes of those surrounding the king and Cromwell left me bewildered.

"Doctor Barnes had *protection*—he possessed a second good friend besides Martin Luther, and that person is Thomas Cromwell, our newly elevated Earl of Essex," Gardiner said, near to choking on his bitterness. "When I criticized Barnes's heretical statements last year, Cromwell used it as a way to persuade the king to ban me from the Privy Council. Then at Easter, it was Cromwell who instructed his puppet to mock me before the entire court."

Suddenly, violently, Gardiner broke his branch into pieces, heedless that a flurry of splintered bark now clung to the bottom of his white robes.

His eyebrows furrowed, he said, "Do you relish being called Papist, Joanna? Of living in fear that the king will take those final steps toward abominable heresy, and knowing that when he does, your soul will be lost forever?"

"No," I said, anguished. "No."

He reached out and laid both his hands on my shoulders. He had touched me in this manner before—it meant the moment had come to pray. I closed my eyes, my fingers leaping to the chain around my neck holding the crucifix.

But then the bishop pressed down, with those same hands that had clawed a branch to pieces. He would have me kneel before him. His grip was so strong that I had no choice but to buckle. The ground felt cold and hard beneath the thin fabric of my borrowed dress.

"I pray to God that no harm in word or deed befalls you, Joanna Stafford," he said. "For I fear that much hangs in the balance on what occurs today."

11

It was not Master Thomas Culpepper but a royal page who escorted me to dinner with the king and queen. I recognized him from the inspection parade, for he was the fairest of the pages and perhaps the youngest, fourteen at most. He had not seen me, masked and hiding in the shadows. His gaze was nothing but respectful. Blank.

Wearing the finest of the dresses His Majesty had pressed on me, I followed the page to the vast hall I'd passed through when I first arrived in Whitehall. At that time it had been filled with gentlemen I did not know. I realized now that the ministers and high noblemen were already in place in Westminster, and now, since they never wanted to be too far from the orbit of King Henry, they gathered in this hall.

I soon perceived that there were two groups of equal size. The Bishop of Winchester stood with the Duke of Norfolk on one side of the long room, surrounded by lords, gentlemen, and clerks sympathetic to their position. I could feel Gardiner's stare on me from far away. He did not turn as I walked the length of the room; his head never shifted. But those eyes tracked my procession. Closer to the archway that the blond page led me toward was Cromwell's party. He, too, was flanked by supporters; I recognized Sir Thomas Wriothesley and Richard Rich.

Conversations faltered across the hall as men caught sight of me. Sir Walter Hungerford's curious questioning was but a harbinger of what was to come. I could no longer attribute the staring to interest in Thomas Culpepper or Catherine Howard. I was becoming notorious.

As I neared the chief minister's party, I kept my eyes on the bobbing red doublet directly in front of me. I did not want to risk any sort of confrontation with Thomas Cromwell. The words I'd exchanged with Bishop Gardiner in the garden had unnerved me enough. Even a few words of forced greeting—or a bow—from his rival, Cromwell, could destroy my fragile courage.

A stream of workers carrying trays and boxes and bottles blocked our path to the stairs. Feeling the eyes of a roomful of ruthless men on me, I turned, desperate, to face the wall. I would have to make a show of examining whatever was displayed there.

Two large and lavish tapestries covered this wall, with a small painting in between that I now scrutinized. Its first point of distinction was that it was not a portrait. Almost every painting in the palace was of a member of the Tudor family, or of Henry VI, the saintly Lancaster king the Tudors venerated. But this was a painting of a group of people, none of them known to me. They clustered before a castle. One man looked to be royal, wearing fine robes and a crown, accompanied by courtiers. Two people struggled to reach this ruler: a woman and a child in rags, pleading. He seemed oblivious to them.

But that was not the most disquieting thing about the painting. It was that a final figure hovered above the destitute woman and child. Not a person. A smiling skeleton, reaching with bony fingers for the arm of the wealthy ruler.

Why would such a painting be displayed in Whitehall?

When we were finally able to pass through that archway and ascend a winding staircase, even as I entered the privy chamber of the queen of England, I was haunted by that question.

This was the most lavish of all the rooms I had seen so far. The wall tapestries were woven with gold-edged thread. Plates and goblets sparkled on a long, thick table at which we would presumably eat. Scented rushes covered the floor; above, a carved and painted ceiling loomed.

But what struck me most of all was the near-blinding brilliance of the room. The queen's privy chamber was located in the middle of the second floor of the palace—there were no windows. Nonetheless, it was brighter than if windows stretched ceiling to floor in the midday sun. Yellow flames leaped in a large fireplace; a fully lit silver chandelier hovered; candles soared everywhere, from table to sideboard.

The page bowed and departed. He had completed his assigned task. The only persons in the queen's privy chamber were a dozen men hurriedly preparing the table or replacing the cushions on the chairs.

No one spoke to me—no one seemed to notice my existence—and I felt incredibly awkward as I stood in the corner, alone. Not for the first time I worried about what I would say to the king. Because he'd had the head of my family, the Duke of Buckingham, executed, the Staffords were sure to be a sensitive subject. And Gardiner was right: my having served as a novice in a priory could not possibly please him, either.

I don't know how many minutes I waited—it might have been very few—when a woman slipped through a door on the other side of the room. As she walked toward me, a sour taste filled my mouth. For it was Lady Jane Rochford, the widow of George Boleyn. If this was the kind of company I would soon be keeping, then the skeleton of the painting was most definitely an omen.

"You are looking very well, Mistress Stafford," she said, and smiled. Just as when I first met her, that broad smile triggered in me a strong desire to run in the other direction. "I am sorry no one was here to greet you. I've only just been made aware of your presence."

I murmured a greeting, fighting down my instinct to recoil.

"I am appointed one of the queen's principal ladies-in-waiting, did you know that?" she asked, preening. "I remember when I met you, it was at Gertrude's London home and we were all wondering who would be queen and who among us would be chosen to serve her. And now"—her smile deepened—"here we are."

How tasteless she was to bring up Gertrude Courtenay here, moments away from the arrival of King Henry, when it was the king who ordered the arrest of the Courtenays for treason, and Gertrude and her son still languished in the Tower of London. She went on to tell me who the other ladies and maids of the queen were. I recognized none of their names but Catherine's.

"And how do you like Whitehall—is it not beautiful?" she asked. Without waiting for an answer, she said, "I was with them the first day they walked through this palace, when they took possession from Cardinal Wolsey."

I did not know what she meant by *they*. Something in her watchful expression told me that Lady Rochford longed for me to ask, and, not knowing what else to talk about, I asked whom she referred to.

"The king—and Anne," she said, her voice lowering to conspiratorial. "My sister-in-law. They toured Whitehall before they were married. The king was so in love with her then. This was her favorite palace, and everything you see here, the furnishings and the paintings, even which plants would be grown in the garden, was her choice. Her taste. When she was queen, there was a portrait of her in every one of the grandest rooms. All destroyed. Every image of Anne Boleyn was burned at the order of the king."

The Boleyns were the very last people I would ever wish to discuss, and so I was flooded with relief to see the arrival of the new Queen Anne—the fourth of his consorts— followed by a group of ladies. Lady Rochford threw her shoulders back and took her place in the queen's train.

I made my deepest curtsy, one that would have made my mother proud.

"You are welcome to court, Mistress Joanna," said Queen Anne, with a dignified tilt of the head. Her accent was thick, her words halting. But I was impressed that after four months, she spoke English this well. On the boat from Calais to Dover, she had possessed not a single word.

She looked different and it was not just her wardrobe. Anne of Cleves wore English fashions now; that strange hat and sleeves were gone. She was still a pleasant-looking young woman—the widespread rumor that the queen was too plain to attract the king was nonsense. But she was paler than I remembered. And thinner, too.

"Will you stitch with me?" she asked. "With stitches, you . . . are good."

"I would be honored," I said, curtsying again. I could not help but be flattered that she remembered my fondness for embroidery.

And then came the king. Henry VIII filled up the room with his presence: tall, broad, a crown atop his red hair, and draped with a diamond-laden pendant. We all of us made our obeisance, and he limped to the table, nodding. Queen Anne sat at the other end of the table from her husband, with my place halfway between.

At first the king said little. His attention was on neither the queen nor myself but on the food. He was quite intent on a certain course—the stuffed capon—and visibly relaxed when it appeared, just after the civet of hare. Some worry he'd had over its sauce disappeared with the first bite, and his heavy jowls shook as he consumed slice after slice.

Six ladies attended the queen, bringing her food and serving her wine. Catherine was not among them, but Lady Rochford was. George Boleyn's widow saw to my dinner service as well, which meant that I was frequently treated to that unfortunate smile. Such rich, heavy dishes were not to my taste, but I did not want to appear rude and so did my best to keep up. The odors of the food mingled with the burning wax of many candles and the king's own scent, the musk and lavender and orange water—this was not conducive to appetite.

Peeking down the table, I detected, even in candlelight, a tenseness in Queen Anne's expression. A certain wariness. She ate even less than I did.

"Madame, you have met our guest before?" said the king to his wife after the capons were cleared. "We are told that our cousin Joanna made your acquaintance in France."

Queen Anne swallowed and said, "Yes, Your Grace, I knew—I knew . . ." She paused and faltered. A man surged forward, listened

to a flood of Anne's German, and then explained to the king the circumstances of my meeting her.

"You are fortunate to be able to travel abroad," the king said to
me. "In truth, we envy you. If we leave the kingdom, it's assumed we
are planning war. We'd have to raise taxes, muster an army, and set
fire to the Scottish border before we go. A high price to pay for trying out the stuffed capon in Calais."

The room erupted in laughter, and, to my own amazement, I
joined in. I had heard from my relations that King Henry had the
power to charm, that he was witty. Now I experienced it for myself.

One person failed to laugh. Queen Anne's translator had conveyed the king's joke to her, but perhaps the humor did not survive
translation. She did nothing but frown.

I was not the only one who noticed that the queen was at a loss.
The king sighed and then drained his goblet. "More wine," he called
out sharply, and men scurried to obey. A silence fell over the table
again.

They were so ill at ease with each other. Would this have been
a harmonious couple even if he hadn't been sickened at the outset?
There was no way for me, for anyone, to know.

As soon as his goblet was replenished, King Henry sipped from
it, nodded, and then turned to me. "Cousin, we should now like to
hear about your tapestry enterprise. First of all: Who precisely taught
you to weave?"

12

Henry VIII had ordered the destruction of the monasteries, thus ending a way of life held sacred in England for a thousand years. How could I tell him that it was the nuns who taught me to weave? But as he drummed his fingers on the table, growing impatient with my silence, I had no choice.

"I learned it while I served as a novice at the Dominican Order of sisters in Dartford," I said.

I waited for him to erupt, to bellow. Here would come the famous, feared temper. But the king stroked his beard and said, "They had a loom, correct? Your work was not done with needles, I think."

"No, Your Majesty. I mean, yes. We used a loom."

"Your work was first-rate on the phoenix tapestry that the queen our wife purchased," said the king. "It shows a certain delicacy, an interpretation of myth, that is too often lacking in these triptychs from Brussels."

My cheeks hot, I said, "Thank you, Your Majesty."

"And you have begun another?" he said, leaning toward me across the table, his eyes alight with interest.

I explained that I'd ordered the design for *The Sorrow of Niobe*, a Greek queen who lost everything to the gods.

It would not seem possible for King Henry to look at me more intently, but that piece of news seemed to trigger some deep contemplation.

"Hubris, ahhhh," he said. "You have made an interesting choice."

"Pardon me, Your Majesty?"

A smile playing on his lips, the king said, "Niobe's children were slain by the gods because of hubris. She had defied them, saying that her children were superior to all. For her pride and arrogance, for her overestimation of their importance, she was punished."

I had seen the word *hubris* in relation to this myth but not understood its full meaning. Now my stomach twisted as I realized my choice could be seen as celebrating defiance of the gods. If King Henry saw himself as a sacred being—which seemed likely—then this tapestry would offend him.

"Pride is a sin, Your Highness," I said.

"Very true, Cousin." He sipped some wine and asked, "Will you use a living woman as your model for Niobe the queen?"

"I know that near the end of a weave, when finishing the faces, some have been known to use paintings or even living subjects as models," I said, relieved at the change in course of conversation. "I suppose it is possible."

The king beckoned for a servant, who shortly after darted away, and suddenly Master Thomas Culpepper appeared at the table. He bent over so that the king could say something to him alone. He nodded and then withdrew from the table. I tried to catch his eye—it felt wrong to fail to acknowledge Culpepper, my greatest friend at Whitehall after Catherine Howard—but he did not look in my direction.

"There is no substitute in art for experience," said the king, approvingly. "Bearing that in mind, tell us what you think of our collection of tapestries. You see only a portion here at Whitehall, but we are proud of what is so displayed."

And so went my discussion of tapestry with the king of England. As the sovereign worked his way through three more courses of food, we talked of the series I had seen thus far. He was eager to hear my opinions. The one in the main hall turned out be called *The Fall of Troy*. Most of the king's tapestries told tales of classic Rome or stories of the Old Testament. "Our prize is still *The Story of David*, we purchased it twelve years ago," he said. "We've assigned a man in Brussels. And scouts in Italy and France and Flanders. We hate to think of losing a good tapestry, particularly if it's to the king of France."

This was a world I had not imagined. Of course I knew that the largest tapestries were woven in Brussels and that the wealthiest families prided themselves on their possessions. But this sprawling community of artisans and weavers, fueled by new ideas and techniques, financed by the competitive kings of Europe—I'd had only an inkling.

"Our grandfather, Edward the Fourth, built up a strong collection," the king explained as he dove into the next course, one of roasted pig. "The king our father added to it; he had a perceptive eye for tapestry, as he did for all things. When he died, the Crown owned four hundred pieces of tapestry."

"Four *hundred*?" It did not seem possible.

"The royal collection now stands at eighteen hundred tapestries." He smiled proudly. "We had it inventoried. We do so periodically. We like to know exactly what we own." He turned his head to the group of servants standing behind. "Fetch Sir Anthony Denny."

Not a moment later, a thin, red-haired gentleman appeared, and the king ordered him to commence with a new inventory of the tapestries of Whitehall.

"Your Majesty, if I may?"

With a start, I turned toward the queen, who had called out to her husband in her quavering, heavily accented voice. I was overcome with shame at my incivility. I had been embroiled in conversation with the king for some time, and had made no effort to include the queen.

"Sire, I know—that you love the music," she said slowly. "I have surprise."

The doors swung open and four men strode in, carrying musical instruments. They were all dark, resembling each other to an unusual degree. With one graceful movement, the quartet bowed low to the king and queen.

The queen's translator announced on her behalf, "These are the

Bassano brothers, come to court from Venice at the queen's invitation, to entertain Your Majesty."

King Henry looked truly taken aback. But he gathered himself and pointed at one of the brothers and asked what instrument he carried.

"It is called the violin, Sire," the man answered in French.

I will never forget the performance of the Bassano brothers in the queen's privy chamber. It could have been the potency of the wine, or my jangled nerves over conversing with King Henry, or my constant and underlying fear of the Palace of Whitehall. Perhaps it was all of those things. But I found the piercing, soaring, aching sound of that violin, the principal instrument in the quartet, so powerful that it was at times hard to draw breath.

I loved music—I used to play a *vihuela*, taught by my mother— but it had been a long time since I'd heard instruments play. When was the last occasion? It took me a moment, and then I remembered, with a twist of my heart. The wedding of Agatha and John Gwinn just a year ago. I danced at that wedding, the last one with Geoffrey Scovill, who admitted more than he should have of his feelings for me. Although I had always known—always. How much Geoffrey and I had hurt each other. And the Gwinns said he would leave Dartford. What if he'd already done so—and I'd never have the chance to speak to Geoffrey again.

The Bassano brothers finished, and the queen clapped her hands, well pleased. As for the king, he had gone still as a statute, his small blue eyes a touch bleary in his fleshy face.

We waited for his reaction. Surely he must be impressed.

Henry VIII cleared his throat and said, "Such music is not appropriate for a small dinner of family in a privy chamber."

The queen's face fell. I could not believe that His Majesty, known for his passion for music, did not appreciate what his wife had done. Standing behind her, Lady Rochford smirked.

The king continued, "Still, we shall be sure that these brothers from Venice are fairly compensated."

I was in an odd way grateful for his coldness to Anne of Cleves, for it broke the spell. During the long discussion of tapestry, I had found it hard to hold on to my hatred of the king. It had almost seemed as if we *were* family, speaking of a common interest. His depth of knowledge of tapestry, his references and insights, were so exceptional that I had been quite carried away. But now I'd returned to earth. The king was a tyrant who had ordered the deaths of people I loved. He could never be my family.

The king rose to his feet with a groan, pulling himself up by gripping the top of his high-backed seat. He had eaten and drunk so much. It was surprising he was able to rise without assistance of strong-backed menservants.

"We bid you good day, Madame," he said to his wife. "We have another matter of tapestry to discuss with our kinswoman, Joanna."

Anne of Cleves said quietly, "Good day."

I rose and curtsied to the queen. To prolong my time with the king was a daunting prospect. I'd hoped to be free of him by now. But at least this meant we would soon finish our business and I'd be able to leave for Dartford.

The king moved with difficulty from the queen's privy chamber. He had been sitting a long time; his leg seemed now a source of utter agony. I wasn't sure what was wrong with him—Master Culpepper had said something about open sores on the king's leg requiring the constant attention of a physician.

We passed a portrait of his third queen, Jane Seymour, hanging on the wall. How pale and pensive she looked, as if she knew she would die before the marriage was two years old. I wondered which ghosts walked with King Henry along the passageways of Whitehall: the first wife he spurned; the second one he had killed; or the third one, whom he lost after she did her duty and produced a male heir. Perhaps it was not so strange the king showed no interest in Queen Anne, for he could well be a man worn down from being husband to the trio who preceded her.

Now that I stood close to him, that singular odor filled my

head. Aside from the fruit and floral extracts and the musk was the same indefinable smell—familiar and animal-like and somehow disgusting. At dinner I'd thought it came from one of the myriad dishes of meat. But we were far from the table now. In trying to place it, my mind skipped to a memory of Edmund treating a wound in the Dartford infirmary and then I had it—what I smelled was infected flesh. As much as he tried to cover it up, the king's leg wound stank.

We finally arrived at the destination the king had in mind: the chamber housing *The Story of David*. It was undeniably magnificent, each glittering tapestry in the long series depicting an episode of the ancient king's life. We stood side by side, saying nothing, for a few moments.

The skill of the weavers, undoubtedly working in Brussels, astonished me. In their hands, flatly woven wool and silken threads took on the appearance of curved, shiny battle armor; of a shimmering meadow of pink, red, and violet flowers; of the deep, soft folds of a lady's gown; of the radiant sun itself.

"We come here often, for only this king of the Israelites could understand our destiny," said Henry VIII, very solemn. "We are another David, chosen by God."

I stole a glance at him. Did he truly believe this? King Henry's face was red and slick with sweat, whether from the long meal in the candlelight or the stabbing pain of his leg, I did not know. "We must lead the people from the darkness and ignorance of papal superstition to truth and goodness," he announced.

I clutched my hands tight, to keep them from trembling.

Although he did not turn from *The Story of David* to look at me, the king must have sensed my fear. "Do not be troubled, Joanna, for you were not at fault for seeking to become a nun. You are clearly a woman of intelligence. What you require is our instruction."

I did not like the sound of that.

Sir Anthony Denny approached and, to my relief, reminded the king of a council meeting, but King Henry waved him off. "We shall be there soon enough," he said in that high, sharp voice. Then, his tone gentler, he said to me, "Tell us, Cousin, what you think of the paintings of Whitehall? You are knowledgeable about tapestry, we would like to discover what else you can speak to."

"I appreciate art but know little of its technique, Your Majesty," I said. "When a painting moves me, I am not sure of the reason."

"And has a painting of mine moved you?" He turned to inspect me. "Ah, yes, one has."

When I described the painting I had seen in the hall just before dinner, the king laughed a little. "You *are* a woman of surprises," he said. "That is one of our favorites. It is adapted from a series done years ago by our court painter, Hans Holbein, called *The Dance of Death*."

"Then the skeleton in the painting is . . ."

" . . . death." Henry VIII finished my sentence. "It appears in each one of the series, but to different people: a nobleman, a poor man, a merchant, an abbess, even a king. You understand, Joanna, death comes to all."

I felt a chill. And for a fleeting second I thought I glimpsed fear in the king's face, too. To believe yourself chosen by God to be another David, and yet to quake before mortality, what a strange state. Or was it guilt that haunted him, guilt for the monasteries he'd destroyed, the parade of martyrs he'd created?

The king said firmly, "We did not ask for your company after dinner to speak of death. Put Holbein and his fancies from your mind. We wish to commission your next tapestry, *The Sorrow of Niobe*, but we have a condition. We would choose the subject whose face you model Niobe's on."

It took me a moment to grasp what he was saying. "But Your Majesty, my loom is in Dartford. I do all my weaving there. Unless you plan to send this person to Kent, I don't understand how it will be possible."

"We have a proposal as to where you will weave," he said. "Many thoughts have come to us on that. But first, we would have you meet your Niobe. We think you will agree she is worthy of admiration."

To my shock, a fond smile played on his lips, the like of which I hadn't seen this entire day. It was in anticipation of the Niobe I would now meet. Once he learned of my tapestry, he'd arranged for her to be brought to this unknown room.

So he was *not* weary of women. Although he was a man of some fifty years of age, married to a fourth wife, fat and near lame, Henry VIII was behaving like a love-struck swain.

The king gestured, impatiently, for a servant to open the door to a room on the passageway. With a dread approaching nausea, I walked toward it.

Inside was a small, windowless study. A cushioned stool was put in the center of the room, and a young woman perched on it, her skirts spread in a perfect circle, her cheeks flushed as her eyes met mine.

Catherine Howard.

13

You are wrong, Joanna. I am only His Majesty's friend." That is what Catherine insisted as soon as we were back in her chamber and alone.

The king had, thankfully, not spoken to her besides making an introduction. I managed to stammer a greeting as she lowered her gaze. And that was all. Catherine was merely displayed to me as if she were one of the royal tapestries.

Sir Anthony Denny had forestalled anything more by pleading, "Sire? The council?"

The king said, "Yes, we shall attend, but first, Cousin, know our plans." He turned, reluctantly, from Catherine to me. "We would have you weave your tapestry here, in London. It shall be the first of many."

"But I could not work in a palace," I protested. "And doesn't the court move to a new palace every two or three months? A single tapestry requires at least six months, even with four weavers."

The king waved my concerns away with a sweep of his plump ringed hand. "There is a workshop in the city, a large and well-maintained place. Our servants take tapestries there for cleaning and mending. It would be the ideal spot. You shall hire your workers and proceed with our plans."

With that, he departed with the fretful Sir Anthony.

His plans were upsetting, but not nearly as upsetting as learning that Catherine was the object of Henry VIII's lust. She must have been pushed toward the king, and I had a good notion by whom. The Duke of Norfolk was notorious for pandering to the king, of using young women to bind himself to Henry VIII. Everyone knew he'd done it with another niece, Anne Boleyn, to the infamy of both.

As soon as I could pose the question without being overheard, I asked, "Is this your uncle's doing?"

"The Duke of Norfolk is pleased that the king enjoys my conversation." She raised her chin. "And that is all it is—conversation. His Majesty says no one has ever taken his mind off affairs of state as I do."

No doubt.

I took a deep breath and asked the question that must be asked. "Have you lost your virtue to the king?"

"No," she cried, now the deepest crimson. "I swear it on the soul of Saint Anne."

"He has never touched you?"

She shook her head, violently, but did not meet my eyes. I was certain she was lying. It was truly sickening, to think of the king kissing or fondling her.

Panicked, I grabbed hold of Catherine by the arms and shook her. "You must listen, Catherine. I beg of you to listen. I've not lived a worldly life, I was a Dominican novice and before that a sheltered girl in Stafford Castle. But I do know something of what I speak. You must not submit to the king, for you will be lost forever. Shamed."

"What makes you so sure I would be shamed afterward?" countered Catherine. "Be assured, Joanna, that I have no such ambition to be a mistress, but if—if I did, for the sake of argument, you know that Elizabeth Blount, the first queen's lady-in-waiting, was married honorably after she had the king's son? She and her husband received properties and pensions."

So that was what Norfolk had told her. After she shared the king's bed, she'd prosper.

"Oh, Catherine, no—no," I said brokenly. "You must *not* believe what the duke says."

Pulling herself from my grasp, Catherine said, "I am expected in the queen's chamber," and she hurried off.

Somehow I made my way to Catherine's room, guarded as usual by her servant, Richard. Catherine did not return for hours. Whether she spent her time with the queen or the king, I had no idea. As sunset approached, I ignored all thought of supper—I was still so full it seemed impossible I'd eat again—and continued to contemplate my impossible situation.

I had no desire to leave Dartford and weave a tapestry in London. I would have to either purchase a house in the city or become part of the king's court, bound to follow him from palace to palace.

On the surface, the proposal had strong advantages. If I were to fill an official position in the king's household, then my cousin Henry Stafford would be more likely to send Arthur Bulmer down. If, however, I decided to defy and enrage the king by refusing this offer and retreating to Dartford, it could ignite such a fury that I'd never reclaim my cousin's son. Moreover, I might have a difficult time finding another buyer for *The Sorrow of Niobe*. My tapestry enterprise could dwindle to nothing, and I'd be left with only the modest pension allotted me, and all other novices, at the dissolution of the Dartford priory.

But how could I remain at court, knowing the king was on the verge of making Catherine his mistress? If I were to feature her face and figure in my tapestry, it would imply my approval of—if not collusion with—this affair. The only way I could possibly serve King Henry was to prevent the further corruption of Catherine Howard.

I just needed to come up with a way to do that.

When Catherine returned that evening, a trifle sullen, I did not resume my accusations. All they would accomplish would be to provoke lies and justifications. I must try other methods to turn her from this terrible course. If only there were someone to help me. But as I thought back over the last three days, I realized that everyone from Bishop Gardiner to Thomas Culpepper must be aware of the budding affair and was doing nothing to stop it.

I cleared my throat. "Will you go to chapel with me, Catherine? I've been here two days and not prayed before the altar."

She brightened at once. "Of course I will. Such a lovely idea. And the Chapel Royal has candles lit until very late."

Her vow by Saint Anne's notwithstanding, I knew that Catherine was none too pious. It wasn't a deliberate flouting of God's laws. Her religious education had been neglected, as had her lessons in other subjects. The Howards cared little for learning.

This meant that Catherine could be unaware that adultery was a grave sin. Saint Paul wrote that those who were guilty of grave sins, committed with intent, could not enter the Kingdom of Heaven, for they destroyed the grace of God. Would she risk the fires of hell for a sordid affair with the king? Only a woman who was blinded by desire would do that. King Henry could not possibly attract a seventeen-year-old girl. She must be receiving intense pressure from the Duke of Norfolk—and was perhaps flattered by kingly attention—but there could be no real feeling in her heart. That should help my cause.

Catherine led me to the Chapel Royal, on the east side of the Great Hall. I stepped inside and dipped my fingers in the stoup but then paused, stunned. The king had made himself head of the church and since this was Henry VIII's place of worship I expected it to embody his laws of faith: fewer candles, adornments, and statues. Had not the king and Cromwell forbidden pilgrimages and offerings to saints, reduced the people's cherished feast days, frowned on prayers with rosary beads and truncated the holy fasts? Yet here, in the Chapel Royal, throbbed the beauty of traditional worship: four bay windows of diamond-shaped stained glass in a hundred colors, delicate clouds of lavender incense, and candles lit here, there, everywhere.

The Chapel Royal was empty but for choristers and boys gathered around a gleaming organ. A psalm was announced and the boys' voices warbled in earnest harmony. Listening to their psalm, inhaling the incense, my feeling of bewilderment and anger receded. No matter how hypocritical the act, the king had formed a chapel devoted to God, and I was grateful for it.

Near the back, Catherine and I knelt, side by side, and I began to pray: "Oh, Lord, give us the wisdom to know your will and to live righteously . . ."

Noises bursting from the side interrupted me. Two pages were preparing the way for the king. He, too, had decided on a nighttime prayer.

King Henry appeared, flanked by Sir Anthony Denny and other courtiers. At the sight of us, he came to a halt, and then called out, "My lords, is this not a fit sight—two comely women moved to worship?"

"Fit indeed," echoed Denny.

The king took one last look at Catherine. I found it most unsettling, his bloated, aging face transformed by such adoration. His Majesty then limped to the king's closet at the other end of the chapel, a place for private worship.

Next to me, Catherine closed her eyes to resume prayers, but even as she obediently murmured the words, a smile quivered in the corner of her mouth.

This was not going to be easy.

14

The next day I received two invitations. The first was to attend a banquet at Winchester House, the palatial home of Bishop Gardiner, in one week's time. The second was to call on court painter Hans Holbein at my earliest convenience.

The thought of dining at the bishop's house left me cold. But even beset by all my troubles, I could not turn down the offer to meet the man who'd painted *The Dance of Death*. Greatly curious, I sent a note to Master Holbein, and before the sun had risen midway in the sky, I was escorted to his workshop. To my astonishment, it was located in the front gatehouse of Whitehall. I climbed two sets of winding stairs to reach the passageway leading to his place of artistry. When I'd arrived at the palace and looked up at those rows of windows, I peered at the quarters of Hans Holbein.

He was not ready for our appointment, however. Although his door was tightly closed, a conversation sounded through the door. Two men spoke French, and one very loudly.

"This is intolerable," screamed a voice. "She is of the highest rank in Christendom. The House of Cleves is connected to the princes of Germany and to Burgundy and France; the queen's older sister is married to the Duke of Saxony! And he will not have her crowned. He does not say more than a few words to her. Why? Because she is a proper princess and not a whore? What kind of king is this!"

The door crashed open. A man appeared wearing a triangular feathered hat and a face as dark as thunder. He brushed past me to stalk down the passageway. A moment later, a second man, plainly dressed, peered out of the doorway. He was of middle years with a broad, homely face. His hair thinned on his head, but his beard sprouted thick.

"Mistress Joanna, you are most welcome to my workshop— please enter," he said in English, with an accent. "I have sweet wine to offer, and cake."

As I entered, a bevy of smells encircled me. Some were familiar, like the lye we'd once used to cleanse the cloister floors. But some were new to me and so noxious that my eyes stung. Easels stood everywhere, with paintings mounted but cloths tossed over so that none were visible. Opposite the tall windows was a shelf for books and maps. It was a place that would ordinarily have fascinated me, except that I was shaken by the other man's angry words. I greatly feared that he meant Catherine Howard when he said "whore." This was what Catherine failed to understand—the irreparable damage to her good name.

Holbein said gently, "Are you not well, Mistress Joanna?"

"I am well," I said quickly. "It is only that . . ." My voice trailed away.

Master Holbein reached out to take my hand, even more gently, "Perhaps you understand French?"

"I do, sir."

Holbein sighed. "Allow me to attempt an explanation."

He steered me to a seat near the window. It was open; I could hear the milling throng from the King Street and courtyards below. He sliced some brown cake and poured me a tall goblet of wine. I did not touch either.

"The gentleman who came to see me is an ambassador," Holbein said. "His name is Doctor Karl Harst. He represents Duke William of Cleves in England and is quite upset about the status of the duke's sister, our Queen Anne. We Germans are a passionate people, Mistress Joanna."

"The ambassador seeks you out as a fellow countryman?"

"I left Augsburg long, long ago," he said. "But I did know the queen before she came to court. I painted her in Cleves, so that King Henry could see what she looked like before deciding on her as consort." He pulled on his beard. "Some now say I did a poor job, that I showed the king a lovely young woman who did not exist."

Holbein's tone was light, but there was an edge of worry to his words.

He continued, "It all goes beyond appearance. Doctor Harst does not want to accept this, but the Cleves alliance is not as important as it was six months ago, regardless of the queen's charms. The ambassadors of France and Spain each court His Majesty. Ambassador Chapuys is fully back in the king's favor."

"Ambassador Chapuys is *here*?" I asked, aghast. "But that can't be; he left court—he was recalled last year. He lives in Antwerp."

"No, Chapuys returned to England."

I had seen no sign of the Emperor Charles's ambassador, nor heard the whisper of Chapuys's name.

"When?" I could not hide the desperation in my voice. "Do you know the date that he arrived?"

"Perhaps a month ago," answered Holbein. "But may I inquire as to why this concerns you so? Eustace Chapuys is a man respected throughout Christendom for his diplomacy, learning, and culture. Have you ever met the imperial ambassador?"

"Yes," I murmured. "My mother was Spanish."

I was horrified but not shocked. This was what I'd sensed, ever since I learned that the man who attacked me must have stolen a page's doublet. A plan that clever, it reeked of Chapuys and the amoral man sent to spy on me and then train me: Jacquard Rolin. Jacquard's twisted lessons were with me still. My telling Holbein the truth about knowing Chapuys, but only a small part of the story, that was what Jacquard taught me to do. "Tell the truth whenever you can," Jacquard always advised. "It is stupid lies that will ensnare you."

But I wasn't certain. There was also a recklessness, a difficulty, to the plot against me that did not seem like something Chapuys would sanction. He was so careful. And still I did not understand why I should be attacked at Whitehall instead of in Dartford. If it were true he'd been in England for a month, that would have allowed enough time to dispatch an assassin. Nothing about this made sense.

Holbein was saying, "You favor your mother in your coloring, then. I was wondering. Forgive me, but you do not resemble the king nor any of his children."

"You are most assuredly forgiven," I said.

Hearing that, Holbein shook with a laugh, swiftly suppressed. "Tell me, Mistress Joanna, how I may best be of service today. I believe His Majesty wishes me to discuss tapestries and your weaving of them."

"Oh, yes?" I felt disappointed. I'd hoped otherwise. The grinning skeleton reaching for the ruler, that image haunted me, even with all of my fears and problems. I ached to know what spurred him to paint it and all those other skeletons the king described. This courteous man who spoke gently and took such pains to make me comfortable, I could not connect him with *The Dance of Death*.

"Tell me of your plans," Holbein said, trying again to coax me into conversation.

"They are not *my* plans. The king wishes to commission me to weave my next one, *The Sorrow of Niobe*, here, in London."

"That is most exciting, and I congratulate you," said Holbein. "I am sure it will be the first of many more commissions."

What a horrible future he painted for me: bound to the king forever, a poor relation trapped in the orbit of the court.

"Mistress Joanna, I do not pry into the feelings of others unless they wish me to, but why such sadness?" Holbein asked. "You are a woman of tragedy here in my workshop. And although that interests me—any artist would be intrigued—I am concerned, too."

"Did the king tell you that he wishes me to use a living woman as the model for Niobe?" I asked. "And that the woman, Catherine Howard, is a maid of honor to the queen?"

I had my answer at once. Holbein sighed and then laughed, but not the deep joyful sound of before. It was a weary chuckle. "Of course, of course. When he is like this, the king does not see clearly, he does not perceive the position of others," he said. "He is sensitive only to himself, and to the lady in question. Sometimes not even her."

"This lady," I said quickly, "is a friend of mine. She is not the sort you may assume her to be, Master Holbein."

"I apologize for any offense given," he said, squeezing my hand in his fatherly fashion. "Then you plan to use Mistress Howard as your subject?"

I shrugged. "The timing is difficult. The faces of a tapestry are finished at the end of the weave. I have already purchased a design from Brussels, and certainly the face can be modified to resemble a specific person. But it will be months before I reach that stage."

Holbein pleaded with me once more to have cake and wine. Once I'd relented, he poured himself a tall goblet, too. "For digestion," he said, and sipped with appreciation. The cake was dense but moist; when I broke off a piece, not a single crumb floated to my plate. It was more sugary than anything I'd tasted in months, so sweet my tongue ached. As for the wine, it was light and reminded me of straw-berries, a welcome change from the heavy wine at the king's table.

"Would you require a subject to sit for you?" he asked. "Unless you are trained in portrait drawing, it might not serve your purpose. I would think a sketch or painting of Mistress Howard—as close a likeness as possible—would better serve."

"Yes, that makes sense. However, there is none that I know of."

Holbein said, still musing, "I could draw her for you, but it would require a portion of Mistress Howard's time."

An idea, fully formed, jumped into my head. "How much time?" I asked.

Holbein said, pulling on his beard, "I was able to paint Christina of Milan when given no more than three hours of her time, but ide-ally I would like four days, in a row."

"Can you begin at once? And of course you must inform me of your fee."

Holbein waved his hand. "I am paid a handsome wage by King Henry, I do not need to extract coins from you, Mistress Stafford. I wish to help you—but I have no assistant at present. His mother is ill and I have excused him from his duties until May Day."

"I am terribly ignorant, but could I serve as apprentice?" I asked.

After a moment's hesitation, Holbein agreed because a drawing that used chalk would not require as much assistance as paints.

In the midst of my expression of thanks, an obstacle occurred. "Doctor Harst, the Cleves ambassador, will perhaps not be pleased with this commission or others, too, if word should spread."

Holbein threw his head back and laughed louder than I'd heard him yet. "Word shall spread, be assured. But artists do not shun controversial subjects, Mistress Stafford. This is what we live for."

Less than an hour later, when I told Catherine of the plan that she sit for a portrait sketch by Master Hans Holbein, she cried, "What an honor. I would never, ever have thought Holbein would be interested in me. Thank you, Joanna."

She embraced me. I could tell that Catherine was grateful for more than the opportunity to sit for a sketch. She interpreted this as a healing of the breach between us since she'd been presented to me by King Henry. She had no idea how I planned to use it as a weapon in my private war.

"This will require every waking minute," I told her. "You'll have to be excused from your duties in the queen's household."

"Oh, *that* will be no difficulty," she said. "Lady Rochford will see to it."

I should not have been surprised that Jane Boleyn, Lady Rochford, was in control of Catherine's comings and goings in the queen's household. She must be in league with Norfolk. What an unsavory person she was: Lady Rochford had supplied the evidence Cromwell desperately needed to condemn not just Queen Anne Boleyn but her own husband, George Boleyn. As much as I detested Lord Rochford, it was a chilling act by a wife. And, most ominously, Jane Boleyn trafficked in the black arts. I knew it was she who told Gertrude

Courtenay of the necromancer Orobas, and where he could be found.

But I was determined to not be intimidated by Lady Rochford or the Duke of Norfolk or even Bishop Gardiner. *We have done all we can to make sure the king continues to detest his wife.* That is what the bishop told me in the Whitehall gardens. I had no idea that a critical part of their plan was to use a seventeen-year-old girl as bait, drawing the king away from the queen and the architect of her marriage, Thomas Cromwell.

For the next three days, I effectively removed Catherine from their corrupting grasp. Once I'd delivered her to Hans Holbein in the morning, I did not leave her side until after nightfall and we went to sleep, protected by the Howards' servant Richard. I put myself at Master Holbein's disposal, and in so doing became more familiar with his workshop. I learned that the strong smells were either for cleaning brushes or mixing pigments or treating the paper. For Catherine's image, he drew on a paper tinted a faint pink. His tools were a row of chalks: black, gray, red, and shades between. I sharpened them to his specification.

My other task was to keep her still. Catherine bubbled with a hundred questions, but as Holbein explained, he could not sketch her while she spoke or moved. I seized the opportunity to read aloud from a prayer book. She listened quietly, but I feared her expression was more obedient than rapt. When breaks permitted, we ate our meals in Holbein's workshop. And then, after he lost the light from those tall windows, I accompanied Catherine to the royal chapel. Thankfully, we did not encounter the king there. I selected the prayers to be recited with great care. I didn't dare say the word *adultery* to her—that would be too obvious. But I prayed with her for guidance in seeking out God's grace and went so far as to ask the Virgin Mary to protect us from temptation to commit fleshly sins.

Through it all, I never mentioned her "friendship" with Henry VIII, and she made absolutely no reference to it. I watched her for signs of contrition in chapel. She knelt next to me, hands clasped, earnestly praying. It almost seemed as if some other girl were in dan-

ger, not my friend. But it *was* Catherine Howard, and I was determined to save her. All other thoughts, from my distaste for the king's
commission to my fear of an unknown enemy in Whitehall, were
thrust aside. This had become the most important objective.

I was certain that Catherine charmed Master Holbein. She made
him laugh so loud that it seemed the walls shook. And he was not offended by her flurry of questions, such as when she pleaded with him
for gossip about the famous personages he'd painted. She was much
more interested in the stories of queens and duchesses than in those
of humanist scholars such as Desiderius Erasmus, whom he'd had
the honor to paint three times in Basel. Catherine even coaxed out of
Holbein the details of his own background: his youth in Augsburg,
a free Imperial city in Bavaria; his apprenticeship under his artist
father, Hans Holbein the Elder; and his marriage to a widow named
Elsbeth, who lived in a house in Basel with their four children. With
a delicacy I was pleased to see, Catherine did not press him for reasons why his family never joined him in England. I suspected there
was some problem, perhaps even estrangement, there.

Late in the afternoon of the third day, a messenger appeared to
inform Catherine that the seamstress was in her room, prepared to
do the final fitting of her dress. Apparently Bishop Gardiner's banquet, which Catherine looked forward to much more than I did, was
the sort of affair that required fine clothes and jewels.

I encouraged Catherine to go on without me; this would afford
a moment for me to make sure that Holbein had formed a high
opinion of her. I very much wanted him to see the best in Catherine.
For a time, I helped the artist clean his workshop. I felt rather guilty
that he would not be paid for his labors and kept trying to make it
up to him. He commented, not for the first time, that he'd never
seen a woman of gentle birth take to cleaning so well. I thanked him
without revealing that as a Dominican novice, I had performed such
labor every day. I did not know Master Holbein's religious beliefs,
but if he was from Germany, there was a chance he was Lutheran
and would recoil from my service to God. He might even be ac-

quainted with Martin Luther or his English follower, the Doctor
Barnes whom Bishop Gardiner hated so fervently.

As I straightened his chalks, I said, "You see how kind Catherine
is, how caring of other people."

"Yes, I see that," he said and continued to clean his hands with a
strong-smelling cloth.

That was not enough for me. "Master Holbein, then, you perceive
how those who say she is the sort of girl who would serve as mistress
are wrong."

He said, "Do you think that mistresses are cruel and terrible? In
my experience, most of them are quite kind."

I stood in the middle of his workshop, staring at him, speechless.

In a gentler voice, Holbein said, "Mistress Joanna, I believe that
you are someone who sees the world in black and white. But I am an
artist." He held up a palette dotted with blobs of dried paint. "I see
many, many colors."

"Another way to put it is that you are a cynic."

He sat down, heavily, by the window. Looking out, he said, "I
came to England, with a letter of recommendation from the scholar
Erasmus, to the house of Sir Thomas More. He was my patron and
a great man. A great friend. And he was beheaded in 1535, by order
of the king. It was difficult, but an artist must have a patron, so I
found my way into the favor of Anne Boleyn. And I grew to like and
respect her very much indeed—until she was beheaded in 1536, by
order of the king. Now my chief patron, besides the king himself, is
Chief Minister Thomas Cromwell. A wise and dedicated man—with
a long list of enemies."

He shook himself from his melancholia. "We shall have our cake
and wine, Mistress Joanna," he announced. Once again the intense
sweetness of cake coupled with the light tartness of wine left me
comforted. Holbein spoke only of benign topics. Nothing of mistresses, or dead patrons. Neither of us wanted to delve into any of
that again. I understood better now his strange life, the loyalties he
formed and the shifts he felt he must make.

It was twilight when I left Holbein's workshop. The sound of the crowds outside the gatehouse had died away. All those petitioners so desperate for Cromwell's favor must have gone home. There were few people inside the gatehouse. I passed no one in the passageway leading to the winding stairs at the end.

I realized this was the first time I'd been alone anywhere since Culpepper delivered me to Catherine's rooms five days ago. *Promise me you'll never be alone*, Culpepper had insisted.

I was starting down the stairs, framing a silent apology to Thomas, when I heard a soft footfall on the step somewhere above.

It made me smile. What exquisite timing—I realize I should not be alone and seconds later I am pursued. Of course it wasn't the case.

I glanced over my shoulder. If this were a typical staircase, I would be able to see someone behind. But because the stairs were winding and dimly lit—there were no fixed candles on the wall and I carried nothing myself—I saw no other person.

I continued to the second floor, determined not to give way to my nerves. I couldn't hear anyone descending behind me, until I stopped, abruptly. There were two more soft steps above, and then that person halted, too. As if he were waiting for what I would do next.

My throat tightened; I could feel the sweat break out on my brow.

Through a slit of a window, the last fading rays of a grayish-orange dusk filled the square space. Before me stretched a long passageway empty of people. This part of the gatehouse was used during the day, but not at night. Master Holbein might be the only person left in the entire structure. If I screamed, I was sure he would hear me, but would he be able to reach me before . . . before . . . I forced such ghoulish thoughts from my head. No one was following. This was nonsense.

I leaned toward the wall and peered up, craning my head, to see, once and for all, if someone hovered above me. My eyes scanned back and forth. There was nothing.

Until a dark form detached itself from the side of the stairs and started toward me, coming fast.

I didn't scream as I hurtled down the rest of the stairs, half running, half falling. But I'd never moved so fast in my life. Not even when I was attacked by the "page" had I felt such terror.

"God's wounds!" cursed the hulking manservant whom I crashed into at the bottom of the stairs. I spun off of him and fell to the floor.

"Someone's on the stairs! On the stairs!" I cried.

"What—someone after ye?" he groaned, holding his arm. Seeing how frightened I was, he said, "Show me where."

I scrambled to my feet, looking toward the stairs. There were torches on the main floor and it was obvious no one followed me all the way down.

The manservant peered up the stairs, holding a candle as high as he could. "See for yerself, there's not a soul here," he announced.

I crept toward him and peered up, as far as the light would permit. He was right. Whoever had followed me, who waited just above, was gone.

15

It was the next day, the fourth day, the day that Master Holbein finished his drawing of Catherine Howard, when I asked about *The Dance of Death*.

I woke before dawn, exhausted from a night of half-formed creatures ravaging my dreams. I'd been shaken by what happened on the winding stairs of the Whitehall gatehouse. Yet the more I thought about it, the more I was convinced that it could not have been a second attempt at harming me. That would mean someone—whether it was the man who impersonated the page or another—followed me everywhere, just out of my sight, waiting for the moment when I'd be alone to pounce. Which was absurd. No, it must have been some shy servant, pausing on the stairs, not wishing to overtake a woman of unknown status. Nothing more. I felt ashamed that I, a daughter of the Stafford house, had given way to such panic. Living in the palace of Whitehall for a week had addled my mind.

Spring nights were usually quite cool, but it felt warm and airless in this bedchamber, even with open windows. While Catherine slept, I knelt on the floor, hands clasped, desperate to feel the grace of Christ and His mercy. Was I pursuing the right course in the way I tried to save my friend? It would be so beneficial to talk to someone about Catherine, about the king, about the man who attacked me—everything. I considered seeking out Thomas Culpepper but then decided against it. He was a good man, but I was certain he could not fully understand all of my feelings. Only with Edmund had I felt that level of understanding.

As if my spirits were not low enough, I ached for the loss of Edmund. Not the self-pitying sulk of a woman who lacked a husband, but a wish to benefit from all of his wisdom, his good qualities. He had insight into people that I sometimes lacked, and deep compassion for everyone, too. Everyone but himself.

I heard Catherine stirring in the bed. "Joanna?" she said, plaintive as a little child.

"I am praying."

She propped herself up. "Today is the last day we shall go to Master Holbein's workshop?" she said, her voice thick with sleep. "I am sorry for it. I've liked being with him—and with you, Joanna."

"I feel the same," I said. And then, the words burst out of me in a rush: "Why don't you leave London with me tomorrow? I've room for you in Dartford, and enough money for us both to live on."

She didn't say anything for a moment. It was too dark for me to read the expression on Catherine's face.

"That is good of you," she said. "Joanna, you are the only friend I have ever had who cared for me, for myself, without expecting anything in return."

What a sad and rather ominous thing to say.

"Then you will come?" I pressed.

"Oh, but what would I do in Dartford? Do you know how many people try their entire lives to win a position at court? This is the center of the kingdom. I can't possibly leave."

I feared I'd lost. How could a few days of friendly companionship and prayer, of distraction in an artist's workshop, count against the enticing glamour of the king's court? But I bit my lip to stop from saying anything more. This was not the right moment.

Catherine was distracted while sitting for Master Holbein that day. For one, it was warm, more like July than April. I assumed she also felt excitement over Bishop Gardiner's banquet that evening. I regarded the banquet as I would an appointment with the barber surgeon to pull teeth. But the instant Catherine had let slip that the king would attend, I'd resolved to go.

Once this banquet was behind us, I would make the strongest case possible to deter her from sharing the king's bed. I
knew Catherine was subject to pressure, but the Duke of Norfolk
couldn't literally force her to commit this sin. My hope was that
once she expressed unwillingness to King Henry, he'd move on to
someone else.

And then there was the question of my own fate. I couldn't keep
living in Catherine's rooms. I wanted to return to my home in Dartford, but that would be difficult now that I had accepted the royal
commission and was expected to work in London. Because without
doubt that is what I'd done by arranging for Holbein to draw Catherine. Complications loomed in all directions. I felt angry with myself—at critical junctures I'd taken all the wrong turns.

In this wretched state, I posed a question: "The painting on the
wall of the Great Chamber—the skeleton reaching for the ruler—
what is the meaning of it, Master Holbein?"

The artist frowned, his eyes narrowing, and at first I thought I'd offended him. But then I realized he was calculating something. "Fourteen years—or is it fifteen?" he murmured. "Such a long time ago."

I said, "In that painting, it is as if the skeleton reaches for the
man."

"Does not death reach for us all?" Holbein mused. "I read a poem
once where Death takes the shape of a companion who says to a
youth, 'Come on, good fellow, make an end / For you and I must
talk.'"

Catherine cried, her voice shrill, "No, stop, Master Holbein
please. I beseech you. It's too frightening." Her cheeks flushed, she
ran her hands up and down her arms. "I'm cold," she said, trying to
laugh but not quite able to.

Holbein laid down his chalk at once, and fetched her sweet wine.
I wrapped a shawl tight around her shoulders, although it was a
warm spring day, the warmest yet.

The artist said to her, reassuringly, "It was but a book, Mistress
Catherine. I designed the illustrations for it, through a series of

woodcuts. The Whitehall painting that Mistress Joanna refers to, it was a commission to expand on one of the woodcuts. But the book was created long ago, when I lived in Basel. That part of the world, it was torn by great upheaval when I did the work—it was the conflicts over religion. All over now."

I said, "Are the conflicts over? It seems to me they've just begun."

Holbein shot me a look, a forbidding one. Whether it was because of Catherine's trepidation or some other, darker reason, he would say no more.

About an hour later, the portrait sketch was declared finished. Or rather, Catherine's part of it was finished. Master Holbein said he was not ready to unveil it, but would soon. He was surprisingly unmovable when she pleaded to see.

"An artist is vulnerable when the work is complete, and I must have a day to restore myself," he said. "Then you will see. And I hope you will be pleased." He turned to me. "Both of you."

So we took our leave of Master Hans Holbein, myself with regret. It had been something of an idyll—I knew I would miss those acrid scents and sweet flavors, the pleasure of watching the great artist observe Catherine: his gaze steady, his left hand making quick, precise movements on light pink paper.

There could be no other such idylls in our future.

We changed our garments and then, when the hour was upon us, we walked, arm in arm, to the royal landing of Whitehall, where boats would convey guests across the Thames. I tried as hard as I could to conceal my dread and my dismay, for a new necklace shimmered on Catherine's bosom. Her maid, Sarah, had presented it to her after she'd donned her deep blue bodice and skirt. The golden necklace was set with a violet gem, one I believed to be a sapphire. It was obviously a gift—either from the king or from her uncle the Duke of Norfolk to best adorn her for the king. Either option made me feel as cold as Catherine did when she heard the poem of *The Dance of Death*.

Something happened as we walked along the passageway leading to the river. Catherine's fingers lightly resting on my arm tightened into the grip of a frightened child. She bubbled with smiles and greetings to those we passed, but her fingers dug into my arm, deeper and deeper. I did not flinch. I wanted Catherine to know that I would not leave her side, now or later.

The wide landing stretched from the palace wall out into the Thames. Boats jostled for a place, with oarsmen eager for pence shouting to one another. The bishop's guests wore blinding finery. A dozen shades of velvet, silk, and brocade flitted in front of the bluish-gray river. All those jewels, dangling at throats or sewn into doublets, caught the rays of the sun trembling atop the London horizon. I hoped that sunset would bring coolness to this uncomfortable day.

An expectant trill danced in the voices of the women; the men stamped their boots as they laughed at their own jokes. A peculiar smell wove its way through the crowd. It took me a moment to determine its origin: the stench of the Thames, cut with scented oils that the noble guests had drenched themselves with before setting out for this party.

"Shall we go to Dartford, Joanna?"

Catherine said it so softly that at first I wasn't sure I'd heard the words at all. Her lips curled into a smile but her thick-lashed eyes brimmed with fear. My mind raced to come up with a plan.

"There you are, Catherine," shouted the Duke of Norfolk. He bore down on us in seconds, flanked by his son the Earl of Surrey, Catherine's brother, and about ten other men, all on the move, headed for a grand river barge at the front of the line manned by oarsmen wearing Howard livery. To my chagrin, Catherine's moment of doubt was lost in the tumult of her arrogant and ambitious family, and we were swept up—conveyed to the edge of the landing.

In less than a moment, the men had all jumped aboard the barge; now it was our turn.

Catherine had to let go of me when the Howard servant lifted her onto the barge. The men handled her as gingerly as if she were a piece of Venetian sculpture. I recognized the growl of the duke as he spoke to her, but I couldn't understand his words.

I waited for someone to turn and lift me onto the barge, too.

Instead, there was the *thwack* of ropes thrown onto the landing, and the unmoored boat pushed away. I watched a solid line of men's backs gliding past me; there was no sign of the diminutive Catherine. Only the tallest of the men, my cousin the Earl of Surrey, looked back at me, his face scrunched with shame. Leaving me behind was no oversight.

It had gone very quiet on this part of the landing— until a man snickered behind me. Another hushed him, quickly.

I felt the gentlest tug on my elbow. I turned, my cheeks flaming, ready to take on whoever was set to make a mockery of me. But it was Thomas Culpepper. He made a deep bow.

"I'd be honored to escort you to Winchester House, Mistress Stafford," he said.

I murmured my thanks as he led me to a much smaller boat and, with a few words, ensured that we would be ushered aboard next. The gentleman of the king's privy chamber and the lady he escorted took precedence.

Once we were seated, side by side, Culpepper said, his voice low, "I have been most worried about you. Have there been any other attempts to—?"

"None," I said firmly. Someone hovering above me on the stairs hardly rose to the level of assassin—that was what I had decided.

"I confess, I thought you would be back in Dartford by now, not attending parties, particularly not this one," he said. "I was surprised to see you among the guests tonight."

"But I was invited."

"Illness can be feigned. It's served others to avoid attending a party such as this."

"Such as *what*?" I turned to face him, but Culpepper stared straight ahead, not answering or looking me in the eye. His disapproval, followed by his refusal to explain himself, stung. I flashed back at him with: "I'm surprised, too, Master Culpepper. To find you colluding with all these other men, encouraging a young girl without protection of parents to submit to the king. It's a dishonorable business."

That forced him to meet my gaze. "I *don't* encourage it," he said.

"I had nothing to do with putting Catherine Howard in the king's path. But I obey the commands of my sovereign, as I'm bound to do. As we are all bound to do."

I gripped the wooden seat with both hands. We said nothing to each other for a time. The oars slapped hard in the dank water, bearing us closer to the bishop's palace across the Thames.

Culpepper broke the tense silence. "This business with Hans Holbein—you were attempting to keep her away from Norfolk and Gardiner, weren't you?"

"You are aware of the sketch by Holbein?" I said, surprised.

"The whole court knows of it. You don't understand—everyone watches everyone else, nothing is missed. Everyone makes use of one another."

"You are saying that by commissioning Master Holbein to sketch Catherine for the tapestry, I am making use of him? I would hardly describe it in such a way."

Exasperated, Culpepper said, "No, Mistress Joanna, he makes use of *you*. Holbein hadn't received a royal commission since the king married Anne of Cleves. Now he is a man in the center of things again. He'll abandon the queen and all her party, using this sketch of Catherine Howard as a way to switch sides and worm his way back into favor. Holbein must have been so eager to win your commission, I wager he didn't charge you more than a few pence. And he's *always* desperate for money."

Could this appalling interpretation be correct? Master Holbein's friendship had seemed genuine, but there was no denying that what Culpepper said had sense to it. I stared bleakly at the nearing riverbank. The Howards were disembarking from their barge. We would be next to arrive.

"Mistress Joanna, I'm sorry," Culpepper said. "I can see I've offended you. But I fear for you—and not just because the man who attacked you is still at large. At Whitehall, people get hurt in all sorts of ways."

I swallowed. "I am aware, Master Culpepper."

He said quietly, "I fear I was mistaken about your role in this for a time. I thought that you knew about Mistress Howard from that first day. When I came to speak to you in her rooms, to convey the king's invitation to dinner, you looked distraught. She hadn't told you then?"

I shook my head. We were merely a moment from the shore.

"But you were weeping. Are you sure that Mistress Howard did nothing to cause you sorrow?"

That grim disapproval in his voice that always curled around her name—it grieved me. "Catherine is a friend, a kind person," I insisted. "My tears were for myself. I was planning to be married last year, and it did not—it did not take place."

Culpepper sat back in the boat. "Now, that surprises me more than anything else. That you, Joanna Stafford, would seek marriage."

"Because I was a novice in a Dominican order?" I asked.

Our boat eased to the pier of the landing of Winchester House. Ropes were tossed and secured. Those around us prepared to disembark.

"Perhaps that is it," he said. "I don't know. All the young women who arrive at Whitehall, they want husbands, titles, jewels, lands. You're better than all that, I saw it from the beginning." He hesitated, and then said, "You are like someone from one of the ancient stories. A fierce Artemis with her bow."

Before I could respond to this, Culpepper was on his feet, his hand stretched down to help me out of the boat. Where others stumbled or crouched as they departed the swaying boat, his every movement was as sure and graceful as ever.

On the landing to the bishop's property, Catherine waited for me. She stood under a freshly lit torch, her auburn hair golden in the reflection of the leaping flames. I hurried toward her, relieved. Now we could finish our conversation.

She said, "I was most concerned when my uncle's river barge pulled away without you, Joanna. I was inconsolable. But I see there was no need."

Culpepper, coming up behind me, bowed and said, "Mistress Howard, I trust you are having a pleasant evening."

She didn't answer him but turned to me, her eyes glittering as hard as the sapphire dangling from her throat. "My uncle has gone on ahead," she said. "Will you walk with me to Winchester House, Joanna? I don't believe you know the way."

I had been to Bishop Gardiner's London residence before, but under circumstances I didn't wish to disclose. So I accompanied Catherine, surprised by her unprovoked rudeness—yet again—to Culpepper.

Greater surprises lay ahead.

Between the river and Winchester House stretched a garden park, dotted with gleaming white statues. We fell in behind other courtiers walking up the well-manicured path slicing through the middle of the park. As if of one mind, Catherine and I slowed our steps so that those who walked ahead could not hear.

I said, "Catherine, what you said before—I hope you know that—"

She stopped me from continuing. "You are accustomed to cautioning me, but I watched you on the river, Joanna, and don't be too angry when I am the one to caution *you* on a certain matter."

"Angry? About what?"

"Every girl who comes to court loses her head to Master Thomas Culpepper," Catherine said. "I wouldn't want you to make that mistake and end with feeling foolish."

"Is that what you think?" I couldn't help but laugh. "I am not smitten with him. Master Culpepper is a friend to me. That's all."

"The way he looked at you—and spoke to you—and the way you looked at him, it was more than a courteous conversation. You seem to know each other quite well."

It was on that path, as the sun set over the trees fringing the bishop's park, that I finally understood.

"You are in love with Thomas Culpepper," I said.

"No, not ever," she fiercely. "I did . . . admire him, I admit it, and he seemed to feel the same. Now, don't rush me to chapel for more prayers, Joanna. He did not trifle with me. He never did more than kiss my hand. Because, you see, I wasn't good enough for the exalted Thomas Culpepper. He has never seen a woman he'd wed, and although I was foolish enough to think he cared for me, he turned away from me, too."

We had reached the archway to the Winchester House courtyard. I drew her off the path—there was much to say now that I knew the truth, a truth I should have detected before now.

"I'm sorry, Catherine."

She tossed her head. "Do not feel sorry for me, Joanna. I am the most envied woman of the court. I shall be honored, not disgraced. You'll see—and so shall Master Culpepper."

A woman's voice shouted, "What a lovely dress, Catherine." I recognized the voice as Lady Rochford's, and I tried to think of some way to repel her long enough to continue to speak to Catherine. But as Jane Boleyn neared us, I was struck dumb by her bizarre appearance. She wore a tight crimson dress with a low square neckline—her exposed bosom and throat and face were rendered chalky white, whiter than any complexion I'd ever witnessed, with two bright red spots rubbed onto the tops of her cheeks. She looked like a malevolent puppet.

Other women sprang up around her, one of them as chalky white as Lady Rochford. They surrounded Catherine, cutting her off from me as effectively as the Duke of Norfolk had earlier on the river. All of them loudly admired her gown and necklace. I recognized two of the women from the dinner with the king and queen. Anne of Cleves was on no one's mind tonight.

Bishop's pages threw open the main door to Winchester House and called to us to enter. I followed the others into the looming manor house, my head bowed. We were ushered into the long gallery I remembered, lined with exquisite paintings and tapestries. It seemed that we were all of us expected to wait here; the banquet hall must not be ready to receive this horde of courtiers. Pressed among the others, it was unbearably hot in the gallery, with the shrill laughter of Lady

Rochford making my head throb. I backed away from the other guests, spotting a door to a dimly lit side room that might offer a respite.

To my joy, it was a chapel, lit by fresh white candles behind the altar but quite empty. A painting of the Virgin—dressed in light blue, hair flowing long and hands outstretched—hung in an oak frame layered with golden leaf.

I knelt before the altar. Despite this being the official establishment of a bishop, I had rarely felt more out of place than among such guests. The revelations of both Thomas Culpepper and Catherine Howard left me unsettled. Prayer could calm my disordered thoughts.

Father, you alone are truly good. Hear the prayers I address to you. Grant my petitions, and give me more than I dare to ask, I prayed.

Because the door between chapel and gallery hung open and the guests talked so loudly, I wasn't aware for a time—I will never know how long—that someone else had stepped inside. It wasn't until I heard the undoubted creak of floorboard behind me that my prayers faltered. My body tensed, as it had the night before, on the stairs of the Whitehall gatehouse. But this time I pushed down the fear. No one would seek to harm me so close to fourscore guests of the Bishop of Winchester.

I crossed myself, rose, and turned, chin held high.

Sir Walter Hungerford, the man who had unsettled me with his musings on evil, was on his knees, two pews behind.

"My lord," I said, dipping the shallowest of curtsies, eyeing the doorway behind him.

But he did not rise. Sir Walter said, "When I look at you here, Mistress Stafford, I think of my book on the teachings of Aristotle. He wrote so eloquently of his classifications. Every single creature on earth was classified. But how could Aristotle—or anyone else—ever define you?"

What possible answer was there to such a question? Remaining silent, I stepped into the aisle of the chapel.

Rising at last, he said, "I was a witness to the Duke of Norfolk's poor conduct on the other side of the river. I tried to make my way to you, to offer myself as escort, but Tom Culpepper got to you first. With the women of the king's court, Culpepper is always quarry. Only with you do I see him in pursuit."

I hated the way this man could make anything, any action, seem sordid.

"I intend to join the other guests now," I said.

But Hungerford stepped into the aisle, blocking me. "You are a woman of high birth, an obedient daughter of God, modest, disdainful, but when I look in those black eyes, I know you are something different. You have *seen* things, my lady. Things I have seen, too."

Repelled, I tried to dart around him, to reach the door of the chapel.

Hungerford grabbed me by the sleeve and spun me around. His bearing was not lustful, nor mocking, but strangely respectful.

"You have great courage," he said. "I have seen it. Not at Whitehall. On Tower Hill."

I pulled my sleeve from his fingers. So Hungerford was there, among the onlookers, when Edward Courtenay and Lord Montagu were executed. That was the occasion when he first saw me.

"You said a prayer that helped a man to the other side," he said.

The other side? I had never heard of anyone describe death like that.

"Joanna Stafford, you know that there is a different conduit for man to achieve power," Hungerford said. "Not just through prayer to God or service to the king."

"I don't know what you mean," I said.

"That's not true," he insisted, and then said: "The covenant is made. The guide secured and the others are chosen. But no matter what the priests say about the frailty of woman, you would be the perfect companion for the journey."

A covenant? It offended me—and frightened me, too—that Hungerford used that word. I realized it could be used to simply describe an agreement between men, but it had a holy meaning, too, one from Scripture. Man made a pact with God to accomplish a deed, a difficult and punishing deed, by forming a covenant.

I spat the words: "If you do not release me, I will scream, and I am quite capable of screaming loud enough for every single person in Winchester House to hear."

His grave, hollow-eyed expression sank into a sardonic smile. "I'm sure you are," said Sir Walter Hungerford, and he let go my arm.

I rushed into the gallery, horrified by this encounter, which seemed not just bizarre but blasphemous. No one noticed my state, though, for their attention was on the far end of the hall. Sir Anthony Denny had appeared and was saying something.

"His Majesty requests the presence of a certain lady in the receiving room of Bishop Gardiner," said the king's gentleman.

A titter rose and Lady Rochford, standing close to Catherine, called out, "Sir Anthony—I believe that we have the lady at hand." Catherine had the grace to blush.

Exchanging smirks, the men and women parted in the gallery, pressing themselves back to allow Sir Anthony to make his way to Catherine and her party. Once the gentleman of the privy chamber reached her, she stepped forward, curtsying gracefully.

"Not her," said Sir Anthony. He turned and searched the faces around him until he spotted me.

"The king requests the presence of Mistress Joanna Stafford."

16

As I followed Sir Anthony Denny, every single person in the gallery scrutinized me: some curious, others contemptuous. None of their reactions were as strong as Lady Rochford's when I was requested instead of Catherine. She was incredulous, furious, her eyes traveling up and down, taking in my dark dress and plain hood, my lack of adornment beyond a pair of tiny pearl earrings, the only jewelry I possessed. Catherine rapidly concealed her surprise at my name being called, but Lady Rochford could not manage to do the same, as if my summons were a personal affront.

I was delivered to this same receiving room two Novembers ago. On that tumultuous night, Bishop Gardiner and the Lady Mary sat side by side in high-backed chairs on a platform, with the Duke of Norfolk pacing between the windows. Two of those same three people were here now, but instead of the Lady Mary, it was her father, King Henry, who sat on the platform, with both Bishop Gardiner and Norfolk standing before him. The king wore cloth of silver and a pendant heavy with rubies and diamonds. His leg rested on a scarlet silk stool set before him. But his mood was anything but restful. He was deep in serious conversation with the duke and bishop. This seemed more an impromptu council meeting than a banquet.

Why on earth was my presence required? A feeling came over me that this was a dreadful mistake, and I tried to capture the attention of Sir Anthony Denny to ask him. He never acknowledged my attempt, his pace respectful but steady as he neared the king with me in tow. I was now close enough to hear their conversation.

The Duke of Norfolk was speaking. "Your Majesty, what Bishop Gardiner is trying to say is—"

The king interrupted, his voice pitched higher than usual: "We need no interpreter, for we are well aware of the bishop's meaning, Norfolk. He judges ill of our stance toward Doctor Barnes. Is not the man imprisoned in the Tower? What else could be required of us, Bishop?"

Norfolk said hastily, "It is more than sufficient, Sire."

"And so you continue to speak for the Bishop of Winchester?" demanded the king, his eyes narrowed to slits in his heavy face.

A tense silence mounted. Bishop Gardiner faced the king, so I could not gauge his reaction. The Duke of Norfolk, for years his friend and closest ally, clenched his hands. Plainly, this was the moment for the bishop to say what King Henry wanted to hear.

But to my amazement, he did not. "My concern is that Doctor Barnes has twice been released from prison, free to resume the spread of his heresies and lies," said Bishop Gardiner.

King Henry pounded the arm of his carved and gilded chair. "God's wounds, was there ever a vainer bishop?" he roared, spittle flying through the air. "You care only for your own pride, Gardiner. You are not capable of understanding what we require, that at times a man close to Luther is needed to communicate with those German princes. But your diplomacy has always been flawed—always— by such vanity. Is it any wonder you are banned from our Privy Council?"

I'd heard stories all my life of the king's anger, as deadly as plague for those who provoked it. Even though he was not angry with me, I felt frightened by this display, even a little sick. Norfolk grimaced, also dismayed. As for the bishop, he bowed, stiffly. "My concern is for the immortal souls of those who dwell in your kingdom, Your Majesty." I braced myself for another royal outburst, astounded that Bishop Gardiner still did not submit himself. His choleric humor was in direct conflict with his own advice to me not to provoke the anger of Henry VIII.

The king took a series of deep breaths, as if struggling to rein in his temper. When he spoke again, his voice was calm. "Fear not, Bishop, all our subjects' souls shall be rendered safe from Doctor Barnes soon enough. You shall have your wish—and more. *Much more.*" With those last two chilling words, his lips curved into a tight smile. I preferred the shouting to the smile.

It was at that moment that King Henry took notice of me and Sir Anthony Denny.

"Sit beside us, Cousin Joanna," he called, his voice nothing but friendly. "Gardiner, has our special guest arrived?"

"I shall inquire, Sire," said the bishop, who turned, his head tipped, and hurried from the room, so quickly he nearly stumbled over me. For an instant, he glared at me with pure loathing. What must it be like for a man such as Stephen Gardiner to realize that I had heard every word of the king's lashing out? I'd just glimpsed the bishop's true feeling for me, not the "You will always be my Sister Joanna" of the privy garden.

Wishing I had a choice, I took a seat next to the king. He nodded with approval, though I had no idea why. When I dined with him, his mood had shifted over the stretch of hours but nothing like this. Such lightning-swift changes in humor were most disconcerting.

I was also rendered uncomfortable by the room's warmth. Not only were the windows tightly closed but also flames flickered in a fireplace. No doubt the servants who'd set the fire did so expecting a typical April evening and did not want to risk the king's growing cold. No one could have predicted this bizarre wave of warmth that would not subside.

Henry VIII might have felt it, too, for he drank deeply from the goblet perched next to him. He wiped his lips with the back of a jeweled hand and then said, "Two of our fellow monarchs, the most eminent monarchs, are blessed in a certain regard, Joanna. The emperor Charles possesses a widowed sister, Mary, who has declined

all offers to marry again in order to serve as his regent in the Netherlands, and with great dedication. My ambassador tells me she barely
sleeps at night because of all the work. The king of France, too, has a
sister who has always helped him. Marguerite of Angoulême was responsible for soliciting poets and artists to come to the French court.
It was she who negotiated Francis's release when the emperor held
him for ransom."

The king paused to take another sip. "Our own two sisters are
with God now, may they rest in peace. Though even while Margaret
and Mary lived . . ." He did not finish the sentence, but bestowed on
me a rueful smile, as if I knew what he referred to. I nodded, uncertainly, stealing a glance at the Duke of Norfolk. He wore a slightly
puzzled, guarded look. Thomas Howard understood the point of this
discourse no better than I did.

The king continued, "We are lacking in relations to assist us in
our efforts to rule this kingdom. It is a perpetual source of regret."

Because you've had them killed, I thought, while trying to keep my
face devoid of expression. Most of his cousins in the House of York,
his mother's family, had been executed. Especially hard for me were
the deaths of Henry Courtenay, Marchioness of Exeter, and Henry
Pole, Baron Montagu. Those were the executions I witnessed on
Tower Hill, and Montagu was the man I prayed for, publicly, while
others watched, including Hungerford, it seemed. They had been
arrested on false charges and beheaded because their share of royal
blood made them a threat—everyone knew that. Courtenay's widow
and son and Montagu's mother had not yet been released from the
Tower of London. I prayed every day for their release, while fearing
that a spasm of royal suspicion could send them to the block.

The king reached over and patted my hand. "You have shown by
your humble desire to weave tapestries for our court that you wish to
serve in any capacity, and do not insist on a position of high standing, as do so many other women. Are you willing to do more than
create one or two tapestries for us, to serve the Crown as an example
in a way only you can do?"

An example?

I felt the blood rushing from my head—would I faint before the king in the Bishop of Winchester's house? I had difficulty drawing breath in this suffocating room.

I forced myself to say, "Yes, Your Majesty."

The king called out to Sir Anthony Denny, "We are ready. Bring him to us."

My hands crept up to grip the armrests of the chair. I tried to think of who this person could be. In the privy garden, Bishop Winchester had said, *King Henry never does anything without having a secret purpose to it and usually two purposes ahead.*

Sir Anthony Denny reappeared, a taller figure looming behind him.

"Your Majesty, the imperial ambassador, Eustace Chapuys," announced the courtier.

I flinched in my chair, but there was no place to go—no escape for me. Yes, the trap was closing. The king, no doubt with the help of Cromwell, might well have discovered the conspiracy to kill him and deliver the kingdom to his half-Spanish eldest daughter, Mary. It was I who was meant to kill him—the prophecy said I would set the course of the kingdom—but instead I had taken the chalice from his lips after only a sip. In so doing, I'd defied the spymaster, Chapuys, who now stood in this very room, and Jacquard Rolin, his shadowy operative.

The last time I saw Ambassador Chapuys was eight months ago in Flanders. He looked significantly older, with deep creases around his eyes and new gray hairs. He exhibited no reaction whatsoever to finding me beside Henry VIII.

The king had said moments ago he wanted me to help him. Did that mean I must now disown the ambassador—provide details of the deadly conspiracy? I had once been more devoted to the erudite Eustace Chapuys than to any other man save my father, but that was before Jacquard Rolin told me the ambassador was willing to imprison me, even turn me over to the Inquisition, if I did not cooperate.

I owed no more loyalty to Ambassador Chapuys.

Henry VIII said in melodious French, "Good Chapuys, you know how we rejoiced when you returned to our kingdom. Your withdrawal to Flanders was a loss to our court and to the cause of diplomacy throughout Christendom."

Chapuys bowed with a flourish of his right hand, an imperial obeisance.

The king continued, "Peaceful relations between England and the empire of your master, Charles the Fifth, have always been our heartfelt wish."

Chapuys bowed again and said in his own rapid French, "Your Majesty is the cherished friend of the emperor."

The king leaned forward in his chair, his leg visibly quivering on its silken stool. "But this was not always so," he said slowly.

Now it comes, I thought. My heart slammed against my chest. A trickle of sweat rolled down my back, and I braced myself for the charm and affability of the Tudor monarch to darken once more to rage. But instead Henry VIII said, "There were many grievances, many misunderstandings, during the life of the princess dowager."

A nerve danced in the side of Chapuys's thin face. That was the hated title that Henry VIII gave to his first wife, Katherine of Aragon, after he annulled that marriage in defiance of the pope. She was no longer styled queen but princess dowager, the widow of Henry's elder brother, Prince Arthur. It was a title that proud lady never, ever answered to, and I knew for a fact that Chapuys detested it.

The ambassador said nothing. But it was not fear that quieted him; he was nothing like the men and women I had seen quake in the king's presence. What became more and more clear with each second he maintained his silence was his independence. He bore the prestige of Charles V, whose empire stretched from the Netherlands through Burgundy, Germany, Austria, and Spain and off to discovered lands across the sea filled with gold, spices, and new peoples undreamed of. Compared to this, England was but a tiny island.

Finally, Henry VIII broke the silence by half turning toward me. "You are acquainted with my cousin Mistress Joanna Stafford?"

Chapuys bowed to me. This could well be the moment of accusation. But he exhibited no trepidation, and his steeliness filled me with new strength. I nodded toward the ambassador and sat straighter in the chair.

The king said, "This lady's uncle, the Duke of Buckingham, was a foul traitor and punished accordingly. Which meant the Staffords, including her father, were broken. Her mother came from Spain as a maid of honor to the princess dowager. Which one could say makes Joanna your master's subject as well as ours." The king smiled that same menacing smile as when he promised the bishop a solution for Doctor Barnes. Yet Chapuys showed not a jot of emotion; he didn't even blink.

The king continued, "Several years ago, Joanna attended the princess dowager, as her mother had before, and when the household was broken up, she returned to Stafford Castle. Joanna then entered the Dominican Order in Kent as a novice, but as part of our just and legal reforms, the priory was found wanting and thus dissolved. Considering all of these events, does she show bitterness toward us? Not in the slightest. She has come in all humility to serve us, eager to weave a tapestry."

I had never sat through such a humiliating summation of my life, one twisted with distortions and outright lies. Tears of helpless anger pricked my eyes. Not wanting to look the ambassador in the face, I glanced at the windows instead—and the Duke of Norfolk who stood before them. A sneer widened across his craggy face.

Chapuys said in elegant French, "Mistress Stafford's abject loyalty must bring you great satisfaction, Your Grace."

"Oh, it does, Chapuys, it does," said the king, smugly. "And shall be rewarded. Henceforth, Mistress Joanna Stafford will serve as the permanent Tapestry Mistress of the court, to oversee, maintain, and add to our collection, which is the finest in all of Christendom."

I did not realize that the king and ambassador's conversation continued for a few minutes, for this news sent me into shock. The king did not accuse me of conspiracy or treason. I should have been relieved. But an official court position? This went far beyond weaving a single tapestry. I had no interest—nor, when it came to it, the requisite knowledge—for such a task, which would most definitely chain me to the court. But the king had not asked. He had proclaimed.

"Joanna? Joanna?" That was Henry VIII's voice, rising in impatience.

"Yes, Your Majesty?" My voice was a half croak.

"I said the ambassador shall escort you to the banquet hall while I settle a few things with the Duke of Norfolk. Sir Anthony will show you the way."

And so he did, leading me and the ambassador through a series of rooms to the banquet hall. Chapuys stuck out his dry, cool hand and I rested mine atop it. It felt incredible that, after what we had been through last year, I walked with him through an English bishop's house, moments after learning of a court post I'd be forced to fill.

"I both wanted and did not want to be invited to one of these evenings at Winchester House," Ambassador Chapuys said in Spanish. I had long thought he knew every language—except English, which he had learned only a little.

"Have there been so many?" I asked, also in Spanish. If he wished to pretend as if we had never conspired, I was willing to go along.

"There have been at least five banquets that I know of," said Chapuys. "The bishop has no other way to do it, to promote the seduction of the Howard girl. Cromwell has such a tight hold on the palace and employs so many hardworking spies. Only Gardiner's residence could do as the setting for her corruption. It is deeply distasteful and, of course, it will not work."

"You do not believe Cromwell can be brought down?" I asked, glancing around. Very few people spoke Spanish in England, but still, ours was a highly dangerous conversation.

"Not this way. If the king discards Cromwell, it won't be because a seventeen-year-old girl suggested it, a girl stupid enough to believe her family when they say that if she shares his bed, she will be made queen."

"Her name is Catherine and she is not stupid," I said, coming to her defense, but more from habit than anything else, for I was reeling over what Chapuys said. Is that what they'd told Catherine? *Do not feel sorry for me, Joanna. I am the most envied woman of the court. I shall be honored, not disgraced. You'll see—and so shall Master Thomas Culpepper.* Now it made perfect sense.

Chapuys said musingly, "My counterpart, the French ambassador, believed Cromwell about to be toppled and said so, openly. Then he looked a fool when Cromwell was made Earl of Essex. Marillac doesn't get things right—well, what can you expect? He's French. He still thinks some crisis is imminent, that the rivalry of Gardiner and Cromwell cannot continue at this pitch without one of them being arrested. But why not? The king enjoys pitting his people against each other. And who could possibly fill the treasury with as much skill and ruthlessness as Cromwell?"

We neared the banqueting hall, teeming with guests, all of them talking and laughing so loudly that a roar cascaded over us. We would not be able to continue with confidential conversation unless we spoke louder, which was risky. I could not be sure that no one else spoke Spanish. But Chapuys's extraordinary lecture on English politics begged a question of the ambassador of the Holy Roman Emperor.

"You *admire* Cromwell?" I asked.

Chapuys surveyed the room, taking stock of every single person within it. "I've enjoyed my dinners with Thomas Cromwell," he answered. "He is a man of the world, a rarity in this kingdom. His words are fair, though his deeds are bad. Anyone who determines to act in all circumstances the part of a good man must come to ruin among so many who are not good." He perceived my deepening confusion and leaned down to say in a low voice, "That is a quote from the philosophy of a cunning Florentine diplomat named Machiavelli—not yet translated to English. And yes, it is possible for me to admire the man while abhorring what he's done. Just as it is possible for me to have some degree of fondness for you, Juana, even after you betrayed us."

"'Betrayed,'" I repeated, stunned.

Chapuys for the first time looked at me, truly looked at me, and I saw pain mixed with anger in those intelligent gray eyes. "You do not approve of the court of the king?" he asked, his light, musing tone replaced with something raw. "You do not enjoy being made an example of abject loyalty to me? Perhaps you do not wish to serve the king as tapestry mistress. But everything that you hear or see around you—the tyrant king, the corrupted Howard girl, the cruel ministers, the destroyed priories, the exiled monks and friars begging in the streets—*you* are the agent. You are the cause. Without you, nothing would be as it is."

Chapuys stalked away, as I struggled to hold on to my composure.

A few moments later, the king came into the room and took a seat at a grand table on the dais, with space enough for the monarch and three others: Bishop Gardiner, the Duke of Norfolk, and, at the right side of the king, Catherine Howard. This was the rightful place for the *queen*. Yet no one else seemed surprised to see Catherine at his side, where Katherine of Aragon, Anne Boleyn, and Jane Seymour presided, one after the other. Where Anne of Cleves should sit now. Was it indeed possible that Catherine would become his fifth queen? The other commoners who had managed it—Anne Boleyn and Jane Seymour—were years older than Catherine when they married Henry VIII. They were both well educated and, while wise to the ways of the court, protected by vigilant parents. Catherine was orphaned, poor, scarcely able to read, and so very naive.

Yet she seemed perfectly calm and poised on the dais. Catherine held up her hands and said, "None of the men will stoop to pullin' at weeds, so they employ such as me, with small hands that are right strong." She was telling the king the story of the girl in the garden. For the first time, I saw the king's suspicious features soften. He looked younger. The sight of my stout, aging sovereign finding contentment thanks to Catherine's genuinely youthful sweetness sickened me. The horrible story flashed through my mind of the ravishing Andromeda chained to a rock, intended as a human sacrifice to a powerful and hideous creature of the sea.

My place at the banquet was among the younger Howards, which had the great advantage of no one bothering to draw me into conversation. The plates came and went: a quartet of stag, sturgeon wrapped in parsley, roasted pigeons, jellies, cakes. Goblets brimmed with wine, voices trilled with laughter. But I did not eat, drink, or laugh. All I could do was bear reluctant witness to the king of England making a prolonged spectacle of himself with Catherine. Leaning toward her, smiling, kissing her hand. Had someone discreetly placed the silk stool beneath the table so he could rest his rotting leg while he flirted? I wondered, and then shuddered at such a savagely mocking thought. *You are the agent, you are the cause*, said Chapuys, who had left Winchester House before the meal, claiming his gout. It might be true that I had changed the king's court, but another truth was that in a short span of time, the king's court was changing me. Would the transformation continue the longer I stayed at Whitehall? A year from now, I could be unrecognizable from the woman of Dartford.

"You do not drink wine, mistress?" brayed a nasal voice. A tall, broad-shouldered young manservant holding a pitcher regarded me and my untouched goblet with a strange smile curving below his swollen nose.

I shook my head and he lumbered along, enjoying some private joke.

A cry went up across the banquet hall as a quartet of dark-haired men walked in, carrying musical instruments. "Excellent," boomed the king. "Bishop, you will not regret inviting to your festivities our latest discovery, the Bassano brothers of Venice. Pay special attention to the sound of the violin. Exquisite."

Poor, poor Anne of Cleves.

At the other end of the banquet hall, servants moved tables aside to make room for dancing. Guests began to mill about again, and

I considered slipping away. A woman should not walk through the bishop's garden park at night alone nor seek out her own boat across the Thames, but this banquet was unbearable. And what, after all, could be accomplished by remaining? Impossible to speak to Catherine when she was the companion of the king. Tonight, when she returned to her room in Whitehall, I would have it out with her at last.

As I eyed the doorway, calculating the best way to leave unnoticed, I saw a man standing near it, a face so unexpected that I gave a soft cry. I shot to my feet and hurried across the length of the hall. Among all these people whom I had no wish to speak to, here was, incredibly, a friend.

I'd spotted John Cheke, the young Cambridge scholar and friend of Edmund's who had come to Dartford last summer to attend our wedding. He was moving toward the door to leave.

Thomas Culpepper tugged on my sleeve as I passed. "May I partner you in a dance?"

I glanced up at the dais. Sure enough, Catherine watched us, her perpetual smile in eclipse. "It might not be wise," I murmured.

Culpepper cocked his head. "Wise?" he asked.

But I darted off without explaining—I did not want Master Cheke to slip away. I had to pick up my skirts and run those last yards, which made heads swivel. It was hardly the behavior of a gentlewoman.

"Master Cheke, wait," I called out, breathless, to his slender departing back.

John Cheke turned, bowed, and said, "Mistress Joanna, it is good to see you again. Are you well?"

I realized with a sharp pang that Cheke exhibited so little surprise, he must have already seen me at the banquet—perhaps during my conversation with Ambassador Chapuys—and hadn't been planning on approaching me before he left.

"I thought you at Cambridge," I said.

"I have not left it," he said. "But an opportunity arose for me to be appointed to the Cambridge chair in Greek. I cannot be confirmed without the approval of Thomas Cromwell, which was given, and Bishop Gardiner, who insisted I come for a month, to be questioned at his convenience." He frowned; I could see the resentment this summons created.

"Where are you lodged?"

Cheke pointed toward the ceiling of the banqueting hall.

"Here?" I exclaimed. "With the bishop's staff?"

"There are scholars' quarters upstairs. They are not uncomfortable. But I am also expected to appear at functions such as . . . this." He gestured toward the line of dancers now leaping and twirling across the floor to the music of the Bassano brothers. Master Cheke wore a plain doublet and hose, not suitable for a royal banquet. But I sensed it was not his threadbare wardrobe that gave him misgivings.

"The king's presence here disturbs you?" I asked.

"I would very much like to have a conversation with His Majesty," said Cheke earnestly. "He supports the study of Greek and could sanction my version of how it should be taught, regardless of what Bishop Gardiner believes. But I would want such conversing to occur in the proper place, in the presence of the king and queen, not here, with . . ." His young face tightened with distaste as he gazed across the hall at the dais, where Catherine Howard threw back her head, laughing merrily.

"I understand you," I said. "In a way, I was compelled here, too. I found that—"

Cheke held up his hand. "Mistress Joanna, I wish I could stay to speak to you for longer, but I cannot. I cannot. I have an appointment tonight. If you will forgive me, I will say good-bye."

Before I could even bid him farewell, Master John Cheke had ducked out of the room. Was it speaking to me that had filled him with such distaste? I had wanted to ask if he'd heard from Edmund, but there was no opportunity. While I didn't understand how I'd offended him, there was no other explanation for his cold and abrupt departure.

The Bassano brothers' violins soared ever higher, to the delight of the dancers. Lady Rochford sashayed sideways, coming close enough for me to reach out and touch her—should I wish to do so, which I decidedly did not. It was so warm in the banquet hall that her unnaturally white face shone like wet paint, the red spots once centered on her cheekbones sliding toward her jaw.

I glanced up at the dais. King Henry VIII gave no attention to any person in the banquet hall besides Catherine. He reached out and slowly caressed her shoulder, his fingers straying higher, to finger her white throat.

I backed away from the sight of the king and Catherine, from Lady Rochford and the other dancers, until I touched the wall. I wanted to cover my eyes, cover my ears, seal myself off from everything in this room.

A hand seized mine, and I instinctively pulled away. It was my cousin Henry Howard, Earl of Surrey, and he would not let go. "You will now dance with me, Joanna," he said.

"I've watched you tonight and you have the face of someone listening to a dirge," he continued as he led me to the floor. "Yet I hear you've been granted an official position, one that is dear to the king's heart. Celebration would be more in order."

We stood opposite each other in a long line. The music exploded; the people stamped, turned, and pirouetted. I followed, using the steps of memory. My mother had drilled me in dance.

The next time I was close enough to him to speak, I said, "I do not wish to serve at court."

"No? Well for someone who dislikes it, you are making a sensational impression," he said.

"My lord Surrey, we have a request," the king's voice rang out.

My cousin bowed with a flourish.

The king said, "A love poem—I know that is within your capacity."

The musicians stopped playing and all dancing and talking ceased. Many people would have been overcome by such a force of attention. Not my cousin, who offered to share his translation of

Petrarch's *"Sonetto in Vita"*—from memory, of course. He stood in
the middle of the dance floor and recited:

> *"Love, that doth reign and live within my thought,*
> *And built his seat within my captive breast,*
> *Clad in the arms wherein with me he fought,*
> *Oft in my face he doth his banner rest.*
> *But she that taught me love and suffer pain,*
> *My doubtful hope and eke my hot desire*
> *With shamefast look to shadow and refrain,*
> *Her smiling grace converteth straight to ire.*
> *And coward Love, then to the heart apace*
> *Taketh his flight, where he doth lurk and plain,*
> *His purpose lost, and dare not show his face.*
> *For my lord's guilt thus faultless bide I pain.*
> *Yet from my lord shall not my foot remove:*
> *Sweet is the death that taketh end by love.*
> *We were forced to part again."*

I wondered at the earl's recklessness—a "coward love" that "ta-
keth his flight"? How like his grandfather he was. The Duke of
Buckingham had relished every chance to subtly mock King Henry,
and had paid for it with his life.

But this same king did not seem to hear the darker part of a
poem that ended with a parting. He thanked Surrey, commanded
that the music resume, and took Catherine's little hand in his, kissing
it in his own display before us all of "hot desire."

Revolted yet trapped in this cage of a royal court, I turned in the
design of the dance to extend my hand to the next gentleman, and
came face-to-face once more with Sir Walter Hungerford.

"Ah, so I see you are a favorite of Ambassador Chapuys?" he said,
eyes gleaming.

"No," I said.

"A pity," said Sir Walter. "I was hoping you could obtain me an

invitation to his library. For years I've longed to see *that* collection."
He laughed at his own bizarre private joke. Fortunately, the dance
sent me on to another partner.

It was not until the dance was over that I could speak again to
Surrey. I was so agitated that my words emerged in a tumble: "I have
remained at court not to seek favor but because of my fears for Catherine, a defenseless girl. A concern shared by no one in her own family." Surrey winced, but I could not stop now. "Is this the only remedy
for the disease of hating Cromwell, to sacrifice Catherine's virtue? You
have no more honorable way to increase your influence with the king?"

Surrey said, "There is another way to put an end to Cromwell,
though it be anything but honorable. I can say not a word to you
about it. Only that, someday, when all has changed, I hope to redeem
myself in your eyes, Joanna."

My young cousin spoke with such dignity that I felt almost
ashamed. I stepped back as the music began and people chose new
partners. Surrey bowed before a young lady who was thrilled to be
chosen and they took their places in the next lines. I had had enough
and moved away from the place of dancing.

His words sent off a deep warning inside me. My cousin had a
secret and I wondered if it would be possible to coax it from him.

A manservant was studying me, his beefy arms wrapped around
a tray. The same young man who'd smiled when I turned away wine.
He *still* smiled. This, at least, I could do something about.

"You have something to say to me?" I demanded.

I'd meant to banish that hateful smirk, but instead it deepened.
"Yes, mistress, I do, and something ye might find of interest," he
whined. I saw that his nose had been broken and assumed that was
why he spoke this way.

"My name is Tom," he continued, "and if I were to tell ye that
a man has been asked to watch out for ye, to inform on yer movements, would that be of interest to ye or yer kin?" he asked.

"Who is informing on me?" I demanded.

Tom slid toward me, lowering the tray, and picked up a plate left behind on the table shoved against the wall. Making a show of examining the plate, he said, "Do ye see yonder a tall man with a long black beard, at the dais, standing behind the bishop? Don't be obvious in yer surveying, I beg ye. He's a mean, base creature."

At the far end of the dais, towering behind the bishop, I did observe a man of that description. He stood tall, a hand on each hip, as he looked to the right and then the left, surveying the crowd. When he reached my part of the banquet hall, his gaze halted as he settled on me, and then, after a few seconds, resumed his sweep.

I swallowed and said, "Tell me who asked that man to watch me."

Tom chuckled and said, "I don't know the other man's name but I know where to find him. He's in Winchester House, hiding. For a price, Mistress. I will take yer kinsmen to him."

"Kinsmen?"

Tom answered, his eyes glistening, "Ye be a Howard, aren't ye? And they are a rich clan. This news be of worth to them."

Now I understood Tom's motives. It was too bad for him that he dealt with a lone Stafford, not a Howard. I said, "First tell me about the man who wants me watched. Did you see him?"

"I did."

"Give me his name."

"Oh, I do not think he gave that in my hearing."

My heartbeat quickening, I said, "What did he look like?"

Tom thought for a moment and said, "He's a tall man, could be thirty years of age, light brown hair. A beard."

It was he—the man who'd attacked me that first day—and he was in the same building as I.

Pleased by my reaction, Tom said, "He pointed you out and then asked yonder foreman if he would send word when you left Winchester House. Gave him a few pence and said there would be more when word was given. I heard it all. Seems to me he wishes to follow ye, mistress. I'd hate to see a lady such as yerself come to harm this night."

It took me a moment to gather myself. I desperately wanted to find out who was directing the actions of the man who sought to harm me. From the first day, I had known that this was the only course that would free me from fear—discovering who and why. Then I could mount a defense.

"Tom, have you a knife on you?" I asked.

He proudly patted his doublet pocket. "Always, mistress. And a sharp one, too."

I pulled the pearl earring from my left ear. "I will give you this, Tom, if you take me to this man concealed. No Howards. No one else. Just you and me. And we go at once."

17

It took both of my pearl earrings to persuade Tom to lead me to the room where my assailant hid. He was grievously disappointed that my name was not Howard. Even if I weren't part of the sprawling clan, surely I could take this matter to one of the men in the banqueting hall for a bit of business?

When I ruled that out because of the matter's private nature, he leered, "Ah, mistress, he's a man of yer past, eh?"

"In a manner of speaking," I said, through gritted teeth. Just as he wished I were someone different, I wished I didn't have to join forces with such a repellent ruffian. But I must make use of either Tom or the hard-faced brute who stood behind Bishop Gardiner. They were the ones who knew where my enemy was.

"Bear in mind that this won't be a happy reunion upstairs," I said. "You may need to make a show of your knife while I speak to him."

"You won't want me to drag him downstairs?" Tom said.

What a fitting end to the bishop's banquet that would make, I thought. Particularly since the man who directed the attack could be in this very room. After tonight, I'd never again doubt that the Bishop of Winchester, the Duke of Norfolk, and the imperial ambassador all detested me enough to wish to see me harmed. Within the hour, I could discover which one.

"But he did look a strong fellow," said Tom. And then: "I have a remedy for this. I shall return in a moment, mistress."

Tom's "remedy" was a fellow servant named Roger, an absolutely massive man with bleary blue eyes and whiskers that shot in all directions on his shiny red chin. "Roger'll help me, won't ye?" said Tom, with a clap on his broad back. Roger grunted and strained to scratch the place on his back where he'd been thumped.

Since we did not want to suggest that I was departing the banquet, I left the main hall in the opposite direction of the door leading out of Winchester House and walked instead through a large study where people not inclined to dance were lounging and drinking wine. After a few moments, Tom beckoned from the narrow door in the corner and I hurried down a long passageway snaking past the kitchens and storerooms and cold pantries. At the end was a set of worn stairs.

While climbing the steps leading higher into Winchester House, I tried to plan what I'd say. With Tom on one side and Roger on the other, I'd demand an explanation for the attack in Whitehall and his lying in wait for me tonight. I had no illusions that it would be a simple matter to learn my enemy's name. But at least I'd have the upper hand, and a series of options, including sending for Thomas Culpepper and turning the man over to him. I still worried that making this an official matter could lead to questions and expose my most dangerous secrets. But now that I was more intertwined with the court than ever, I couldn't continue at Whitehall with an enemy in the shadows. It was possible that this man would escape punishment for hurting me that first day—but at least I'd deal a blow to the plotters against me.

The size of Winchester House became even more apparent as Tom led me farther and farther in. Roger carried the candle to light the way as we moved from the servants' stairs to the main corridor of the second story, and passed a well-appointed library, where a half dozen men—priests and scholars, I guessed—read texts by candlelight. This was the purpose of the Bishop of Winchester's London residence, not the bacchanal downstairs.

"The room be right down there," whispered Tom, pointing down a passageway with his right hand and gleefully shaking my earrings in his left. Roger's response was yet another grunt.

"The man is hiding here?" I asked, surprised that he'd choose a second-story room so near a library. A hiding spot closer to the banquet would have made more sense.

Tom nodded, licking his lips.

A loud confrontation now seemed inadvisable. Did I want a group of scholars listening?

"Have ye lost yer spirit for this?" Tom hissed. "Now will ye want me to fetch some of the Howard men?"

I shook my head.

My throat was tight, my hands clammy, as I followed Tom the rest of the way, Roger lumbering behind us. I'd pressed for this—I'd paid for this—but now I dreaded looking at the face of the man who tossed me across the storeroom in Whitehall. And did these two servants possess the strength and speed to contain him?

There were three closed doors on this passageway. Tom strode to the third one. "Hold up the candle, Roger," he whispered. The light revealed that the door had a number carved on it: 41. Tom nodded, and looked at me, licking his lips again. I so wished he wouldn't do that.

I gave the signal with a terse nod.

Tom rapped on the door, twice. "There's a matter requiring yer attention, sir," he said, all unctuous.

I tensed at the creak of floorboards on the other side of the door. It opened a few inches—and Master John Cheke peered out into the corridor, blinking in the bright light of the candle Roger had thrust close to the door. At the sight of me, his eyes widened.

"You've made a mistake," I said, furious, rounding on Tom. "This is not the right man."

"No, he isn't the right man—but *this* be the right room," insisted Tom.

"And there's no mistake," said a second man from inside the room. My whole body tightened in response to that voice, one I knew so well.

But he couldn't be here. It wasn't possible.

The floorboard creaked again. The door opened all the way. Directly behind John Cheke stood Geoffrey Scovill, the constable of Dartford, the man who had saved me, and fought with me, and loved me, suffering so much when I chose another. He looked exactly the same, except he'd started a beard. Tall and broad-shouldered—no wonder Tom hadn't relished confronting him—Geoffrey was scrutinizing me with light blue eyes.

Cheke said, "Joanna, what are you doing here?" He mopped his face with a cloth, distressed.

"Joanna never stays where you put her," said Geoffrey matter-of-factly.

I finally found my voice through the shock. "Geoffrey, what is happening? Why would you pay someone to spy on me? How could you do such a thing?"

Geoffrey sighed. "As much as I don't want to explain, I see I will be required to. But first, let's put something in order." He crooked his finger to Tom and Roger, who had been listening gape-mouthed to the whole exchange. In less than a minute, I had my earrings and the menservants had the boot, along with a stern constabulary warning about preying on guests of the bishop.

In John Cheke's small room, filled with towering stacks of books and papers, there were but stools, and I planted myself on one. Nothing about this made sense, but I had no intention of leaving until it did.

Cheke began: "I sent word to Geoffrey to come here tonight, not knowing about the banquet until too late. He saw you when he entered Winchester House along with the other guests and didn't want you to see him."

I felt my cheeks redden. I knew I wasn't Geoffrey's favorite person but when had it reached this pass?

Watching me, Geoffrey said, "It's not a matter of antipathy, Joanna. Master Cheke had sensitive business to discuss with me, and I didn't wish to involve you, to upset you. I asked that servant of Gardiner's to come up here and let me know when you left so I wouldn't run across you on my departure back to Dartford."

"So you *are* still in Dartford?" I asked. "I'd heard otherwise."

Geoffrey glanced at John Cheke. Some sort of silent message hovered between them and then Geoffrey said, "I shall be leaving, but it's not yet clear when."

Growing frustrated, I said, "What could Master Cheke possibly have to do with your departure, your livelihood? And what sort of business would you have to discuss? I don't remember the two of you even being acquainted, except the day of . . ."

I couldn't come out and say the words "my wedding." My union with Edmund Sommerville never took place, because, as I'd tried to explain to Catherine, moments after we arrived at Holy Trinity Church, news came of the Act of Six Articles, forbidding marriage to those who'd ever taken vows of celibacy in a monastery. The painful memory rose of Cheke urging us to marry anyway and then seek official approval, until Geoffrey, acting as the legal representative of the town, forbade the ceremony.

It was as if Geoffrey read my thoughts, for his face grew mournful, too. The bright, curious light in his eyes dimmed. A new apprehension clawed at me.

It was Cheke who said, "Yes, Joanna, this concerns Edmund."

I covered my mouth with my hands, looking at these two men, for their countenances were so serious, I *knew*.

I lowered my trembling hands to whisper, "He's dead, isn't he? Edmund's dead?"

"No," said Geoffrey quickly.

"To be completely honest, we don't know if he's dead or alive," said Cheke. "That's why I've asked Geoffrey to help. Edmund has been gone for almost eight months and no one has heard from him in six months."

"But Edmund is in Europe—in Germany," I said, and regretted it instantly.

"How do you know that?" Geoffrey asked, all intent again. "Has he written to you? I thought you'd received no letters. That's what you told Mistress Gwinn."

"So you *are* spying on me," I said, my voice rising.

Cheke intervened, his hands outstretched, "Joanna, please do not be offended. I asked Geoffrey to make such inquiries. I've hired him to search for Edmund—that was a part of the task. This is a delicate matter. Very delicate. I know that what happened with your wedding and everything afterward was extraordinarily painful. But, Joanna, he is my friend. For years he was a friend—with all due respect to you, for years before you even met him. I must find Edmund, or at least learn if he is dead or alive. I cannot go on without knowing."

John Cheke looked so distressed, snatching up the cloth to wipe his face, that I felt wretched for not realizing that Edmund's well-being mattered to others beyond myself. While both lived at Cambridge, Cheke and Edmund found they shared an interest in ancient Greek texts, and a friendship of humanists had deepened, in spite of their differences in religion.

His arms folded, Geoffrey said, "You will please tell us how you know Edmund is in Germany if you've received no letters from him." I knew that tone well; there was no possibility of his giving up.

What an agonizing dilemma. When I'd refused last year to go forward with my part in assassinating the king, I was imprisoned by Jacquard Rolin for months at Het Gravensteen, a stone fortress in Ghent. Persuasive arguments followed by vicious threats didn't force me to comply, so one day Jacquard revealed their plot to find Edmund and drag him to the same prison.

It wasn't Geoffrey's badgering that weakened me, but John Cheke's eyes, full of pleading. I said, "In the early autumn, I was told that Edmund had requested permission to leave England, it was granted, and his boat reached a port in some part of the Holy Roman Empire. Then, in November, I learned that Edmund was believed to be in the Black Forest of Germany, but no one knew where. As of early December, that had not changed."

"It fits, Geoffrey," exulted Cheke. "Those dates confirm the letter from Paracelsus."

"Who is that?" I asked.

"A Swiss man whose birth name is Philippus Aureolus Theophrastus Bombastus von Hohenheim—but he is known as Paracelsus," Cheke said happily. "Edmund saw him in his home in Salzburg, in Austria. After that, we are not sure where he traveled to, though we think a part of Germany."

But Geoffrey was not sharing in the celebration. He said, "I cannot assess the soundness of Joanna's facts without knowing the source."

I stared back at him, resolutely silent.

Geoffrey said slowly, "I know that you traveled to Flanders for several months, Joanna. At one point you told Agatha that it was to look for Edmund, but that you were unsuccessful. A little later, you denied that was the purpose of the trip and were simply vague. I suspect that you traveled to Flanders to find another priory to enter, to resume your life as a Dominican nun. There are many cases of nuns and friars and monks doing so after our king dissolved the monasteries. Is that how you learned of Edmund's movements—through friars who knew of him?"

Outraged, I said, "My life is not a domain for inquiry, Geoffrey. Why are *you* doing this—helping John Cheke locate Edmund? He cares about him, but you? I don't follow this. What does it have to do with your leaving Dartford? If he is in Germany or Austria, that's the end of it. You can't travel there."

"I can't?" Geoffrey said.

I began to laugh, but it died in my throat as I saw both men were serious.

"You plan to wander a vast land of duchies and kingdoms and impenetrable forests, not knowing the language or a single person who lives there?" I asked.

Cheke protested, "It's not as mad a plan as that, Joanna."

I took a step toward Geoffrey. "Tell me the true reason you are doing this. We both know you never liked Edmund—not since the beginning, when he was still a friar at Dartford. *You* were the one who prevented our wedding. Now you're going to abandon England, in order to search for him?"

Geoffrey slumped onto a stool, running his hand through his hair. For the first time I saw his exhaustion; his cheeks were hollow, and I'd never seen him so thin. Something was causing him considerable anguish—perhaps his grief over Beatrice's death prevented him from sleeping or eating. I regretted my harsh words, but before I could soften them, Geoffrey spoke.

"My reasons are my own, Joanna," he said in a flat, dull manner. "Your life is no domain for inquiry, and neither is mine."

"Then I believe our conversation is at an end," I said.

It was such a small room that a few short steps led me out of it. I could bear no more of this painful encounter. I'd almost reached the scholars' study when footsteps thundered behind me. I braced myself for another bout with Geoffrey, but the man who caught up to me was John Cheke.

"Joanna, I am so sorry," he said, miserable. "That must have been terrible for you. I beg you to allow me to escort you to the banquet. We won't speak of Edmund again if you don't wish it."

I returned to the hall of the king and his court by a different way than I came. John Cheke steered me down the main corridor to a wide set of marble stairs. Halfway down, the sound of music and laughter wafted up, and I hesitated on the steps.

"You don't wish to return?" Cheke asked.

I shook my head.

"I must admit, I was surprised to see you in such company," said Cheke. "But then I never foresaw myself in a bishop's residence, begging for approval for the chair in Greek. We both tread quite different paths than we did last May, when we met." He hesitated, and then said, "So does Geoffrey Scovill, I think."

I could not stop myself from asking, "Why did you commission Geoffrey, of all people, to locate Edmund?"

"Joanna, you don't understand. Geoffrey came to *me*."

"But why?"

"To that point, I cannot speak. It's up to Constable Scovill to explain himself, should he wish to. If you two ever speak to each other again."

For the last fortnight, I had been melancholy over Geoffrey leaving Dartford, but after spending just a few minutes together, we'd quarreled. The usual painful jumble of emotions seized me. When he questioned me so unrelentingly, so suspiciously, it made me furious. But a part of me wished I could lay down my defenses and tell Geoffrey all. I knew of no one shrewder.

When Cheke opened the door leading from Winchester House to the courtyard, we stepped into a night as warm as July. It was well after midnight. He insisted on escorting me through the garden park, his arm protectively around me as we left the bustling torchlit courtyard for the dark and silent park. Looking up, I saw a sky hung bright with hundreds of stars.

We'd almost reached the river when we heard voices. One man said, "It's too soon." Another man said, his voice familiar, "But it must be May Day, I tell you. That is what Lady Rochford specified."

I paused, signaling to Cheke. We were partly obscured by a large hedge. Several yards away was a statue of an angel. A trio of men huddled on the other side of it. My eyes straining in the night, I recognized first the tall, lanky form of my cousin the Earl of Surrey; then the slender figure of Master Thomas Culpepper; and finally, the outline of the oldest of the three, Lord Hungerford. It was he who had spoken of Lady Rochford.

"We pledged ourselves to a covenant," said Thomas Culpepper. "We must do what is required, no matter what."

In the unearthly warmth of this spring night, a chill raced up my arms and I shuddered. With a nod to John Cheke, we hurried forward.

A covenant? Sir Walter Hungerford had used the same word in the small chapel. I strained to remember his exact words: *The covenant is made. The guide secured and the others are chosen.* Were Surrey and Culpepper the others?

With the churning waters of the Thames coming into view, John Cheke said, "I hate to think of you in the company of men such as Sir Walter Hungerford, and so would Edmund, if he were here."

I stopped short on the pathway. "You know Sir Walter?"

"I do," said Cheke. "I hear many things at Winchester House, and I've been privy to stories of Sir Walter Hungerford long before I came to Southwark. I would tell them to you, but they are too sordid for a young lady's ears."

"Master Cheke, I laid down my novice habit long ago," I said. "I was forced to come to court, and for certain reasons am finding it impossible to leave. If I am to protect myself, I need to know as much as possible about the people who surround me. Please, tell me what you know of Sir Walter."

Even with nothing but moonlight to illuminate him, I read disgust on John Cheke's face. "It concerns his wives," he said.

"He has more than one?"

"Sir Walter's present wife is his second. The first one was . . . executed."

Thinking of my cousin Margaret Bulmer and other blameless female victims of the king, I said, "You must not condemn her."

"I don't," Cheke said. "I condemn *him*. For his first wife was arrested, tried, and convicted for attempting to murder Sir Walter. And the whispers are that his depravities drove her to such a terrible act, the details of such I would never share with you no matter how much you pleaded."

My mouth dry, I said, "Christ deliver us."

Cheke said, "He didn't deliver the first Lady Hungerford."

I was too horrified to chastise Cheke for his blasphemy. My mind again ran back to what I'd overheard. What sort of covenant had Hungerford made with Culpepper and my cousin Surrey? If Lady Rochford were involved, its purpose was most certainly a dark one.

A single man, slumped with exhaustion, waited on the river landing for a boat inching toward shore. John Cheke insisted on accompanying me across the river and to my rooms. When I pointed out that Geoffrey Scovill had come to see him this same night, Cheke said firmly, "He will wait, since it is your safety that is of concern."

The riverboat reached the landing, and we three boarded. The boatmen were an odd pair: a thin man, stooped of shoulders, with snowy white hair, and a hale lad no older than fourteen.

In no time our fellow passenger fell asleep, his chin bobbing with snores on his jeweled doublet. I was bone tired, no question of that, but my mind twisted and turned with uneasy thoughts.

John Cheke said to the old man steering the boat up front, "It is very late to be on the river."

"Aye, 'tis late," said the boatman. "But we must earn all we can now, for the time lying ahead."

"Isn't summer the most prosperous time for the riverboats?" asked Cheke.

The boatman chuckled. "Not this summer. It will be a time of want and pestilence. The lady of the river told me."

"Which lady?" Cheke asked.

"Grandfather, don't," pleaded the young man pulling oars behind us. "'Tis nonsense. Forget it, sir."

The older man laughed again. "He's too young to know about the lady. But she speaks to a-many of us grown men. We know how to listen to the river."

Cheke leaned forward. "If I tried, could I hear her?"

The boatman turned around, painfully, and scrutinized John Cheke. Perhaps he thought he was being mocked. Satisfied at last, he said, "Of course ye could. The truth is plain enough. The air like a fever. The weeds withering. The smell of death when ye put yer head within an inch of water."

I shook my head, dismayed. Why was Cheke encouraging such unpleasantness?

"Just one question to ask yerself," the old boatman said, grinning at us both in the moonlight. "When did it last rain?"

With that he turned and resumed his steering of the boat, humming a tuneless ditty.

I said in a low voice, "His grandson is right—that *was* nonsense."

Cheke was silent for a moment, and then said, "I will tell you who would disagree that it's nonsense, and that is Paracelsus. The man whom Edmund traveled to see in Austria."

"The man who wrote you the letter?"

"Yes, a single letter, and that is the difficulty. He confirmed that Edmund saw him and that afterward he sent him to the Black Forest. But he won't respond to any of the other letters I've sent subsequently—more than a dozen—or to correspondence sent at my request from the master at Cambridge. Did he return to Austria? Did he go somewhere else in Germany? We have no idea. Many letters have been sent, without leading to answers. That's what Geoffrey plans to do: go to Paracelsus, find out any details he can, and then pick up the trail. Last year Edmund wrote me he would be gone three months at most and yet—"

"Edmund writes to you?"

"Yes, or rather he did. The letters stopped, and that is why I am so greatly concerned."

I don't know why it should have hurt me so, that Edmund wrote to John Cheke and not to me after that first note he left me in Dartford, saying I would not see him again. I took a moment to be sure my voice was steady before I said, "Paracelsus is such an odd name."

"He is a physician of great renown. Or perhaps I should say notoriety. Many do not agree with him. He is sometimes chased from town to town by those who fear and hate his beliefs."

"Which are?"

"That the mysteries of nature can heal us, and more than that—that they hold the answers to all existence. He writes that a work of nature constitutes a visible reflection of the invisible work of God." He paused. "Those who believe as Paracelsus does say, 'As above, so below.' Whatever occurs on any plane of reality, corresponds on another. Everything is connected."

My head hurt from trying to understand such beliefs, which

seemed, at the least, heretical. What attraction did they hold for Edmund?

The boat slowed as we approached the landing on the other side of the Thames. Against the inky black sky, the stone palace possessed an unearthly white glow, even in the middle of the night and with only a few candles burning in all of those windows.

I said, "I cannot comprehend why should Edmund go all the way to Austria to speak with a physician who has such bizarre opinions. He is an apothecary himself, and knows more of healing than most physicians who practice."

John Cheke said, "One of Paracelsus's areas of knowledge is the use of opium, the drug of the red poppy. I believe that's why Edmund went to him, in a desperate quest for help from his affliction."

I suddenly felt so very tired. I did not say another word to Cheke as he helped me from the boat because I was gripped with the pain of remembering my wedding day. The last time I saw Edmund his eyes were blank and sleepy, his words slurred. How cruel, that my final memory of Edmund Sommerville was seeing him enslaved by opium.

John Cheke said, "It was all my fault, Joanna. I pushed you to leave, to allow me to cope with Edmund that night. But I believe that if you had remained, and been the one to console him when he recovered from the opium—or chastise him—then he would not have left Dartford, covered with shame. He needed *you*. I didn't understand that."

I shook my head. "Edmund made his own choices, Master Cheke. Do not take this upon yourself."

John Cheke said nothing more but walked me through the dimly lit palace to Catherine's rooms. Her servant Richard slept before the door, as he always did. I nodded my thanks to John and slipped inside. Catherine's maid Sarah, too, was sound asleep on her pallet on the floor.

I changed into my shift and curled up in bed. I meant to stay awake for the return of Catherine, but in a few moments I was asleep. My dreams were stalked by ghouls: a woman who crawled out of the river, a skeleton that reached for me, grinning. A girl wailing as she struggled to free herself from a rock.

I woke up with a start, sitting upright in the bed. Sunlight flooded the room; it looked to be midmorning.

Catherine's bed was untouched, the blanket neatly turned over. She had never returned.

18

It took me a few moments to realize that there was more to this than Catherine's failure to come home last night. Her clothes and jewels were gone and so was her maid, Sarah. While I slept, all had disappeared.

I got dressed as quickly as I could. I'd send word to the Earl of Surrey to discover what happened to Catherine. I could see the hand of his father, the Duke of Norfolk, in this.

When I yanked open the door to the passageway, I was surprised to find Thomas Culpepper talking to Catherine's servant Richard. My mind was still thick with traces of sleep and I was certain I looked the worse for the night before, but as always, Thomas Culpepper was meticulously groomed and composed.

"Good morning, Mistress Joanna, and I am afraid you don't have much time," said Culpepper.

"For what?"

"The king wishes you to meet this morning with his keeper of the wardrobe to discuss your duties as tapestry mistress."

A wave of dread washed over me. So much had happened at the bishop's banquet, I'd thrust out of my mind the king's pronouncement. It hadn't seemed real, somehow. Much more like another piece pushed forward on the chess board by the king to impress or confound others—in this case, the imperial ambassador, Eustace Chapuys. But now, looking at Thomas Culpepper's serious young face, the gravity of it hit.

I said to him quietly, "The truth is, I am not suitable for such a position."

"It is for the king to decide who is suited to perform which duties at court, and he has decided on you for this," he said.

Glancing at Richard, whose stolid expression had given way to something approaching interest, I said, "First I wish to speak with you on another matter in private, Master Culpepper."

He joined me inside Catherine's room, the door left open a few inches for propriety's sake.

Before I could even ask, Culpepper said, "She has been moved to Howard House."

I was relieved by this explanation. I'd feared something much more reprehensible happened to Catherine last night than her being taken to the London house of the Duke of Norfolk. It raised certain questions, however.

"How can she serve the queen if she doesn't lodge in the palace?" I asked. "Or is Catherine no longer a maid of honor?"

The shutter of grim disapproval came down. "It would be accurate to say that Catherine now serves the king, not the queen," he said.

"No," I said, so loudly that Richard stuck his shaggy head in the room to inquire after my well-being.

Culpepper said, "Mistress Stafford has just received a piece of unpleasant news, you may continue to wait outside."

Richard retreated, and I said, struggling for calm, "The appointment with the Keeper of the Great Wardrobe shall have to wait. I must go to Howard House at once."

"It's too late for that."

"What do you mean?"

"I mean that the act that you sought to prevent has occurred, Mistress Stafford. Catherine Howard is now the king's mistress."

Horrified, I turned away from Culpepper. If anyone would know such a thing, it would be this gentleman of the privy chamber. And so I had failed. My efforts to prevent this seduction were nothing pitted against her family's ambition and the king's lust. It was almost as if Whitehall itself, this vast stone city within a city, had willed it to happen. Yet I could still feel her fingers digging into my arm as we walked to the river landing. I'd missed what could have been my only chance to rescue Catherine from disaster.

Culpepper said, "She is now under the total and absolute control of the duke, his stepmother the dowager duchess, and the other Howards. Her submission was sealed with gifts. The goods and chattel of two men of Sussex, indicted before the coroner, have been seized by the Crown and deeded to Mistress Catherine Howard."

"What was their crime?" I whispered.

"Murder."

My stomach turned over, and for a moment I thought I would be sick. After sucking in three deep breaths, it passed.

"Mistress Stafford, listen to me, please," said Culpepper. "You must come with me to the Keeper of the Great Wardrobe. It's time to take up your duties."

I whirled around, enraged. "Have you lost your wits? You expect me to serve the king *now*?"

"Yes, I do, and for two reasons," he said, undaunted. "First, you should remain at court to be of support to Catherine when the king discards her. You can be sure that her family will not care what happens to her then."

"So you are not among those who think Catherine could become his wife?"

"A *fifth* queen?" Culpepper said. "It is unheard of for a king, for any man, to take that many wives. And, even more important, Anne of Cleves cannot be dislodged. The king used an affinity to annul his first marriage—Catherine of Aragon was married to his older brother. Even with that in his favor, it took him years to rid himself of her. He has no such legal grounds for annulment now. Anne of Cleves would never go the way of Anne Boleyn, either. Her conduct is absolutely blameless, and her family in Germany is too powerful to let her be charged with trumped-up crimes."

Everything he said made sense. "What is the second reason for your thinking I should serve the king?" I asked.

He said earnestly, "Because you should seize this opportunity in order to look after yourself, Mistress Stafford. The king intends to pay you significant wages—you will be able to hire servants and create a household. Your future will be assured."

"None of that means anything to me," I said. "I know this may be hard for you to understand, Master Culpepper, but I wish only to lead a quiet life. If I cannot serve God in a priory, then I will follow my calling as best I can outside monastic walls, as others do who once were nuns or monks or friars."

"What about your family?" he persisted. "Wouldn't your filling a court position help the Staffords, who have been so eclipsed in the affairs of the kingdom?"

Arthur.

I heard his name as clearly as if someone shouted it from atop Whitehall Palace. Culpepper was right, this position could assure my standing. I'd finally be able to persuade my cousin to send Arthur Bulmer back down. I'd have the money for a tutor and the connections to help him regain his family honor, when the time came. For Arthur's sake, I must continue to stomach this life at court.

"Very well," I murmured. "Lead the way to the Keeper of the Great Wardrobe."

As we walked down the passageway, Thomas Culpepper explained that certain arrangements had been made concerning my situation. It was not yet settled if the king wished me to form a part of the permanent royal household, moving with the court among his principal residences. Perhaps a home in London would suit. But until such decisions were made, I must live at Whitehall. Catherine's maid, Sarah, would stay close to her at Howard House, naturally. And Richard had been reassigned to serve me, and would run errands and sleep outside the rooms, as a protector. Culpepper said that word *protector* with great emphasis. Now I understood why Richard had taken new interest in my welfare. But I still felt uneasy.

"Who made these decisions?" I asked.

"The Duke of Norfolk—and myself," he answered, his cheeks reddening ever so slightly.

"Why would Norfolk wish me protected?" I demanded. I was certain the opposite must be true; the duke would relish my coming to harm, or at the very least rejoice to see me banished from court.

"It's true that the duke bears little fondness for you," Culpepper admitted. "He is a practical man, however. He sees you high in the king's favor, and so would not gainsay my proposal that Richard be transferred to your staff."

I glanced sideways at Culpepper. His solicitude on my behalf was most kind—certainly no one else was looking out for my interests in such a way—and we both knew that the mystery of who attacked me the first day in Whitehall, and why, was unsolved. However, I felt certain that representing me in negotiations went beyond what a gentleman of the privy chamber should do for a woman he was not related to. Some sort of gentle reproof was called for.

The passageway we hurried down had become quite crowded, though, and this was not the time or place to take the matter up, even if I knew what to say.

The Keeper of the Great Wardrobe, the man who directed all of the purchasing and maintaining of the king's clothing, armor, furs, velvets, canopies, and tapestries, occupied a large chamber, crammed with men, off the Great Hall. I felt a fool, remembering how the man impersonating the page had persuaded me that such an important office would be located in a small building on the outskirts of the palace.

I was not sure which one of the men was the keeper, for in the center of the room stood a foursome of finely attired older men studying a series of books spread open. A line of a half dozen other men, looking like grooms or clerks, waited to gain the attention of those huddled at the table. Others busied themselves with duties, rushing in and out.

Thomas Culpepper commented, "There is much work to do, with the tournament next week."

"A tournament?"

Culpepper laughed. "Mistress Stafford, you amaze me. You must be the only living being at Whitehall unaware that the king ordered a tournament joust on May Day, the first to be held in four years. Everyone else thinks of nothing else."

A shiver ran up my spine. "May Day?" I asked carefully. "So that is the day of a joust? Nothing else?"

Culpepper slowly turned toward me. "What else could there be?" The amusement died in his eyes.

"Is that not the day something will take place that you've planned with my cousin the Earl of Surrey and Sir Walter Hunger-ford?" I asked.

I suspected he would not appreciate the question, but Culpepper's reaction astounded me.

He grabbed my arm, his expression one of horror verging on panic. "How do you know about this—how?" he choked.

"I heard you in the bishop's garden park last night," I whispered.

"You must forget what you heard, and say nothing to anyone else, do you promise me, Mistress Stafford?"

"But what—?"

His grip on my arm tightened. "Promise me, Joanna," he begged. "If you value my life, and your own, you must not repeat a word of it."

I nodded, genuinely frightened.

Culpepper called out, "Sir Andrew Windsor, Mistress Stafford is here to speak with you, by the king's command."

The heads of the gray-haired men shot up, but Culpepper did not lead me across the room to be introduced to Sir Andrew or any-one else. Instead he turned on his heel and fled, moving faster than I'd ever seen him go—and he always moved like quicksilver.

Swallowing hard, I walked toward the quartet of court officials at the table. The closer I got, I realized two things. The first was that two of these men were very old indeed, at least seventy years of age. And the second was that they regarded me with a common distaste. I felt like a new mistress sent to take charge of a resentful flock of novices—except that these novices were my grandfather's age.

"I am pleased to make the acquaintance of the lady His Majesty has appointed to take charge of his arras collection, the preeminent one in all of Christendom," said the most elderly of them all, which must mean he was Sir Andrew. The way he said "pleased" suggested just the opposite, and he used the formal term for Flemish tapestry, to drive home the prestige of the collection.

I curtsied and told him how pleased I was, as well.

The second elderly man said, with a foreign accent, "We understand you had great difficulty locating the chamber of the keeper of the wardrobe."

This must be a reference to my summons to Whitehall and what happened the first day, how I failed to find my way here after being attacked and then encountering Cromwell in Westminster Hall. I had never thought about how my actions would be perceived by these men in charge of tapestry.

My cheeks warm, I said, "I regret there were . . . complications."

Sir Andrew cleared his throat—a genuinely alarming gurgle—and said, "Be that as it may, we are taxed with the inventory of the Whitehall collection, Mistress Stafford. It comes at a difficult time, when we must prepare for His Majesty's tournament, the greatest pageant the court has put on for years. Following which, the royal household departs Whitehall for Greenwich."

So that explained the disapproval in the air—they resented the inconvenience.

The second man said, scowling in accusation, "Mistress Stafford, the order for inventory was in response to a remark *you* made?"

"I made no such remark, or request," I replied.

The men looked at one another, silently dubious.

My temper flaring, I said, "If you feel the king has erred in requesting an inventory of his own arras, I can convey that sentiment the next time I am in his presence."

The man who'd accused me of prodding the king recoiled, visibly shocked. Out of the corner of my eye, I saw two clerks ribbing each other. Sir Andrew said, more mildly, "You must forgive my colleague. Master Jan Moinck is the king's agent for acquisition in Brussels, recently returned. He has a role in supervising the arras. He has labored long hours to perform the inventory, with few clerks to spare."

"You are from Flanders, sir?" I asked Master Moinck. If we were to work in tandem, which seemed inevitable, I must get our acquaintanceship on a better footing.

Chin trembling, he responded, "How did you know that? Are you one who distrusts all foreigners, Mistress Stafford?"

"I hardly think so, being that my mother was born in Spain," I said, exasperated. I took a breath. Best to try again. "I recognized your accent and I am also aware that those from Flanders possess discerning taste when it comes to furnishings and decoration and—"

Jacquard Rolin. That was how I pinpointed his homeland and how I knew of the Flemish reputation for excellent taste. He spoke with the same accent. I hastily shoved the imperial spy from my thoughts.

Sir Andrew stepped in again. "Mistress Stafford, we should have the inventory ready for you by the day of the tournament."

"May I be of assistance?" I asked.

"How exactly do you propose to assist?" asked Master Moinck.

"By taking it on," I replied. "I will complete the inventory. You said you are unduly taxed with preparing for the tournament and other duties. If someone can instruct me, I shall begin today."

Sir Andrew silenced Master Moinck's scoffing noises with the order for the books to be brought to me here, at the keeper of the wardrobe's chamber. Master Moinck himself stalked away to oversee the transfer.

Sir Andrew said with a wistful glint in his eyes, "I was a friend to the Duke of Buckingham, and I must tell you that you remind me of him in several respects." He lowered his voice to just above a whisper. "But you were also a novice of the Dominican Order, correct?"

"Yes," I said. Searching his face for condemnation, I saw none and continued: "As you must then know, service in a priory means I am not afraid of work."

Nodding, Sir Andrew said, loudly enough for everyone in the

room to hear, "After the tournament, I will see that you are welcomed at the tapestry workshop in London. I have been informed that you have your own tapestry to weave. You shall receive all necessary assistance."

The inventory books were assembled and explained and I politely declined the offer of a clerk to assist. Like it or not, I now had my own servant, and the least Richard could do was carry books for me as I made my way around the palace.

Sir Andrew's final words, delivered as he escorted me out of the chamber, carried a warning. "Master Moinck has his reasons for being reluctant to welcome a newcomer to the keeping of His Majesty's tapestries. He shall not be your ally at any stage of your enterprise."

"Understood," I said.

Another person at the king's court who wished me ill. The list grew lengthy.

I did my best to ignore the stares of the courtiers as I performed the inventory of Whitehall's tapestries over the next four days. There were more than two hundred pieces hanging in this palace alone. Others were either part of the permanent collection of Henry VIII's many castles or stored in the tapestry workshop, for repair or cleaning.

To my surprise, Richard showed enthusiasm for the task. Up and down and around we progressed, stopping at every tapestry, large and small, to note the placement, dimensions, design, and present condition. Up until now, he'd been used as the lowest level of servants for the Howards—a strong back for the guarding of family members. But he was capable of more. And Richard never complained, no matter how long I asked him to stand nearby, balancing a book for me to write in. It could be hot work, too, for this uncomfortable dry spell continued, just as the strange old riverboat man had predicted.

But the clammy warmth of the palace was the least of my troubles. As much as I labored on the inventory, making notes in the books about this tapestry and that one, I could not quiet my fears. Thomas Culpepper's near-violent reaction to my May Day question haunted me, every hour of the day and deep into the night. What sort of dangerous conspiracy had he formed? He and Sir Walter Hungerford both used the word *covenant*. Did it have anything to do with hatred of Thomas Cromwell—that is what I sensed. But why must some unknown action take place on the day of a tournament joust? I had not seen Culpepper for even a moment since he delivered me to the keeper of the wardrobe, and I strongly suspected that he was avoiding me.

Just as unfathomable was Geoffrey Scovill's plan to travel to Germany to track down Edmund. Not only did I find it baffling that Geoffrey would do such a thing, I also feared anew for Edmund. I'd never understood why he'd journeyed to an impregnable corner of Germany and now I found it chilling that his friend John Cheke shared my apprehension. I ached that Edmund suffered from the ravages of his opium craving to the extent that he must travel for months on end to seek help—and was he safe from its power now? No one had heard a word in six months.

And, though I knew full well that it was unfair, I blamed Geoffrey and John Cheke for the renewal of my suffering over Edmund Sommerville. An old scar had been ripped open. But also I couldn't block from my mind the sight of Geoffrey, hollow with exhaustion and sadness, slumped in Cheke's room. It made me feel that something should be done—but what? I would have wagered that I was the last person Geoffrey would accept help from. The weight of these troubling thoughts was so heavy that it was as if I carried the tapestry books up and down stairs, not Richard.

Still, it was another matter altogether that brought me to tears, and Master Hans Holbein was the agent.

"I've heard such fine stories of your enterprise, Mistress Joanna," said Holbein when he came to see me. "But they come as no surprise to me—were you not my artist's assistant for four enjoyable days? How I have missed you since."

"And I have missed you," I said, and meant it. It brought a moment of real happiness to see his broad, smiling face and hear his soft German voice.

"I suppose you are impatient for the tournament in two days' time?" he asked.

"No," I said, and waited for him to exclaim over my foolishness in not embracing the grand pageant. But Master Holbein said somberly, "The last tournament was something I can never forgot—but for reasons less than pleasant," and then shook his head, as if to banish some memories. His tone turned teasing. "It's not often that work is commissioned of me and then forgotten. I decided it was time to call on you with my sketch."

He unfurled the image of Catherine Howard.

Holbein certainly captured the blessing of Catherine's beauty: smooth pink-and-white complexion, even features, and shiny auburn hair. A dimple danced low in her right cheek, as if she verged on one of her bursts of giggling. But in those green-gray eyes a shadow lurked. Staring at her image, I felt as if she were trying to tell me that she knew all such blessings would recede before something that could not be charmed or appeased or, finally, forestalled.

"Forgive me, Catherine," I gasped through a harrowing sob. "Forgive."

Holbein enveloped me in a hug, a fatherly comfort I'd not experienced for years. I was grateful and, resting my head on his broad shoulder, I found it impossible to rein in my regret and grief.

Holbein leaned down to say something in my ear, and said it softly, with restraint, as if he were afraid others could hear him even though we were utterly alone.

"I'm afraid for her, too."

He patted me soothingly, until my weeping finally died down, and we could hear the faint roar of the court in the crowded palace on one side and the rivermen shouting on the Thames on the other.

19

How many toppled priories paid for the May Day tournament? It was impossible not to wonder about this as I walked with Master Hans Holbein to the tiltyard of Westminster, just outside the palace walls. After living in Whitehall for thirteen days, I was no stranger to King Henry VIII's taste for pomp. But neither was I ignorant of where the funds for it came. After the king spent the vast inheritance of his own father, he faced an empty treasury. It was Thomas Cromwell who filled it again with gold—the spoils of the abbeys. Henry VIII was able to indulge with a fury his passion for seizing and rebuilding castles. He owned more homes than he could possibly make use of. The luxurious furnishings, all the servants' wages, the epic dinners, his perpetual adornment in furs, jewels, and crowns—all made possible by sacked shrines and plundered acres.

My mind had not been on today's grand event, but rather on the tapestries. I'd labored through the night on Thursday so that the inventory would be ready by the appointed time. Sir Andrew Windsor had promised me his cooperation, but when I sent word early Friday that I was prepared to present my work on the agreed day, he sent back a curt message of postponement: "His Majesty wishes to receive the inventory of arras on the day after the tournament's end, the Fifth of May."

I read the message three times, stunned, before tossing it on the floor.

Hans Holbein, who'd become a frequent visitor since comforting me over Catherine Howard, chuckled at my ill temper.

"You had better accustom yourself to the king's whims," he advised. "Take relief from a postponement, for I have seen it work the other way. The king can be most impatient and demand to see something finished that no earthly power could have completed in the time he allots."

"It is all grossly unfair."

"There is only one man in the kingdom who can decide what is fair, and at present he is occupied with the tournament," Holbein said. "Which is another reason why you and I must attend, and be seen to attend."

And so I agreed to accompany him. The sport of the joust did have some meaning for me, because my father made a name for himself in the king's tournaments, before I was born. He once said that Henry VIII and his favored companions had a lust for war that fueled their love of the tiltyard. Of course, the days of the king himself donning armor and holding the lance were finished. It was a sport for the young.

Moments after we set out that Saturday morning, I asked Holbein, "How will we even be noticed in this great a crowd?" I'd heard that the king sent word to France, Flanders, Scotland, and Spain for all comers to "undertake the challengers of England." The entire court was expected to assemble, its nobility hosting the knights and burgesses of the Commons, the Mayor of London, even the city aldermen and the richest cloth merchants. After the tournament, the most esteemed were expected to feast at nearby Durham House.

"The king always knows who is missing at such events," said Holbein in that instructional voice I would surely find irritating were it not coming from a trusted friend. "He took note of every person who failed to appear at Anne Boleyn's coronation, and in time each of them was sorry for it."

I was about to say that nothing could have induced me to cheer that particular coronation when a strange sensation took hold. We had just come out of the doorway of the king's gallery, onto the grounds leading to the tiltyard. A stream of people pushed forward, as would be expected, but I felt that among the mob, someone watched me in particular. It was as if eyes burned holes into the back of my head and my shoulders. I stopped and carefully looked in all directions, but no one met my gaze. Neither did I spot anyone acting suspicious.

It was similar to the feeling I'd had when riding into London with my friends weeks ago. Then, hours later, I was attacked. I had never connected those two things before. Doing so made me feel odd. A link was impossible. The man who impersonated a page awaited me at the gatehouse; he couldn't have watched me as I approached the city. Moreover, how could I be at risk here, today, with Master Hans Holbein in this jubilant crowd? Anyone would laugh to hear of my fears.

My steps faltered as I thought of one person who wouldn't laugh. Elderly Father Francis, the chaplain I'd sought out for confession this morning, whispered afterward, "Be careful, Mistress Joanna, this is a day when not all may be safe." I glanced at him, surprised, but his lip fastened like a button and he hurried the next penitent into the confessional.

What had the priest meant?

The king's gallery faced the tiltyard. On the other side of it stretched the fields of Westminster. On those fields workmen had raised a series of enormous white tents for the use of the knightly challengers and defenders. The flags and streamers mounted at the high points of the tents, all in the Tudor red, hung limply. This was the hottest spring day yet, and a singularly still one, too. The tournament tents languished, like ships at Gravesend, waiting for the wind to fill their sails.

Just as Master Holbein and I found our places along the side of the ninety-foot-long tiltyard, trumpets blared. In strict order of precedence, the members of the court shuffled onto the open gallery, to take their places. Here came Bishop Gardiner and the Duke of Norfolk, together as always, but filing in before them were their hated rivals for the king's favor, Chief Minister Thomas Cromwell and Thomas Cranmer, Archbishop of Canterbury. It was the second time in my life I'd glimpsed the archbishop and I was taken aback by his mild expression and unassuming stance. Not what I expected.

To the cheers of the crowd, the king strode out, wearing cloth of gold. He took the hand of Anne of Cleves and led her to their places in the gallery as if he were the most devoted of husbands. How lovely the queen looked. She wore a gown of the royal purple, its French cut flattering her figure. I finally saw that smile again, the one that brightened her face on the boat from Calais but had been starkly absent at our Whitehall dinner.

With some nervousness, I watched the queen's attendants, led by Lady Rochford, find their spots alongside the queen, but there was no sign of Catherine Howard.

Reading my thoughts, Holbein said, "Oh, she won't appear at a great function such as this. That is not the king's way. He is very discreet."

"There was little discretion at Winchester House," I said sourly.

"That was different. Here you will see Parliament, the bishops of the church, and all sorts of ambassadors and dignitaries of the courts of Europe, with Cleves among them. Everyone must play their part. There is no place for Catherine."

I could not decide who I felt worse for, the queen deceived by this spectacle into believing her husband cared one whit for her, or the girl who loved parties and pageantry, sitting miles away at Howard House.

One of the king's chamberlains made a speech to the crowd: "It having pleased God to establish between Christian princes more concord than ever there was, so that in the idleness of peace there is danger that noble men may themselves fall into idleness or give occasion of idleness to others; and as, in the past, feats of arms have raised men to honor, both in God's service against his infidel enemies and in serving their princes; and as there are six gentlemen, naming themselves knights of blood and name, who, without pretending to excel all others, feel bound to do what they can to further this object, they intend, by the grace of God, Our Lady, Saint George, and all the Court Celestial, and license of their Prince, to defend . . ."

The rest was drowned out, as the crowd gave a great "Ahhhhhh" at the sight of the defenders: six men rode the length of the tiltyard, wearing polished suits of armor and carrying lances, their horses' saddles hanging with white velvet. A page walked alongside each of them, toting the helmet, shield, and other gear of the chosen athlete.

This celebration of the "feats of arms" made me feel strange. No matter the bloodlust of his youth, I knew quite well how much Henry VIII feared a real war, the invasion of his island by the Catholic powers of France and Spain that hovered over him the last two years. He'd fortified the kingdom, mustered his citizens, even taken a foreign bride whose family would, if it came to it, defend England. But that was not enough. In a frenzy Henry VIII had the nobles he imagined disloyal arrested on false charges and killed.

"*That* is interesting—Sir Thomas Seymour comes first," said Holbein, and then in a tone of explaining, "Seymour is the brother of—"

"I know him," I said shortly. Was there ever a prouder man than Thomas Seymour, his shoulders thrown back, grinning, his reddish-brown beard quivering, as he led the defenders? I was sure he would take full advantage of his leading position later, with boasts and careless flirting

Holbein said, "Next comes Lord John Dudley. What intrigues me about him is his father's history, for—"

"I know it," I said, shuddering at the sight of his handsome face. I could never forget the man who pounded on the door of the Courtenays' house to make arrests that November night, or who charged Canterbury Cathedral when Edmund and I scrambled there on our quest to protect the bones of Thomas Becket.

His voice dancing with laughter, Master Holbein said, "I see you are better acquainted with the young gentlemen of the court than I

understood. Do you also know Anthony Kingston?" He gestured at
the next challenger.

Swallowing hard, I said, "Is he related to Sir William Kingston,
the constable of the Tower?"

"His son," said Holbein.

As the memories of months of imprisonment in the Tower of
London took hold, I turned away from the tiltyard course. Each of
the three men caused me some level of distress. Holbein, perceiving
that I was genuinely disturbed, ceased his teasing.

I did not think it safe for me to look upon the tournament until
the horn blew and the next batch of knights announced. These were
the men who would joust with the defenders today.

Even from across the length of the tiltyard I recognized the red-
gold Plantagenet hair of my cousin the Earl of Surrey. A ways behind him rode Thomas Culpepper. Now my fears churned again, but
for different reasons. What were they up to? What was the covenant
they'd pledged, something so secret that if I knew of it, my life would
be at risk, as Culpepper had insisted?

"Mistress Stafford, I have found you at last," said a man's voice in
the crowd.

At first I could not believe it. I had seconds ago puzzled over the
pact formed by the Earl of Surrey, Thomas Culpepper, and a third
man—and Sir Walter Hungerford materialized right in front of me,
among the spectators. It was incredible, as if he had been conjured
from my very thoughts. But, as I took a closer look, my surprise
turned to disgust. Each time I'd been in his presence before, Sir
Walter had observed decorum of dress. Now I looked at a man with
dirty hose and a torn right sleeve. Sweat covered his face, more than
was warranted even for this warm day. Some say that the evil within
the soul must show itself outwardly, and knowing something of Sir
Walter's depravity, such disarray seemed inevitable.

No one else existed for him in the crowd but me. Wringing his
hands, he cried, "Only you could understand our journey, only *you*."

"Calm yourself, sir," I snapped, but that only seemed to agitate
him further. Heads swiveled to see what the fuss was about.

"Can I be of assistance?" said Master Holbein. Sir Walter turned, slowly, to examine him. His eyes, which were bloodshot, took a moment to focus on my companion.

"Master painter," he finally said, "you are also a propitious sight, for you embody the wisdom of Germany."

Stepping even closer, Holbein said, his strong hand clamping round Sir Walter's wrist, "Desist, sir. This is not the time or place to speak of Martin Luther."

To my further amazement, Sir Walter Hungerford threw back his head and laughed—a horrible laugh, hysterical, piercing. More curious heads turned. We were becoming of greater interest than the jousters on their fine horses.

"*That* is not the man whose wisdom I follow, oh, you are mistaken," said Sir Walter. "I revere other Germans—such as the genius Heinrich Cornelius Agrippa." He burst out laughing again, a diseased howl.

"Hungerford!"

It was the Earl of Surrey, on his horse. He had reached the closest point to us, and must have heard the disturbance. He guided his mount to the perimeter of the running course, holding the reins tight. The earl looked furious. Not only that—I could see, from the purplish-yellow bruise covering his forehead, that Surrey had already suffered some sort of blow.

Behind him, Thomas Culpepper nudged his horse to get closer without breaking the line of procession.

"Go home, man," shouted Surrey. "For the love of Christ and the Virgin, go home."

With a final howl of amusement, Sir Walter stumbled back, and then, pushing and shoving the spectators out of his path, he charged away from the tiltyard. "That man was *drunk*," commented one spectator, and a titter of laughter went round the mob.

Surrey and Culpepper rejoined the line of challengers and rode on, followed by more knights. The bizarre behavior of Hungerford was forgotten in the reflection of men wearing such glittering armor.

But not by me or by Hans Holbein, who was more upset than

I had ever seen. He muttered to himself in German, pulling on his beard. After a moment at least of this, he said to me, "That man, that Hungerford, I'm not sure that he was drunk. That was not his malady. Why did he seek you out, Mistress Joanna? Do you know the man he spoke of?

I shook my head. "I've never heard the name before. It *is* German, isn't it?"

"It is. And even though speaking too favorably of Martin Luther can get you burned in half of Europe, I would rather discuss Luther any hour of the day with you than Agrippa, for he is twice as dangerous."

"More dangerous than Luther? That is not possible."

The horns blew again, the crowd cheered, and the challengers and defenders circled back to their tents. The promenade was at an end; the first challenger would soon tilt against a defender.

"Who is this man Agrippa?" I pressed.

"Not here," said Holbein. "Not now."

I could hear the voices in the bishop's garden park: *It must be May Day. It must be May Day. It must be May Day.* At a crowded tournament such as this, what could Surrey, Culpepper, and Hungerford possibly plan to do? I glanced at the royal gallery. King Henry beckoned to Thomas Cromwell, and the chief minister leaned over to better hear what his monarch said. Anne of Cleves pointed at something on the tiltyard, her smile even brighter, for each of the challengers and defenders had saluted the queen of England. The Duke of Norfolk leaned against a wooden pillar, nodding at the Bishop of Winchester. The nobles and ladies who ranged across the galley looked expectant, haughty, supercilious. A few even appeared bored.

Yet every instinct I had, every feeling of unease and observance of ill omen, screamed that this *was* a day of some planned action. I struggled to remember precisely what Surrey had said at the bishop's banquet: *There is another way to put an end to Cromwell, though it be anything but honorable. I can say not a word to you about it. Only that, someday, when all has changed, I hope to redeem myself in your eyes, Joanna.* Three of them formed a covenant, but I sensed that Sir Walter Hungerford was the architect of the plan. Surrey said it was "anything but honorable," and among the first words Hungerford had ever said to me were "But what if I have no honor?" It must be a dark plan indeed. I studied the chief minister from my place below the royal gallery. Cromwell looked perfectly calm and secure, still in conversation with King Henry. No man could be safer from harm.

"Master Holbein, I've never begged you for anything—I'm not a woman disposed to beg—but please tell me why Sir Walter thinks this Agrippa wise," I said.

He seemed about to answer me when a herald shouted, "For England!" The crowd roared its loudest yet. On the course, two men, their heads now concealed in helmets, galloped toward each other from opposite ends of the course, lances quivering.

They charged closer . . . closer. The spectators tensed.

There was an ear-splitting clap, like thunder—one of the men fell from his horse, struck down by the force of his opponent's lance. This pitched the crowd into a frenzy of excitement, an emotion I did not share. And neither, I detected, did Master Holbein.

I gripped his arm and repeated, "Tell me."

Holbein pulled me close, as if we were father and daughter or even man and wife. I could smell the sweet wine on his breath, feel the scratch of his wiry beard. But I was so desperate to learn the truth that I clung to him tightly. Holbein whispered in my ear: "Agrippa is a scholar and a physician who has written certain books that are most dangerous."

My entire body, head to toe, froze in the noonday heat. "What are the books about?" I managed to ask.

"Agrippa wrote of the magical world, Mistress Joanna. How to interpret and harness its powers. His most famous work is *De Occulta Philosophia Libri Tres.*"

De Occulta. The occult.

Trembling with nausea, I said, "So Agrippa is a necromancer."

"No, Joanna. He is of a much higher order. He is a magus. A high priest of magic and sorcery."

The crowd around us cheered again, for the fallen man had been pulled to his feet and was waving. Abashed but alive. The man who vanquished him tore off his golden helmet so that we could see him and know him: Sir Thomas Seymour.

Holbein gently released me. He made a show of joining in the applause for the vainglorious Seymour. But I could not make a sound or clap my hands. Nothing—for I was staggered by this discovery. My cousin the Earl of Surrey and my friend Thomas Culpepper had made a covenant with Sir Walter Hungerford and it was guided by a master of the occult.

As workers prepared the tiltyard for the second pairing, I turned to Holbein once more.

"What do you know of today—of May Day?" I asked.

He looked down at me, puzzled. "It's the day that the king often chooses to begin such festivities," said the painter. "Everyone knows it's for making merry. It's the same in Germany. The peasants love it more than any other day."

"Why does everyone love it so?"

"Why, it is a holiday for welcoming the spring, celebrating the power of the fertile earth. You call it May Day. We call it *Walpurgis-nacht* or *Hexennacht*."

Struggling to keep my voice calm, I said, "Is that a form of the word *hex*?"

Squinting at the jousting field, Holbein said, "Yes. It is to do with witches and their spells and hexes. I'm not sure, but I believe, in the time before Jesus Christ, there were ceremonies in the forest for making spells. But that's long past—" He stopped short, and whirled to scrutinize me. "You don't believe that man, Hungerford, meant *Hexennacht* when he spoke of his journey?"

I lamented Master Holbein's quickness of mind. I could say nothing; I'd promised silence to Culpepper.

"Sir Walter may not be drunk, but his babblings are nonsense worthy of the tavern," I said, aiming for the sort of arch tone of voice I often heard around me in court.

"Are you sure he is harmless?" Holbein persisted. "He was intent on you, Mistress Joanna."

"I met him briefly through my cousin the Earl of Surrey, who does not always choose his companions with temperance and wisdom," I replied.

"True enough," grunted Holbein, and, to my relief, turned to look at the action on the tiltyard.

The next challenger thundered down the field, and as Holbein's head tracked his approach, I backed away, as carefully as I could. Everyone's being transfixed by the athletes of the field made it easy to snake my way through the crowd. Once I made it to the field, I held up my skirts to hurry as fast as I could, drawing curious glances as I went.

There was no way of knowing which tent contained Thomas Culpepper, so I had to ask questions, and of a lot of people. No one could help. The fourth man I asked, standing outside a white tent, leered at me. "You wantin' to wish him luck as only a pretty lady can?" he demanded.

"Never mind that," I said. There was no time to pay back his offensiveness with any sort of retort or just punishment. "Just tell me where Master Culpepper can be found."

The man gestured toward an entranceway flap.

The light filtered strangely through the material of this soaring, windowless tent. The sun bore down with such strength that it created a golden-grayish tint. About a dozen men occupied this tent, each of them attended by a page or servant. There were other servants, too, serving goblets of wine and trays of food. A trio of musicians played a jaunty melody. The tent resembled a party except that not a single woman attended. This changed when I stood, breathless, inside the hanging flap of a door.

A blond knight having his armored sleeves adjusted called out, "My lady, your presence is irregular. Does an errand compel you?"

"I seek Master Culpepper," I replied.

The tent instantly surged with men's laughter, and not the nicest sort of laughter.

"Why is this not a surprise?" said the blond knight. He lifted his goblet high, as if toasting, and then took a drink.

Although no one had denied his presence, I could not see Culpepper among the men for a moment. He'd walked toward me along the perimeter of the tent, saying nothing until he was right in front of me. No one else could see his expression but myself, which was fortunate. His face was pale, his eyes fiery with anger.

"If you've come to give me a favor, you're too late, mistress," Culpepper called out, loud enough for everyone to hear. "Lady Lisle insisted I ride as her champion. And I agreed. We all know there's no female as grateful to a young man as an old man's darling."

The others in the tent laughed even louder. Such a comment must be meant to mislead his companions as to the true nature of our friendship. Still, I hadn't thought Thomas Culpepper capable of saying such a coarse thing.

To the disappointed jeers of his fellow jousters, Culpepper pulled me outside of the tent, his armor banging against my arm. We went to a place where no one could listen.

"What are you doing here?" he hissed.

"When Sir Walter Hungerford spoke to me today, I put it together," I said. "I know that you plan to seek out someone to perform some sort of occult rite, something to do with Thomas Cromwell. Please, please, you must *not* proceed. I cannot say why or how, but I know something of that world, and . . ."

The words died in my throat. In the sunlight, Culpepper looked worse than I'd ever seen: deep gray shadows under his eyes, complexion like white chalk, lines in his forehead where they'd never existed before. He had not slept a moment last night—and not only that. I thought of the German words Holbein had used: *Walpurgisnacht* and *Hexennacht*. I knew that the German language was not so different from English. *Nacht* must mean "night." The performing of hexes and spells did not happen the evening of May Day but the *night before*.

"It's already happened," I whispered. "I'm too late."

"What's done is done, and I have no regrets," Thomas said roughly. "You should never have come here. I tell you to say nothing, to forget what you have heard and may think you know, but you won't listen to me, Joanna. You keep asking questions, demanding answers. You pay me no heed whatsoever, do you? No wonder men attack you."

I stumbled back a step, shocked by his cruel words. I knew I'd made Thomas Culpepper most angry, and that rash things could be said in anger. In a moment, he would apologize, and I would be able to really talk to him about what happened last night.

But Thomas said, with great articulation, as if I were slow of mind, "I won't speak of what happened—not ever. Nor in future will I speak to you of anything beyond what my duties as a gentleman of the privy chamber compel."

"Master Culpepper, I only—"

"No. Say nothing more. Just leave me be."

With that, he stomped away, his armor clanking as he reentered the tent.

It took me a moment to gather myself, but after I did, I knew there was nothing left to do but rejoin Master Holbein at the tilt-yard, making some excuse for my absence. I did not walk nearly as fast. My throat burned and salty tears pricked the corners of my eyes.

I paused at the top of a shallow hill. From here I could look down on the scene: the next armored challenger preparing his horse at the end of the tiltyard, the hundreds of people drunk with spectacle, the king and queen flanked by their courtiers surveying it all. Behind them rose the massive buildings of the Palace of Whitehall. The gray-blue Thames glittered beyond.

"What has happened to me?" I said out loud. In a short time I'd become so immersed in the court that its intrigues, both romantic and political, consumed me. In my house in Dartford, in those quiet moments before Gregory tapped on the door to deliver the royal summons, could I have foreseen such a transformation? From this perspective, looking down, I tried to imagine that I knew nothing of the people milling about below. I broke free of them; my life was simple, honest.

"Are you unwell, Juana?"

I shook myself from my reverie at the sound of my Spanish name, used at the end of a sentence spoken in French. It could only be Ambassador Eustace Chapuys, and here he was, his wariness mingling with curiosity as he surveyed me from a short distance.

"I am quite well, Ambassador," I said with a quick curtsy.

"No, I believe you've lost your color," he said. "I was on my way to convey the emperor's good wishes to a Spanish knight who answered England's challenge, when I observed you, looking somewhat unsteady and talking to no one. I thought perhaps you withdrew from the joust to recover from some woman's ailment. But to move about the tournament grounds alone like this, with no companion or servant . . ." He looked to the right and left, driving home his point. "Some might consider it unwise."

I took one step down from the hillock, then another, to draw closer to the imperial ambassador.

"And some might consider it an opportunity, wouldn't you agree?" I asked.

Chapuys cocked his head while he examined me. The crowd roared over some feat performed. I fought to keep any hint of fear from showing. This was my moment to throw down the gauntlet, to challenge him to admit to any role he had in the attack on me in the palace. It was a more dangerous challenge than anything attempted on the tiltyard below.

The ambassador finally said, "If you think yourself in danger, it could never be from me."

"No?"

"The Emperor Charles himself has commanded it—no harm shall come to Joanna Stafford at our hands." Chapuys's mouth quivered, and I sensed regret, whether over revealing the commands of the emperor or not being able to order my assassination, I couldn't decipher.

Then he was gone, walking quickly toward the tents.

Was it relief that seized me?—I did not know. Waves of some sort of emotion rippled through me as I trembled in the bright Westminster field. I had faced down Eustace Chapuys at last, and he denied being the one to plot against me here in the palace. Perhaps my legs shook because of the knowledge that the most important ruler in all of Christendom knew of my existence—and had decided to allow it to continue.

I forced myself forward, to return to the sidelines of the joust. I did not realize how light-headed I was, perhaps from going without food or water in the heat, or from the emotion of these encounters. I had only managed a half dozen steps when I stumbled. My ankle turned on a knot of ground, tangling me up in my skirts, and the next thing I knew, I sprawled facedown in the grass. Greatly embarrassed, I sat up, trying to straighten my crooked headdress before rising.

A smooth hand in a fringed sleeve appeared before my eyes. I peered up, but the sun was in my eyes and it took a few seconds of blinking before I could focus on the person's face. When I realized who it was, I recoiled, falling back on the palms of my hands.

Señor Pedro Hantaras chuckled. "May I not offer you assistance, mistress?"

"No." I realized it was ridiculous to refuse him. But I could not help it. The most trusted operative of Ambassador Chapuys, Señor Hantaras had, in a partnership with Jacquard Rolin, trained me for my role in their conspiracy. He was well versed in spying, in codes and falsifying letters. And he knew every trick of doing harm, be it with poison or knife or rope. When I turned against the group of them and refused to kill the king, Señor Hantaras knocked me unconscious, drugged me, and would have gone further if I hadn't escaped from him in Rochester.

His brown eyes gleamed as he said, "Then you shall have to be more careful." He backed away, his legs carefully scissoring on the ground, as if I were royalty that he could not turn his back on. But there was mockery in his face and something else, too. Something

twisted and hateful. This should not surprise me. I had made a fool
of him by escaping and stabbed his mistress in the leg to do it. These
things did not make for friendship.

Then Señor Hantaras turned his back on me and moved along,
in the same direction as Chapuys. He was never at Chapuys's side at
public functions— but never far away.

After a few moments, I spotted Holbein, who was searching
through the crowd. It must be for me. Surging with guilt, I babbled
apologies, but the painter waved them away. "I am quite relieved to
find you, mistress. Your disappearance caused me some distress because of the day's events."

Something about the way he said *events* struck a chord.

"You refer to the tournament?" I said.

My friend shook his head.

"Just a short time ago, a man was arrested," Holbein said. "It was
Sir Walter Hungerford, and he did not go quietly."

20

The news of the arrest of Sir Walter Hungerford pitched me into a state near panic. Had the king's men discovered that Hungerford, Culpepper, and Surrey performed some sort of occult rite before dawn? Did they know its purpose—which I assumed was the annihilation of Cromwell? If so, trial and execution for treason were sure to follow. And those close to them could be swept up in the arrests. For the first time since learning of the conspiracy, I felt the sharp twist of fear for my own survival.

I managed to ask Master Holbein, "What were the charges?"

"No one knows why he was arrested, only that when soldiers took hold of Sir Walter, he tried to fight them off with a knife and screamed curses most blasphemous," said Holbein. "It caused a great stir in the crowd."

I blurted, "I must leave you to change my dress, for this is not fit to wear to the open household at Durham House."

Puzzled, Holbein said, "You are intent on attending the banquet at Durham House?"

"You do not think we would be welcome there?" I asked.

Pulling on his beard, he said, "The royal painter and the cousin of the king will surely be welcome at Durham. But you abhor such gatherings."

I said, growing desperate, "I am famished, Master Holbein. You must be as well."

"I am always famished," he acknowledged.

Of course I did not wish to go to Durham House. But what better place than a banquet of courtiers to hear fresh gossip? I needed to discover how much the authorities knew, and if a connection had been established to my cousin the Earl of Surrey. And no matter how much I tried to convince myself otherwise, I cared deeply about what happened to Thomas Culpepper.

Durham House lay near the boundary of the city of London. It was one of a row of grand manor houses that fronted the Thames, near enough to Whitehall Palace for their owners to attend the king. Holbein and I joined a cluster of gentlemen hiring a barge to row the short distance up the river. On the wharf and in the boat, the talk was entirely of the bravery of the day's knights. One would have thought that a genuine battle had taken place that day.

We joined the stream of people heading into Durham House. The great hall seethed with guests diving into their meals. The air was so warm and thick that it was like a cloud lowering over the long wooden tables—one pungent with the odor of roasted capons and venison and beef.

The king presided on the dais, with his wife by his side this time and not Catherine Howard. Even from across the vast hall, Queen Anne's smile sparkled. But equally striking was the grim visage of the Cleves ambassador who sat on the other side of her. Holbein clucked his tongue and said, "Doctor Harst will never get her crowned that way."

"Crowned?" I echoed.

"The Cleves party grow restive that King Henry does not arrange a coronation for his wife," he explained.

Would Henry VIII command a crowning for Anne when the marriage was unconsummated? It seemed impossible. But I had learned that it was not widely known that the marriage had fundamentally failed. Clearly, the king did not dote on his queen as he had on his other wives, but some at court attributed the coolness to its being an arranged diplomatic match and to Henry VIII's advancing age.

"Master Holbein!" shouted a bearded man, beckoning. He was with a small group at a table near the window overlooking the river.

I was introduced to three bearded men, the esteemed heads of the guild of merchant tailors. Holbein had painted the oldest of them when the artist lived in the household of Sir Thomas More years ago and was still held in the highest regard. As I picked at the capon on my plate and sipped the wine, I listened to the merchant tailors talk to Holbein. They had a different view on the court than any I'd heard before. They were most pleased to be welcomed to the joust and to the feast, yet it all seemed to amuse them, too. Said the youngest merchant tailor: "Seymour looks to be the favorite. But then, the brother of the king's favorite queen has enough gold to buy the best armor."

The next turn of conversation seized my attention.

"There is one similarity to the tournament of 1536," said the red-bearded merchant-tailor, tearing off a chunk of manchet. "Just as on that May Day, an arrest was made."

"Ah, yes, Sir Walter Hungerford," said the oldest man, the one who had beckoned to Master Holbein and myself.

My fingers tightened on my goblet of wine.

Master Holbein said, "Do any of you know what the man was charged with?"

"I have heard," said the same older man, "that the king's men discovered Sir Walter harbored secret sympathy with the Pilgrimage of Grace."

It was the very last thing I expected. That popular rebellion, which raged in the North of England four years ago, opposed the king's reforms of religion, called for protection of the monasteries, and demanded the ouster of Thomas Cromwell. The failure of the Pilgrimage of Grace not only hardened the king's heart against the abbeys but also destroyed the lives of scores of people. My cousin Margaret Bulmer, who rose up against the king with her Northern husband, was burned at the stake at Smithfield, that day that forever changed my life.

The red-bearded merchant-tailor said, "But Sir Walter is known for his devotion to Cromwell."

After draining his goblet of wine, the older man said, "The theory is that is all a pose. Sir Walter made a show of leading a company of soldiers to defend the king's rights in the North, and in so doing arrested a man of God. But instead of turning that man over to the justices, he brought him south and secretly made him chaplain in Farleigh Hungerford Castle."

Master Holbein said, "This all hangs on his harboring a chaplain?"

With the relish of a man delivering a choice tidbit of gossip, the older man said, "Oh, I'm told that there were all matter of things going on up at Farleigh Hungerford Castle. Quite shocking. The chaplain may have been part of a group that conjured magic, and one of the conjurings was to learn how long the king is expected to live. Not only that, Sir Walter even—" He broke off, with an apologetic look in my direction. "There are other crimes, not fit topic for conversation in proper company."

I cared nothing for tales of Sir Walter's sordid private life. What horrified me was that it was publicly known he dabbled in magic. What a dark and pitiless world, controlled by forces far from Christ's goodness. I vowed to turn away from all such practices for the rest of my life. Yet here, in the court of King Henry VIII, the most treacherous place in all of England, I found myself pulled in again. Without my saying a single word, Sir Walter had somehow perceived how close to the flame I once danced. In the chapel of Winchester House, he said, *When I look in those black eyes, I know you are something different. You have seen things, my lady. Things I have seen, too. And will see again.*

Culpepper had told me that everyone watches everyone else, always. I looked up from my plate, heaped with untouched food, and nodded at whatever the heavyset merchant-tailor was saying. I even managed to force a smile.

Master Holbein met my smile with one of his own but his eyes were puzzled. He was probably wondering about my true connection to the now-infamous Sir Walter Hungerford.

I raised my goblet to Holbein in a toast to our friendship and then drank from it. The greatest gift I could bestow on the artist was to tell him absolutely nothing, just as with Geoffrey Scovill. Ignorance would become a shield of protection for them, stronger than any that a knight clutched on the field.

Shortly before the king and queen took their leave of Durham Place, the Earl of Surrey and Thomas Culpepper strode down the middle of the vast hall. Surely they, too, knew what happened to Hungerford, but they showed no sign of fear. They were a popular pair. Dozens of men—and not a few women—called out greetings and they turned this way and that, full of light cordiality. They seemed content to move slowly but steadily through the maze of tables. All would see them as joking and gay.

As they progressed to a table of courtiers near to me, one young man shouted, "Look at that bruise, Surrey. You let them get the better of you today?"

The earl clutched his forehead in mock pain and then cried, "It won't happen again, my lords!"

The surrounding tables burst into laughter. Culpepper joined in, but at the same instant his roving gaze found me, among the merchant-tailors. For a few seconds we stared at each other; then he turned away, laughing harder than ever.

Said my red-bearded neighbor, "Those two swagger as if they hadn't a care in the world."

"They do indeed," I said, in as normal a voice as I could manage. At the same time, I gripped the edge of the table to stop my hands from trembling. No blow during the tournament caused that bruise—I'd seen it on Surrey's forehead when he rode in the procession of challengers. Which meant that something violent took place during their secret gathering.

Each day of the tournament passed like this: I wore a mask of good cheer and, each time I glimpsed Culpepper and Surrey, they did as well. But every single minute I felt encased in dread as thick as the armor worn on the field of the tournament.

In seeking out a foretelling of the king's death, Sir Walter committed high treason. King Henry had a violent fear of prophecy. He was only the second of the Tudor line and possessed as heir one three-year-old son—and two daughters, Mary and Elizabeth, whom he'd deemed bastards. I'd heard whispers for years that the Tudors were not as secure on the throne as Henry VIII wished the foreign rulers to believe.

But what if the men questioning Hungerford learned that was not all? It was one thing to summon the means to look into the future. To strike at the king's chief minister *now*? I shuddered when I thought of how the king treated Henry Courtenay and Lord Montagu—both of them his close relations—when they had done nothing wrong. Look at what the covenant trio had aimed for. How swiftly the three men's hatred of Cromwell would become a plot to take down the king himself. After all, the Earl of Surrey possessed a splash of royal blood. Their covenant would be condemned as a group of rebels intent on replacing the king.

As I watched the armored men joust and fight in the cloudless heat, as I dined at the interminable banquets, one question pounded in my brain: *What was Sir Walter Hungerford telling his inquisitors?* I had been inside the room used for torture in the Tower of London, and I knew how impossible it would be to hold out forever.

I did learn two things that brought new complexities to the matter of Sir Walter Hungerford and May Day. The first was relayed to me by Master Holbein, who shared gossip on another reason for Sir Walter's fall.

"The Hungerfords are rich, and the rumor is that the royal treasury is dwindling again," the artist told me in a quiet moment. "It is unwise for a wealthy man to display anything other than abject loyalty to the king."

"He did not seem that wealthy," I said, adding quickly, "not that I knew him well."

"The man I saw on May Day had lost control of himself, yet the family is brave and prestigious," mused Holbein. "I have learned that a Hungerford was the first speaker of Parliament, another fought beside Henry V, yet another killed an officer of Richard III's in hand-to-hand combat at Bosworth. The present Sir Walter has amassed one of the finest private libraries in the kingdom, up at the family seat, a truly enormous castle. There is a London property on the Strand, too."

After a moment of silence, pulling on his beard, Holbein said, "Perhaps there is no other explanation than that he's gone mad."

Or something drove him mad.

My instinct told me that whatever happened in the hours between midnight and dawn on the first of May was so foul and abhorrent that it had addled Hungerford's mind, injured Surrey, and turned Culpepper cruel. I couldn't imagine what. I'd been frightened each time I heard prophecy, but no one hurt me. Whatever dark place the covenant took them to was far different than what I had witnessed.

The only person I could think of turning to for more knowledge of the practices of May Day was Father Francis. If he warned me, he must know something.

After making my confession to him, I lingered in the chapel the third day of the tournament. "I thank you for telling me to be careful on May Day, Father."

He shook his head. "I cannot understand why good Christians tolerate pagan practices," he whined. "The maypole is terribly indecent."

He feared a maypole? Sagging with disappointment, I murmured, "I understand your disapproval, Father."

"I am happy to hear it, Mistress Stafford. I only wish I could persuade His Majesty to cease all his acknowledgments of May Day, particularly the custom of lighting the Beltane fires."

"Which fires are that?"

"In the centuries before Christ in His Mercy blessed England with wisdom, there were all manner of terrible practices committed on our island. One is lighting a bonfire the night before May first to worship the goddess of the earth and pay homage to her power—can you imagine anything more blasphemous? Yet the kings of England always light a small fire to mark this 'holiday.' His Majesty doesn't seem to appreciate the real *danger . . .*"

The instant he said that word, his mouth shut, the same as the first time he spoke to me of May Day. But this time I was determined to pull more knowledge from the priest.

"Father Francis, I agree with you wholeheartedly, but if I am to help you in your mission, I must know more," I said.

The king's chaplain remained silent.

Out of the corner of my eye I spotted a lady of the court hovering, no doubt waiting to enter the confessional with Father Francis.

"Please, Father, I am the king's cousin once removed, as you well know—I wish to protect him from all danger," I pleaded.

Father Francis signaled for me to follow him to the shadow of a square pillar in the chapel.

"It touches on an incident from my personal history, and I must have your word you will not repeat it," he insisted.

After I promised my silence, the priest took a deep breath and began his story: "I was a boy who loved nothing more than study, but my two brothers taunted me for it, endlessly. They forced me to go with them that night, the thirtieth of April, deep into the woods. They'd heard from people in the village—the worst sort of people— that strange fires could be seen in a certain place. We walked for hours, and it was cold. Nothing like the way it is this year. But my brothers would not let me return home."

Father Francis must have been forty years of age, but the mistreatment by his brothers marked him still. His eyebrows gathered; his face grew more pinched.

"We reached the forbidden place—and there they were. Five people, two men, and three women, lighting fires, chanting, doing a dance that was . . ." He flushed scarlet red . . . "highly indecent. They threw something in the fire and made it leap high—as high as the flames of Hades, mistress. I swear it."

I crossed myself, quaking at his evocation of Hades. "Were you hurt?" I whispered.

"No, no, no. I ran from that place, ran as fast as I could, away from the evil rites, from my brothers. I became lost, of course, and did not find my way out of the forest until dawn. My father beat my brothers senseless, and the two of them never forgave me."

Such memories brought him no pleasure, and Father Francis cleared his throat, regarding me with some measure of resentment. He then looked beyond me at the impatient lady who waited.

I was drawing closer to something, but I still didn't have the truth.

"Father, the people in the forest, what were they doing?" I asked. "Were they performing a spell of some sort, a hex?"

"Who told you that?" he demanded.

"No one. I guessed, Father. I'd heard that in, in Germany the night is called *Hexennacht*."

He waved his hand at me. "I know nothing of what they do in Germany, but yes, it was a spell for certain. The night before May Day is, according to these disgusting beliefs, the night when a spell, be it a love charm or a hex to harm, is at its most potent during any day of the year. You and I may agree that it's pagan nonsense, but many a young scholar fancying himself a humanist studies books and dredges up these secrets—secrets that should be left undisturbed. This study of nature is an offense to God. Now I must go, Mistress Stafford, and let us never speak of this again."

21

"Finally this tournament ends, and we can return to our normal lives," announced Master Holbein as we found a place near the tiltyard. He'd told me his apprentice had returned and he was eager to take on his next portrait commission. I would present my tapestry inventory to the king tomorrow.

But Sir Walter Hungerford's life would not resume. He was now imprisoned in the Tower, I'd overheard. I continued to act as if none of it had anything to do with me, and so did the Earl of Surrey and Thomas Culpepper.

The only time one of us slipped was on the tournament field, after one of the challengers, Cromwell's nephew Gregory, bested Culpepper in a hand-to-hand staged combat. He threw Culpepper to the ground with a resounding crash. When he managed to struggle to his feet, Culpepper showed a face distorted with humiliation. He even cursed. A murmur of surprise ran through the watching crowd. It was uncharacteristic behavior for Culpepper, a favorite for his handsomeness and chivalry.

Finally, the tournament concluded. All of the competitors had ridden their horses onto the tiltyard and amassed before the king and queen. For this closing ceremony, they had cleaned and polished their armor. To see more than fifty men side by side, mounted, waiting, was like beholding a giant chess set, poised for play.

King Henry and Queen Anne, wearing jeweled crowns, sat on their thrones in the gallery. Cromwell stood behind and slightly to the side of the king's throne. He had stayed close to King Henry during the length of the tournament. If the three men conjured a spell against Cromwell, it was a remarkably ineffective one.

The six "challengers" were very much out front: Thomas Seymour, John Dudley, Anthony Kingston, Gregory Cromwell, and the two others. In one of the most celebratory moments of the joust, Kingston and Cromwell were knighted on the field the day before. Thomas Cromwell showed a rare public smile when his athletic nephew rose as a knight. The crowd murmured afterward that it was another sign of how much King Henry valued his chief minister.

The chamberlain called out, "His Majesty King Henry the Eighth is well pleased. The king gives to each of the six challengers of England and their heirs forever a reward for their valiant activity of one hundred marks a year and a house to dwell in."

The crowd gave a collective gasp. Then a deafening roar—cheers mixed with applause and stamping feet at the king's generosity—shook the tournament grounds. It had to be loud enough for all of London to hear, and wonder over.

I did not cheer. I thought of the hundreds of nuns and thousands of monks and friars, cast out of their homes with small pensions. The sisters in Dartford who huddled together in a farmhouse outside of town could barely survive on their pooled pensions.

It was all so incredibly unfair.

The next day, the day I was to present my inventory to the king, was hotter than the five days of the tournament. The night before had been stifling—the air in my room was as thick as if a thunderstorm were imminent. But lightning never split the sky. I slept no more than an hour before morning came. I knew that food and drink would strengthen me, but I had no appetite at all.

I climbed the steps to the section of the palace housing the king's privy chamber. Richard carried the inventory book, his face expectant. I wished I could share a quarter of his enthusiasm.

To reach our sovereign, we must first pass through the presence chamber. I was inside this room a week ago, when I examined its tapestries. The weaves hanging off the walls were fine indeed, but the room's most notable feature was a majestic throne under a canopy of estate. When the king received ambassadors or presided over certain court functions, he sat on the throne. But the room was empty today except for a line of Yeomen of the Guard on either side of the stone-faced King's Chamber Usher.

A short passage connected this room to the privy chamber, accessible to only a handful of the chosen. The rest of the people attending court could not get by the usher without an express invitation, the sort I now clutched in my hand. I'd never stepped inside the chamber in my life, not even for my book. Its tapestries were recorded by my predecessor.

After reading the invitation, the usher sent a guard down that passage. My face felt flushed and hot; beneath my velvet dress, the drops of sweat sliding down my back threatened to turn into a stream.

Sir Anthony Denny appeared, with the guard who went to fetch him.

"Mistress Stafford, you are expected," Denny said and beckoned for me alone to follow.

"Give me the book, Richard," I said. To my horror, my voice cracked as I said *Richard*.

Bearing the bound book before me like a sacrifice, I trailed Denny. The passage opened into a long room that glowed with an unearthly light. The walls and ceiling were painted gold. I took a few halting steps into the privy chamber but froze at the sight of the painted mural that covered the wall to my right. It was a life-size depiction of the royal family. Next to his submissive third wife, Jane Seymour, the muscular king stood tall, hand on his hip and feet wide apart, staring out from the wall, cold and conscienceless.

"Master Hans Holbein's creation takes a bit of getting used to," said someone.

I swallowed and turned to face a man wearing the same red livery as Denny but who smiled most kindly and said, "I'm Sir Thomas

Heanage, chief gentleman of the privy chamber and groom of the stool."

I looked past Heanage to the group of men clustered at two tables at the other end of the room. Three young men wrote in open books with furious speed; I imagined they were royal secretaries. At a separate, gilded table sat the king of England. He was dressed in the same jewelry and finery he always wore, but exhibited little of the bravado of the figure on the wall. The light pouring in through the windows exposed a bloated, tired face. Thomas Cromwell stood by the side of the king, as always. A stack of letters curled atop the table. Cromwell was pointing at a sentence in one and murmuring something, while the king nodded.

Heanage glided over to the table, bowed and spoke; the king and his chief minister looked up.

"Welcome, Cousin Joanna," said the king. "The business of the kingdom demands our attention, but we gladly take reprieve to examine your work. We are told you have been most diligent."

I curtsied low and approached the king and Cromwell.

Once I'd reached them, I paused and shifted from one foot to the other, the book heavy in my arms. I wasn't sure whom precisely to give it to. A gentle tap on my elbow, and Heanage took charge. He placed the book, spread open, at the corner of the king's table.

Cromwell said, "Shall I review it and summarize the most salient points, Your Majesty?"

"No, no," said the king, irritated. "Let us look at it now. Nothing is more important than our tapestries."

I don't know how long King Henry studied my book. The room fell into complete silence as his slightly bloodshot eyes traveled up and down the columns. When he'd reached the bottom, he slowly turned the page. I noticed for the first time how swollen red and cracked white his fingers were, beneath his gold rings set with diamonds and emeralds. The sight made me feel rather sick, like opening the door to an exquisite painted cabinet and discovering a shelf of rotted cheeses.

I suddenly looked up. Cromwell scrutinized me with the same icy mix of curiosity and contempt I always seemed to inspire. His skin was grayish white, as if he had never stood in the gallery with the king and nobles or walked the grounds of Westminster, watching a tournament for five days. Cromwell was a creature most suited to rooms like this: deep inside the palace, the coiled center of power. I knew that turmoil existed behind his imperturbable mask, though. I could never forget that I witnessed him disintegrate in the room at Westminster Hall, and I knew he would never forget it either.

"Cousin Joanna, what does this mean?" said the king.

His puffy finger pressed down on a phrase I'd written. As I came around the table, I saw it was the description of the *Fall of Troy* tapestry in the Great Hall.

I read aloud, hesitantly, "'Lower edges are soiled, perhaps from smoke damage. Smells of food.'"

"You personally saw this?" the king asked quietly.

"Yes, while I was performing the inventory I took note of it, Your Majesty." There was a space allotted for the condition of each one. I took a breath, and continued: "But in the case of the *Fall of Troy*, I was already aware."

"How is that possible?" said the king.

"The first day I came to Whitehall, I passed through the Great Hall and I stopped to look at the tapestry and examined it pretty closely, though for less than a moment. I noticed its state then."

Henry VIII took not one breath, or even two, but three deep inhalations, and as he did, his skin mottled red in an appalling transformation. "Soiled?" he roared, spittle flying through the air. "Our tapestries are *soiled*? And so degraded that a cursory glance made by a person walking through a room could detect it?"

"I'm sorry, Your Majesty," I stammered.

He gave no sign of even hearing my apology, which I had offered to quiet his terrible outburst, not because I had committed an offense. No one else reacted. Cromwell said nothing; Heanage looked as calm and benevolent as ever.

"This is the last blunder I will tolerate by Moinck, Cromwell," he shouted. "He's a careless old fool—he should on no account travel to Brussels to bid on *The Triumph of the Gods*. Joanna should go in his place, she has five times his powers of perception. Moinck cannot be trusted."

Travel to Brussels in his place?

The king continued to rant. "Sir Andrew Windsor has protected this fool from Flanders, I wager. He should be tossed out along with Moinck."

Cromwell cleared his throat. "Sir Andrew has served since before your first parliament. He was appointed by Your Majesty's father as a man showing great promise."

"Windsor may retain his position—for now," the king said, sullen. "But Moinck must go."

Cromwell said, "Of course, Your Majesty. We should inform Master Moinck forthwith. I believe he has been grooming his eldest son to succeed him for at least ten years. He needs to know this is no longer a possibility."

"But I cannot deprive a man of his livelihood," I protested.

The king frowned as he picked up a letter. "This not *your* doing. You serve our will, Cousin Joanna, do you not? You agreed to do that at Winchester House?" Cromwell's eyes narrowed at the name of his enemy's house.

"Yes, Sire," I said, "however—"

His face beginning to turn red again, the king said, "There are no *howevers* at our court."

I wanted more than anything in the world to tell King Henry VIII that I would not take this position, that his tapestries were not my concern, that my return to Dartford must take place today, this hour. But I couldn't do it. His rage—the rage I'd been warned of by so many for so long—was just too intimidating.

I made an uneven curtsy. "Yes, Your Majesty."

Pointing at me with a quill on the table, Henry VIII said, "You will go to the Great Wardrobe in London tomorrow morning and make arrangements to inspect all tapestries stored there as well. Following that, we will decide on the details of the position, your annual allotment and size of your household, and the most effective strategy for acquiring *The Triumph of the Gods*. Our sources in Brussels hear that it could be the most magnificent series of arras ever woven. I will *not* lose it to the Emperor Charles or to King Francis."

Without waiting for my response, he took up the letter again, and Sir Thomas Heneage was once more at my side, guiding me away from the king's table.

"Mistress Stafford, it was a great pleasure to make your acquaintance," he said, and then handed me over to Sir Anthony. Apparently Heneage himself did not ferry people to and fro—that was for Denny. As to Thomas Culpepper's role in this group, I couldn't even guess. He had never appeared, doubtless because he had heard of my appointment with the king and was still determined to shun me.

But I could not dwell on Culpepper now, for my own situation was too disastrous. Each time I came into the presence of King Henry VIII, he demanded more of me. My resistance to filling the tapestry position did not come from lack of confidence. I loved everything about the weaves, and if I were honest with myself, had found the inventory a project holding great fascination. I was face-to-face with the finest collection of arras in Christendom. Yet this livelihood meant I would always revolve around the man who had demolished the monasteries, signed the orders of execution for my uncle, cousin, and friends, and had corrupted Catherine.

How could I serve the king and God at the same time?

As much as I pleaded for direction from God— I must have prayed the Rosary five times—I had found no clear answers when the moment arrived to ride to the Great Wardrobe. There was nothing to do but obey. But I vowed that as soon as I learned the details of my position, I'd send my most forceful letter yet to my cousin Lord Henry Stafford, requesting the return of Arthur. I would extract one benefit from this sorry situation.

I'd charged Richard with securing horses from the Whitehall stables and escorting me to this London destination. He responded joyfully—it was clear that this was one young man weary of the palace. After I took the reins of my mare and we set off, I have to admit that I, too, felt a bit . . . lighter. I dreaded facing the Moincks, father and son, at the Great Wardrobe, and I'd slept little yet again. Sound sleep had eluded me for weeks. But still, I welcomed any sort of stab at freedom. To live at Whitehall was an oppressive, taut business. The court would soon move to Greenwich. I looked forward to leaving Whitehall behind, although there was no sound reason for thinking my troubles might lift. How much difference could the place make if the people remained the same?

"Mistress Stafford, there's Scotland House," Richard called to me, pointing at a grand manor house on the Thames. "The king's sister Queen Margaret lived there for a time."

Richard identified Charing Cross and other points of interest as we went, proud of his knowledge. He was a true Londoner. We passed Durham House and other grand properties on the Strand that sloped down to the river, and then the road turned away from the Thames. Churches, inns, shops, and brick-and-timber houses jammed the sides of the streets. I could no longer enjoy Richard's pointing out sites, because the din was too loud to hear him. I had to nudge my horse to follow his closely on the street crowded with others on horseback, people on foot, and even some wide wagons. I kept my eyes fixed on Richard's tawny-colored doublet—he had never abandoned the livery of the Howards—so that we would not be separated.

"Thomas Becket! Thomas Becket! Thomas Becket!" Not one man shouted the name of England's saint but many. I pulled on the reins, rather frightened. Why would anyone call out for the long-ago martyred archbishop of Canterbury? I pulled up next to Richard. It was not easy to do, for the street was thicker than ever with people. Through them I saw a curtained platform jutting out into the crowd.

Shading his eyes from the sun, Richard said, "Ah, it's a company of players, mistress. But they've picked the worst place possible to set up their stage. That's the street leading to Baynard's Castle, and the Great Wardrobe is beside it. Now blocked."

I looked to the right—in that direction the street curved without end for quite a way. But to the left, there was a narrow opening to a lane that presumably ran parallel to the street blocked to us. "Why don't we try it?" I asked, pointing.

Richard peered farther down in that direction. "I know of another route," he said. But just as he kicked his horse, a crowd of mummers, wearing all manner of costumes, appeared at the top of the street, presumably on their way down to meet with the players now scrambling onstage. Richard shrugged. "So much for that. Yes, we'll have to try this lane and see where it empties out. The market's not far from here, and we don't want to get caught up in *that*."

"But we are now close to the Great Wardrobe?" I asked.

"Oh yes, mistress, and we shall get there," said Richard.

A man onstage bellowed, "I am the king and that troublesome priest has offended me."

I could not help but turn in the saddle to watch this unfold. I found it strange that the death of Thomas Becket would become fodder for players and mummers on the streets of London. Was this not a sensitive subject? The pope had excommunicated Henry VIII in part because of his defilement of the shrine of Saint Thomas. When I was a child I'd seen many performances in my uncle's castles. But nothing that touched on a controversy of a king.

The "king" onstage had to be Henry II, that other monarch who had clashed with the church. He bore no resemblance to the real Plantagenet. I had a memory of being taught as a child that Henry II was tall. This player was short and sallow, wearing a fur around his shoulders despite the heat and a huge ostrich feather in his hat. He was ranting to the crowd about the disobedience of Becket.

Four "knights" stepped forward in unison. The first dropped to one knee. "Can we serve you, Sire? It is our duty to serve you."

The "king" waved them off. "There is nothing you can do to help me, for Thomas Becket is the Archbishop of Canterbury." He then turned from the knights and stepped forward, so that he stood on the edge of the stage, and shouted at the top of his lungs, "Will no one rid me of this troublesome priest?" This was the famous question

posed by Henry II, in which he set loose the murderers of the Archbishop of Canterbury without specifically ordering their deaths.

I had heard more than enough, and I turned away from the stage
to speak to Richard. But he was not by my side. It took me a moment to find him in this ever-thickening crowd, now jammed with
the mummers, too. I spotted his Howard doublet, he was just about
to guide his horse through the mob and onto the lane.

By the time I'd steered my horse to the same lane, Richard had
ridden a portion of the way up. It was a long, narrow lane, not nearly
as busy as the streets we'd just come from. Eager to serve me, he
must be taking advantage of the open way forward, to see if this was
the way to the Great Wardrobe.

"Richard!" I shouted. "Tarry for a moment until I catch up."

He stopped and raised his hand to wave in acknowledgment
without turning around. I shook the reins to hurry my mount along.
With each clap of the horse's hoofs on the cobblestones, the smell
of a market grew stronger. Richard was right, we were nearing a
place where meat was sold. I shook my head, for I'd always hated the
stench of freshly slaughtered animals. This was a dirty, ugly lane, too.
I was sorry I had pressed Richard to try it.

For a second, I thought I heard my name called from behind.
But that was absurd. No one knew me back on the street.

"Joanna!"

I swiveled to look back, for this shout could only be for me. To
my astonishment, Geoffrey Scovill ran toward me, waving his arms
as if in warning.

"Come back—come back *now*," Geoffrey shouted. "Turn your
horse around. That's not your servant!"

What was Geoffrey talking about? I glanced back up the lane.
Richard had stopped but, strangely, he did not turn to face me or
speak. How unlike my eager servant.

Could it have happened again?

It hit me with force strong enough to leave me breathless. He
wore the exact same doublet as Richard, the Howard gold, but the

man now several yards away was *not* my manservant. He sat taller on the horse. After we stopped to watch the players, he'd been replaced.

I yanked on the reins with all my strength, to turn the horse around. But not all horses were easy to turn around in a narrow space, and she was one of them. She stiffened and then balked. I kicked her sides, frantically. "Turn, turn, turn," I begged.

A figure streaked by—it was not the man impersonating Richard but someone who had sprung from a doorway, a small figure, more like a boy than full-grown man. I felt the force of his hand slamming into the haunches of my horse and then he kept running, up the lane.

My mare screamed a fearsome whinny and then wheeled around, but too fast for me to control. I grabbed the saddle to keep from falling. Geoffrey had reached my part of the lane on foot, but he was forced back, flattened against the wall, as my horse began bucking. I surged up and down. I'd never been atop a horse bucking this violently.

"Geoffrey—help!" I shouted.

My horse twisted and bucked again. I was trying to keep hold of the saddle but I couldn't hang on. I was flying—flying off the horse. But I was flying slowly. I saw everything in those last few seconds. Geoffrey reached up as if to catch me, and there was bright red blood on his hands.

He was not quite close enough to catch me. The brick wall came to meet me and the last thought I had before slamming into it was how filthy this lane really was.

22

The man who bent over me, frowning, wore a black cap that fit his head as tightly as a second scalp. I wanted very much to speak to him, but a heavy object pressed on my own head, crushing it. I couldn't make my eyes focus, and a deep ache pulsed through one of my arms.

"Her eyes are open," said the man to someone else, though I couldn't see whom.

"I can't be late," I said. Or I thought I said it. I didn't hear my own words.

The black-capped man by my side said, "Late to what?"

Relieved I'd been understood, I said, "The Great Wardrobe. I must ride there today." I swallowed and then said, my voice croaking, "His Majesty willed it."

He stood up and walked over to the second man, who I now could get a glimpse of. He seemed older. He wore a cap, too, but also long sweeping robes. There was insignia woven into the robes but I couldn't tell whose, because my eyes weren't working properly. I blinked and blinked but everything in the room was fuzzy. I did grasp that I was in bed in my room in Whitehall wearing only a shift and suddenly I felt humiliated by the presence of two strange men. What were they doing here while I lay abed?

The older man approached.

"Mistress Stafford, I am Doctor William Butts, physician to the king," he said in a soft but deliberate voice. "The man you just spoke to is Samuel Clocksworth, the principal barber-surgeon of the court.

You set out to the Great Wardrobe this morning. It is now the afternoon." He paused and then continued, "There was an incident in London. Do you understand what I am saying?"

"No, I am sorry. That's not correct." I tried to take control of this state of affairs. "Please fetch my man Richard, he must be just out in the passageway. We must prepare to ride."

The two of them exchanged a significant look and withdrew a little, as if to enter a private discussion. They made no effort to fetch Richard.

Everything about this was wrong, and I had had quite enough of the confusion. I pushed myself up—and plunged into a pit of fiery, stabbing pain. Crying out, my head and my left arm and shoulder in agony, I fell back, fighting waves of dizziness and nausea. There was nothing pressing on my head, I knew now: just bandages.

Master Clocksworth rushed to my side. "You must not move," he said sternly. "Do not do that again."

"My arm," I said, half groaning and half weeping. "What happened to me? How will I weave tapestries?"

As he struggled to calm me, the door burst open and Catherine Howard appeared, shouting, "She is awake, she is awake. Why did no one tell me?"

The barber-surgeon put out his hand as if to push her back, but Catherine ducked past him and threw herself onto the floor, so that her face was inches from mine. Through my pain, I was glad to see her, though she looked quite unlike herself, with a red nose and tear-ravaged cheeks.

"What's wrong?" I managed to force out through the nausea.

At that, Catherine broke down, weeping and laughing at the same time. "What's wrong? My dearest friend in the world nearly died—that is all. They told me that you were lucky to be alive, that you might never awake from such a blow to the head. It's been an hour since you came back to court. Yet here you are, speaking to me. I shall give prayers of gratitude to the Virgin morning and night."

From a distance, I heard Doctor Butts trying to silence Catherine, to halt her near-babble. But it didn't matter, because in that instant it all rushed past me, like the pages of a book ruffled quickly. The ride with Richard to London, the players on the street, the near-abduction in the lane, and, last, my being thrown off the horse. I must have lost consciousness when I hit the wall. But what actually happened in that lane?

"Geoffrey," I said, "I need Geoffrey."

"We must help her to be calm," said Doctor Butts. "She seems to be remembering now, but if she is lost to wild passions and to sorrows, it could be very damaging."

"Geoffrey was hurt," I said, "There was blood."

"Hush," said Catherine, stroking my arm. "Hush."

Master Hans Holbein was the next one to push his way into the room. After a few words to the king's doctor, he took a stool to sit beside me. He tried to put Catherine onto a stool as well but she insisted on kneeling on the floor.

"Be assured that Constable Geoffrey Scovill was not hurt," Holbein said.

"But then where is he?"

"Constable Scovill brought you here, Mistress Joanna. It seems he witnessed your injury?"

I said nothing and Holbein continued. "He dressed your head wound and he persuaded some men to put you in their wagon and bring you back to Whitehall. Catherine was in my studio—we heard the shouting when the guards would not let him past the gatehouse with you."

Catherine said, "I was curious and I looked out the window. I heard someone shouting your name—'Joanna Stafford, this is Joanna Stafford'—and I realized it was you lying there senseless in the back of a wagon . . ." And with that, fresh sobs shook her small frame.

Holbein said, "With some effort I was able to get him admitted to the verge of the court. Catherine raised the alarm in the king's household, and these illustrious men of medicine took charge of you."

I tried to take it all in through the dizziness and pain and nausea. Frustration welled up inside me. "But I saw blood on Geoffrey," I repeated.

"It wasn't his blood, Mistress Joanna," Holbein said.

A horrible truth began its descent, like a falcon coming to ground.

"Where is Richard?" I asked.

"That's enough talking for now," said Doctor Butts.

"No," I cried. "No. Richard is terribly hurt, isn't he?"

Catherine said, her voice trembling, "You are a woman of God, you must cleave to your faith and be strong, Joanna."

"He's dead?" I choked. "Richard's dead?"

Catherine bowed her head.

The horror of this, that Richard, only twenty years old and my servant for a fortnight, had been murdered, overwhelmed me. The faces of all of the people who crowded around began to run together. A faint roar vibrated in my ears. I was losing consciousness—but I did not want that. I sucked in deep breaths.

"Tell me," I croaked.

"He was killed by the same terrible men who tried to rob you," said Holbein. "Constable Scovill was in London and saw the two of you on your horses near the actors' stage. Then Richard dismounted in a way that I gather was suspicious. The constable came forward, found Richard gravely injured, and then rushed to help you."

This did not sound the way I remembered it, but there were blank patches in my memory. And now, even though I lay flat on a bed, the room rocked as if I were aboard a ship. I sucked in more deep breaths. Once I was confident that I would not slip into sense-lessness again, I said, "No one robbed me."

"But that is what they were trying to do," said Catherine.

"No," I said. "That wasn't it."

Master Holbein said, "The high sheriff of London has been notified as well as the lord mayor. We understand that every undercon-stable of the city is searching for the men who tried to rob you."

"No, I—I need to speak to Geoffrey. I need to speak to Geoffrey now."

A man's voice said, "Who is Geoffrey?"

Thomas Culpepper stood in the doorway.

He moved toward me, past the physician and the barber surgeon. His face was as tired and strained as when he spoke to me last in the tournament tent, but his brown eyes asked a fierce question.

Catherine touched my arm, protectively. When I winced because that was my injured arm, she didn't notice, because she was glaring at Culpepper.

I said, "He is my friend. From Dartford. But he is in London now." My head swam. "As it was before, Geoffrey is in London. He first saved me in London. At the burning. I met him at Smithfield. He wouldn't let me run to the flames." I closed my eyes; why was I telling them this? I took a breath and forced myself to focus. "I don't know why he isn't here."

Holbein said, "As soon as you were in the hands of the physicians, Constable Scovill said he must go back to where you were injured, to secure some answers."

"This Geoffrey is a constable?" Culpepper asked.

"Yes," I said.

Culpepper began to back out of the room. "I shall find him for you, Mistress Stafford, and tell him you are awake and have asked for him."

Catherine said, "Surely a messenger could be sent? Why must *you* go?"

Without acknowledging she had spoken, Culpepper was gone. Catherine's lips tightened and an angry flush stained her cheeks.

"Richard," I moaned. "What of his family? They must be told."

Catherine said, "My uncle the Duke of Norfolk is seeing to it, and to all the arrangements."

"No," I said. "I must do that."

"The duke hired him and paid his wages, Joanna. Richard's stepfather was an East Anglian man—you know how much that means to my uncle. Come, you may not like him, but, Joanna, this is what he does. The duke always takes care of his men."

"As I did not."

At that, Master Holbein and Catherine Howard rushed to assure me that it was not my fault. How could I be responsible for the actions of criminals? Or have been able to predict that thieves would prey on us? I did not say anything while they comforted me. Nor did I make a sound as the barber-surgeon examined me while Doctor Butts observed. He raised and lowered my left arm and then probed every inch of bone with his long fingers. After more consultation with the king's physician, he placed my arm in a tight sling, the bandages soaked in foul-smelling comfrey paste.

As skilled as he was, everything he did caused searing pain, but I welcomed that, for it helped drive away my disorientation. I must gather all of my wits now. What happened today was no robbers' assault but a second attempt at my abduction and, considering what happened to poor Richard, my eventual murder. It was an even more terrifying attack than the first, for someone had gone to the trouble of securing a Howard doublet and then followed me, waiting for an opportunity, such as the play actors setting up a stage on the street, to spring their trap. How did my enemies know I would ride through London? The king just gave the order yesterday. If only this sickening dizziness would cease and I could *think*.

Everyone in the room perceived my distress, though they did not know the entire cause. To soothe me, Catherine read aloud from a book of psalms. She was far from an accomplished reader, but the sound of her determined young voice—and the warmth of her presence—did keep me from breaking into outright panic. Once I appeared calm, Doctor Butts and Master Clocksworth took their leave, but not before the barber-surgeon asked a question.

"What could slow your recovery is that you are alarmingly thin, Mistress Stafford, and I must inquire whether you've been abstaining from food?"

"No," I said.

"She ate next to nothing when she stayed with me and I fear that turned into nothing after we . . . we parted," said Catherine. "And then there is her propensity for fasting. But that will all change, do not fear. She will eat the finest meats roasted in the kitchens of Whitehall. I will take care of her."

Master Holbein, who had been so sad and quiet, said, "And I, too—I will bring her sweet cake, which I know she does enjoy."

The barber-surgeon insisted they wait some time before feeding me meat and cake. After my dizziness and nausea passed entirely, I was to have a bowl of plain gruel and some sweet wine. And with that, the two medical men finally left, to give report to the king.

"His Majesty is most distressed," Catherine informed us. "He's commanded the mayor of London to attend him tomorrow morning to discuss the question of safety in the city. In the last few years, it has become so dangerous that people are robbed and killed when they ride through the city in daylight!"

Even with everything that had happened, it saddened me to hear Catherine speak with such knowledge of the king's temperament, knowledge that came from her being his mistress. But that was nothing compared to the impact of what came next.

"As soon as you have recovered enough to cross the river, we will take you to Howard House," Catherine said.

"No," I said, my voice louder than at any other point.

"But you can't be alone in the palace now, without even a single maid and unable to move, and we have everything there to take care of you, Joanna," she said. "My uncle and grandmother employ a personal physician. Lots and lots of servants. As soon as you are able, you can oversee the tapestries perfectly well from Howard House."

Hans Holbein said, "This makes good sense."

"I am sorry, but I refuse to consider it," I said.

At that tense moment, the door opened and, finally, I looked at the face of Geoffrey Scovill. It was a weary face, reddened by the sun;

his dark blond hair, dampened with sweat, clung to his forehead. His clothes were dirtier than any commonly seen in the rooms of Whitehall—but a glance at his hands revealed that he'd washed Richard's blood away. I shivered.

"How are you, Joanna?" Geoffrey asked, as if no one else were present.

You saved my life again, I wanted to cry. *Everything in this room was pain and fear and confusion until you walked into it.*

"I am well," I whispered.

Catherine exclaimed, "She is *not* well, she is weak and in pain, with an injured head and a broken arm." She stood up from the stool, smoothing her skirts. The diamond pendant at her throat sparkled. "Constable Scovill, we were just discussing where she should be moved to. I see that you are Mistress Stafford's friend, and I would very much appreciate it if you helped me persuade her to join the household of the Duke of Norfolk during her recovery."

I didn't care for the imperious tone that had crept into her voice, as if she were addressing someone of inferior rank. Which he unquestionably was, but still—after everything Geoffrey Scovill had been through, it seemed most unfair.

Geoffrey gave Catherine a long, somber look and then said, "I am afraid that plan won't do. It's imperative that Mistress Stafford return to her home in Dartford as soon as possible."

Both Catherine and Holbein offered with vigor all of the reasons why I should not leave the orbit of the court. The best medical men in the kingdom were here, at the king's command. As soon as I was able to pick up my tapestry work again, I could do so at Howard House. Dartford was simply too far away from London. Were there physicians, barber-surgeons, and apothecaries to attend me? No, it was a small town, inadequate to my needs.

Geoffrey did not give way—he simply kept insisting that I must go. No one even looked at me and realized what was happening, until Geoffrey saw me weeping.

"We should stop this," he said. "Joanna is upset."

Catherine flew to my side once more, dabbing the tears from my cheeks. "It will be all right, hush," she said. But I couldn't stop weeping; the sobs were so strong, I couldn't even speak at first. I had to fight for calm, to say what must be said.

"I want to go home," I choked. My simple house, my old friends, the honest daily customs of the town, I longed for it all.

"Of course you are homesick, Mistress Joanna," said Holbein. "But we must wait—"

"No—I beg you, no," I said, my voice rising. "Take me home, Geoffrey. I want to go. *Please* take me home."

He said quietly, "I will do it."

And so, reluctantly, Catherine Howard gave way to my determination to leave Westminster. As soon as I was strong enough, I'd be conveyed to Dartford for my convalescence. Until that time, Geoffrey said, I must be guarded every moment, by either himself or John Cheke. Master Holbein immediately offered to serve as a third guardian.

Frowning, Catherine said, "I agree that Joanna should not be alone, but you're proposing to guard her as if the criminals of London were plotting another attack. She is safe here. There is no safer place in the kingdom."

As I listened to his cool, careful tone while he worked out the hours of protection, I suspected that, like me, Geoffrey realized this was no robbery attempt. He was a constable and knew better than anyone in the room, perhaps better than anyone in the palace, what a common thief was capable of. That was not who I encountered this morning.

Catherine refused to leave my side until two hours past sundown. She fed me gruel and fussed over my comfort, asking me over and over if I were better. I assured her I was, although the relentless pain in my head and arm meant that true comfort was impossible and sleep should prove elusive.

A moment after Catherine finally kissed my cheek and left, Geoffrey Scovill took the stool beside my bed.

"I know you are weak and in pain, but, Joanna, you must tell me more than what you've disclosed so far," he said. "If I am to save your life, I must know what you know. Hold nothing back. Because even if you tell me absolutely everything, the odds are not necessarily in your favor. If you keep lying to me, the odds drop to your having no chance at survival at all."

I swallowed, and said, "But these underconstables of London—won't they find out who killed Richard and tried to kill me?"

"No, they won't. They are searching for thieves, and you and I both know the men in question were not thieves. I told them of the man wearing a Howard doublet just like Richard's leading you up the lane, but they don't believe me, a country constable. It is too fantastical, they say. But I know what I saw."

"But—but if you guard me, you and the others, will I not at least be safe here?"

He said, "Your friend Thomas Culpepper told me everything."

"Everything?" It was impossible to hide my shock.

"That's correct, Joanna. So you should abandon this pose. I know that someone impersonating a page led you through Whitehall and attacked you in a storeroom. Since the method of the crime is so similar, it is definitely the same men who attacked you today."

"'Men'? You think a group is at work?"

"It's obvious that a group is working to kill you, one whose members possess intelligence, daring, experience—and money. And they are familiar with the streets of London *and* the layout of the palace. I had the devil of a time gaining admittance to Whitehall, while these men move about it with impunity."

I covered my eyes with my right hand, and pleaded, "Stop, you're frightening me."

But Geoffrey lifted my hand and placed it back by my side. "I want to frighten you, Joanna. It is the only way I can think of to break down your stubbornness and to make you grasp what is happening. This is a game of cat-and-mouse such as I've never seen in my life. And, Christ's blood, what a cat you've got after you."

Geoffrey ran his hand through his hair. He was exhausted. But there was more to it—he, too, was afraid.

"You know who it is, don't you?" I said.

"I have a pretty good idea, yes," Geoffrey said. "Joanna, the men who want you dead must be King Henry the Eighth and Thomas Cromwell."

23

The master spy Jacquard Rolin taught me that when you are trapped in a corner with someone who demands to know things, things you do not wish to disclose, one way to buy more time is to make a gift out of a choice selection of your secret. "Think of it as a portion of cake—share the sugar topping so your opponent will be so delighted with his delicious morsel, he may never ask for the whole slice."

Geoffrey Scovill was saying he was certain that the king and his chief minister lured me to Whitehall under the pretense of desiring a tapestry. And then, when the first attempt on my life failed, they'd devised a second. Who else, he said, possessed both the ready resources and the advance knowledge of my traveling to London besides the men at the very top?

I said, "I find I cannot agree with your theory, Geoffrey, but to explain why, I will have to tell you something that I've disclosed to no other person, including Thomas Culpepper. If I tell it to you, it must be under the condition that you tell no one else, not even John Cheke—on your honor."

Geoffrey said, "Of course I give you my word, you need have no fear of that." His eyes shone with eagerness. I felt guilty for my feint.

I said, "Did Master Culpepper tell you that Cromwell ran across me in a room in Westminster Hall and dragged me into the great hall where Parliament waited, to see him made Earl of Essex?"

"Yes," he said. "Is that not true?"

"I was dragged into the great hall, yes, but there was more to the way we met. Master Culpepper left me in a small, empty room while he set out to attend the ceremony in the hall. What happened was that Cromwell himself stepped into the room and, while I watched, unobserved, he gave way to a moment of great distress."

"What sort of distress?"

"He buried his face in his hands and he groaned and said, 'Oh no.' He was quite upset."

Geoffrey was as astounded as I thought he'd be. "Why would the Lord Privy Seal, valued above all other men by the king and on the brink of being raised to an earldom, be upset?"

"I don't know. But what I *do* know is that he was deeply shocked and then angry to see me in the corner of the room."

"Perhaps he was surprised because he was the one who devised the plot against you and did not expect to see you alive and at liberty."

"No," I said. "His anger came from embarrassment." I hesitated, trying to find the words to explain something I'd been brooding over for quite some time. "It's as if Cromwell and I have made an unspoken pact with each other. I shall remain silent about what I saw, and he shall not move against me as long as I do."

Geoffrey said, "Now I have a better understanding of why you insisted to Culpepper that the attack against you not be reported once the two of you discovered that someone stole a page's livery. You were trying to maintain this delicate balance, to not bring more attention to yourself."

I nodded, relieved that Geoffrey took this attitude.

But then he pushed on, saying, "The summons to appear at Westminster was signed by Cromwell but it was the king's command. Perhaps it is all the king's idea, not Cromwell's. Wouldn't this be the perfect way for King Henry to eliminate another Stafford, a family he is known to despise?"

I understood why Geoffrey seized on these theories, but his reasoning was flawed because of his lack of firsthand knowledge of the court of Henry VIII. Something that I now, somewhat unfortunately, possessed. "It's true that my family has fallen from favor, but that is not the king's way," I said. "If he wanted to strike me down, he'd have me arrested on trumped-up charges and sent to the Tower. I've personally witnessed him do that to others."

Glancing back at the door to make sure no one could hear him, Geoffrey said in a low voice, "But this king is known for deviousness."

"Yes, he is, but, well, King Henry is also an impatient man. I've witnessed that, too. If he were unhappy with me, he'd have me punished immediately. To sanction these conspiracies that take weeks, if not months, to bring to fruition? No."

Geoffrey ran his knuckles up and down his cheeks, as if trying to keep himself awake. He was not ready to give up. "King Henry loathes the people of the monasteries, and you were once a Dominican novice. I find it hard to believe that he would put aside his feelings against the abbeys and against the Staffords, to obtain some tapestries. Nothing you weave could be *that* extraordinary."

That statement stung. I remembered now that my tapestry enterprise always seemed to puzzle Geoffrey, and that he had never had the faith in my abilities that Edmund had.

Geoffrey did not notice that I was hurt and continued, "To plan the ambush takes time, and the king is the one who set the date of your ride into London. He and Cromwell were the only ones who knew when you would leave Whitehall."

I said wearily, "No, they weren't. Sir Anthony Denny and Sir Thomas Heneage, gentlemen of the privy chamber, were present when the order was given. Royal secretaries were present." A thought occurred. "How did you know, Geoffrey? These others have accepted that you happened to be in London on the very street where I was nearly abducted. But I know you must have followed me."

"I don't deny it," he said stoutly. "John Cheke heard about the ride to the Great Wardrobe from your artist friend, Master Holbein, at dinner in the great hall yesterday. Cheke was at the same table as Holbein and a Sir Andrew Windsor. He told me when I came to see him later. I could see that you were hiding something at Bishop

Gardiner's palace, and I had a feeling—a strong feeling—that you were in some sort of danger. I thought I would wait for you to leave the palace and follow, while keeping a bit of distance, just to be sure."

At least Geoffrey had the grace not to point out how right he was.

"But if you could learn of my leaving Whitehall the next day, so could others," I pointed out. "It was spoken of at a table in the great hall. News spreads very fast in a palace. Everyone knows everything about each other."

Geoffrey sat back. The candle lit in the corner flickered low behind him and I couldn't read the expression on his face, now in shadow.

"Very well," he said. "Who do you think is behind these attacks? You must have your own ideas."

"I don't know," I said, frustrated. "I truly don't."

For once Geoffrey did not get angry that I failed to give him an answer. He was quiet for another long moment and then said, "Who hates you in the palace, Joanna? Who are your enemies? We shall try to address the problem that way."

Here I was, back in the same corner, with the shrewd and relentless Geoffrey Scovill asking all the questions I dreaded.

I blurted, "Let's just say that I would have rather recovered from my injuries in the open road than at the house of the Duke of Norfolk."

Geoffrey gave a low chuckle and said, "Joanna, I must agree, since the first time I met His Grace the Duke of Norfolk, he was in a cell in the Tower of London, and the second time, he said he would hang me if he ever found us together again."

It was impossible not to laugh, though pain shot through my left arm as I shook with it. "Stop, no, Geoffrey, I can't laugh."

"Sorry." He smiled, and pressed his hand on my right shoulder to still me, as if I were a rocking horse that must stop rocking.

I realized at that moment that I had not been alone with Geoffrey like this for a very long time. He got to his feet. Had his thoughts been running along the same lines?

"You must rest, Joanna. I will be just outside this door until Cheke comes to relieve me."

He said the words quickly and with that, he was gone.

I was grateful to have Geoffrey's protection, but there was no rest. The pain from my injuries was too severe for me to sleep, yet my mind and body were extraordinarily fatigued. I kept sinking into a fragmented dream state, and visions would run past me: a man wearing Howard livery who waved in a jaunty way at the top of a lane, a horse that wouldn't stop bucking, a short man with a peacock feather in his hat who screamed at a huge crowd of Londoners, yet his words seemed just for me: *Will no one rid me of this troublesome priest?*

The pain in my head and arm pulled me out of this vision as with all the others, and hurled me back into my narrow bed in the warm, airless palace. Hours passed this way until dawn broke and Catherine Howard returned. One look at me, and she ordered that the barber-surgeon be called for. Then she busied herself with making sure I ate some freshly baked bread. I had no appetite at all, but did my best to oblige her.

"I never would have expected that a crime on the streets of London would bring us back together as friends, Joanna," she said timidly.

"I was always your friend, and I always shall be," I said. "I only wish I had helped you when you required it most."

"What do you mean?"

My voice shaking, I said, "I should have protected you from the king. I failed to do that and now—"

Catherine's face turned scarlet but she did not weep or bluster. She said, "I know you have suffered at the thought that the king took my virtue."

"And he has not?" I said in disbelief.

She whispered, "I was not a maid when the king took me, Joanna."

I could not speak for the shock of it. A girl of tender years and of good family, how was such a violation possible? I had never known of a daughter of a noble house being despoiled before marriage. But the Howards were careless, immoral people. They had not taken proper care of a motherless girl. And, knowing she was damaged goods, they had not hesitated to push her toward the king for further soiling.

"You do not know the man, and it ended just before you and I were together at Howard House. I can say no more—please, promise me you will tell no one," Catherine pleaded.

I promised her silence, my heart aching with pity. Her childhood had been a grievous one. Now she had fine clothes and jewels; important people like Doctor Butts and the barber-surgeon came when she called and Master Hans Holbein painted her portrait. But that would all change when her stint as royal mistress was over. Without husband or parents, it would be as if she were Mary Magdalene, fending off stones thrown in the street. More than ever, I intended to be of support and help to her when that time came.

The barber-surgeon was not as alarmed as Catherine by my appearance. He focused on the fact that my blurred vision and dizziness had eased. It was now safe to give me potions to help me sleep, he announced. The first herb to ease my pain and bring me true rest was a pot of comfrey tea. I recognized its foul smell from the days when I would brew batches of it for Edmund, to give to his customers in Dartford.

"You should be well within the fortnight, Mistress Stafford, though your arm will need bandaging for a month and be stiff for a time afterward," said the barber-surgeon. "Doctor Butts's fear was of infection and fever from your arm wound, which is almost always fatal. But do not be troubled—I assured him, as I do you, that no one can set a bone better than I in the Palace of Whitehall. The king's physicians never touch a patient, yet they consider themselves wiser than those of us who do."

The physicians and the barber-surgeons always quarrel, and both of them look down on the apothecaries. That is what Edmund always used to say to me. I took a deep, shaky breath. Why was Edmund Sommerville so often in my thoughts as I lay, injured and dazed? When

John Cheke arrived to take his turn at my bedside, I resolved to raise the subject of my former betrothed.

"Do you think that this German physician, Paracelsus, has found a cure for Edmund's affliction—is that why he traveled so far to seek him out?" I asked.

Cheke said, "I've wondered that myself, but none of the inquiries I've made in the last six months indicate that Paracelsus has found a cure. My best guess is that Edmund sought him out for discussion of his opium craving, yes, but also to speak of healing and of philosophy. Edmund was not alone in making such a pilgrimage, you realize. For a generation, others have turned to the wisdom of Germany, and by that I do not mean the teachings of Luther. They seek the secrets of the magical world."

At first I could not believe it, that words so close to Hungerford's came from the lips of Cambridge scholar John Cheke.

"Who dispenses this wisdom?" I asked, as beads of sweat rolled off my forehead.

"Ah, well, there was John Trithemius, Abbot of Spanheim. He wrote a book about magic, about communication with spirits. A scholar and alchemist named Johann Georg Faustus travels the country offering to conjure up demons, if not Lucifer himself."

I crossed myself.

Cheke said, "Then there was another man, a scholar and astrologer, who seems to be the most venerated of them all. He's dead now—been dead for at least five years—but for a time it was the fashion in Europe to try to gain an audience with him or purchase his books. Even Englishmen traveled to see him."

One of the few advantages of being wounded and bandaged, stretched out in bed, is that when something distresses you, no one realizes it.

"Don't you know the man's name?" I asked.

"Let me think. It's a peculiar one that doesn't sound completely German, just as with Paracelsus."

He pondered, squinting, and then brightened. "I have it! His name was Heinrich Cornelius Agrippa."

Not wanting to raise any suspicion whatsoever, even in John Cheke, I counted to five before I asked, "This Agrippa and Paracelsus, are they of like mind and philosophy?"

"Yes, there is a group of them throughout Europe, loosely connected, who seek knowledge from the same sources. Physicians, scholars, astrologers, alchemists, even monks. Some call it the invisible college."

"Why do they hold such influence, these men—and why would anyone, whether it be Edmund or others, travel to see them or read their books? The magical world is so dangerous. Don't they fear the Inquisition?"

Cheke thought for a moment and said, "Do you know that in the last twenty-five years there have been junctures when a great many people believed that the world was coming to an end? They sold all their goods and gathered in wait of the apocalypse. These are harrowing times we live in, Joanna, times of discovery and learning but also the greatest turmoil of faith in a millennium. There are the wars, some religious and some for power alone, such as the sack of Rome that unleashed such atrocities. The most horrific of them all took place in the south of Germany, when the peasants revolted to overturn the order of the world. Thousands upon thousands died. In the face of such a revolt, and the rise of Martin Luther and John Calvin, that part of the world is where people search most desperately for answers. And there will always be those who step forward to supply answers to the desperate. For a price, though. If not coin, then a man's soul . . ."

Cheke shuddered, and then gathered himself. "Ah, but these are becoming matters of academic interest alone, since I do not believe Geoffrey Scovill will be traveling to Germany and Austria to search for Edmund. I find I lack the funds to outlay the expense of such a trip."

I honestly did not know how I felt about the journey foundering. I'd been disturbed by the idea—and Geoffrey's being the one to find Edmund made no sense whatsoever—but the thought of Edmund lost to these strange and blasphemous doctors and occultists, wandering through the forests of Germany, was terrible. Particularly since I knew that this sort of dark magic could be what Sir Walter Hungerford drew on in his May Day gathering with Culpepper and Surrey.

The only thing I could think of to say was "It is costly to travel."

Cheke said, growing agitated, "I had planned to use my salary as Greek chair of Saint John's College to pay for Geoffrey's expenses, but it no longer seems probable that I will be appointed to the position. That's what brought Geoffrey back to London—we met to attempt to come up with a way forward. But how can we make plans when I don't know what sort of wages I will have? The Bishop of Winchester does not say yes or no, but continues to pose questions and to delay a decision. He disputes my writing on the proper pronunciation of Ancient Greek. I am convinced that the words from the texts of the philosophers should not be pronounced in the same fashion as someone living in Greece today, but the bishop disagrees. I am not given leave to return to Cambridge. Gardiner is the most maddening man I have ever encountered."

"He is that," I agreed. "But tell me of your writing."

It could have been the comfrey tea, it could have been the nasty-smelling dilution of mandrake that the barber-surgeon dosed me with—or perhaps fatigue finally overtook me. But while John Cheke sat by my side and spoke of his passion for the Greek world, I slid into a dreamless slumber that went on for many hours. I opened my eyes, and it was night, not day, and Master Hans Holbein sat by my side, not Cheke.

"How fortunate I am," I murmured.

"What did you say, Mistress Joanna? What did you say?"

"My friends," I said. "I am fortunate in my friends."

But before he could respond, my eyes closed once more. This time my rest was unnatural. My eyelids were heavy and my lips dry; I was not asleep all of the time. I could hear snatches of conversation in the room. I wanted to speak to my friends, but it was too hard to open my eyes; I drifted and drifted.

And then I heard Geoffrey say, "How is her condition?"

Holbein said, "She's slept for a long time. The barber-surgeon said it was to be expected. But I fear it is going on too long."

"The hour is late, Master Holbein. Allow me to relieve you."

"No, I think I should stay. I am most concerned about Mistress Joanna."

I wanted to reassure them, but I began to spiral down again, to a deeper state in which I heard nothing around me. But just on the brink of the descent, I heard Geoffrey's low laugh.

"Be careful, Master Holbein. *You* may be at risk of developing a disease for which there is no cure."

"What do you mean?"

"In just under a month, Joanna has made her mark. Yesterday I met a Master Thomas Culpepper, a young courtier who was consumed with fear for Joanna Stafford, a woman of great mystery. I tell you it was as if I looked at myself in a glass. And now you?"

Holbein said, his voice tinged with amusement, "I cannot speak for Master Culpepper, but I have no romantic intentions toward Mistress Joanna, if I take your meaning, Constable. I am just old enough to be her father."

"I am not describing a romance necessarily. You've heard the word *obsession*? It means to be besieged by a feeling."

Still amused, Holbein said, "I know the word. When did it begin, your besieging?"

Geoffrey said, "Almost three years ago to the day. Here in London. Or just outside London—Smithfield."

"Joanna said something, when she was at her most distressed yesterday, when she kept calling for you over and over, about a burning at Smithfield. Is that what you are speaking of?"

"Joanna said that?" The weary, cynical edge had fallen away from Geoffrey's voice. He sounded quite startled.

"Yes, she did."

There was silence for a long time. I felt more alert now and I wanted to open my eyes, to put an end to this humiliating conversation, but if I did, they could realize I'd overheard them already.

Holbein said, his voice very gentle, "Constable Scovill, you honestly can't see that you are in love with her?"

"No, I'm not," Geoffrey said roughly. "Once I was—Christ, how I suffered. And others suffered, too, Master Holbein, because of it. Now, yes, I care what happens to her. I always will. I will protect Joanna with my life, if it comes to it. But love? I will never, ever endure that sort of suffering again."

24

Five days after being injured in London, I left the Palace of Whitehall, stretched out in a curtained litter attached to a pair of horses on one end and a wagon on the other. I'd never been in such a conveyance before. Litters were intended for ladies of royalty or the highest nobility, or for those too ill to sit up while traveling. I fit into the latter group more than the former. Under normal circumstances, I'd certainly not be traveling so soon after being knocked unconscious and breaking my arm. But my circumstances were anything but normal.

I saw nothing outside my narrow, rectangular litter during the entire journey. I could hear the voices of those on the road all around me, but making out words was difficult. A sentence or just a phrase from a stranger would shoot past and I'd feel the mood behind what was said—joyful, irritated, furious, and pragmatic—before each speaker was reabsorbed into the din.

Two days earlier, Geoffrey Scovill found an opportunity to speak with me again alone, and what he said frightened me more than anything that had come before.

When I first looked at Geoffrey, fear was not uppermost in my thoughts. The conversation that I'd heard between him and Master Holbein left me shaken, humiliated, and sad, too. I knew I'd hurt Geoffrey in the past and more than anything, I didn't want that to continue.

I said too stiffly, "I've reconsidered my course of action, and perhaps I should stay in Whitehall and you should return to Dartford. I do not wish to be a burden."

As if I had not even spoken, Geoffrey said, "Joanna, I need you to tell me everything you remember about the day you rode into London."

Not this again.

I murmured, "It is a day I'm desperate to forget."

"I would not ask if it weren't terribly important."

A closer look at Geoffrey revealed a new grimness. I knew that he had spent hours each day in London, searching for clues to the identities of who'd killed Richard and attempted to ambush me. Whether the underconstables of London still combed the area I didn't know. Clearly the criminals had not been apprehended by anyone.

I forced myself to re-create for him the details of that morning's ride: how the manor houses on the Strand turned into shops and taverns and tiny churches and narrow homes as we veered away from the Thames and into the heart of the city. And then came the chaos caused when the players put on their show. My heart thudding in my chest, I told Geoffrey about listening to the beginning of the performance and how the man with a feather in his cap cried out in imitation of Henry II, then I looked for Richard but did not see him in the mob, until I spotted a man wearing a Howard tawny-colored doublet entering that fateful lane.

"You know the rest," I said.

"Did you ever notice someone following you, anyone watching you?" he asked, very intent. "I am not talking about riding into the lane, or even the period immediately preceding when you observed the men on the stage. Before that, in the course of the day, did you notice anything or anyone that suggested you were followed?"

I stared at Geoffrey, and then said, "No, not that day."

"But you have noticed it at other times?" he said quickly, seizing on the manner in which I answered him. "You *must* tell me. Please, Joanna, this is critical."

Although I'd attributed my feelings to nothing but fancies—or to the lingering wariness that came from being trained as a spy by Jacquard Rolin—I told Geoffrey about the times that I'd sensed someone watched me: when I rode into London in April and, weeks later, when I approached the tournament grounds. He listened to every word very carefully, so much so that it made me uncomfortable.

"What are you making of this?" I asked. "Why do you ask?"

Instead of answering, Geoffrey said, "Is there anything *else* that struck you as odd or frightening since you came to Whitehall? You are observant, Joanna, more so than I've given you credit for, perhaps. Search your mind, through every day of every week, Joanna."

"There was an episode on the stairs in the palace gatehouse," I said slowly. "But I am quite sure it is not connected to what happened to me in London."

"Dismiss nothing," he said. "Tell me."

Feeling even more uncomfortable, I told Geoffrey of my hearing soft footsteps above while leaving Master Holbein's studio later than usual that day, and my breaking into panic when I thought someone was moving toward me.

"But there was no one on the stairs when the manservant lifted the candle, and so my fears were without foundation," I insisted.

Geoffrey clasped his palms together and stared at the floor, tapping his forehead.

"Tell me, *please*," I cried. "Tell me what you are thinking."

Continuing to look at the floor, he said, "Joanna, despite all of my efforts and the efforts of half a dozen men of the law in London, men who know the city extremely well, the players acting out the murder of Becket have not been found."

I didn't understand the importance of their disappearance and told him so.

Geoffrey said, "I found Richard bleeding to death at the side of their stage. They were so close to it all. Questioning them could have helped me learn who lured Richard off his horse. Two underconstables searched for the company of players at Blackfriars." At my startled look, he explained, "Since the king suppressed it, that vast monastery, now empty, and the liberties surrounding have served as a hive for companies of strolling actors and all manner of disreputable men."

A wave of sadness washed over me. The largest English monastery of the Dominican Order, the place where Edmund and I once went in our quest to learn the meaning behind prophecy, was now a refuge for men of light morals.

Geoffrey was saying that he, too, searched through Blackfriars, questioning everyone he could. He met those who put on performances all over London, miracle and mystery plays mostly. The life of Saint George or Saint Nicholas. The Expulsion of Adam and Eve. The Raising of Lazarus. Such stories had diverted Londoners for hundreds of years. But in the last ten years, it had become steadily riskier to put on such tableaus in public. After all, Cromwell and Archbishop Cranmer, the arbiters of faith in England, called for an end to the veneration of saints. Even a New Testament story could offend. A play actor never knew now when a performance could lead to not a shower of coins but a stay in the stocks. That is why the choice of the story of Henry II and Becket left them flabbergasted. It was so dangerous. No one had ever acted out the murder of Thomas Becket before in London, and not one of those Geoffrey spoke to, experienced in the life of the stage, were acquainted with the company of strolling actors who had brazenly performed it.

"What does this mean?" I asked, puzzled.

Geoffrey said, watching me carefully, "The play actors did not perform the story of Saint Thomas Becket for the benefit of the London crowd."

"I'm afraid I don't know enough of the lives of these sorts of people to understand why they *would* do it then." I was growing frustrated. "Won't you just speak plainly? Your gravity of manner suggests you have formed some sort of dire theory. Speak the words."

"Very well, Joanna. That performance was part of an elaborate trap laid just for you."

I burst into laughter, saying, "That is absurd."

"No, it isn't. It's extremely clever, when you work it out. Those who wish to harm you discovered that on the following day you would ride to the Great Wardrobe in London and assumed—rightly—you'd have your one servant with you. Ladies don't ride into London alone, but you don't have the means or the rank for a group of attendants. If you had continued along the street that Richard meant you to, you'd have soon reached the Great Wardrobe on the other side of Baynard's Castle. That street is the obvious choice. But next to it was that lane, narrow and not nearly as populated. A perfect place to lure you in and take hold of you—if Richard could be removed from your side. So, first they'd need to block the main street, and second, prompt you to linger, attention drawn, while dealing with Richard. I think you'd agree that, considering your history, the murder of Becket is a tableau you'd have a hard time hurrying past."

"I don't believe it," I said, although a cold, sick feeling stirred. "How could anyone know that we'd pick that particular lane? Richard at first planned to ride higher up the street to find another way."

"But he didn't—because the moment he looked in that direction, a crowd of loud mummers started moving toward you, making it a daunting prospect for those on horseback to ride in the opposite direction, passing through them essentially. I noticed them, too, Joanna. And I was able to find one of those mummers later in the same day, and through him spoke to the leader. A man paid him well to gather a group and move down the street, but not until the man waved a flag near the stage. *Then* they'd start their fuss. The timing was critical—and I believe they picked the time when you and Richard approached the stage. So the lane became the only choice. And that's where they must have been waiting for you."

I resisted what Geoffrey was saying—I desperately did not want to believe in this scenario.

"Why don't you find that man who paid the mummers and waved the flag?" I asked. "Couldn't he shed some light?"

"Vanished. He paid the mummers in full before they came down the street—which is unusual." Geoffrey took a deep breath. "And then there's your horse."

"My horse was frightened by some boy who ran past and slapped her haunch to get out of the way," I said. "Although I was grievously hurt, I suppose I should be grateful for it. Otherwise, I might have ridden farther up the lane, away from you and toward . . ." My voice died away. "I haven't asked—who took charge of the horse after I fell? Were there difficulties?"

Geoffrey said flatly, "Your horse is dead, Joanna."

"Dead?"

"That boy wasn't trying to get around you. In some sort of last-ditch effort to harm you, he stuck a dart into the horse that caused her great pain and panic—that's why she kept bucking violently. A moment after you were thrown, the horse collapsed. In ten minutes she stopped breathing. I believe she was poisoned. I found a horse master who has some familiarity with their diseases and took him to examine the dead animal. He'd never seen anything like the state of that corpse. I took the dart to an apothecary and alchemist who could not identify the dried substance on its tip."

The cold, sick fear spread to my heart and clutched it. With some effort, I put my question into words: "Do you think that the times that I have felt myself watched—and followed on the stairs in the gatehouse—that it wasn't fancies?"

"Joanna, I believe you have been under nearly constant surveillance since you rode into London in the middle of April. The conditions in a palace such as this make it uniquely difficult to murder anyone. Not only has the king made any act of violence, no matter how small, punishable with the severest of measures, but those who live within it are rarely alone. The first time you left Westminster in a month, they pounced."

That was when I fully capitulated to Geoffrey's theory—one that terrified me beyond measure. Someone wanted to kill me with such determination and I didn't know why. I agreed to return to Dartford with him as soon as possible.

"I can't protect you here without knowing whom to trust," he said. "And my status in Whitehall is too uncertain, too low, to question anyone I wish. But in Dartford, I know the worth and honesty of every man and woman. I know when a stranger enters the town. I can keep you safe."

I was not so afraid for my own skin that I couldn't make one last protest, remembering what Geoffrey said to Holbein while they thought I slept.

"You can't spend the rest of your life standing guard over me, Geoffrey," I said. "I understand from John Cheke that you no longer intend to travel to Germany, but still you must—"

"Joanna, you are worrying about the wrong matters," he said. "I am the constable of Dartford and so your safety is my charge. Let us take this in stages. First I extricate you from Whitehall and return you to Dartford? Then you regain the use of your arm and your strength. Afterward, you can decide what is to be done."

And so I found myself heading south to Dartford, lying in a litter lent to me by the Howard family. The conveyance, and an escort of four men armed with halberds answering to Geoffrey, came courtesy of Catherine, of course. She'd been dismayed that I said I could not wait until I was stronger to leave the palace, but finally agreed.

An hour after dawn, Catherine and Master Holbein walked me slowly to the courtyard, where Geoffrey and the litter waited. There were the warmest of embraces and promises of many letters. "You will be back *soon*," Catherine kept saying.

Just before I stepped into the litter, I glanced at the intricate gatehouse, the same one that had so fascinated me when I first came to Whitehall. It seemed fitting that it would be the last thing I looked on now.

There was a flash of movement on top. I tensed. Some final attempt to attack me before I left court? A man definitely watched me from above. But as I craned my neck to better see, I recognized him: Thomas Culpepper. What a lonely silhouette he made atop the rampart. Before I could make a gesture of farewell, Culpepper disappeared. My friend was gone.

The distance between London and Dartford can be covered in a few hours riding briskly, but in this litter it took the entire day. I spent the hours in a daze, alternating between prayers and snatches of sleep. It was yet another dry, hot spring day. For safety's sake, Geoffrey had ordered the curtains be fastened, so I saw nothing. We stopped frequently to rest the horses carrying this heavy contraption and for Geoffrey to peer in and check on me. I drank when it was offered. But it was still an ordeal of heat and of dull, pounding fear.

Someone wanted me dead. Someone wanted me dead. As I stared at the shifting wall of my litter, the sun hurling strange shapes against the cloth, I wondered what kind of mind could conceive of distracting and delaying me by means of putting on a play. And not just any play, but the story of Archbishop of Canterbury Thomas Becket being murdered by knights wishing to please their king. A rush of dread moved through me as the identity of my would-be killer began to take form. I know you, I gasped. But as my mind made a final leap, I fell back into confusion. My enemy remained a shuddering outline without substance within, like the hidden forms dancing against the litter cloth.

I was too weak to manage a full Rosary but repeated over and over, clutching my crucifix, the bit of psalm beloved by Saint Dominic: "Oh God, come to my assistance. Oh Lord make haste to help me."

The moment finally came when the litter stopped, the curtains were unfastened, and, when I peered outside, there rose the buildings of the High Street of Dartford.

"I thank God and the Virgin for bringing you home to us!"

Such were the teary words of welcome from Agatha Gwinn, who was the first of my friends to embrace me, gingerly. Perhaps it was because the hour was near twilight—or because we'd left behind the crowds of London and Westminster. But whatever the reason, it felt so much more pleasant here. What a relief to see Agatha and the five Dominican sisters, all gathered to greet me, for Geoffrey had sent word ahead. Even Gregory our former porter stood among them, with his young wife. She gamely smiled in welcome while looking bewildered. It must have been a strange sight—the vestiges of the priory of Dartford gathering one of their own back into the fold—to anyone who had not endured what we had endured. I knew from their exchanged glances how dreadful I must appear: head and arm wrapped in bandages, face flushed and sweating, moving slowly out of the litter and toward my house. But no one said a word—for a few moments, at least.

Once over the threshold of my little house, freshly swept and tidied by these dear friends, Sister Eleanor, who outside Holy Trinity Church had pleaded with me not to go to Whitehall in the first place, could no longer contain herself.

"Sister Joanna, what have they done to you?" Her voice ripped through the cheerful murmurs.

Agatha Gwinn said, with a tight smile, "Come now, Sister Eleanor, that isn't helpful, is it?"

Moving toward me as if Agatha had not spoken, Sister Eleanor stared into my eyes, her brows gathered in a scowl, and then pressed her palm to my forehead. After a few seconds she removed it, alarmed.

"Sister Joanna," she said. "You are burning up."

"The ride was long and the day is hot," I said.

"No," she said. "You have fever."

25

How do I explain the next month and a half of my life? The first fortnight I could barely describe to anyone—a jumble of delirium and aching pain, not just in my head and arm but all the joints in my body. I was dimly aware of those who cared for me: Agatha and Sister Eleanor primarily. Agatha because she still felt like a mother to all the novices she trained, and Sister Eleanor because she had served as healer at the priory—that is, before a friar named Edmund Sommerville arrived and set up infirmaries for convent and town. Neither Edmund nor the sisters had ever put much stock in leeches and other popular remedies used to treat disease, such as a plaster of honey and bird dung. No, my friends washed me with cloths soaked in vinegar and made herbal poultices of sorrel and chamomile and pressed them on my forehead. They beseeched me to sip liquid or nibble bits of bread. The virulent fever went on day after day, and without sustenance I could not hope to outlast it.

Geoffrey was there much of the time, his eyes clouded with worry. "Perhaps we should send word to Whitehall," he said one day to Agatha and her husband, John, gathered by my bedside.

"No, no, no," I cried out, teeth chattering, for that was during a spell when I was fairly lucid but shivering as if it were winter outside and not blazing hot. "If it's an infection of bone, I shall die. And if it's an ailment, it is possible I will live. It's in the hands of God."

Agatha crossed herself and murmured prayers. But Geoffrey,

looking even more troubled, said, "It's not that I don't have faith in God—I do as much as the next man. But you must fight, too, Joanna. You've always been a fighter. *You* must fight to live."

I was silent. I had no wish to deceive Geoffrey. The truth was, I had given myself up to God's will entirely. As I suffered the agony of this prolonged fever, I became convinced it was the culmination of a series of divine punishments. First there were the attempts on my life, then the cruel injuries, and now this ravaging disease. I had offended God—there was no question of it. Geoffrey was right, my nature was obstinate and hot-tempered. I was a fighter. But was this not part of my offense? A true daughter of Christ accepted God's wisdom. I sensed that I was being put to the test now, and I would display to God true submission.

As the days ground by, I found it harder and harder to speak. I was aware of Agatha weeping beside me, and I struggled to comfort her but couldn't form the words. "I used to pray for patience in my dealings with you," she said brokenly. "You were one of my most trying novices. So headstrong. Prioress said from the beginning she saw great promise in you, but it took me months to see it, to grow to love you. I admit that in the beginning I prayed to God to tame your spirit. What I would give to see a shadow of that spirit now."

I tried to speak, to comfort her, but I could not.

One evening the fever that boiled my blood seemed to reach a new, excruciating level. There was a crackling, followed by a rushing in my ears. "Help," I cried, but I was alone in my bedchamber and no one heard me downstairs. Then the heat fell away and I was soaked in sweat. My face, my arms, my chest, even my legs. Something stirred in me, something new.

Slowly, using the headboard to pull on with my right hand, I sat up. I did not faint, nor cry with pain or confusion.

God had decided in His Mercy to spare me.

"Oh, Christ's nails!"

I heard a man's booming voice, full of anger, and then shoes pounding up the steps. Geoffrey exploded into the room, his face frantic. At the sight of me sitting up in bed, his mouth fell open.

"Geoffrey," I said.

He raced toward me, a smile lighting up his tired face.

"I believe—I believe I'm hungry," I said.

He burst out laughing. "You shall eat, Joanna. A feast!"

I'm told that in Holy Trinity Church, prayers were said the next morning in gratitude for my fever breaking. Both Agatha and Sister Eleanor insisted it was nothing short of a miracle. "I thought twice I should send to Father William for Last Rites," confided Agatha. "But I know how much you detest him, so I postponed it."

Father William, bending over me, gloating over my demise as he proclaimed *"In nomine Patris et Filii et Spiritus Sancti . . ."*

"Oh, thank you," I said. "I would not wish his to be the last face I see."

The recovery from such a virulent illness promised to be lengthy, made even more of a challenge because of my tender skull and aching arm. But, thanks to the steadfast nursing of my friends, I made progress on all fronts. Sister Eleanor praised it as an excellent sign when I complained one day of boredom. Even I, who loved Scripture, could bear only so much being reading aloud to. I wanted to study my own books, sit at my tapestry loom, and walk along the High Street.

Most of all, I did not want to impose on my friends any longer, and a solution was found in a brother and sister who'd recently begun working for the Gwinns. Pierre and Aimée were French; they'd come to London with a merchant but were left stranded when their master died suddenly without leaving instructions or money for the servants. Due to Londoners' distrust of foreigners, they found no employment and were destitute when Master Gwinn came upon the siblings and brought them to Dartford. He offered me their service while I remained in town, a service I insisted on paying for. It was a comfort to have people living in the house: Pierre was capable of any task, and Aimée loved practicing her

English with me. It was left vague about how long they'd be needed. None of my friends thought I should return to London—and they didn't even know about the plots against my life. Only Geoffrey and I knew what happened to me, and one day when he came to visit me, he shared with me a curious observation.

"I've been meaning to ask you: Why did you curse on the stairs that day?" I asked.

"Because you were completely alone," he said. "It seems there was a mistake in my communications with Mistress Gwinn and she did not know I counted on her to be with you that night."

"How long had I been alone?" I said, surprised.

"You were unprotected for at least four hours," he said.

We stared at each other for a moment. "Then my enemies have not followed me here," I concluded. "For surely if anyone observed that I was alone in my house, they would have taken the opportunity to . . ." I couldn't finish the sentence.

"I have not seen anything amiss since we returned," he said. "No suspicious strangers in town and no evidence of anyone observing you at all."

"Geoffrey, there was never any trouble here in the months before I journeyed to court, either," I pointed out to him. "And I was alone much of the time. Which is part of the reason I didn't believe at first that anyone plotted to harm me. Wouldn't it be a simpler matter here in Dartford to dispatch me?"

Geoffrey's eyebrows shot up at my choice of phrase, but he agreed. "You are correct. It's only when you leave Dartford and go to London that these incidents occur."

We both of us pondered that unsettling realization for a while, trying to make sense of it. And were unable to. I thought of the moment in the litter, coming down from London, when I'd felt close enough to perceiving who was trying to kill me, based on the choice of Thomas Becket's murder as the subject of a play. But now there was nothing but a blank. That rush of recognition must have been a product of my fever, nothing more.

"Well," Geoffrey said with a sigh, "if you're strong enough to take on the question of attempts on your life, you're strong enough for your correspondence."

He handed over five letters that he had been saving for me. Three from Catherine Howard, one from Sir Andrew Windsor, and one from my cousin Lord Henry Stafford.

I read Catherine's first. She apologized profusely for not visiting me in Dartford but promised me that she prayed continually for my health. In each of the short, hastily written letters, she hinted at big changes soon to come. "Be assured, you shall rejoice that Catherine Howard is your friend," she scrawled in the third.

Shaking my head, I turned to the letter from Sir Andrew. He inquired after my health and asked that as soon as I was fully recovered, I make arrangements to receive the king's instructions regarding his tapestry collection. Also to be resolved was the question of whether I should travel to Brussels to make inquiries about the new series *The Triumph of the Gods*.

I could feel the king's impatience quivering through the careful script of the letter. If only I had a sound plan for how to proceed on the tapestry position—or anything else. The wrath of the king would flare once more if, after all he had said of the value of his collection and the need for family to help, I did not take up my duties. I then opened the fifth and final letter, the one from Stafford Castle. I didn't see how it could upset me more than Sir Andrew's. I was wrong.

My dearest and most beloved cousin,

The Duke of Norfolk, my esteemed brother-in-law, informs me of the terrible accident that befell you in London. He conveys that you are expected to heal completely and I thank God for it. We will light candles of thanks in chapel. But taking this into consideration, it would be unwise to send Arthur down and into your charge. Perhaps in one year the question can be taken up again . . .

I threw down the letter, tears of disappointment filling my eyes.

When he knew the cause, Geoffrey expressed sympathy. "He is a hale boy, I miss his brand of mischief. But at least you can try again with your relation next year. In the meantime—"

"*Meantime?*" I cried. "What is to be my meantime? I cannot take up my tapestry position at the court for fear of an assassination. Am I to live here in some sort of limbo, without livelihood or Arthur to care for? It is intolerable!"

He said, "I see I was wrong to give you this correspondence."

"I cannot live like a child, shielded from unpleasant news."

"Oh, I don't know about that," he said lightly. "I have sometimes thought that your life would be much happier had you experienced a little more shielding."

I loosened my grip on my foul mood. "Geoffrey, you know I am grateful for all you have done for me. But in all seriousness, I must repeat what I said in the palace: I cannot be a burden to you."

"And I repeat, Joanna, that you must wait until you get your full strength back and then make all your decisions."

I continued to recover. I even managed to put on a little weight, to the joy of my friends. All the dizziness and soreness of the head disappeared; one wonderful day, Sister Eleanor removed the splint from my arm. It was stiff but, with practice, I should regain its full use, she assured me. After my repeated pleadings, Agatha took me for a short walk on the High Street, but it was less than enjoyable. Even though the hour approached Vespers, it was blazingly hot. The first time I attended church I heard, among all the well-wishers' greetings, distress from the townsfolk over the drought, which began in spring and had worsened.

In the last decade Dartford had already been pummeled with change. This was once a town that revolved around religion and not just because of the existence of my Dominican priory. The inns on the High Street had always catered to the pilgrims on their way to Canterbury. Now that the king had destroyed Saint Thomas Becket's shrine, far fewer people were stopping at Dartford. In the last two years, the construction of a new manor house on the rubble of the priory employed many of the townsfolk. The manor house was complete—it stood luxuriously empty—and so that source of work petered away. All that was left was the land itself. If the harvest suffered, poverty was sure to follow. I thought about what the old boatman said the night of the bishop's banquet: *This summer will be a time of want and pestilence. The lady of the river told me.* I had been so caught up in my own frights, and so isolated from the town because of my illness, that I hadn't realized how much the people were hurt by this unrelenting and unnatural heat. With the bulk of the summer before us, there was palpable dread in Dartford: What was yet to come?

After another fortnight passed, I woke up one day feeling completely restored in strength. I broke my fast with a slice of manchet prepared by Aimée, and then I searched for the drawings for my new tapestry I'd purchased from Brussels months ago. I carefully placed the main one, the one meant to serve as background for the weave, on the loom. The beautiful long form of Niobe stretched across the wooden poles and boards and pulleys. I'd brought down with me Hans Holbein's sketch of Catherine, but I wasn't ready to inspect it again. I had no choice but to use it, yet I regretted incorporating my friend's face in the weave. Niobe's was a story of punishment by the gods and death.

Still, surveying my loom, I felt a new determination. I wasn't sure where, or how exactly, but I must take up my responsibilities as tapestry mistress. It wasn't a calling—my calling for the life of a nun died with the priories—but it was an affinity. My future was in tapestries.

I wrote a note asking Geoffrey to call on me and gave it to Aimée. He had not come to visit me much of late—perhaps my sharp tongue had driven him away, or he was simply busy with his resumed constable duties. But this could not wait.

The sun had reached its highest point when I heard a sharp rapping at the door. I was surprised to find on my doorstep not just Geoffrey but two visitors come from court: John Cheke, whom I'd not been expecting, and Doctor Butts, even less so. They were good friends, it seemed, despite their disparity in age.

In the parlor of my house, Doctor Butts looked me over himself, an uncalled-for honor from the royal physician. "Mistress Howard wanted to be certain of your recovery, and I am most relieved that I will not disappoint her," he explained.

Perhaps it was because I'd been away from the court and its flowery phrases, but such deference to Catherine seemed excessive.

"Yes, I am myself again, and I regret that you came so far on this errand," I said.

John Cheke cleared his throat and said, "Before we return, you should see the church in town, Doctor Butts. It's of great interest— I've been told that Henry the Fifth's funeral ceremony was held there."

"Oh, I should very much like that," the doctor said immediately.

"Geoffrey, would you mind escorting the doctor?" Cheke asked.

Frowning, Geoffrey said, "Me?"

Doctor Butts insisted that he did want to see Holy Trinity Church, and Geoffrey, with a reluctant bow, led him out of the room. There was something strange about it, as if Cheke and Doctor Butts had worked out this plan in advance, but hadn't told Geoffrey. Once they'd left, Cheke turned to me with a look in his eyes of barely suppressed excitement.

"I don't have much time," he said. "I must ride back to London today."

"I am surprised to see you at all, Master Cheke, for I'd thought you back in Cambridge."

"I did return to university, yes, but four days ago was summoned to court again. Bishop Gardiner officially offered me the position of chair of Greek at Saint John's College."

I congratulated him, but that agitated look persisted. As much as this must be a pinnacle of his career—a most prestigious post for a man of his humanist learning—I suspected that sharing this personal advancement was not why he came to Dartford.

"Do you have any idea of what's happened at court?" he said. "Has the news not spread here yet?"

I shook my head and braced myself. But nothing could have prepared me for John Cheke's next words.

"The king has turned on Cromwell. He is arrested, imprisoned in the Tower of London, and it seems certain he shall die."

26

Impossible," I cried. "This all occurred since I left court in May?"

"It took place in the last three weeks!" Cheke exclaimed. "Just before a meeting of the Privy Council on the tenth of June, the captain of the guard stopped Cromwell, and the Duke of Norfolk stripped him of his Order of the Garter insignia—as he stood there, he tore it off his doublet. No one had ever seen such a thing or heard of it before. Norfolk shouted that a traitor could not sit in the council, and the guards dragged Cromwell away, as he shouted to all he passed that he was no traitor. But no one would listen, and the constable himself took Cromwell to the Tower of London. He writes letters begging the king for mercy."

Although the last stage of dizziness had receded weeks ago, this report made the room spin, and I fell into a chair. Cromwell had served the king as his right hand, the second most powerful man in England, for more than ten years. What could possibly have made Henry VIII turn against him?

Cheke wiped the sweat from his brow with a kerchief and said, "Even as I tell you what happened, Mistress Joanna, I can't believe it myself."

I heard the voice of my cousin, the Earl of Surrey: *There is another way to put an end to Cromwell, though it be anything but honorable. I can say not a word to you about it. Only that, someday, when all has changed, I hope to redeem myself in your eyes, Joanna.*

"The covenant," I whispered.

Cheke said, "What did you say, Joanna?"

I shook my head. "Nothing." And then: "Who shall replace him?"

"Bishop Gardiner has finally taken back his seat on the king's council; whether he can entirely fill the role of Cromwell remains to be seen. He's also expected to be elected as the next chancellor of Cambridge—that is why a decision was made about my future. Gardiner works in tandem with the Duke of Norfolk, whose son, the Earl of Surrey, celebrated in the palace for days on end the arrest of the 'foul churl,' as he calls him." John Cheke wrinkled his nose in disapproval. "The Howards are ascendant as never before, now that they have disposed of Cromwell and shall have a Howard queen."

All of the breath left my body.

"Mistress Joanna, are you ill again?" said Cheke, alarmed. "You've lost all of your color."

"What did you say?" I choked. "A Howard queen?"

"I assumed, since you are such true friends, that you're aware that Catherine Howard is poised to become the king's fifth wife. They are said to be secretly engaged. Everyone at court knows it."

"He *has* a wife—Queen Anne of Cleves," I said.

"The queen was sent away from court to Richmond House six days ago," said Cheke. "The king's counselors visited her and presented the grounds for divorce—a previous engagement of hers to the Duke of Lorraine, a man she never met. I'm told she wept but makes no objections. The divorce should be speedy. The king seeks out Catherine Howard whenever he can, and openly. She shall soon be elevated, the Howards tell everyone at court."

It was hard for me to take in the impact of all of these changes, some most precipitous. Poor Anne of Cleves. So Norfolk did not lie when he told Catherine she could become queen. He knew what sort of man the king was, after all. I should have been proud of my friend's dramatic rise, but all I could feel was fear. Through divorce, execution, or childbed fever, the king had gone through four wives. Catherine was the youngest of them all. And by far the least prepared.

"The gossip at Whitehall is that the king turned against Cromwell because he'd favored the German marriage and lagged in arranging a divorce. Cromwell did not want Anne of Cleves replaced with Catherine Howard, the niece of his enemy," Cheke said.

I thought about how King Henry and Cromwell behaved when I saw them last, in the royal privy chamber. The chief minister did everything he could to serve his master and they seemed a close pair; he practically finished the king's sentences.

"It is hard for me to believe that if His Majesty commanded Cromwell to procure for him a divorce, he would be refused," I said.

"I agree with you, and certainly the divorce was easily obtained once initiated," Cheke said. He bit his hip and studied me. The nervousness was still there.

"What is it, Master Cheke?" I asked.

He said, picking his words with evident care, "I would like to know your plan for Geoffrey Scovill."

His question plunged me into a defensive stance.

"I have no plan for him," I said. "Why do you think I would?"

Instead of answering, Cheke scuttled back to the window and peered outside. "Good," he muttered. "They haven't left the church yet."

"Why was it important you speak to me alone?" I asked. "Everything you've said to me could be said to all. I don't understand this."

He turned and said bluntly, "I want you to release Geoffrey."

I could feel my face flush red. "Master Cheke, he is worried about my safety for various reason, but Geoffrey is not mine to release. He is not my captive."

Cheke said, "Forgive me, Mistress Joanna, but now that I have more serious wages to draw upon, I can finance a trip to Germany. I very much want Geoffrey to find Paracelsus, to pick up the trail of Edmund. I could send someone else, there are men available to be hired, but they don't know Edmund and there is no portrait to lend. And I do believe Geoffrey to be highly intelligent and resourceful. If Edmund's alive, Constable Scovill will find him. I fear he's the only one who can."

"I see."

Once again, Cheke went to the window. This time, he grimaced. "Ah, they emerge. And I've run out of time with you. I didn't have a chance to—wait, I still wish to—it could make a difference . . ." John Cheke practically danced with indecision before pivoting toward me, his hand once more in his doublet.

"I have considered giving this to you a hundred times," he said rapidly, pulling out a set of worn parchments. "Geoffrey wrote to me that you almost died of fever, and I lambasted myself for not sending this to you already. I always felt it would be a betrayal of a sort. But, considering all that has happened, please—take it now."

Two pages of parchment dangled open. The ink was faded, but the writing was quite legible. The letters were beautifully formed. That would be expected from someone who spent his youth in the scriptoriums of prestigious monasteries.

Yes, it was written by Edmund Sommerville.

I took the pages, my heart pulsing in my head, my ears, my throat. The letter was missing the earlier pages; these two were the last part of the correspondence. I read as quickly as I could.

It is difficult to end my missive to you, John, for today I feel more alone than ever before in this country far from England. The people have suffered in ways that can hardly be imagined and yet they show a good heart to a stranger. It is not that which makes me wish we could speak to each other tonight. I caught sight of a young woman carrying a bucket of water who had thick black hair, and it put me into a humor of melancholia. I fear that Joanna will never agree with me that her life will be a happier one if I am far away. Her compassion and patience for my manifold weaknesses were always more than I could deserve.

I cannot stop thinking about the first weeks that I knew Joanna and I find I want to describe them to you. Our circumstance of meeting was very strange. We were brought together by Bishop Stephen Gardiner on a mission. I doubt you would believe the mission's purpose.

I will pass over it. But we served in the same priory in Dartford after my Dominican order in Cambridge was dissolved. I soon perceived her quickness of mind and her warm heart for her friends. Some of my fellow friars take the position that women are so inferior that we should not converse. I never accepted this disdain of women. We took vows to go out among the people, we are not monks. But the danger in speaking to women is of succumbing to temptation to commit mortal sin. I have learned to recognize the signs of a female becoming too avid for my company and how to handle these dilemmas with tact and compassion. Why do I picture you smiling, my old friend?

I began to see these signs in Joanna and prepared the words I would say to her and the actions that must be taken. But to my consternation I found that I did not want Joanna to cease feeling the way that she did. It was the first time I experienced such a desire. I will not describe what ensued, for those experiences belong to me and to Joanna, and are not mine to share solely. These memories, I will carry with me for the rest of my life. They are painful to me but quite precious, too. I shall soon put the parchment away and prepare myself for sleep, always with the prayers for forgiveness for all whom I have wronged, and the principal person is Joanna.

The door to my house opened and Geoffrey and Doctor Butts came back in. I can only imagine the expression on my face, for both of them expressed concern.

"Master Cheke brings shocking news from Whitehall," I said in explanation, bending to pick up an imaginary speck, so that Geoffrey would not perceive just how distraught I was. "I need a little time to absorb it."

"It's shocking, yes," said Geoffrey, but he sounded intrigued, as most men are by tales of power lost and claimed.

The three of them resolved to share dinner at the town's best tavern, and then Cheke and Doctor Butts would set off back to London, avoiding the worst heat of the day. I bade them farewell, attempting to answer the question in Cheke's eyes with as much reassurance as I could summon. Turning from him, I said, "Geoffrey, would you come to see me before day's end, for I need to speak to you."

"Certainly," he said, smiling, and the three of them disappeared up the street.

I could not let go of the letter. I held it in my lap as I sat by the window, the chatter of the folk on the High Street humming beneath my thoughts. Ever since I'd recovered from my virulent fever, I'd felt a growing restlessness. What purpose could I serve with this life God spared? I exercised all caution here in Dartford to evade those who wished me harm and it was effective. Following Geoffrey's advice kept me alive. And I'd been grappling with the idea of taking on the tapestries of the king as commanded. But to what higher purpose? Merely to exist was not enough—it could not be enough.

I assumed that John Cheke showed me this letter of Edmund's to reawaken the love in my heart, so that I would "release" Geoffrey Scovill to search for Edmund. What occurred was more complicated than that, and more unexpected. In reading his words, I heard Edmund speak as if he were in the room with me, a sensation I'd been deprived of for many months, and to my own astonishment, I found my way back to caring for him without the grief and anger. Edmund was right: the memories were painful but they were precious, too. There was one in particular that enveloped me.

It was the first summer we all spent in Dartford after being forced from the priory. Such a difficult matter, reentering the world we'd each of us withdrawn from with such conviction. The cloister was gone, and the refectory, the dorter, the library, the tapestry workshop, all the places we knew and loved. Even worse, the hours of worship and service had vanished: Matins, Lauds, Prime, Terce, Sext, None, Vespers, and Compline, all were gone. We were like sailors taught to navigate by the stars staring at a black sky. I was more fortunate than most, because the demands of Arthur filled my days. Yet I still found moments here and there to go to the infirmary that Edmund opened in Dartford. The truth was, I seized any excuse I could to go to the infirmary. My feet would as good as fly along the High Street when I was on my way there. Because I would be with Edmund.

"Look what I found this morning," he said as I slipped in the door. He waved fistfuls of spiky yellow flowers at me, a smile warming his pale features.

"Is it blessed thistle?"

"Joanna, you remember—how wondrous," he said. "Yes, the flower is uncommon as far north as England. We are most fortunate."

Half of the flowers were set aside for drying; working in companionable silence, we chopped the petals and stems of the rest for immediate remedies. As I cleaned up, Edmund toted buckets of water into the infirmary. Although it was a hot day for lighting a fire, Edmund didn't want to miss the opportunity to brew fresh teas with blessed thistle. He knew a few townspeople with ruined digestion who would benefit.

"Brother, it hurts—can ye help me?" sounded a man's voice. It was Peter, a young man who worked in his father's shop. He held up a burned right forearm, clumsily bandaged. He'd hurt himself the night before at Saint Margaret's Fair, held every July a short distance from Dartford.

While he struggled not to scream, Peter had his wound properly cleaned. Edmund then prepared his favored burn remedy of a paste of chopped onions, to ease the pain.

"I know what I did was stupid—trying to juggle the fire sticks," Peter muttered. "But Madge was watching and I couldn't look a coward in front of those louts from Rochester."

Edmund said, applying his paste on Peter's arm at the table, "I am certain Madge could have no such opinion of you."

"She used to look at me like I was ten feet high, but of late I fear she tires of me." He shook his head. "I shouldn't be bringing this sort of trouble to a friar, it's not fit. And . . . ye wouldn't understand."

Edmund said, "I understand how when another person looks up

to you, thinks well of you, it can be as important as food or drink. More so, because . . ."

His words trailed off. Edmund leaned down even lower over Peter's arm.

I could barely breathe. What Edmund described—that was how I felt about *him*. I strove to better myself not only because it was proper and Godly but because Edmund would take note of it. But who was he talking about? Was it possible that I was that person, that he sought to impress me? It seemed incredible.

The water in the pot hanging over the fire popped and bubbled as I waited for Edmund to say something more. His hair had grown in where once it was shaved to create the tonsure. These wayward fine blond curls hung far enough down that I couldn't see his eyes or read his expression as he worked.

Peter shifted at the table, and Edmund looked up, meeting my gaze for a few seconds, nothing more. Then we both turned away—ecstatic and terrified, in equal measure. Nothing more was done or said that day, but I carried the details of it with me for months afterward, reliving each word and glance.

Edmund must be found; he must be helped.

A plan eased into my mind, a bold one, but as I turned it over, it grew in practicality. When, some time later, I heard Geoffrey whistling outside, I took a deep breath.

"You are better?" he asked once in the room with me, his eyes bright with the ale downed with Cheke and Doctor Butts.

"Geoffrey, did John Cheke come here to ask you to go to Germany?"

"Yes, he did."

Geoffrey's buoyant mood sagged, and I regretted that I'd sprung my question on him straight away. I should have eased into it. But it was too late to change my tack now, and so I plunged on with "What is your answer?"

"Regrettably, my duties here make it impossible for me to leave for such an extended time."

"But you were set to leave before. You and Cheke agreed. It was only lack of funds that stopped you."

Geoffrey folded his arms. "Your point?"

"What's changed is *my* crisis, my being attacked at Whitehall and retreating to Dartford. You don't want to leave me unprotected. But I have Pierre and Aimée—and you concede that no one has come to threaten me here. You need not stay on my behalf."

"As if you would remain in Dartford! The boat wouldn't have left Gravesend before you'd be on your way back to Whitehall. You have a dangerous tendency to overestimate your ability to deal with a situation."

"I'm glad to hear you have so little faith in me," I said.

"Oh, Joanna, you know I did not mean it to be taken that way. But can't you see that the enemies you've made will go to great lengths to capture you?"

"Capture? Don't you mean murder?"

He regarded me cautiously. "Well, that could be your eventual fate, but no, I am convinced that these people want you alive for a time. The first man, the false page, it sounds to me as if he tried to subdue you. If he wanted you dead, why not kill you the moment he had you alone? And even more so with the confrontation on that lane—they murdered your servant Richard without hesitation, and could have stabbed you, too. But they were leading you up that lane for a reason, and I think it was to snatch you and take you somewhere else."

The details of Geoffrey's imagined scenario repelled me. "Stop it," I said through gritted teeth. "It's too much to bear, too frightening."

"Good," Geoffrey said. "I want you to be frightened—it will drive this Germany business out of your head." He started to the door. "Now, if you will excuse me?"

"No," I said. "I will not."

"You will not excuse me?" he asked, with a smile breaking out.

"No." It took an effort to stamp out my smile that was curving in response. I needed to be serious. "Geoffrey, I'd like you to listen to a proposal. What if you could travel to Germany and not have to worry about my safety because I'd be out of reach of danger? Would you consider taking Master Cheke's commission?"

"I might," he said after a moment. "How could that be guaranteed?"

"The king has already said that I should go to Brussels to make inquiries about a tapestry series he is interested in acquiring. I will take up the royal commission. You and I would travel there together to Brussels, and I'd stay in Brussels while you made your way to see this Paracelsus. Flanders borders on Germany; it's not all that far. These enemies of mine, you can't believe they would book passage to Flanders to eliminate me."

Geoffrey stood stock-still, his head tilted, a seriousness darkening his eyes.

After a moment, he said, "I must know what John Cheke said to you."

"He said that now that Bishop Gardiner has granted him the position at Cambridge, he has the money to finance your trip and he wants very much for you to go."

"Nothing else?"

"Just that he thinks you are best qualified to succeed. Those are the only things he said to me." Which was true, although I felt a pang over the duplicity.

He shook his head. "I could be gone for a long time, Joanna. Paracelsus is in Salzburg, which is *not* near Brussels. Depending on what I learn, I might search for months for Edmund. Six, perhaps. You can't remain in Brussels six months. Won't the king wish you back far sooner?"

"Brussels is the center of tapestry production in all of Christendom. If I am to serve the king effectively, I must immerse myself. A long stay would be expected."

"Would it? Well, you have certainly concocted quite an interesting plan, Joanna. But I should like to know—why is it so important to you that I locate Edmund? At Winchester House, when you first learned of it, you acted just the opposite of how you seem now."

I'd feared he would detect my change in course. "I've always wanted Edmund to be safe," I said. "No matter what passed between us."

Geoffrey walked to the window. Peering outside, clenching his hands behind his back, he said, "I wish to know, Joanna, if I am able to find Edmund and persuade him to return, what would be your intent? Parliament forbids marriages between those who'd taken monastic vows of chastity, but exceptions have been made, too, as with Agatha and Oliver Gwinn."

This was *not* what I had anticipated.

"Oh, Geoffrey," I whispered.

"You mistake me, Joanna," he said, still not looking at me. "I am not putting myself forward as your husband. I've had a wife—a devoted and loving wife—and shall never have another. I'll die a widower. If it would please you to reconcile with Edmund Sommerville, that would help me."

"Help you? Why?"

"That's my business," Geoffrey said. He cleared his throat, and turned around, his face perfectly calm and composed. "Very well, Joanna, I shall take up the assignment to travel to Germany, and with you along for part of the journey. Perhaps, in the end, we will both find what we seek."

27

Less than two years ago I stood on Tower Hill, my heart breaking, as first Edward Courtenay and then Baron Montagu knelt
before the executioner. That cold, rain-soaked day was the first time I
laid eyes on Thomas Cromwell, whom men praised from all sides as
the all-powerful Lord Privy Seal who had freed the kingdom of traitors. Today, in the baking sun, it was Cromwell's turn to die.

I had not intended to witness this. In fact, Geoffrey and I agreed
that I would stay away from London, using my health as excuse,
until the time came to board our ship.

I resolved to use the time to weave *The Sorrow of Niobe*. I asked
the sisters of Dartford to sit at the loom with me, one or two at a
time, and begin the weave. I was examining the work performed so
far when my cousin Henry Howard, Earl of Surrey, materialized on
my doorstep, talking about the details of Cromwell's execution, set
for the end of July.

"I don't know why you're telling me this—you can't possibly expect me to attend," I said.

"Cromwell does not die alone," Surrey said.

It took only a few seconds for me to know who it must be.

"Sir Walter," I said, and shivered.

"I managed to obtain permission to visit him in his Tower cell,
and he didn't make a great deal of sense, but he was clear on one
request—Sir Walter wants you to pray for him at the moment of his
death, as you did for Lord Montagu."

"Oh, Cousin, that is too much to ask," I protested.

"You've seen such sights before," Surrey pointed out. "We stood side by side for Courtenay and Montagu."

"That was different! Henry Courtenay was my cousin, Montagu my friend. I would pray for them as I would for any other of God's creatures, but I harbor no friendship for Thomas Cromwell or Sir Walter Hungerford. And you know that. So why have you come?"

Surrey said, "It may calm Hungerford if you are there to, as he put it, help him to the other side. And it may quiet him. I am afraid of what he may say on the scaffold."

Now I understood.

I asked, "And what is it that Sir Walter Hungerford could say that causes you fear—and that sends you all the way to Dartford to badger me?"

"Nothing—nothing," the Earl of Surrey insisted. "I do not want the man to shame his good name. He comes from an old and honorable family. I didn't think I was badgering you to convey a condemned man's request. Sir Walter asked for you in the name of Saint Dominic."

I took a deep, shaky breath. Leave it to Hungerford to find the one means of persuasion I could not refuse.

"Very well, I shall attend. But you must tell no one I will be there—I must have your promise." I asked Surrey to put both my name and Geoffrey's on the list of those with permission to witness the executions.

Geoffrey opposed this, of course, but once he realized I'd simply go by myself if need be, he agreed to come. However, this time he extracted from me a promise that I would not go to London or Westminster again before we left for Antwerp.

After giving it some thought, Geoffrey decided that instead of horse, wagon, or litter, we'd hire a small boat from Dartford, timing our journey to suit the tides. It wouldn't be possible for anyone to follow us without being detected.

We left before dawn and disembarked a distance from London

Bridge. We hurried on foot the rest of the way, moving so fast that a stitch stabbed my left side and sweat trickled down my back. We didn't know what time the executions were set for and there was a chance we'd come too late.

We found our way to Tower Street, quiet and orderly. In moments, we'd reach the appointed place for execution of those of noble blood. Not that Cromwell possessed a drop. His earldom, conferred less than three months ago, granted him the privilege of a death at the Tower, rather than the squalid fields of Tyburn.

As we walked along it, Tower Street began to unnerve me because of its very normality. Such a short distance from the site of deep suffering, of torture and death, and yet these shopkeepers smiled from their windows. We passed a fine church, its tiny green bordered by white and pink flowers. At one cross street we halted, along with the others, as a string of wagons filled with merchants' fragrant goods rumbled up from the wharf. Men's oblivious laughter crashed out of the window of a freshly painted building bearing the sign *Rose Tavern*. Just two doors down from the tavern stood All Hallows Barking Church, where the executioner's victims were carted for burial. Sometimes the families later quietly arrived to claim their loved ones' bodies for more honorable burial. And sometimes they didn't.

My heartbeat quickened as we walked past All Hallows, for now our destination came into clear view. Tower Street was the only permitted entrance to the spectacle of death. A brown, grassless hill rose between the eastern outskirt of the city of London and the dominion of the Tower of London. On the center of that hill stood a permanent wooden scaffold. With a rush of nausea, I wondered if Baron Montagu's and Courtenay's blood still stained the platform boards. I forced myself to look away from the pitiless structure.

Between where we paused and the scaffold stood row after row of stone-faced men. Tower Hill swarmed with sheriffs and constables and soldiers. There were more men of the law present than the last time I was here—did they fear an attempt to rescue Cromwell? Peering past them, I spotted perhaps fifty spectators, clustered in silent groups.

Something brushed against my arm, something as light as the wing of a butterfly but with the glancing warmth of a human touch.

I whirled to see. Odd. There were about a dozen people behind us on the street, but no one stood near enough to have made contact.

"What is it?" asked Geoffrey.

"I thought someone touched me," I said. "But it was my imagining."

"Dismiss nothing, Joanna."

"But there was no one there," I said. "It could only have been a . . ."

The words faltered in my throat, for a new sensation came over me. "Geoffrey," I whispered. "Someone—someone is watching me. I feel it. Someone behind us."

"Don't turn around," he ordered.

Geoffrey Scovill slung his long, muscular arm across my shoulders, in protection. He peered behind, looking this way and that. "The trouble is, everyone is looking this way, for it's the only way to Tower Hill. No one seems out of sort." He tightened his grip on me, so much that my shoulders ached. "Surrey must have told others you would be here. This is a serious mistake, Joanna. We will double back, go into the church for a time, and then—"

"What is your business here?" demanded a soldier, armed with a picket. For a few seconds I thought he questioned someone else, but then realized he edged toward us. Turning back from Tower Hill would be dangerous now.

Geoffrey said to me, shortly, "Show him the paper."

I thrust forward my authorization, conveyed by the Earl of Surrey. The soldier nodded when he read the signature at bottom.

"Send these two through," he bellowed.

His arm still around me, Geoffrey led me past the row of soldiers, all of them scrutinizing us as if we'd committed the crime. Once we were out of earshot, I said, "In this place, nothing can hurt *me*, Geoffrey, surely."

"No, but we will be here for a time, clearly visible, and must afterward file out with all the others the same way we approached, down Tower Street, as visible as knights in a damn tournament," he said. "That will give them time to plan."

Them.

Although it was unbearably hot on the treeless Tower Hill, I began to shake as violently as if freezing with cold. This was the last place someone should give in to weakness, and I said a silent, vehement prayer to Saint Dominic. I was here in his name—the founder of my order would protect me. Determined to see it through, I tried to take in who was around us.

At first I recognized no one. I'd thought to see Bishop Gardiner and the Duke of Norfolk, or perhaps the king's friend the Duke of Suffolk. They were now the highest-ranking men of the land, expected to attend an important occasion such as this. But there was no sign of them. Finally I recognized the courtiers Thomas Wriothesley, avid with curiosity, and John Dudley, circumspect as always. But no one higher. And certainly no other women.

"Mistress Joanna?"

By his accent, I knew him before I turned around to face him: Master Hans Holbein. Any happiness I felt over seeing my friend was extinguished by the misery carved in his countenance: bloodshot eyes, haggard features.

"This killing ground is no place for her," the artist said to Geoffrey, in reproach. "Why did you bring Joanna?"

Geoffrey shook his head, exasperated. "She brought *me*, Master Holbein."

I said, "Do not concern yourself, for I've been to Tower Hill before—and Smithfield, too. I am more worried for *you*. Are you ailing, Master Holbein?"

"Not in body, no, but in spirit, perhaps," he answered quietly. "I have not slept more than an hour in three days. Thomas Cromwell was my patron, as was Queen Anne Boleyn before him, and Sir Thomas More before her. I pay my respects to them—no matter the cost."

"I understand," I said. And I did.

Holbein stared away from Tower Hill, toward the barren fields stretching north, dotted with forlorn buildings. "It has not rained in the month of July, not a single drop," he said. "It must mean some-thing, it must . . ."

There was a stirring along the top of the ancient wall, the same I remembered from before. The officials of the Tower of London brought the prisoners down, to be handed over to the men of the City of London, who ruled this sorry piece of land. First came Sir William Kingston, greatly aged, his hair snow-white and his gait so stiff he moved like a wooden puppet.

Geoffrey's hand closed around my arm, not a firm, guiding grip but a spasmodic tightening of fingers. Looking up at him sideways, I realized that Geoffrey feared what was to come. More than that, he stared at the walls of the Tower with something approaching horror. Of course—the king's men arrested him along with me at Smithfield and he spent two days inside those walls, being interrogated, before Norfolk deemed him harmless and ordered Kingston to release him. Whether it was two days or two months, no one fully recovered from imprisonment in the Tower. I hadn't given a thought to Geoffrey's pain over what he'd gone through. Guilt over dragging him back here enveloped me like a suffocating blanket.

All the mutters and whispers on the hill died away as the prison-ers emerged along the walkway to Tower Hill.

First appeared Thomas Cromwell, Earl of Essex and Lord Privy Seal and chief minister to the king of England for more than ten years. Like any other condemned man, he wore a shabby white che-mise and plain dark hose—stripped of the chains, the brocades and leather, the fineries of high office. Without the dignity of his doublet, his loose belly swung beneath the torn chemise, yet he did not seem the slightest humiliated. He approached with a strong step, his head high. As much as I hated him, I had to concede Cromwell's courage. The anguish I'd witnessed in that room in Westminster Hall was gone. Somehow he had found a measure of peace.

An odd keening sound ripped across Tower Hill.

"No, it cannot be—it cannot be!" And then the sound again, a high-pitched laugh turning to scream.

Sir Walter Hungerford stumbled into view. While Cromwell

walked, proud and untouched, between the rows of guards, Hungerford was being dragged to his death. He twisted this way and that, the whites of his eyes rolling like a panicked animal's.

"Christ, have mercy," I breathed, as Hans Holbein muttered something in German. On the other side of me, Geoffrey's grip on my arm tightened even more.

Hungerford was a pitiable sight but a grotesque one, too. I'd heard more details of his crimes. Geoffrey had learned that Sir Walter was formally charged with "unnatural vice"—acts committed with certain men of his household. And there was more. His wife broke free after Hungerford's arrest with a harrowing tale. She claimed her husband beat her, imprisoned her in Farleigh Castle for three years, and tried to poison her.

"Hello, Cousin Joanna," said another voice. At last the Earl of Surrey materialized beside me. "It's fitting we should be here together—again," he said, with a fierce nod toward Cromwell. Dark violet shadows pouched young Henry Howard's glassy eyes. Although Cromwell was his hated enemy, he'd not slept any more than Holbein had in the last few days.

"Where is your father—and the bishop?" I asked.

"At the wedding," he answered.

I stared at him, blank.

With a bitter smile, he said, "The king marries Catherine today."

I simply couldn't believe it.

"To be joined before God—the same day as an execution? How can a marriage prosper, to begin in such a fashion?"

Before Surrey could answer, Sir Walter Hungerford screamed some senseless babble, and a soldier's arm rose, as if to strike him. Another blocked him. They both turned toward Sir William Kingston, who said and did nothing. No one knew how to control Hungerford. My prayers to convey him to God were the last thing he could be thinking of now.

"God's blood," said Surrey, anguished, beside me. I could not begin to imagine what this was like, to see his partner in conspiracy executed while he went free. Hungerford must never have told his interrogators about the covenant, or else Surrey—and Thomas Culpepper, too—would now be in line for the ax, too. I wondered where Culpepper was. If Surrey could bear this horror, he should be able to as well. But then, with a twist, I realized that a gentleman of the privy chamber might be required to attend the king on his wedding day.

"Wait," called out Thomas Cromwell. Even now, condemned, he gave commands. Incredibly, they were obeyed. The soldier moved back, and Hungerford sagged to the ground, sobbing.

Cromwell said something to the guards I could not hear. They stepped back a few more feet and he leaned down, to speak to Hungerford. He laid his hand on the wretched man's quavering back. After a couple of minutes, Hungerford stilled, nodded, and looked up, his face wet with tears. Whatever Cromwell said had calmed him.

Cromwell said loudly, "Now we may proceed."

Geoffrey and I looked at each other, struck with wonder at what we had witnessed.

In a short time, Cromwell stood on the platform, his shrewd gaze as steady as ever as he surveyed the assembled crowd and then said his last words, clear and strong:

"I am come hither to die and not to purge myself, as some think that I will, for if I should do so, I would be a very wretch and miser. I am by the law condemned to die, and thank my Lord God that hath anointed me this death, for my offense. For since the time that I had had years of discretion, I have lived a sinner and offended my Lord God, for that which I ask him hearty forgiveness. And it is not unknown to many of you that I have been a great traveler in this world and being but of a base degree was called to high estate, and since that time, I have offended my prince. For that I ask forgiveness and beseech you all to pray to God with me, that He will forgive me."

Cromwell held up his hands as if he were in fact beseeching us and then said, "O Father, forgive me, O Son, forgive me, O Holy Ghost, forgive me."

My lips moved in response. I noticed a man standing in front of us and to the side, closer to the scaffold, cross himself. Something about his gesture seemed familiar, but then another man shifted to stand in front of me, so I could no longer see.

Cromwell cleared his throat and continued, "And now I pray you that be here, to bear my record, I die in the Catholic faith, not doubting in any article of my faith, nor doubting in any Sacrament of the Church."

Shock rippled through the crowd. No one seemed to have expected that—least of all myself.

His voice edging into anger, Cromwell said, "Many have slandered me and reported that I have been a bearer of such and have maintained evil opinions, which is untrue but I confess like as God by His Holy Spirit doth instruct us in the truth, so the devil is ready to seduce as, and I have been seduced, but bear me witness that I die in the Catholic faith of the Holy Church."

He paused, and a sadness shuddered through his square body, driving out the anger. "Like God by His Holy Spirit does instruct us in the truth, so the devil is ready to seduce us, and I have been seduced, but bear witness that I die in the Catholic faith of the Holy Church. And I heartily desire you to pray for the King's grace, that he may long live with you, may long reign over you. And once again I desire you to pray for me, that so long as life remains in this flesh, I waver nothing in my faith."

Cromwell stepped back from the edge of the scaffold. A man wearing the headsman's hood knelt before him, seeking his forgiveness, and Cromwell nodded, jerkily. The others stepped away as Cromwell then knelt on the platform, before the small wooden block.

"Close your eyes," whispered Geoffrey, but he did not need to, for my eyes were clamped shut. If only that could obscure the horrific deed—but I knew from experience it was not just sight but sound that left its mark on the souls of those who gathered at Tower Hill.

Sure enough, a dreadful ten seconds or so of silence were broken by a crashing thud. I heard oaths and cries all around us—more than

I'd heard when I was last here. I took a deep breath, and just as my eyes opened, a damp hand clamped over them and Geoffrey said, "No, Joanna, it's not over!"

Incredibly, there was a second thud, a third—and a *fourth*. Geoffrey threw his other arm around me, holding me as tight as he could, as if he wanted to shield me from it with his very body. I could feel his heart pumping, light and fast, in his chest.

There were no more crashing noises. Cromwell was in God's hands now.

"That axman should be whipped," said a man behind us. There was a string of German singsong in my ear—did Holbein chant a prayer? My poor, poor artist friend. This was too much for him to bear.

Geoffrey slowly released me, and my eyes fluttered open. Would this now be too much for me to bear?

At first there was nothing but ferocious white sunlight, burning my eyes. I blinked and blinked. I managed to focus on men rushing around the scaffold platform now, bumping into one another, as they frantically tried to recoup from the disaster of what had just occurred. All but one: Sir William Kingston. He stood stock-still, staring out at us, gone blind and deaf and dumb. This execution, the latest in God only knows how many he presided over, seemed to have annihilated his mind.

One of the men stumbled and fell on the platform, and with a sickened rush, I realized what felled him: Cromwell's arm. The axman had cut him into pieces.

I heard a coughing and then a splash behind me—a man was retching onto the ground. The stench of it made a sour thrashing rise in me and for a moment I thought I'd be sick, too. I dug my fingernails into my palm, and willed myself not to vomit. A few moments passed as I stared down—they must be carting away the remains of Cromwell.

"Hungerford," groaned Surrey on my other side.

It was the turn of Sir Walter Hungerford to die, and he had lost his calm. Who could hold on to courage after watching Cromwell beheaded thus? Hungerford fell back against the railing of the scaffold and quivered there. He said nothing, made no noise, but his mouth opened and closed like a frightened bird's.

I searched my mind for the correct prayer and then began. No matter whether he knew of my presence or not, I must carry out my promise.

One man took his right arm, the other his left, and they propelled Hungerford forward, toward the headsman that more than a hundred people now knew to be incompetent.

"Is there no pity here—none?" screeched Sir Walter. He looked out across the crowd, as if frantic for a rescuer.

My cousin the Earl of Surrey tensed beside me. "No," he muttered. "No." What did he fear—some final betrayal in the form of a screaming confession on the scaffold? Would the covenant be revealed?

Hungerford's terrified searching gaze froze when it came to Surrey. I braced myself for what we were about to hear. There was a part of me that prayed Hungerford would say something too insane to be understood. But there was another small part that craved to know the truth about their covenant, though its revelation would surely destroy two people I cared about, Surrey and Culpepper.

With a start, I realized it was not Surrey whom he stared at but me.

"Joanna Stafford, help me—can you not help me?" Hungerford wailed. "Only you can save me now. Come closer, I beg you."

28

As all heads turned in my direction, Geoffrey, distressed, said, "Why does this man cry for you? In the name of the Virgin, what does he expect *you* to do?"

"Prayer," I said. "Sir Walter Hungerford needs me to say the Dominican blessing. As I did for Baron Montagu. That is why I am here."

"You can pray from back here," said Geoffrey. "You should not be any closer to the scaffold."

I glanced at Surrey's pleading eyes and said, "I'm sorry, but I must do this."

"Mistress Joanna, no," pleaded Master Hans Holbein.

I turned away from them and took a step toward the scaffold. I realized I was too far back for Sir Walter Hungerford to hear me, that is why he begged me to get closer.

But I was so terrified of the scaffold that I couldn't move. It was as if an invisible barrier pushed me back. Every spectator on this side of the platform stared at me; Sir Walter Hungerford stood atop it, his arms quivering at his sides. Desperate and waiting.

It took every scrap of willpower to force my right leg to move, and then my left. *Forward*, I prayed. *Mother, Mary of God, help me forward.*

The men in front of me silently shuffled back to afford me a path to the scaffold. Some stared at me, uncomprehending.

I made it ten more steps and then stopped. A repugnant odor wafted from the scaffold—rotted wood and dirt and sweat, and much worse. There was the sickly sweet smell of blood and the horror of a man's loosened bowels.

"May God the Father bless us," I said, but my voice was raspy and broken. I coughed and then forced myself to continue: "May God the Son heal us. May the Holy Spirit enlighten us and give us eyes to see with, ears to hear with, and hands to do the word of God. Feet to walk with and a mouth to preach the word of Salvation with."

I glanced, self-consciously, to my left and caught the gaze of Eustace Chapuys, imperial ambassador. He was the one who had crossed himself at the beginning of Cromwell's speech. Behind him was Señor Hantaras.

I turned back to the scaffold. I was now near enough that Sir Walter looked down on me—and his lips moved.

"Agrippa, Agrippa, Agrippa," he said in a rushed chant.

I almost buckled. Did anyone else understand that he spoke a name—and know that it belonged to a German occultist?

Much louder, desperate to drown him out, I said, "And the angel of peace to watch over us and lead us at last, by Our Lord's gift, to the Kingdom."

When he realized I'd come to the end, Hungerford's mouth fell open and he stiffened. At that moment, two men leaped forward and pulled him back toward the center of the platform. One kicked in his knees from behind so that Hungerford slammed down, on his knees, in front of the block. Another pushed his head onto the block. Sir Walter would not be given the chance to say last words.

A hand gently but firmly pulled me away, back to where I'd stood. "That's enough, Joanna, that's enough, shhhhh," Geoffrey said, as if he were soothing a skittish horse. I couldn't help but be grateful for his taking charge, for my feet were unsteady.

And so my back was turned when the ax crashed onto the neck of Sir Walter Hungerford. It took only one blow to do it. Presumably, the executioner had practiced enough on Cromwell to do it correctly on the next man.

When I returned to Hans Holbein, his head was bowed, hands

clasped, and he was weeping hopelessly. The Earl of Surrey was no longer in our group. I caught a glimpse of him racing away, toward Tower Street. There was no opportunity to discover if he had heard Hungerford chant Agrippa's name.

The spectators all silently headed toward Tower Street. There had been no effort to rescue Cromwell from death—it seemed to me ridiculous that anyone would dare such a thing. We who came to observe his and Hungerford's deaths did so for our own private reasons, and were now most anxious to get away, though none fled as openly as Surrey.

I was under no illusion that my prayer would be enough to spare Sir Walter Hungerford from God's judgment. As a novice, I had seen terrifying pictures in our priory's devotional books of Purgatory. Hungerford's many sins condemned him to a long and fiery time in that celestial prison. But now I must turn from the afterlife to the needs of the living.

Geoffrey had one arm around my waist, and I realized he had also linked arms with Master Holbein, who must be helped along. Although it was dangerous to show grief at the deaths of traitors, the royal artist could not conceal his feelings and was in great difficulty. The three of us shuffled forward, awkwardly.

What would Geoffrey and I do now? If there were enemies waiting for me west of Tower Hill, how could we anticipate their next move? I was so dazed, so horrified, by what I'd just seen that my mind could not form any sort of defensive plan, although I knew one was urgently needed.

As Geoffrey and I escorted the broken Hans Holbein away from Tower Hill, I felt no one's eyes seeking me out, sensed no imminent danger. The sun blazed from on high, meaning there was scant shade on the street. "If only I'd brought a flask—I'm a fool," said Geoffrey. "He is suffering from the heat and a drink could make all the difference." Holbein seized on that, pointing weakly at the Rose Tavern, halfway down Tower Street. "I am acquainted with . . . the tavern keeper," he said. "Could we not rest there a time?"

I nodded to Geoffrey. I was feeling light-headed myself, whether from the heat or what I'd endured. Although the tavern was no place for a woman, racing down the baking hot streets of London was impossible.

The Rose Tavern boasted long tables covered with clean cloth. The tavern keeper did indeed know Master Holbein, and he cleared a table in the corner for "the greatest artist in all of Christendom." The establishment was full, the men drinking with a grim purpose I saw more often in the faces of worshippers at Holy Trinity Church. Many were spectators from Tower Hill, their faces reddened with sun. That more than explained the sour spirit.

Tall cups were delivered to our corner, brimming with Lepe, a Spanish white wine fresh from the cellar. Holbein downed his drink in one continuous gulp, ignoring Geoffrey's warning to drink slowly. Wiping his mouth, he sat back in his chair and then, finally, shared with us his thoughts, in a low voice so that no stranger could hear him: "Make no mistake, my friends, in Germany I've seen bloodshed, terrible acts of violence. The Peasants' War swept across the country, with battles that you cannot even imagine. But here—you English— you make a terrible cold business of killing a man in the prime of his life. And you expect him to walk up to the ax, so nonchalant, and admit to crimes he is not guilty of?"

"You're referring to Cromwell's last words?" Geoffrey asked.

Holbein gestured for another wine.

"Yes, what was that all intended to mean?" Geoffrey said. "Cromwell's no Catholic."

Holbein's eyes filled with tears again. Geoffrey patted him on the back and I took one of his knobbly artist hands in mine.

"Afterward, to kill a madman like Hungerford—and why do it the same day as Cromwell?" Holbein said, genuinely baffled. "As hard as it is to watch someone spout lies to suit some strange custom, it's just as hard to look upon a man's pure terror, in the face of death."

Holbein downed his second cup of wine, once again ignoring Geoffrey's advice to drink slower. Only a few sips made my head swim; it was strong wine. I swallowed a chunk of brown bread, and that gave me a little strength.

"How did you do it, Mistress Joanna?" asked Holbein, turning to me. "How did you have the bravery to walk up to that scaffold, and say a prayer for a condemned man in front of so many others?"

Such attention to my actions made me uncomfortable.

"It is not bravery so much as fear," I sighed. "How could I face God our Maker if I had refused such a request—whether it was made to me as a representative of the Dominican Order or not, I had no choice but to comply."

Holbein shook his head. "Your humility does you justice, but such a reasoning is inadequate to the occasion. I've never known a woman before who would do a thing like that."

"There aren't any other women like Joanna," said Geoffrey. His voice was soft, and for a few seconds it was possible to accept the sentence as just another statement of fact, such as the sun shone bright or wine was made from grapes. But as the full import sank in, I felt a surge of happiness. He often seemed angry and suspicious with me, overly protective, just as I was wary and defensive with him. The trauma of Tower Hill stripped away our usual emotions and exposed what lay beneath, perhaps. But Geoffrey had made it clear that he no longer harbored love for me and I'd accepted that with relief, so why should I be happy to learn otherwise? I stole a glance at Hans Holbein. A smile played in the corner of his lips as he regarded us both, then an awkward silence settled on our table.

I shifted in my chair and made a show of craning my neck, as if something had caught my attention. That is when, incredibly, something did. A narrow door swung open to a side room and a serving-woman eased out. Behind her, before the door closed tight again, I glimpsed my cousin Henry Howard, the Earl of Surrey, sitting at a round table.

"Geoffrey, I must speak to my cousin," I said, rising.

"You cannot go anywhere else," he insisted, returning to his usual form. "I can't lose sight of you, Joanna."

I reassured him and then made my way to the room. My gentle rapping on the door called forth a loud "Be off with you," but I opened the door nonetheless.

"Ah, it's you—of course it's you," he said. "Come. Celebrate with me. There's enough for two."

I'd seen only brown bread on the long tables in the main tavern, but Surrey had in front of him a board of manchet and a plate of meats, as well as an apple neatly sliced, its edges just beginning to brown. The smell of wine hung in the air—not the Spanish white we drank but a rich Rhenish red, Surrey's favorite. A bottle of it stood in the center of the table and he poured a second goblet full with a flourish.

"It took much effort to bring down Cromwell," I said, sliding into a chair.

"It did indeed," he said. "Here's to a vanquished Cromwell and a Howard queen." He clinked my goblet in a toast before guzzling it like cheap ale.

I raised my goblet but could not bring myself to drink. As much damage as Cromwell did to the kingdom and to those I loved, I could not rejoice in his horrific death. Nor could I exult in Catherine's marriage, for it brought me nothing but dread.

"What do you make of Cromwell's claiming to be a Catholic at the end?" I asked.

Surrey waved his hand, dismissing the notion. "Cromwell was the most fanatical Reformer in the kingdom—those were the charges against him, not treason but sacramental heresy. He was just trying to wrangle some sort of lenient treatment for his son and nephew, who are defenseless now. Cromwell knows the kingdom will turn Catholic again with him gone and he wants to put them on the winning side."

"Have you seen any evidence of such a change in religion?" I asked.

"Not yet," Surrey admitted. "But it should come soon, my father and Bishop Gardiner are sure of it. Gardiner's expecting Robert Barnes to burn at the stake before the Feast of the Assumption of the Holy Virgin. And he also expects some of the prisoners who've been held for years because of obedience to Rome to be freed."

Surrey stuffed shiny chunks of duck meat into his mouth.

I said carefully, "Many take pleasure in Cromwell's downfall and perhaps many conspired at it, but the principal effort was made by your friend, Sir Walter Hungerford, as well as the principal sacrifice."

Surrey's hand dropped onto the table and the duck tumbled out, smearing his palm. "What do you mean?" he demanded, his voice belligerent.

Despite his height and sportsman's prowess, and his fame across the kingdom, I had never been intimidated by my cousin the earl, five years younger than myself. I leaned across the table and said, "I mean that some might say today's execution was the work of a covenant, three men who pledged to destroy Thomas Cromwell and made their way to the man Orobas, just after midnight on May Day, to accomplish it."

I half expected Surrey to explode, to flip over the table and bellow threats. He had more than his share of the Plantagenet temper. But instead he slunk back in his chair and clasped his hands in his lap like a frightened child.

"I must know who told you," he finally said. "Culpepper? I could see he had a sweetness for you."

"No," I said. "Thomas Culpepper did everything he could to drive me away. He told me nothing. I put it together myself, as others might be able to, Cousin. That is why you must tell me everything, and quickly. I want to help you. I am close to both of you—and I just prayed for Sir Walter Hungerford, as he said the name *Agrippa* over and over."

Surrey flinched as if I struck him.

"You didn't hear him say the name?" I asked.

My cousin buried his head in his hands. "No—no—no," he said.

My tone softening, I reached over to pat his head, those waves of auburn hair. "Quiet," I said. "You can't make a scene here. Just tell me what happened with Orobas—please."

"I can't," Surrey said, his voice still muffled.

"Oh, *why* can't you?" I asked, longing to shake him.

My cousin dropped his hands to scrutinize me and, after making some final calculation of my trustworthiness, said, "Because, Joanna, I wasn't there."

"But the three of you formed a covenant, and you went to Orobas. Do you deny it?"

Surrey drank deep from his goblet. "I was there—but only up to a point." He set down his wine and then, at last, he told me what happened.

"Yes, we swore that we would go to whatever lengths were necessary, even if the journey were to imperil our souls, to break the bond between the king and Cromwell. Hungerford knew of these men in the German lands who were familiar enough with the magical world—who had completed enough research of the ancient Greek texts, along with knowledge of the Jewish Cabbalah and Arabic practices—that they could summon certain powers strong enough to deliver us our result. Agrippa was the most knowledgeable of them all, but he died in 1534. Still, he wrote a series of books, three books that contained everything that he learned about the natural world, the celestial and the divine. The Antwerp publisher feared being burned for heresy, so he would only print twenty of the series and only for a great deal of money. Hungerford had the three—only God knows how he raised the gold to pay for it. But he was obsessed with finding them. It was known, here in London, how much he wanted those books."

"Yes," I sighed. "I gleaned that Sir Walter was obsessed with a dark world. But what about you? As long as I've known you, it's been poetry and revels and sporting and swords. Those are your pastimes. Why did you follow him down this path—why did you put belief in this man Agrippa?"

Surrey's long face grew even longer. True fear quivered there—something I never thought I'd see.

"I've seen the man Agrippa myself, Joanna," he said, glancing at the door, though it was too thick for anyone to hear through. "I know better than anyone in England what he can do."

I swallowed. "But I thought Agrippa was dead."

Surrey ran his hand through his hair. "I was traveling through France and Italy, just before the marriage to Frances that our parents arranged. I'd heard Erasmus was in the court of John George, elector of Saxony, and I was desperate to make his acquaintance. So I persuaded the men my father appointed to my service to take me to Saxony in the German lands. There I met the great Erasmus, yes, but there was another scholar in attendance. Heinrich Cornelius Agrippa. I should have turned away from him, for he was an arrogant man and did not hide his proclivities, but . . . I didn't."

"He is truly a scholar?" I asked, quite skeptical.

"They all are—there's a circle of learned Germans touched by magic. One, Paracelsus, is a physician trained at universities. The other, Faustus, a doctor of divinity."

I shuddered at the name of the man that Edmund went to see, the man whom Geoffrey would soon journey to see, in search of answers. Why did Edmund seek him out to begin with? He was no callow, restless youth seeking the excitement of forbidden knowledge.

"What happened in Saxony, Cousin?" I asked.

He shook his head. "Even to speak of it is dangerous—but all you need know, Joanna, is that Agrippa made someone . . . appear."

Chills raced up and down my arms in that stifling hot tavern room.

"Who?" I managed to ask.

"No, I truly can say no more. Only Sir Walter knows everything I saw that night, and he's dead. I was drunk and he got it out of me. So now it is only myself, and I shall keep it that way until I am in my grave."

"I cannot believe that you associated yourself with Sir Walter Hungerford, that you trusted such a man as him."

Surrey shook his head. "Don't believe all the charges, Joanna. He harbored a priest he saved from the Pilgrimage of Grace rebellion—that is true. And he was the kingdom's worst husband. But the claims of forced buggery? That's invented. It's a trick Cromwell played with Anne and George Boleyn, saying that they committed incest. It causes such revulsion that no one hesitates to believe the lesser charges. Cromwell's enemies played the trick back at him, to heap nefarious claims on Hungerford and then send him to the ax the same day. It lowered Cromwell."

And yet it was Thomas Cromwell who comforted Hungerford, when there was no possible other reason than humanity. How would I ever understand the king's men?

I pointed Surrey back to the conspiracy.

"What happened on May Day?" I asked.

With a deep sigh, Surrey continued. "The three books Agrippa wrote are about his ideas, his philosophies about natural magic, but they don't contain his deepest secrets. They don't tell you how to communicate with the other side, how to channel the forces that are beyond man's reach. Agrippa was not a man who always lived in the shadows. He taught at universities, he mastered six languages, he served the Emperor Charles's father as a soldier and, they say, as a master spy. Agrippa's secrets of ceremony—how to do such things as I saw in Saxony—are in a fourth book that the same printer produced. Well, not a book, but a grimoire."

"What is that?" I asked, not even wanting to repeat the strange word.

"A grimoire is a book of instruction," Surrey said. "It names the spirits, it explains how to do the necessary incantations and conjurations, to create the ancient formulas. It is"—Surrey swallowed—"the key. Some say that Agrippa himself did not write it, that others gathered the darkest secrets of all and turned them over to a printer in his name. Sir Walter was not able to purchase it along with the series of three books. The grimoires have gone underground. None of his inquiries led to anything. But Sir Walter learned several months ago that there are two Agrippa grimoires in England. It was quite a shock. One was in the possession of a necromancer who knew how to use it. He made a connection to someone who led him to the necromancer and—"

I held up my hand. "The connection is Lady Rochford and the necromancer is Orobas."

Surrey flinched. "How could you possibly know?"

"We each have our secrets, Cousin. Leave it at that. So you went to see him in his chamber near the Guildhall? The one deep below the earth, fashioned in an ancient Roman tomb?"

Wide-eyed, Surrey nodded.

"But why bring Thomas Culpepper into it? Surely Hungerford and you were enough for the task."

Surrey looked away from me, reddening with some emotion it took me a moment to identify. Then I had it: my cousin felt ashamed. He muttered, "We needed something of the king's, an article of clothing that had touched his body."

"And only a gentleman of the privy chamber could obtain it." Now it was my turn to bury my face in my hands. "Poor Culpepper. You made callous use of him."

"He wanted to be part of our covenant," said Surrey, defensive. "Thomas truly believes King Henry to be a good man, if only the influence of Cromwell could be removed."

I heard men calling out to one another in the tavern. Geoffrey must be growing impatient. I feared I was running out of time with Surrey—but I must learn all. Who knew when I would be able to coax so much from him again?

"What happened on May Day?" I asked again.

"We arrived at the appointed time; we paid Orobas. But he seemed different—a little fearful. Before he had been so sure of himself. Not now. The grimoire required much study, and diligent interpretation and translation. It isn't written in English, of course. But he swore he had mastered it and said that the ceremony to be performed was dangerous to all who witnessed it. That there would be lingering . . . effects."

The word hung in the air.

"What does that mean?" I asked.

"He was not specific. And while I was in the midst of conversation, I lost consciousness."

"You fainted?"

"No, Culpepper hit me! He knocked me unconscious so that I would be spared the dangers of the ceremony's effects. There was no need for three men, Orobas even said two were enough. Culpepper was determined to take the threat himself and spare me from it."

So that was why Surrey's head showed a bruise before the tournament began.

"Culpepper and Sir Walter Hungerford went forward," Surrey continued. "They roused me afterward. I was angry with them, but what was done was done. I don't know what occurred, whether there was a conjuring. Whether they wrote on the floor and made sacrifices. Nothing. All they would tell me was that a curse—a sort of hex—and been enacted. If it worked, the king would break with Cromwell finally and irrevocably."

My hand groped for the second goblet of wine. "I think I shall need this now," I whispered.

We each of us drank wine, but I felt no comfort from it, only a spreading fear. I fought back with reason.

"The king is a volatile man—that he should spurn Thomas Cromwell, is it really explainable only through magic and necromancy?"

"Come now, you know that the king relied on Cromwell for years, and commanded the arrest of anyone who Cromwell bid him to. And what more proof do you need that Hungerford lost his wits within hours of the ceremony?"

"Sir Walter was never a stable man," I argued. "And Thomas Culpepper? Do you see any sign of madness?"

"Not madness, but . . ." His voice trailed away.

"What? Please tell me."

"Culpepper has changed, Joanna."

I had to admit that Thomas Culpepper showed a coldness and a rudeness after May Day that I'd not seen before. Still, he had been distressed over my attack in London and told Geoffrey of the earlier attack. I remembered the lonely sight of him atop the gatehouse, watching me leave Whitehall. His altered temperament could be caused by the evils of the court—and the strain of Sir Walter Hungerford's arrest—rather than the forces of magic.

"Can you detail these changes?" I said.

Surrey said, "Thomas Culpepper was once a man of chivalry, gracious to all and especially honorable to women. Now he is swaggering and lewd. I've spoken to him of it, and he laughs at me. He's never done *that* before. Then, just a few weeks ago, he committed a crime that defies belief. I cannot even speak of it to you, no decent woman should hear the details."

Gripping the table with both hands, I said, "You must. He is my friend, he helped me in Whitehall. I can never thank him enough for it. No matter what the crime is, I can bear the hearing of it."

"Very well. One night Culpepper attacked a gamekeeper's wife. He ordered some ruffians he now travels with to hold her down. Afterward, her husband sought him out for justice, and Culpepper killed him."

I was torn between repulsion and disbelief.

"Don't say it could not have happened, for it did, Joanna. Everybody knows about it. He didn't even deny the crime. And the king forgave him. What does a gamekeeper's life matter—or his wife's virtue? The rape and murder didn't occur in the vicinity of the court, so the steward brought no formal charges."

Tears smarting in my eyes, I said, "And this is the man who is married to Catherine. Why did you let that marriage go forward? Your father used Catherine to dislodge Cromwell. But once he was arrested, why keep pushing her?"

"It was too late for anything else! King Henry is more besotted with Catherine than with any other woman he's married or bedded. More than even Anne Boleyn. Catherine has given him back his youth, he proclaims."

I was not certain that their May Day covenant had anything to do with Cromwell's arrest and death. But for Culpepper to commit such acts—what other explanation was possible? I took a deep breath, and then another. "Listen to me. We shall go, the two of us, to see Orobas. If it is difficult to find him, we will force Lady Rochford to help. There may be a way to reverse what has been done to Culpepper and we will find it."

Surrey smiled sadly. "You are quick, Joanna. It took me days to think of that. And it is possible that the grimoire does possess some sort of incantation, a ceremony to do just that, to reverse the effects and restore the Thomas Culpepper we once knew."

I stood up. "Then let's go. We must accomplish this at once. I leave England in a few weeks."

"No, Joanna."

"No?" I turned on him in outrage. "After what Culpepper did for you, you won't risk your safety to help him?"

My cousin slammed his fist on the table. "Of course I would! I'd do anything. But we can't go to Orobas, because there is no more Orobas, Joanna. He's dead."

I sank back into the chair.

"Dead? How?"

"Suicide. He hanged himself ten days ago."

I made the sign of the cross. "May God have mercy on his soul."

"That is doubtful, for you know how God punishes suicides." Surrey's words were becoming slurred. I had lost track of how much wine he'd consumed.

"Was it because of your ceremony?" I asked.

"No one knows. He said nothing to anyone and left no letter."

I shuddered at the memory of Orobas, a man who trafficked in the blackest arts known to man. Now, for taking his life, he was doubly damned.

"What about Agrippa's grimoire?" I asked. "If we could find someone else to study it—"

"Clever Joanna again. But that is not possible. Before he killed himself, Orobas burned it. He could have sold it for a fortune, but he burned it, along with all of his other books of magic and necromancy."

"You're sure?"

"I found a woman named Hagar who associated with him; whether she was his common-law wife or his servant or his familiar, who could tell? But I paid her an enormous bribe and she showed me the evidence. I recognized the grimoire from its cover. Everything else was ashes."

"But you said there was a second grimoire in England."

"Yes, but the woman didn't know who might have it. She truly didn't. I could tell she would have happily betrayed anyone for more gold. All she could tell me was that Orobas once said the second grimoire was in the possession of a man of importance."

"Then you must find it."

"Yes, Joanna, that should be a simple matter. Perhaps at the next banquet I'll stand up and ask, 'Who among you keeps in secret a heretical text that contains incantations and spells?'"

Tears of frustration stung my eyes.

Surrey said, "So now you understand my suffering. And you will suffer with me, Joanna. There's nothing we can do but see it all out. It's like a play that we have only the first pages for. The lives of Culpepper, myself, King Henry, Catherine, you, and that constable who follows you everywhere, all of us—we must wait and see what happens when the play ends."

29

When Geoffrey and I booked passage on a Flemish ship bound for Antwerp, we assumed that the rest of the people on board would be strangers. But a friend decided to join us: Master Hans Holbein.

He did not form his decision immediately. When I emerged from Surrey's room, I found the painter inebriated. He wailed in German, half song, half lament. The worried tavern keeper lent us his wagon and three workers to take Holbein to his home on London Bridge. By that time, it was dusk and a sobering Holbein begged us to share his quarters for the night. After some deliberation, Geoffrey agreed, for otherwise we would not reach Dartford until after sunset, a dangerous proposition.

Sleep was impossible. A nightmare filled with blood and shrieking bedeviled me. I wrenched myself free of it to sit up in the bed, breathless, while I struggled to figure out where I was. After I grasped that I occupied a room in the home of Master Holbein, my heartbeat slowed.

I had no idea of the hour, only that it was blackest night. Feeling unbearably restless, I crept to the door and opened it an inch. My room was at one end of the long, narrow parlor. At the other, a candle burned by the door leading to the stairs. Geoffrey sat next to it, his makeshift bed untouched. He was still and alert. The flickering of the candle picked up a shiny gray sliver in his hand. I realized he held a knife. Geoffrey was keeping watch, afraid for my life.

Part of me wanted to rush out of this room, dressed in only the shift I wore under my kirtle and bodice. My fingers trembled on the door. Those words Geoffrey said at the Rose Tavern—it was a declaration that roused some feeling in me I didn't want to have. But then I remembered Surrey saying, *The constable that follows you everywhere*—I hated that my cousin described him so. I didn't want to keep taking advantage of Geoffrey. Traveling together, the two of us—it was wrong. There must be another way to find Edmund while ensuring my safety. I turned and crept back into the bed. I would re-open the discussion tomorrow, I decided.

But when we gathered again to break our fast, Hans Holbein announced he would join us. "I've been needed by my wife and friends in Augsburg for far too long," he said. "I shall complete my portrait of Queen Catherine in the next two weeks in time to travel."

What a jolt that was—"Queen Catherine."

Geoffrey responded with enthusiasm to Holbein's announcement. I suspected that he, too, welcomed the presence of another person, so that we would not travel as, inevitably, a couple. Holbein would be able to accompany Geoffrey through the German lands, which solved many a problem.

Although nothing out of the ordinary happened the night before, Geoffrey told me as we left Master Holbein's that he would take no chances. This time, we'd hire horses to ride the other direction, through the heart of London, and then circle around to Dartford. Wearily, I agreed.

Thus I bore witness to something as terrifying as what I'd witnessed on Tower Hill—and more heartbreaking.

The ride through London seemed like any other until we found ourselves on a narrow, shaded street opening to a much wider one up ahead, mobbed with people waiting for something—or someone. They were packed so tight we'd not be able to ride through.

"We can turn around, or wait for the crowd to dissipate and continue this way," Geoffrey said.

"Let's wait and rest our horses," I said. "At least they will have respite from the sun."

We dismounted and waited for whatever was expected to pass. It did not take long. A ripple of shouting grew louder—jeers mixed with cheers. I felt uneasy. This was no diversionary tactic. No one could herd hundreds of unruly Londoners onto a street with that as motive. But this was beginning to remind me of the spirit of the mob at Smithfield, as the soldiers dragged Margaret to the stake for burning.

"I think we should leave now," I said to Geoffrey. Nodding, he organized our mounts.

We got back on our horses, but that, tragically, afforded me a clear view of the middle of the street over the heads of the mob. If we'd stayed where we were, at the back of the crowd, I'd not have seen anything.

Down the middle of the street a team of horses pulled a hurdle. I was right—these Londoners gathered to witness a procession to an execution. But it was not just one person strapped to the board. No, it was two men, wearing rags, chained side by side. One of them shouted something but the mob screamed so vehemently, I could not make it out. The other, a much older man, had his eyes shut tight, his lips moving.

I sat on my horse, rigid, disbelieving, while Geoffrey spoke to a dark-haired man standing nearby.

"Geoffrey," I said, but he could not hear me in this cacophony. He was too busy taking in what the dark-haired man told him.

The crowd's cheers grew louder. I did not understand it—the pair of prisoners had passed. Why did they applaud now? Part of me wanted to kick my horse and ride away without seeing the cause of renewed excitement. But the devil entered into me—what other explanation could exist for why I remained to gawk down the street, like any other hard, pitiless Londoner?

I saw, and what I saw defied understanding. A second team of horses pulled a hurdle of two men bound together; behind them appeared a *third*.

Seized with panic, I kicked my horse to ride away. There was no choice. I had to get far, far away from this parade of prisoners.

By the time I reached the opposite end of the street, Geoffrey caught up with me. He did not chastise me for bolting. He, too, looked shaken.

"Tell me," I said.

"You may not be able to bear it, Joanna."

I laughed, a mirthless sound. "If you knew how much I have borne already . . ." I forced myself to stop. That was a dangerous path to take. "Please tell me about those prisoners, Geoffrey."

"The soldiers are taking six condemned men to Smithfield."

"Yes, I knew it was Smithfield," I moaned. "It had the same spirit as Margaret's death. You were there, Geoffrey. You remember. Is that what is to take place—will they be burned?"

Geoffrey hesitated, choosing his words.

"Half will be burned—and half will be hanged, drawn, and quartered."

I stared at him, uncomprehending.

"The man who was shouting, who came first, is Doctor Robert Barnes, a Lutheran ally of Cromwell's. He will be burned today for heresy. But the man bound next to him, his eyes shut, is Richard Featherston, he was chaplain to Catherine of Aragon and a tutor to her daughter, the Lady Mary. He will be hanged, drawn, and quartered as a traitor who serves the pope in Rome over his king. The three Lutherans will be burned while the three Catholics are hanged and then torn to pieces."

So King Henry VIII showed his true heart. He did not favor the Catholics, nor did he follow the Lutherans. It was impossible to understand him, to live safely in his kingdom. The removal of Cromwell had not made him a better man. There was something twisted—even diseased—in a mind that would command that the condemned be paired as opposites on the hurdles. How foolish Bishop Gardiner and the Howards were to think they could predict what King Henry would do—or control his actions.

"We need to return to Dartford as soon as possible—by whatever way you think safest," I said. "And then we must leave England. Geoffrey, I don't know if I will ever want to come back."

They were words spoken in distress, but in the weeks leading up to our departure by ship, I did not come to feel differently. All that I had experienced since coming to Whitehall in April—in addition to all that passed before—fired within me a deep distaste for the king whose household I had officially entered as tapestry mistress. The final arrangements for my appointment were made with the keeper of the king's wardrobe. After a visit of up to six months to Brussels, I would take up my duties at court. The week before we were to set sail, a royal messenger arrived with a fat purse of coins—the first install-ment of my wages. Standing in the parlor, holding the purse, I felt unclean.

I will use this money to find Edmund, I vowed.

I did not know what to say to Catherine, child bride to a mon-ster. I could not bring myself to send her anything besides a short and stilted letter of congratulations. She did not reply; no doubt her life was too full of demands to take much notice of my quietude.

It took some doing, but I persuaded the sisters of Dartford Priory who lived in community to accept payment for their labor in weaving *The Sorrow of Niobe*. Sir Andrew Windsor had suggested that the male workers at the Great Wardrobe weave the tapestry in my absence, but I did not know the abilities of these men. I did have every confidence in the women of the priory. They had begun the work with me, and I was well pleased. I made arrangements for the loom and silks and the drawing to be transported to their farm. I would someday finish it personally, using the chalk drawing of Catherine Howard as model for the face of Niobe. But it was hard to picture myself returning.

Geoffrey and I took a wagon to Gravesend that late August morning. My packed belongings filled a large box; Geoffrey brought one satchel. As he pointed out, I'd need to live in comfort in Brussels while he traveled far.

And so there was every reason to feel relief and some anticipa-tion when setting eyes on our ship, anchored at Gravesend. But I didn't. The ship off Gravesend was shadowed for me. What was I doing, making such a trip? How much of the reason was fear for Edmund and how much fear for myself?

A smiling Master Hans Holbein waited for us at the wharf, with unusual-looking groups of people clustered on either side of him. There was Doctor Harst, the ambassador to Cleves, and a quartet of women. I knew one of them: Mother Lowe, of middle years and stout. She had been in charge of the queen's maids. Another woman was of her years but thinner and well dressed. Rounding out the group were two girls who looked about seventeen.

We soon learned that Doctor Harst had made the travel arrangements for the German women and escorted them to the boat to bid farewell. To the surprise of all people I knew, Anne of Cleves had decided to stay in England after the divorce. King Henry announced that if she remained in his kingdom, she was to be treated as his sister, with houses and income, and she'd agreed. But her household could not be as large as a queen's, and so Mother Lowe and these other three attendants returned to Cleves.

On Holbein's other side, a greater distance away, stood a different kind of group: a woman wearing a long, hooded light-gray cape leaned on a cane. I recognized it as the clothing of the blind. A young man hovered at her side, with a servant besides. Holbein told us that the woman, Mistress Collins, was indeed blind and in weak health, and her son had booked passage for her to stay with another son living in Antwerp and take some new cures in Flanders.

There were some fifty passengers in all, and we boarded in an orderly fashion. Doctor Harst waved goodbye to the German women—he was set to remain in England, and continue to look out for the interests of Anne of Cleves. The blind woman's son and servant went further, helping her on board and settling her in her cabin below, and then rowing back to shore.

The passengers milled about the deck, excited. It was a fine ship. The voyage to Antwerp could take anywhere from two days to a week, depending on the wind and weather.

After a bit, Geoffrey took me aside and said, "There's a problem for you. Only one small cabin was set aside for women passengers, and originally that was to be occupied by only you and Mistress Collins. The German women are a late addition, and no doubt the captain was put under pressure to take them. The ship is full and they can't sleep among the men, obviously, so you'll be packed in very tight in that room."

I shrugged. "It doesn't matter to me," I said. "But there is something I need to speak of with you."

"Something's wrong?"

"Not necessarily." I took a breath. "Have you considered the possibility that someone was put on the ship to hurt me?"

Frowning, Geoffrey said, "Your enemy shows resourcefulness, but I think that is going very far. Have you had any feelings of being watched, on the wharf or here on the ship, any hint that you are in danger?"

"None," I admitted.

After a moment, Geoffrey said, "Of course I will take precautions. Do you have any thoughts on where the threat could present?"

Speaking carefully, I said, "Perhaps you could make sure that there is no one hiding aboard the ship. I cannot think that anyone who booked passage is a threat, but if there were a stowaway . . ."

"It will be done," Geoffrey said.

30

The ship set sail, all of the passengers gathered along the side to watch the shore ease away. The winds did not blow as strong as they had when I left England with Jacquard last year. The sails billowed rather than snapped.

Hans Holbein was in his element, striding about the ship, friendly to all, speaking English to us and German to the former ladies of Anne of Cleves. "What I should be doing is teaching *you* German," he said to Geoffrey. "You will find few English speakers on your journey to Salzburg. Some of the men speak French; and some of the clerks and priests, what is left of them, speak Latin. No woman of the German lands speaks anything but German."

Geoffrey replied, "I can hold my own with French and with Latin, and I don't expect I will be needing to communicate with the ladies. It's not that kind of trip."

Holbein erupted into laughter, clapping Geoffrey on the back; both of them cast apologetic looks my way for enjoying a joke that I might deem rude.

Their joking did not offend me in the least, for I had another matter on my mind. I continued to do battle with feelings of unease. Geoffrey told me the second morning aboard that he'd inspected the ship from bow to steer, searching every corner, and found no stowaways. He'd even concocted an excuse to speak with the captain about the passengers in his capacity as constable, and he learned all were vetted to some degree and considered utterly respectable.

But I could not relax. I slept only a few hours in the women's

cabin, where we were indeed packed as tightly as fish boxed for market. My place was against one side, the German women slept in the
middle, and Mistress Collins rested on the far side. Everyone was
careful of her; and in her broken English, Mother Lowe often asked
if the blind woman needed anything: food, drink, assistance to the
stool closet. Anything.

"No, I am fine, but thank you," Mistress Collins would say in her
faint, low voice. She didn't want anyone to be bothered; I saw her
eyes were bandaged within her hood, and felt sorry for her plight.

The second day the winds did not pick up sufficiently to convey
us to Antwerp by evening, and the captain put out the word that it
could require three or even four days to reach our port.

"I don't mind, for I quite enjoy this," said Geoffrey, pointing at
the aquamarine waves foaming and cresting. "It's so . . . open."

He turned to lean backward onto the railing of the ship, sliding
his arms out on either side. Closing his eyes, his lips parted, Geoffrey
tilted his face up, toward the sun, as if trying to eat up its rays. I had
never seen him like this before. There was something . . . intimate
about his openness, and I had to look away, anywhere, toward the
mainland that had not yet materialized.

Later Hans Holbein entertained us, beginning with fond
memories of his youth in Augsburg and spreading to the fantastical children's stories of his homeland. We three sat on boxes at the
bow of the ship sailing to Antwerp and heard about a witch turning
a boy into a fish and his sister into a lamb, of a frog who emerged
from deep in a well to bully a princess before becoming a handsome
prince, of a servant who cut off a piece of a king's snake and could
then understand the thoughts of the animals, the ravens, and even
the fishes, of a wolf pounding on the door of a cottage to entice the
children to come out to be eaten.

"There is an element of transformation in most of your stories,"
I said.

Our ship sailed east, and the sun lowering behind us cast an
orange glow on Master Holbein's face as he smiled, and tugged his

beard, and said, "It's appealing, isn't it, Mistress Joanna, the possibility of transformation?"

"I suppose so," I said, unsure of his meaning.

"For the man Geoffrey seeks, Paracelsus, transformation is a subject of fascination, I believe," Holbein said. "He studies the properties of many things, some say because he is nothing but a money-seeking alchemist. But I think he studies the essence of men, of defining who we are. There is something he is fond of saying that was repeated to me." The artist paused to remember the exact words. "'Let no man belong to another who can belong to himself.'"

Geoffrey asked, intent, "Do you think that a man would have sought out Paracelsus because he did not know his own essence?"

"It's possible," said Holbein. "But if that were the case with your Edmund Sommerville, I can't say. I never met him."

Hearing those words of Paracelsus, I should have instantly recognized whether they'd have some meaning for Edmund, but I felt only confusion. I did know that while Edmund trusted profoundly in God, at times he despised himself, what he perceived as his own weaknesses. A sadness rose in me.

I turned to Master Holbein and said, "The stories enchant me, but there is something that is a little horrible about them, too."

"Yes—yes," he chuckled. "You begin to understand the German temperament, what our essence is, and why we love our poetry and magic more than any other people in Christendom."

I suppressed a shudder at the word *magic*, for it brought to mind a forbidden grimoire and a rite that drove one man mad and a second to violence, and the necromancer himself to suicide.

Geoffrey said, "You make it sound a magical land, Holbein, but we know there is another side. You spoke of it yourself, that day at the Rose Tavern, of the bloodshed of the German wars."

The artist went very quiet and then said, "I did not personally witness a battle, none took place near Basel, where I lived in 1525, but the Peasants' War decimated the German lands, and all who survived it were deeply changed by it."

"'All who survived,'" Geoffrey repeated. "I have heard some un-believable numbers of how many were killed in the Peasants' War."

"Two hundred thousand died—and you can believe that," said Hans Holbein.

"But that number is extraordinary," protested Geoffrey. "And it was all because the people were thrown into a fervor by Martin Luther?"

"You English blame all ills on Luther, as if he were a fiend from hell with powers beyond any man's," scoffed Holbein. "Luther distanced himself from the peasants, he even appealed to the princes to punish them."

I was struck by how Holbein now distanced himself from *us*, even though he'd lived in England for years and years. Drawing closer to his homeland seemed to increase his ancestral pride. "It was the injustice, the starvation and misery, that the peasants suffered for centuries that caused them to take up arms," explained Master Holbein. "It's true that Martin Luther defying the pope opened everyone's eyes to the possibilities of freedom, but the causes of that war belong not in Rome but with the princes and the dukes and the margraves and the knights and the abbots and the bishops—all those who oppressed the common people. Before the war was over, they learned to their great cost that all are equal in the eyes of God."

"And they're equal in death, too," I said. "Isn't that why you created the woodcuts for *The Dance of Death*?"

Holbein nodded, but winced a little. The topic of that book was still troubling to him.

Geoffrey said, "One thing I have never understood is how the peasant armies were defeated when they possessed far superior numbers."

"Ah, but you know so little of the German princes and dukes," exclaimed Holbein. "They've spent generations fighting one another for land and titles, but when a cause unites them, such as marauding armies of peasants, they take all of their military strength and their wealth and become an unbelievable force. The prince elector of the

Palatine and his clan were relentless. The Duke of Bavaria, now that he no longer feuds with the House of Hapsburg, is a man who could take on the armies of France and England. The peasants were no match."

"I've seen hunger and poverty and I hate them," said Geoffrey. "But there must be law of the land, or else what will become of us as civilized men?"

Holbein smiled. "Spoken like a true constable," he said, but in a more amiable tone. His rant was over. "One thing it is very important for you to learn, so that you will come to no harm in your journey, is that there is no one law in the German lands. Each kingdom, each dukedom, each principality, has its own laws. It's easy to make mistakes, but those mistakes can be hard to recover from."

Holbein stood and stretched. "Ah, enough of my frightening you. I have hope, too. Art can be the medium to express, reveal, break down, and rebuild the world. We may be on the way to a new and higher form of life. Let us watch the sun disappear. There's nothing like watching it on a ship." We watched, transfixed, as that glowing ball of fire bobbled on the horizon, then slipped behind it.

Holbein bade us good night, but Geoffrey said he would enjoy the open air as long as possible. I wanted to stay with him, to try to enjoy it, too.

For a long time, we didn't speak, just watched the sky darken slowly, and then, one by one, the stars emerge. The moon, unshrouded by clouds, glowed bright. No one else was above board except for the man steering the ship on the deck, and he wouldn't have been able to see us at all should we move a bit closer to the door leading to the cabins.

It was a beautiful evening, but I couldn't stop thinking about what Hans Holbein had said. The journey to Salzburg sounded more difficult than I'd imagined.

"Geoffrey," I said, "why do you want to find Edmund?"

I waited for him to launch into his usual cryptic explanation, or to refuse to answer. But this time, with the moonlight bathing his face, Geoffrey gave his true reasons.

"I came to believe, after Beatrice and the baby died, that I was cursed, Joanna. I mean, not the sort of curse inflicted by a witch or seer but something I had done. What crime did I commit that would make God take away a young woman's life so cruelly? And one night, I knew: it was what I did in Holy Trinity Church that day, when I said that you and Edmund couldn't be married, that must be the cause. John Cheke is right—Parliament's bill had not been enacted yet, and you should have gone forward and wed. Afterward, there might have been permission granted, as with John and Agatha Gwinn. But I was unable to overcome my jealousy and I put a stop to it, as the constable of Dartford. I believe, in my heart, that I blighted all four of our lives that day. I didn't know about Sommerville's addiction, that he would react in such a manner after our fight. I didn't foresee his disappearance."

How guilt and sorrow over Edmund blighted all of our lives.

Geoffrey looked at me, gauging my reaction. Whatever he saw gave him the strength to push on. "Joanna, I had no inkling that your ruined marriage would set you on the path it did, committing acts I can only imagine since you won't confide in me. Beatrice paid the price of my pride, and our child. It caused me unbearable pain, until I came upon the idea that if I found Edmund in Europe, brought him back, restored his life somehow, that I could find . . . forgiveness. And no one knows which way the king will go—he could easily reverse those laws forbidding those who've taken vows of celibacy to marry. You could still be Edmund's wife."

My heart swelled as I looked at Geoffrey—I felt sadness, and admiration, yes, but something else, too.

What if I don't want to be Edmund's wife any longer?

I wanted to say it, but I couldn't. Not after he had spoken so movingly of Beatrice and all of our losses.

"So it's a vow of sorts to do this—that is what led you to go to John Cheke and begin your inquiries?" I asked carefully.

"Yes, I've come to think of it as a covenant I've made with myself," Geoffrey said.

I shrank from him, grasping the railing of the boat. I couldn't believe I'd heard that word from his lips. Yet it was a word most benign. It was Hungerford who'd turned into something frightening.

"What's wrong, Joanna?" he said.

"Nothing—nothing," I insisted. "I am just surprised by learning this."

He nodded and said, "I think enough has been said for one night. Let me take you below to your cabin."

The thought of that stifling hot, crowded room, with its lack of privacy, repelled me. I needed more time to calm myself. It had been only a coincidence that the same word was used by Surrey, Culpepper, and Hungerford. That was it.

"May I have a few minutes here, alone?" I asked. "I will follow you soon enough."

Geoffrey hesitated, glancing up at the man at the ship's wheel on the upper deck. "Very well, you seem safe enough. But I will come back for you myself. I'll find something to drink first."

After he'd left, I folded my arms and leaned down on the railing, hoping that a few drops of sea spray would fly high enough to cool my face. I needed something to help me order my thoughts and feelings on what I'd just learned.

No more than a moment had passed when I heard a soft step behind me.

"That wasn't very long," I said, smiling a little, and turned around.

There was no Geoffrey. My body froze against the railing as a tall white form floated toward me—resembling some sort of spirit. I opened my mouth to cry out but was too frightened to make a sound.

The spirit was no more than six feet away, hovering, when I recognized the light gray cloak of Mistress Collins. For a few seconds I felt relief, but then spreading confusion. How was she able to walk toward me unaided when she couldn't see?

She came forward a few more steps, and raised an object, swiftly, before darting all the way to my side. A long silver knife quivered at my throat.

"Make a sound and I'll kill you," she said, but her voice had changed. It was stronger, and much lower. Her eyes were no longer bandaged; they glittered deep within her hood.

My throat burned where the knife pierced. With her left hand, she seized my arm and began to pull me closer to the cabin entrance, to the place where the man at the wheel couldn't see. This was no blind, old woman, but a strong and determined assassin.

"When attacked, don't submit." I remembered Jacquard's teaching as if he were whispering in my ear. "Your assailant is counting on you to go limp from shock and fear. Do the opposite."

She's pulling me to a place where she can kill me unseen.

That realization shot through me, and with it, the determination to use one of Jacquard's exercises to save my life.

My left hand was not my lead, but I used it to stick two of my fingers into the woman's eyes as hard as I could. I felt bone and something wet.

"Joanna!" someone shouted behind me. It was Geoffrey. But my focus was on getting away from Mistress Collins, who had let go of my arm, howling in pain and slashing the knife in the air in desperate arcs but not stabbing me because I had scrambled away from her.

"What's happening down there?" called out the man on the deck above.

My attacker clutched her knife, cupping the left eye, which seemed to be causing most of the pain.

"Get behind me, Joanna," ordered Geoffrey, and I did so, as he pulled out his own knife and pointed it at my attacker. "You. Come with me—now. We're going to see the captain."

She didn't move toward Geoffrey. Instead she pulled down her hood and lowered her hand from her eye.

"Mother Mary," I gasped.

This was no woman. I looked on the cropped brown hair of a man of medium height and slender build. A thin line of blood trickled from the eye I wounded.

His mouth quivered in the bright moonlight and, turning to me, he said, "Welcome to the Palace of Whitehall, Mistress Stafford."

I flinched as if he struck me. I knew that voice and, staring at him, I knew the man. He was the page who escorted me that first day at Whitehall. No beard now—but it was him.

He tossed his knife away, groped for the top of the railing, pulled himself up, and paused for a second, straddling it in that long gray cloak of a blind woman. A truly bizarre sight.

"Christ's blood!" Geoffrey grunted, springing forward, hands outstretched. But he wasn't fast enough. With one final determined heave, the man jumped overboard and disappeared into the dark sea.

31

Geoffrey didn't seem angry with me on the ship. No time for it. There was the shock of what happened and then questions to be answered. The ship's captain turned out to be terrified of scandal and determined to keep it from the passengers that a man, dressed as a blind old woman, tried to stab a passenger. "No one will ever book passage on a ship of mine again," he said, wiping his face.

The captain later knocked on the door of the women's cabin and told the German women that Mistress Collins had fallen ill and was removed for the night. The next morning, her condition was publicly changed to fatal. Everyone was told Mistress Collins had died in the night and been buried at sea, as regulations required. Mother Lowe and the others expressed the customary amount of regret for a woman they had known, slightly, for two days.

The captain put more effort into concocting a story to explain the disappearing passenger than looking into the crime itself: "A madman—how else can anyone explain such actions?" he said, throwing up his hands.

Geoffrey withdrew into silence, for he knew, as well as I did, that the man who threw himself off the boat was not mad. Quite the opposite. The planning, the cunning, the ability to anticipate and improvise—these were all indications of sanity and intelligence. Geoffrey asked me if he was the same man who attacked me on my first day at Whitehall, and I said yes. This attack was even more audacious than the others, and revealed, as Geoffrey had pointed out before, the presence of resources. Of men. It was not a single person; far from it.

It's only a matter of time before they succeed. That is what ran through my mind that sleepless night, lying rigid and terrified in the cabin, made slightly more spacious by the absence of "Mistress Collins," now floating lifeless in the sea.

I felt profound gratitude for the presence of Mother Lowe and the three other Germans. If it weren't for them, I would have been alone with my killer that first night, a prospect that was unbearable. To have gone to sleep, unknowing, beside that vicious predator? It made my breath catch in my lungs. And yet he was just a tool. Who was behind this, who would pursue me so relentlessly? Bishop Gardiner had placed a stowaway on board the last time, to watch me. But not to kill me.

It was close to dawn when the realization crept over me that there was something about the character of this attack that seemed familiar. I'd also felt that in the litter being conveyed to Dartford but attributed the sensation to fever. I knew that a disguise of an old blind woman had been used before in some way that I'd not personally witnessed but knew of nonetheless. With a shudder, I remembered: At Dartford Priory, when I was a novice, I'd heard that after the infamous Sack of Rome in 1527, the pope escaped from the Castel Sant'Angelo by use of disguise. One day Pope Clement VII walked out of the castle, in the clothes of a peddler, some say. But others say he was dressed as an old blind woman.

As the water lapped against the side, and the oblivious women snored in the darkness of our swaying cabin, I tried to put a name to this hunt for my life. There was something significant about the choice of disguise of a desperate pope, but I couldn't, try as I might, push my way through to a conclusion. I would bring this nagging sense of familiarity to Geoffrey. Together we could find answers.

That day, the third day, our ship reached Antwerp, one of at least fifty to arrive during the daylight hours. I tried to force myself to act in a normal fashion. I did not want Master Holbein, or anyone else, to know what happened.

As we walked through the city, it seemed even more prosperous than when I'd seen it a year before—the flat, tidy streets teemed with hundreds of smiling, laughing tradespeople. Nothing impeded the flow of goods to the center of commerce for all of northern Europe.

Master Holbein knew of a respectable inn, favored by many English wool merchants, that let rooms for a short time. The plan was to rest overnight and then continue on to Brussels, a three-day ride on horseback. Geoffrey made sure the lock on my door was a good one.

Exhaustion captured me, and I slept deeply the first night in Antwerp. I knew nothing until I heard a pounding on the door. I opened my eyes to full daylight.

"Joanna, dress yourself," Geoffrey shouted on the other side of the door. "Joanna—hurry!"

In a panic, I threw on a bodice and kirtle and unlocked the door. Geoffrey pushed it open with the palm of his hand, and stormed inside my room, his face twisted with fury.

"Do you know what this is?" he asked, shoving a small vial in my face. It contained a deep red powder.

"No," I said. "Why are you upset?"

"This was in the box of the man who tried to kill you, along with a change of clothes, rope, a map of Antwerp and a sizable amount of money. I took the vial to an apothecary and he analyzed it. This is poison, Joanna. Slow-acting poison that is of the highest quality in Christendom—or the worst quality, depending on how you look at it. I had to buy the apothecary's silence. I think he wanted to send for the magistrate after looking at this, he was so alarmed. He might still do so."

I struggled to take it in. "So I was to be poisoned, rather than stabbed and thrown overboard?"

"Well, that would have been the most intelligent way, should your assassin wish to evade suspicion. But once the other women were put in your cabin and he lost direct contact to you, he had to improvise."

"That's why he decided to stab me."

"Yes, and then no doubt throw you overboard. He had to silence you first so you wouldn't scream and then hope no one heard the splash."

Frightened, I tried to back away. But Geoffrey wouldn't allow it. He seized me by the shoulders, and shook me.

"What do you know—what do you know?" he demanded.

"Know what?" I shouted.

"Don't parry with me, Joanna. You know something so danger-ous—or you've betrayed someone so powerful— that there's a plot to kill you the likes of which I have never seen before, never heard of before in my nine years as a constable. But you won't tell me what you've done. I have to try to protect you without full knowl-edge. It's like fighting with both arms tied behind my back. And what an opponent! The person behind it all is so formidable that an operative would throw himself into the sea rather than risk betray-ing him."

I twisted out of his grip. How could I tell Geoffrey all that I knew, of the truth about the prophecy, the plan to kill Henry VIII that I was at the heart of? Or the more recent treasonous plot to destroy Cromwell, using the dark arts of magic? Such knowledge would put him at risk as much as me—more so, if he went to the English authorities, as I feared he would feel compelled to do.

"Who trained you?" he said, his voice as hard as steel.

How did he know about Jacquard Rolin?

"Train me to do what?" I threw back at him.

"To stick your fingers in a man's eyes. It's not what you learned in the priory, is it, Joanna? And when I first knew you—and I saw you in some terrible spots, too—you never defended yourself in such a way. But something happened to you after Edmund left England. Who did you spend time with? And why?"

Geoffrey was closer to the truth than he'd ever come before. For a few wild seconds, I wanted to tell him everything. I wanted to share with him the frustrating feeling two nights past that I knew the person who wanted me dead. But was that the right thing to do for him? I was so distressed, tears smarted.

"I've opened myself to you—I've trusted you with my open heart, not just on the ship when I spoke of my covenant, but before that, several times," he said, anguished. "But not you. You have never put your trust in me, Joanna."

Now the tears poured from my eyes.

"I do trust you," I said.

Geoffrey laughed at me.

"Why don't you leave me to my fate then, Geoffrey?" I asked, a sob catching my voice.

"It is *tempting*," he roared. "But you won't have it that easy, Joanna. You're coming with me to Salzburg."

Wiping my eyes, I said, "No, I will stay in Brussels while you travel."

"You'd be dead in a month," he said. "As soon as word got back to England that the attempt failed, another plot would form, and without me in Brussels or any friend, they'd have a clear path."

"Then I will book passage to London. I'll return to Dartford alone. I've always been safe there."

"True. Though *why* you are safe there has kept me awake many a night, baffled. But you are part of the royal household now, Joanna. How could you possibly defy the commands of the king if he summoned you to court?"

I didn't have an answer for that.

"No, the only place that I am sure is safe for you is the wilds of Europe, which happens to be exactly where I am headed."

I gathered myself. "Very well, Geoffrey," I said, seeing no choice.

He turned and left, just as angry as when he arrived.

Incredibly, the day worsened. Master Holbein came to my room in the afternoon, with a grim Geoffrey in tow, to tell me the alarming news he'd picked up in Antwerp.

"The drought and terrible heat that struck England—it is much, much worse here," Holbein lamented. "No one can remember such heat. Harvests are ruined; the grapes on the vines are dead. The poorest people are expected to starve this winter in the Netherlands, Germany, France, Italy, the Swiss confederation, everywhere. There will be pestilence, they say. The Rhine is so low that boats cannot travel safely on it. They have closed the gates to Venice and other cities in Italy, so that strangers cannot enter and rob them of stored food. You can expect that to crop up everywhere in the next few months."

"What worse time could there be to travel?" Geoffrey muttered.

"*Mein Gott*, it could not possibly be worse," said Holbein. "But I must reach Basel, my wife and my children need me desperately. Geoffrey, be ready to deposit Mistress Joanna in Brussels and leave with me as swiftly as possible."

When Geoffrey informed him that after a week or so in Brussels, I would be coming with them to Salzburg, he could not believe it, and tried his best to dissuade me.

"Mistress Joanna, it is a trip of some rigor when conditions are normal—and they are not normal," said Holbein. "You simply cannot go to Salzburg."

Geoffrey and I were unable to calm Holbein's fears, and in the end, after a long and emotional discussion, Master Hans Holbein left Antwerp alone. He was in a panic over fear for his family's lives—no doubt underscored by guilt over not seeing them for eight long years—and, despite his fondness for us, would not be delayed.

The morning he left us, Holbein delivered final words of warning. "Please, please be careful. The English are not hated in the German lands but I doubt they are loved either, because of King Henry. The Catholic princes despise Henry the Eighth because the pope excommunicated him. But much of the German lands are Lutheran, and they don't trust him, either, because England does not enact true reform. There are more than two hundred German states, and each one follows their own idea of religion."

I said, shaking my head, "I cannot understand it. The Emperor Charles is the most powerful ruler on earth and yet more than half of Germany, the heart of his empire, refuses to follow him in religion. He is the leader of all Catholics but he does nothing about it. In England, the smallest infractions in faith are punished." I shuddered as I thought of those six men, strapped to hurdles and dragged through London on their way to a terrible death.

"You do not understand the German mind because you know so little of the German history," said Holbein. "The emperor does not command the princes, as Henry the Eighth does his subjects. Emperor Charles convenes them, again and again, to conferences we call Diets, so that he can rule by persuasion. I think that after this long and difficult journey, you shall understand us much, much more. Ah, I shall think of you and the good constable every day, and though I am not much of a praying man, I shall pray for you."

Master Holbein enveloped me in a crushing hug and whispered, "Mistress Joanna, please keep your heart open to the possibility of transformation. Promise me?"

I did, still uncertain what he meant. It was hard to say good-bye to my friend Hans Holbein, particularly since I wondered if I would ever see him again. I'd agreed to go with Geoffrey Scovill to faraway Salzburg—what else could I do?—but there were moments, more and more of them, when I feared we hurtled down a path from which there could be no return.

At first there were few signs of trouble. The road leading out of Antwerp was lined with attractive villages. We reached Brussels early one afternoon, and paused to admire the large city, enclosed by a long wall of brick and tower. "We can only spend a few days here, Joanna," said Geoffrey. "It's almost September, and Holbein is right. As people begin to run out of food across the countryside, it's only going to become more difficult and dangerous to travel."

But a short stay was not possible. I was expected to reside in the establishment paid for by the English crown. For years Master Moinck lived there. Now it was mine to occupy, and waiting for me were notices of two appointments I was expected to keep. In a week's time, I was supposed to meet with the head of the largest workshops in Brussels. And in three weeks' time, I must report to Coudenberg Palace to be presented to Queen Mary of Hungary, Regent of the Netherlands.

"This is madness," exploded Geoffrey. "We should be safely out of Brussels in a week at the latest, not a month. And while here, you must be discreet, not presenting yourself to the queen."

"I don't have a choice and you know it," I said. "If I fail to appear at the palace, word will spread. The English ambassador will no doubt write to the king. *That* would be a disaster."

I found them bittersweet, the three weeks leading up to my presentation to Queen Mary. I was frightened by the attack on the ship, and nervous about the journey to come, yet I also found myself dazzled by this city. The glittering brick buildings, meticulous gardens, vast cobbled squares—for the first time in my life, I felt a provincial person. London lacked such glamour. Brussels, smaller than Antwerp, possessed quite a different character from that city as well. The latter was a sprawling port, awhirl in the sights and sounds of the world, in particular the smells: the tart spices of the Indies mingling with the bitter odor of printer's ink. Brussels was more insular, subtler, and capable of deeper pleasures.

My official duties as tapestry mistress came off better than might have been expected. When I arrived at the appointment with the head of the largest workshop, I braced myself for skepticism that a female had replaced Master Moinck. But the distinguished man seemed oblivious to my sex or my years of experience. He was keen to know just one thing—would King Henry VIII continue to be the leading purchaser of tapestries in all of Christendom? Once he'd ascertained that the answer was yes, I conducted my business without any prejudices or obstacles whatsoever.

I found the answer to a problem I'd thought unsolvable while touring the vast tapestry workshops, the heart of the industry in all of Christendom.

One of five men who lived in Brussels worked in the tapestry business, I was told. At the top of it were the ten most prestigious workshops, each employing at least fifty skilled weavers to produce elaborate tapestries for the courts of Henry VIII, King Francis, and the Emperor Charles. Rivals in Europe, the three rulers were willing, if not eager, to lavish fortunes on the most luxurious tapestries.

I inspected the series of tapestries that King Henry craved: *The Triumph of the Gods*. Zeus was complete, two goddesses nearly so, and the one of Hercules a month from being finished. In the Hercules tapestry, a series of feats were depicted, from wresting with a lion to abducting a woman to balancing the entire planet on his shoulders. There were no mythological complexities to be deciphered. Each of the figures simply displayed godlike qualities in the most luxurious threads known to the world. I knew King Henry well enough to understand that this was exactly what he desired.

"*The Triumph of Venus* is our next challenge, and it shall greatly overshadow the one being completed in Paris," announced the master of the workshop.

"So a separate tapestry is being woven, not part of this series, but of a goddess who could take her part in this grouping?" I said, my mind racing with a new possibility.

"Yes, to create a tapestry of Venus is the rage now. In the tiny workshop of Cologne, and in Paris, too, they are racing to complete an image of her. But none of those workshops can offer you the craftsmanship you will find here, Mademoiselle Stafford," he sniffed.

I could not wait to tell Geoffrey my idea. "Remember how we couldn't think of an explanation for Sir Andrew Windsor and King Henry of why I needed to leave Brussels for an extended period but was not returning to England? Now I have it. I shall say I must go to these other workshops to see the other images of Venus. Cologne is in the German lands. And then of course there is Paris, quite a distance from here. I will write to him that I fear his series won't be complete unless he secures the best Venus as part of his *Triumph of the Gods*. It will account for the additional time out of England."

Geoffrey had to admit that my idea had merit. He, on the other hand, was finding it impossible to form a travel plan to Salzburg. Everyone was quite adamant that it would be impossible for an Englishman and woman to ride through that long a stretch of the German lands without a guide and armed protectors, yet there were none willing to be hired. The land was too hungry, too volatile.

We still had no idea how to accomplish our goal when I arrived at Coudenberg Palace, a sumptuous castle of the Hapsburgs.

Mary of Hungary was the sister of the Emperor Charles, and thus first cousin to the Lady Mary of England. After her young husband, the king of Hungary, was killed in battle, defending his country against the Turks, Mary became her brother's representative in the Netherlands. The Hapsburgs' domains around the world were so vast that one man could not govern them. The whole family must leap to it.

I suspected that this summons was issued because the Lady Mary wrote to her, suggesting it, and within the first five minutes of meeting the queen, I was proved right.

"I'm fond of my poor cousin—she's had such a hard life with that horrendous man as a father," said Queen Mary with a forthrightness I enjoyed. I detected little physical resemblance between the English princess and the Hungarian queen. My hostess could be judged a plain woman, with a protruding chin and sallow skin. But she spoke with incisiveness and radiated an energetic confidence that the Lady Mary sadly lacked.

"I am also kept well informed by Eustace Chapuys, one of my brother's most erudite ambassadors," said the queen. "As your mother was Spanish, I assume you are acquainted?"

Trying to keep my face as neutral as possible, I said, "Yes, Your Highness. I have that honor."

"Chapuys has never understood, and nor have I, the English king's refusal to settle on Mary as his heir—there are examples, in my own family, of strong female rule."

None more so than yourself, I thought. Everyone admired the energetic rule of Queen Mary of Hungary.

She tilted her head, regarding me with those large brown eyes. "I find it interesting that Henry the Eighth entrusts you, a relation of his, with his tapestries. Perhaps this is the beginning of a new age, of women taking on responsibility. Were he alive, Cornelius Agrippa himself would be proud. Don't you agree?"

32

I found it impossible to hide my astonishment over hearing that name from the lips of the queen.

Smiling, she said, "I see you have heard of Heinrich Cornelius Agrippa. Probably that he is an occultist, yes? Oh don't believe that such nonsense is all he is capable of. Agrippa wrote a wonderful book called *The Declamation on the Nobility and Preeminence of the Female Sex*. He forwards the theory that we possess no less excellent faculties of mind, reason, and speech than men. I could have a volume sent to you. Yes, he's a fascinating thinker, why else would Chapuys have been such a close friend?"

This was another jolt to absorb. I managed to say I had no idea that the ambassador esteemed the German so highly.

"Yes, I think Chapuys stood as godfather to one of Agrippa's sons," she mused.

At the conclusion of my audience, Queen Mary inquired on my planned date to return to England. When I told her I was considering a trip to Cologne and other tapestry workshops to inspect their work—following the story that Geoffrey and I had worked out—she was most startled.

"To travel by sea, yes, that I can understand, but over land, now, when the German and Flemish country is in misery?"

I did my best to insist that yes, this was my plan.

The queen said, "Well, I think I shall supply you with a 'safe conduct,' in case you should run into any difficulties."

Queen Mary did not seem to actually request that such a document be prepared, but magically, after I curtsied to her and withdrew
from her chamber, a scroll was slipped into my hand bearing the seal
of the Hapsburgs, the most prestigious family in the world.

Geoffrey turned it over in his hands when I showed him the
document. He had news for me as well. He'd found a way out of
Brussels. A party of merchants would leave in two days' time in a
string of three covered wagons, heavily guarded. It was the last such
party scheduled to leave Brussels until next spring. The wagons
would travel east until finding the Rhine and then follow it southeast
for a long time, many days. Our destination was Regensburg, a city
on an ancient north-to-south trade route. From there we would have
to find new transport to Salzburg, which was not too much farther.

"It's incredibly costly," Geoffrey said. "I had to pay them all the
money before we left and it came to half that John Cheke gave me
for the entire enterprise."

"Half?" I said, dismayed. "Why do they demand so much?"

"We will need to bring a lot of food with us. Then there are all
the men. We shall have a small army surrounding us. And also, I had
to pay more than anyone else."

"Because we are English?"

"No," said Geoffrey. "Because I am insisting on discretion, on
extra lengths being taken to hide our names, in the recording book, in
case anyone arrives to search for us. There's another reason, too." He
hesitated as if trying to decide whether to tell me something and then
said, shortly, "The man in charge, Jochen, believes you're bad luck."

Geoffrey looked away as my throat tightened. Was Jochen the
only one who thought I brought bad luck?

It wasn't until the day we left Brussels that Geoffrey explained.
He would ride ahead on horseback, but I must ride in the wagon,
with two old, stout merchants. Others filled in the next two wagons,
a party of nine passengers in total. By day we'd ride as far as Jochen
and his team instructed; at night we'd sleep on the ground or in the
back of the wagon. Geoffrey hastened to emphasize that should I

wish to sleep in the wagon, he would sleep outside it, even though we posed as a married couple. Geoffrey told me that within a few seconds of meeting Jochen, he knew that the safest guise for me would be as his wife.

Jochen, who rode a chestnut stallion, pulled up next to our wagon shortly before we set out. It was impossible to know how old he was; his face was scarred and lined but his hair, tied in a knot, was sleek and black as onyx. He said nothing to us; he glanced at Geoffrey and then scrutinized me. Whatever he saw made him shake his head, lips tight with anger, and kick his horse, to gallop to the front of the line.

Geoffrey said, "He thinks you're bad luck because you used to be a novice in a priory."

"How does he know so much about me?"

Geoffrey said, "After your appointments with the tapestry men, and your audience with the queen, half of Brussels knows details of you. I am certain he doesn't believe we are married, but he declines to challenge me on it."

After that unpleasant news sank in, I said, "Does he hate Catholics?"

"I wish it were that simple," Geoffrey said. "Jochen was a mercenary in several Imperial armies, and I have a suspicion that he encountered nuns in the past."

"Encountered?"

"Joanna, please, let's leave it at that." After a moment he said, much more gently, "I will protect you; no one will touch you, I swear it." Although his statement was meant to reassure me, it stirred the first sensation of real fear on the journey.

As the wagons rumbled along the road leading into the countryside, the charm of Brussels fell away and misery took its place. It was the end of September, yet still very warm, like the peak of summer. But the grass was flat and brown, as it would look after emerging from a hard winter, and the trees stood bare, for the drought had already stripped all their leaves. They lay in dead piles below the bare branches. I saw no signs of harvesting crops. I did glimpse people, on the side of the road. They stood in clusters, watching our wagons and surrounding soldiers pass through their devastated land. Geoffrey, I noticed one day, carried a sword on horseback. I said a fervent prayer for peace on our journey.

And I remembered again the words of the old boatman of the Thames, that spring night after the bishop's banquet: *It will be a time of want and pestilence. The lady of the river told me.* Followed by John Cheke: "As above, so below."

On the tenth day we reached our first German city, a small but prosperous one with churches and guild halls fashioned of dark red brick. I watched Jochen pay for our entry. This must be one of the reasons the trip was so costly. We took rooms in an empty inn, and I sat down to an extraordinary supper.

We'd survived on smoked meat, dried cod, and nuts, washed down with warm ale, and I could not complain of the monotony. So many others I glimpsed on the side of the road, faces gaunt and eyes hollow, were on the verge of starving.

But in this inn, an older woman set a cast-iron pan on my wooden table. *"Rheingauer Hühner,"* she said. Steam rose from the dish, prepared in the pan itself. Thin, delicate cakes embraced a dense mixture of chicken and pear slices, with honey, cinnamon, and another spice I wasn't sure of. Anise?

"Thank you," I said to the woman when she came to clear the pan, and she smiled.

The next morning, Geoffrey told me he'd gone to a bathhouse, a German custom, and then spent hours in a tavern, finding enough people who spoke French for interesting conversation. He was intrigued by the men's views of England and enjoyed the friendly argument that ensued over our king's faith, even laughed off their ridicule over Henry VIII's five wives.

But a day later, back on the road, we suffered an attack. After staring at the brilliant stars through the branches of a desiccated oak, I fell asleep. I'd entered my first dream—I was hurrying to Vespers in the priory—when the peal of the bells summoning us to prayers became the screams of men.

"Wake up, Joanna, wake up," Geoffrey shook me hard. "Get under the wagon."

I crawled under our wagon and watched, in horror, as Jochen and the soldiers beat the men they'd found crawling into our camp to try to rob us. They were easily vanquished, but Jochen didn't send them fleeing. The invaders were punched and kicked by our "protectors" as they cursed and even laughed.

After it was all over, Geoffrey stalked over to Jochen. I heard fresh shouting, and Geoffrey returned tense with anger.

He rustled around inside the wagon and then emerged, holding something: a knife.

"Joanna, keep it with you in the wagon and everywhere you go."

I shook my head. "If there is another attack, surely Jochen and his men can defend us. It would take an army to defeat them."

Geoffrey continued to press the weapon on me. "Keep it with you at all times."

After staring at him for a moment, I said, "You think it's Jochen I should be most afraid of."

"He blames you for what happened."

"How can that be?"

"It is ludicrous, yes. Bad luck? Almost no one in the city even saw you, you went straight to bed. If anyone should be blamed, it's me, talking to a room full of men in a tavern. They all knew strangers were in their city."

The wagon kept going, east and then south, and the mighty Rhine, forlorn from drought, sometimes flashed into view. We entered no more walled cities, both for fear of enticing thieves and because disease galloped through some of those cities. One day I saw dead animals on a field, with people standing in a circle around them, helpless. Holbein's drunken wailing about the end of the world seemed more possible than I wanted to admit to myself.

I lost track of the number of days, but I knew we'd traveled several weeks by the thickness of Geoffrey's beard, for he had not shaved since going to the city bathhouse. The air finally began to cool, and we endured a few days of rain. The thirsty ground soaked in every drop. It was too late for the growing season; all the rain did was soften the roads, slowing our pace of travel. Geoffrey told me one evening that his chief worry was that by the time we reached Salzburg, it would be winter and we would be trapped there until the spring thaw. Our quest to find Edmund stretched out as endless, devouring our time, our money, our very future.

Although the nights grew colder, I still preferred to rest on the ground. It was difficult to sleep soundly, for I did nothing but sit in the wagon all day, conversing with no one. My fellow passengers understood French, but Geoffrey and I agreed that due to the threat that still hung over me, that even here, a hundred miles deep, I should tell no one anything, for someday, when we reached the large cities in the southern German lands, news of my whereabouts could travel. And so my mind was left to turn in on itself, worrying about Edmund and wondering who sent that man to kill me, and fearing for Catherine Howard and Thomas Culpepper and my other friends in faraway England, at the mercy of the king. What would King Henry do if I disappeared for more than a few months, the expected span of time to look at a few tapestry workshops? Time and again, my thoughts circled back to Arthur, too. I felt so far away from my little cousin; I longed to hug him. But when would I ever see him again?

Which is why one night, in a clearing of the forest of the prince elector Palatine, I was awake when the men came.

I jumped to my feet at the first scream, before Geoffrey, before any of the others. The fires had died. I could not see anything in the darkness except for human forms darting here and there—Jochen's men, I assumed. But as I squinted in the moonlight, it seemed there were other men among them, with swords and knives. I was surrounded by shouts and curses, and the sound of steel hitting steel.

Geoffrey pushed me against a tree next to the wagon, and stood in front of me, a sword in his hand, as the fighting reached a pitch.

"What's happening, Geoffrey?" I shouted.

"I don't know," he shouted back.

At that moment a man rushed toward Geoffrey, his own sword flashing. As they fought, I cried, "No, no, no, no, no." I couldn't bear this—it was impossible to live if Geoffrey should be killed.

I raised my knife in my right hand and sprang forward, to stand next to him, to do something.

Boom. There was a deafening explosion, like thunder, followed by a second and a third. An acrid smell filled the air. I gasped from it, choking, as I realized that the men attacking us had backed away. Then they were running, calling to one another, melting into the forest. I couldn't see Geoffrey in the smoky darkness.

"Geoffrey, where are you?" I screamed.

In seconds, he was beside me.

"Are you hurt, Joanna?"

"No," I said, weeping as I clung to him. He was damp with sweat but he was standing, and he seemed uninjured. "I thought they would kill you," I cried.

"Well, I'm not dead, I'm not even hurt," he said, breathless, and wrapped both of his arms around me. Gratitude and a fierce joy charged through me, and I kissed him on the cheeks.

His beard scratched my cheeks, and suddenly his lips were against mine, and my mouth opened as I kissed him. Geoffrey's hands ran up my back and in another instant his fingers tore through my hair, hanging loose over my shoulders. He pulled my hair so hard it hurt, but I welcomed the pain and pressed up against him even harder.

There was a flash of bright light and we sprang apart. Someone had lit torches.

Two men slowly approached us, a boy ahead of them holding a torch. The men held long sticks in their arms that whispers of smoke curled from. I had never seen them with my own eyes, but it seemed to me that these must be guns, and I had heard their firing. Which is how they frightened off the men who attacked us, even though there were so many of them. By the torchlight I saw men lying everywhere, dead or injured. One of them, I realized with a jolt, was Jochen. I saw bright blood on his chest. Jochen could be dying. Our wagon had no leader. And we had no one who could speak for us. We'd have to represent ourselves.

The taller man said something to Geoffrey and me in German, and then repeated it when we didn't answer.

"We are English," Geoffrey said.

He turned to the other man, short and bearded, who said to us in French, "You are English? Do you speak French?"

When Geoffrey nodded, he said, "My name is Arnulf and this man"—he gestured to the tallest man—"is Freiherr von Seckenburg, our lord. Many of your party have been killed and others are wounded. The bandits are desperate men, and if we had not been tracking them on behalf of the prince elector Palatine, you would be dead, too."

I said, "We are most grateful to you, sir."

He frowned, disapproving that I had spoken. Turning back to Geoffrey, Arnulf said, "What are you doing in the Palatine—why do English people travel deep into the German lands so late in the year, when there has been hardship? You tempt hungry people with your wealth."

Geoffrey said, "We are *not* wealthy, and our destination is Salzburg."

That made an impact. The pair spoke to one another in German and then Arnulf said, "Why do you want to go there?"

"To see the physician called Paracelsus."

Now the men laughed at us. "You ride in a wagon for weeks and weeks, to see that old fool? It is a ridiculous statement." He turned to his companions. "We should search their wagon."

Geoffrey protested that we had done nothing wrong, that there was nothing improper about our traveling, but they ignored us as they searched our belongings. To my amazement, von Seckenburg rummaged harder than anyone else. Geoffrey and I could not say a word to each other because Arnulf stayed close, his face hard with suspicion.

My heart stopped as von Seckenburg emerged, excited, carrying my document of safe conduct from Queen Mary of Hungary and the bags that contained Geoffrey's coins, all the money he'd been given by John Cheke. They squatted on the ground and counted it in front of us, as overjoyed as children playing with toys.

"Joanna, this is not good," Geoffrey said in a low voice.

Arnulf turned on us, his eyes now gleaming. "So you are not wealthy? You expect us to believe you are nothing but an English couple seeking the advice of a physician? We are not stupid. You are spies."

"That is absurd," I said. "We are on a journey to find a friend whose last known location was in Salzburg. This man, Geoffrey Scovill, is a constable in the town of Dartford and I am the tapestry mistress of His Majesty King Henry the Eighth. I had an audience with the queen in Brussels and she gave me this safe conduct."

Arnulf translated my words to all the others gathered and the men laughed harder than ever.

"A woman in charge of a king's tapestries?" Arnulf scoffed.

"I tell you, it is the truth," I said, furious. "How could we be spies? Who on earth would we be spying for?"

Geoffrey laid a cautioning hand on my arm. "We have committed no crime in your land. None. Take our money if you must, but allow us to continue on our way."

Arnulf smiled for the first time, exposing a line of brown teeth.

"You will soon learn we don't care for spies in the Palatine. The others can go, all those who survived the bandits. But not you two. You're coming with us."

33

'm surprised they haven't killed us," said Geoffrey.

The two of us, now prisoners, rode in the back of a wagon, sitting in damp straw. Our conveyance was a poor farmer's cart, without a cover. It had rained, briefly, just after we set out, and the chilly gray sky held the threat of more like a giant apron sagging over our heads.

The route we followed was more mountainous than the previous one, and the two horses pulling the cart strained as they trod up the narrow road. The driver kept whipping them to go faster.

"We haven't done anything wrong," I said, for the tenth time, eying Arnulf trotting ahead, out of earshot.

"They had to come up with an excuse to steal our money," Geoffrey said. "In the daylight, you can see their clothes are of wretched quality, even those of their lord. All they possess are those guns. The most intelligent thing would be to shoot us—or stab us, if they don't want to waste the powder—and bury our bodies in the woods so no one will ever question where the money came from."

I shuddered. "Please, Geoffrey."

"Don't turn into a delicate flower on me now, Joanna. I think that when you spoke up before, when you insisted that you are a tapestry mistress to the king of England, he laughed, but it put a worry into Arnulf's mind. He doesn't want to be punished for killing someone who turns out to be of importance. Hold on to that. You must be stronger, and more determined, than you've ever been before, if we are to survive this."

I knew Geoffrey was right.

"What can we do—how will we find someone to listen to us?" I asked.

"Arnulf has the safe-conduct document and I doubt very much he will return it," said Geoffrey. "We must wait, and listen, and learn all we can, and when the opportunity presents, speak up. Hans Holbein was right. We don't understand enough of the German history or the German character. I don't even know if the Palatine is Catholic or Lutheran. All I can say in my defense is, Jochen was not exactly what one would call a teacher."

I thought, with a twist, of our leader, bleeding to death on the ground.

"It turned out I *was* bad luck for Jochen," I murmured.

Geoffrey said nothing, and I could not stop myself from saying, "As I am bad luck for you."

"Don't say that—never say that." Geoffrey slapped the side of the cart, which made the driver turn around, scowling. He raised his whip at us, muttering something foul.

Neither of us made a sound for a good while, until Geoffrey spoke, in a low voice, haltingly. "Joanna, I need to say something to you about what happened last night, what happened between us."

Even in this miserable, cold cart, my cheeks flamed hot.

"It's not necessary," I said.

"Yes, it is. Please hear me out. We know that we're drawn to each other, but still, we don't get on well, Joanna. Too stubborn, the two of us, perhaps. And I know that those feelings you have for me, they are not the same sort you have for Edmund. It isn't love in your heart. I have known that for a while, and accepted it. I am sorry about what happened in the woods. I think it was the relief of being alive, it can make people do things they wouldn't ordinarily do. But I failed to show you respect. Forgive me."

I turned away from him, looking at the gray-and-brown cheerless countryside but not seeing it. At the front of our convoy, one of the men said something that ended in a questioning tone and another shouted back, *"Ja, natürlich."* I snatched up a handful of straw and tried to snap it in two, but it wasn't dry enough.

"How can you tell me what is in *my* heart?" I said.

Geoffrey stammered, "I didn't. I meant that—" He broke off. "Wait. Wait. What do you mean? What are you trying to tell me?"

"You always think you know everything, and perhaps this time you don't," I said. "That's all."

He sat up straighter against the side of the cart.

"When we extricate ourselves from this situation, are you saying that there are things we can plan for ourselves?" he said, still wary.

I could not believe while it happened that I was doing this, but I reached through the straw for Geoffrey's hand. When I touched his warm skin, I intertwined my fingers with his. In response, he pulled me up, to press against him and kissed me, not as he did in the woods, but tenderly, again and again.

"When did you know?" he murmured.

"Always," I said. "Or perhaps three days ago? I can't say."

Geoffrey laughed.

For hours, we said not a word but gripped each other's hands, tight. And the next day, and the one after that, as we spoke of many things, I rarely let go of Geoffrey's hand. Often I rested my head on his broad shoulder, and he would run his finger along the lines of my cap, twirling strands of hair.

Geoffrey said, "When I was fighting in the forest—all those men coming at me with knives and swords—a thought went through my mind, 'I'm going to die trying to take the woman I love to another man.'"

I took that in. "So you've believed all this time that I wish to be with Edmund again? Geoffrey, I have told you, and I meant it, that I fear for Edmund and I care about him, deeply. But we will never be married."

Geoffrey nodded. "I still must find him, Joanna. That hasn't changed. I accepted a commission from John Cheke. When we are able to win our freedom from these men, my search continues."

"*Our* search," I corrected him. And then I put into words a thought that I'd had for some time. "What shall we do if we find Edmund but he doesn't want to return to England, if he is lost on this strange path of his?"

"That possibility exists," he said. "I will do whatever is most just and fair—to everyone, I hope. But first, we need to break free of our captors."

"Yes, you are right." I said.

This bittersweet interlude ended the fourth morning, when Geoffrey and I reunited after spending the night separately, under guard, in a large farmhouse that von Seckenburg commandeered in the name of the prince elector of the Palatine. "I just heard Arnulf talking to someone in French," Geoffrey said. "They're taking us to a place called Castle Heidelberg, to be imprisoned."

"Without trial? Without any opportunity to speak for ourselves?"

"I don't know," he said.

The next day, we emerged from the road through the forest and I looked down upon a town nestled in a valley, on the side of a dark blue river. A castle loomed on a ridge high above the town, surrounded on three sides by a dense forest of leafless trees, low mountains rising behind.

Heidelberg Castle seemed handsome, its long redbrick wings stretching into the woods. But when we drew close, Geoffrey nudged me, pointing to a blackened section of the castle, with one of its walls collapsed.

Arnulf said, "The castle was struck by lightning a few years ago."

Was it God's punishment?

At the side of the castle, we were pulled out of the back of the cart. They parted me from Geoffrey, of course. Men and women prisoners could have no contact. I didn't want to give our captors the satisfaction of seeing me weep, but the truth was that I choked with fear for both of us.

"Be strong, Joanna, and remember what I said about looking for opportunity," said Geoffrey.

We embraced, quickly, frantically, while the men talked of something. Too soon, they pulled us apart. Arnulf led me away first, without permitting us to say a final good-bye, without my being able to look into Geoffrey's face. I saw only the back of his head, his light brown hair tousled from my desperate grip.

The room Arnulf took me to was not a dungeon. I had spent months in cells within the Tower of London and Het Gravensteen in Ghent. This was of a better sort. I had a few pieces of furniture, a bed with a clean blanket, and a window yielding a view of the city and the valley. But there was a lock on the door from the outside. I was in a cell, no matter what one wanted to call it.

I started out strong—Geoffrey could not have expected any more of me. An old man came to bring me meals, and I attempted to ask him questions. But my jailer knew only German, and I'd picked up perhaps fifty words and phrases of the language since leaving Brussels. Certainly not enough to ask if I could speak to someone in authority.

A woman was kept in the room next to mine. I could not see her but I could hear her. She laughed, she wept, she sang—all in German. My attempts to communicate with her in French were met with silence, and then she shouted a string of angry-sounding German words. She was as frustrated with our inability to communicate as I was.

I could only hope that Geoffrey was having more luck.

After a cold night under the blanket, I saw snowflakes drift past the window come dawn. By midday, snow dusted the valley—to anyone else, it would seem a beautiful sight. But I was horrified. Would I be trapped in the castle all winter? Or even longer?

Suddenly I could bear this no longer. I had nothing, I was forgotten, imprisoned, and lost to all I loved.

"I am Joanna Stafford and I've done nothing wrong," I screamed out the window. I waited for something to happen, for someone in the castle to crash into my room and exercise punishment, but no response came. It was as if I no longer existed in this world.

Just before nightfall, as I crouched before the window, a large black bird soared past my window, banked, and dove to the ground to seize a small creature—a mouse, I saw, when the bird wheeled back up with its prey—and the creature was borne off, limp and dying, to some place to be devoured.

34

Another week or so went by before I realized the woman confined next to me had uttered no sounds—it occurred to me she'd either died or was freed. One afternoon I heard something else, something unusual: two men talking in the passageway. I stood on my tiptoes to get the best view out of the barred upper half of my door.

What I saw made me grip those bars, my heart racing.

My jailer was bringing a monk down the passageway. By the brown color of his habit—universal throughout Christendom—I knew him to be Benedictine.

They stepped into the room next to mine, and I heard the murmur of male questions and the very faint sound of a woman responding. While it went on, I tried to plan what to do.

As soon as I heard the door slam in the passageway and footsteps approach, I was ready.

In Latin, I called out into the passageway, "Brother, I need to speak to you. I am a former novice of the Dominican Order. I am English. As a fellow member of a religious house, I entreat you for assistance."

The monk slowly came into view. He was of middle years, and thin, with large gray eyes bridged by a pair of thick eyebrows under his neatly trimmed tonsure. Those eyes slid sideways, fixing on my face in the door. Then his eyes slid back and he hurried to reach the far end of the passageway.

Desperate, I called after him, still in Latin, one of the only rules of the Benedictine Order I could remember: "Not only is the boon of obedience to be shown by all to the abbot, but the brethren are also to obey one another, knowing that by this road of obedience they are going to God."

A door opened and clanged shut. I sat on the edge of my bed for hours, tears easing down my cheeks. He didn't understand me; the gamble was lost.

But the next morning, my door suddenly swung open. The monk took three measured steps inside my room and then stopped. A belt of frayed rope clinched his waist and he wore plain clogs on his feet.

"How do you know the Benedictine Rule?" the monk asked in perfect Latin, studying me with gray eyes.

So he *had* understood me. I clapped, and then forced my hands into a clasp of prayer.

"As I told you, I was for a time a novice of a Dominican Order," I responded.

"And you are English?"

"Yes," I said, and then in a rush: "I am unjustly held here, myself and my friend, Geoffrey Scovill. We have committed no crime and I wanted to—"

He held up his hands, palms out, as if pushing me back, although I was not by any means that close to him.

"I know nothing of you or why you are here," he said. "But I cannot intervene in a matter of law, my abbot was clear on that."

"You told the abbot that I spoke those words of Latin and asked for instruction?"

"Of course. In obedience we find truth. He said it was my duty to learn more because of the nature of your appeal, but not to agree to any sort of intervention."

I was once exactly like this Benedictine monk. Eager to follow the rules, to obey the will of the head of the house. But what happens when the house is shattered and there is no leader any longer?

I said, "So you visit the prisoners held in Heidelberg Castle?"

"Only when we are sent for. My abbot was informed that the woman also kept here, charged with counterfeiting, had not much more time left to her. She has the lung rot. I was providing her with Christian comfort."

I said, "I am most happy to find the Palatine a Catholic land."

The monk gnawed on his lip. "The truth is that most of the people who live in the Palatine follow Luther, but Prince Elector Louis is faithful to the True Church. He asks our abbot to sup with him, often. He protects our monastery. We pray for a long life for the prince, because afterward . . . nothing is certain."

This was the opportunity I needed.

"That is regrettable. But I am sure the prince elector has many years of life remaining."

The monk shifted from one foot to another. "He is advanced in years, and to be truthful, his health has not been good. We pray for him continually, all of us at the monastery. His young nephews, they follow Luther. When one of them inherits . . ."

I hated what I was about to do to him, but this was the way out of Heidelberg Castle.

"I know what that is like, to fear that sort of change," I said. "In my priory, we feared it, and when it came, it was even more sorrowful than our worst imaginings. We were exiled from our house with small pensions, and our priory was torn down."

Fear rippled across his face. "The abbot says that our house, the Monastery of Saint Michael, is too revered to be in danger."

How often I heard the sisters say that same thing to one another at Dartford, in the months leading up to the end.

"I'm sure there is no reason for alarm," I said. "But still, it will be very important for your abbot—and for you—to have important and influential friends, should a change come."

"Yes, my abbot says that."

"Do you not think that Queen Mary, the regent of the Netherlands, and her older brother, the Holy Roman Emperor Charles, would be the best friends to have?"

The monk smiled. "Of course. But every Catholic in Christendom would beseech the Hapsburgs for help. They cannot reach down to us all."

I spread my hands, as if making an offering. "What do you think your abbot would say if I could introduce him by letter to the queen regent, if she were to be grateful to him? I was presented to her in Brussels, and she gave me a passage of safe conduct. My friend is her cousin, Princess Mary of England. Should they hear of my case, both of those women would want to help me. If the abbot were to write to the queen regent in Brussels . . ."

The monk edged toward the door. "That sounds very much like intervention."

"Talk to the abbot," I said. "He sounds like such a wise and far-seeing man. Seek his counsel."

"I will do that," said the monk, knocking on the door, signaling for the jailor to come and let him out.

"What is your name?" I asked.

"Brother Theodoric."

"My name is Joanna Stafford, and I was once called Sister Joanna. God was good to me when he sent you down this passageway, Brother Theodoric," I said. And meant it.

There is a difference between hope with nothing to support it but prayer and longing, and hope with specific cause. The latter is more powerful but also more torturous. I paced the room; I slept in patches; my heart jumped at every sound in the passageway. Each day crawled by, endless. Would my gambit lead to anything?

I had rarely in my life felt such relief as when Brother Theodoric's bushy eyebrows appeared on the other side of the door

"The abbot will help you," said Brother Theodoric. "He has written a letter to Queen Mary, Regent of the Netherlands, stating your case."

In this moment, I loved the abbot of Saint Michael's.

My elation dimmed when Brother Theodoric told me that a letter from the abbot might not reach Brussels until the spring, making it possible that we wouldn't hear anything from the queen until summer. Geoffrey and I looked at six months spent in Heidelberg Castle. But there was no alternative but to wait.

I pressed Brother Theodoric to take a message to Geoffrey. He refused. "No one but you shall know of the letter to Brussels, that is the abbot's wish," the monk said. "Once we have received word from the queen regent, your friend shall also be informed." The way he said "your friend" hinted at disapproval, that a former Dominican novice should have formed any sort of association with a man. He did, when I pleaded, confirm that Geoffrey was still in Heidelberg Castle, held with a handful of male prisoners in another wing.

The days grew shorter, and darker, and colder, as full winter came to the Palatine. The unnatural heat and drought was over; this seemed the usual pattern of the season. I spent my days in prayer and reading, for Brother Theodoric brought me some devotional books. I tried my best to stay hopeful.

When signs of spring arrived, I found it harder to control my impatience. The snow melting, the calling of birds, those first flashes of green below. They were welcome, but they taunted me as well. Life was going on everywhere, but here, in this castle, time stood still for me and, somewhere else within these walls, for Geoffrey.

One day was particularly difficult for me, because I learned that April had come and thus it was a full year since I traveled from Dartford to Whitehall and set so many things in motion.

Shortly after, Brother Theodoric returned with news.

"The abbot received a letter from the queen regent," he said. "She confirms who you are, and your family's standing in England, and your appointment as tapestry mistress to your king. She wrote that suspicions of spying could only be baseless."

I couldn't speak for a moment, I was so convulsed with relief and with gratitude.

I finally said, "Shall your abbot inform the prince elector?"

"Yes, as soon as the prince elector returns from the Diet in the free Imperial City of Regensburg."

Brother Theodoric explained that the Emperor Charles had urged the princes of the German lands to come together with the leaders of the Catholic Church and representatives of other kingdoms to try, once more, to find a compromise, to heal the religious divisions that many feared would lead to war and bloodshed.

"It does seem a worthy cause," I sighed.

Brother Theodoric did not leave but neither did he do anything else; he stood, clogged feet planted in the middle of my room, and gnawed on his lip.

"Is something wrong?" I asked.

"There is sickness in the castle," he said. "Most of the men held prisoner have the disease."

The fear hit me as powerfully as a slap. "Geoffrey Scovill, the Englishman, is he sick?"

He nodded.

Jesus, in Your Mercy, I entreat you to preserve the life of Geoffrey. Let him not be stricken.

"You must help him," I said. "Go to him, Brother, as soon as you can."

The monk looked miserable. "I am not an apothecary or a healer of any sort, but I will try." He paused. "I have learned something that may help you and your friend. Among the distinguished people invited to the Diet of Regensburg is an English churchman who traveled here to represent his king."

That was not what I expected.

"My abbot says this churchman is most impressive, both in his own knowledge of theology and that of the secretary who assists him. His name is Bishop Stephen Gardiner. I don't know the name of the secretary."

I lost the power of speech for a moment and then asked, choking, "He is here? Bishop Gardiner?"

"Regensburg is two or three days' journey, but yes, your bishop is close by. The abbot will send him a letter apprising him of the situation, and it could speed your release, and your friend's, too."

No matter our differences, I knew Bishop Stephen Gardiner would help us, even impoverished and dangerously ill.

I said, "I am sorry, but we need to leave this castle at once. I will take Geoffrey with me to Regensburg."

"How will you reach it?" he asked.

"You will take us," I said. "In a wagon or coach."

Brother Theodoric edged toward the door.

I did not know what would persuade this monk to do something so reckless, I only knew that he was my way out of the castle. There was no other. If I waited for letters and princes and bishops to decide, Geoffrey could die.

"Brother, I know full well what you do not," I blurted. "My priory in England was destroyed. I pray that does not happen to you, but I must be truthful. It is possible, very possible. And when that time comes, one of the things you will discover is that we who serve God have only each other."

He stared at me, frightened.

Too desperate to control myself, I seized his arm and shook it. "We need each other. Don't you understand?"

Brother Theodoric shook me off and hurried from my room, his clogs banging on the floor.

I wept for hours, lost to despair. When, at sunset, the jailer opened the door and slid the tray of food inside, I turned away. I almost missed the note, sealed and placed between plate and mug.

"Be ready to leave Heidelberg Castle before dawn," said the note in perfect script.

I did not know whose decision it was to help me escape from the castle, Brother Theodoric's or his abbot's. He did not explain. The monk helped me out of the castle, leading the way by candlelight. An open coach awaited us outside, with Geoffrey in the back, unconscious, under blankets. I jumped into the coach, next to him, and Brother Theodoric took the reins. It was a four-horse coach, so we would have greater speed.

It wasn't until the sun rose on the road to Regensburg that I grasped how ill Geoffrey was. His beard was long, but underneath I saw a face so gaunt I would not have recognized him. He did not open his eyes until several hours after we'd set out, the horses speeding east, for the road was dry and well maintained. Spring was well under way.

"Joanna?" he whispered. And then: "I'm sorry I could not manage . . . a way out."

"Oh, Geoffrey, we're out now."

"I knew you could do it," he said, and swallowed. The swallowing pained him, and he shivered.

I tried to tell Geoffrey that we were bound for Bishop Gardiner, but it seemed to agitate him, and so I spoke of only soothing things, and tried to make him comfortable.

Late in the afternoon his breathing turned raspy, and red spots flared in his cheeks. "Your friend is worse," said Brother Theodoric.

"How much farther to Regensburg?" I pleaded.

"If the weather holds, late tomorrow," the monk told me.

"Cannot we ride through the night?" I asked.

"Even if it were safe to travel the road at night—and it is not—these horses must rest," Brother Theodoric said firmly.

We found a small village at sunset, with a shrine to the Virgin at the gateway, a lamp burning. This would be a place of safety. I spent a sleepless night tending to Geoffrey, trying to ease his pain and fever with the remedies and herbs supplied by Saint Michael's. I tried to convince myself that he was improving, while a growing dread clawed at me. Geoffrey could die, here, in a Bavarian village. We finally found our way to each other—and I had found a way out of our prison—yet now I would lose him.

At dawn, Geoffrey croaked, "You should . . . have left me."

"Oh, that is ridiculous," I said.

To my amazement, Geoffrey smiled. "From the beginning," he said, "you've been the same."

"I know," I said. "You, too." I caressed his feverish face. "But, Geoffrey, how could I abandon you? You've never abandoned me."

Brother Theodoric and I carried him to the coach, for he could no longer walk. Geoffrey fell into a restless sleep as our coach moved faster and faster. When Brother Theodoric grew too exhausted to control the horses, I took the reins. I didn't want to stop to eat, and only rested and fed the horses because I knew it was necessary. Every moment we delayed was a moment in which Geoffrey worsened.

Through my fear, I saw that a carpet of light green grass covered the ground; the trees were thick with leaves. And vivid flowers, yellow and white and pink, dotted the side of the road. Their scent was so strong, it burned my nostrils. We passed small villages that offered little shrines of prayer, and the countryside was sprinkled with white stone crosses and slender ones of wood, too. A wild and desperate hope took hold: Were these signs of God's forgiveness? Would He bless our journey and spare Geoffrey's life?

Peering over the horses' heads as we emerged from the woods, I gasped at the sight of a wide and tumultuous river, sparkling and blue, with red-roofed houses and gabled churches and gardens and markets crowded alongside it. It was a large city, larger than Heidelberg.

"Is this Regensburg?" I cried.

"Yes, on the other side of the Danube," Brother Theodoric said, and pointed at a stone bridge of many arches spanning the river. "That's the only way into the city."

The abbot had told Brother Theodoric where the dignitaries would be housed, and we made our way to that section of the city, through the thickening crowds. I had never seen so many finely appareled men walking on the streets of a city. Peering down a dark, narrow street that led to a courtyard, I glimpsed row after row of soldiers, in tight formation.

"That is the imperial guard, they travel wherever the Emperor Charles goes," explained Brother Theodoric, who had taken the reins again for our entry into the city. No one gave a second glance to a coach guided by a Benedictine monk; he was the best possible guide.

"Charles the Fifth himself is in Regensburg?" I tensed next to him on the front seat of the coach. It was something I had never expected, to be in the same city as the Holy Roman Emperor.

"That is the Street of the Ambassadors, I'm fairly sure of it," Brother Theodoric said, pointing to a prosperous row of three-story buildings. "Do you see them? Those must be the churchmen summoned to the Diet, with their staff."

A cluster of cardinals and bishops and priests, in the various bright robes and insignia of their countries, talked animatedly in front of a towering residence on the corner, their secretaries and clerks surrounding them in a more sedate-colored circle. They were like a flock of many birds, gathered to cluck over a hill of seeds.

I scanned each of the religious representatives. I was so overcome with the import of finally meeting the bishop, hysteria mounted. I'd finally made it here—and yet where was Gardiner? If he was not among them, how would I find him? I couldn't bear any more obstacles or delays.

A heavyset scarlet-robed cardinal moved away and I saw him: Stephen Gardiner, Bishop of Winchester, wearing white. He was nodding at something the man next to him was saying, a younger man, tall and handsome with shoulder-length, wavy white-blond hair, wearing the dignified doublet of a secretary to an English bishop. At the sight of him, I began to tremble as a rushing noise rose up in my head, as strong as the Danube itself.

It can't be him. The exhaustion and fear, they have addled me.

But I blinked, and blinked again, and the secretary's face came into even clearer focus. There was no doubt. It was Edmund.

35

A t first there was only confusion.

Both Edmund and Bishop Gardiner were astounded to find me alive and before them in Regensburg. It was so odd—all of the emphasis was on *my* whereabouts. The last thing anyone in England heard was that I'd planned to go to Cologne to inspect tapestry workshops. After I did not return to Brussels or send word to anyone, King Henry ordered messengers sent to those two cities, and to Paris, to make inquiries. It seemed I had disappeared. The king and queen were greatly worried.

"But, Edmund, *you* are the one who was missing—no one has had word of you," I said, frustrated. "John Cheke tried for so long to find you."

"I wrote to Cheke last month," said Edmund. "When the Diet officially began in April, I was permitted to do that, before then everything had to be kept secret. I've not had a letter back yet. It takes a very long time for correspondence to reach England."

Bishop Gardiner interrupted to say, "Master Sommerville has been here, in Regensburg, preparing for this Diet and for my arrival, since last November. A level of discretion was called for, due to the sensitivity, the international importance, of this conference. But certainly I've known of his whereabouts for much of last year. Do you forget, Joanna, that I first met Edmund when he was a Dominican friar in Cambridge? I have followed his progress from afar ever since. When Cheke was at Winchester House, he had only to ask me and I would have told him and saved you this extraordinary effort."

I could no longer control myself. It was as if a floodgate opened. I laughed and cried at the same time, and had to stagger back to the coach to hold on to its side to keep from collapsing onto the ground.

"If only we knew," I cried. "If only we knew."

"Mistress Stafford, please compose yourself," the bishop said. "The eyes of the world are upon us."

Edmund followed me to the coach. "Why do you keep saying 'we'?" he asked, glancing, uncertainly, at Brother Theodoric, sitting wide-eyed on the coach. Because we'd said everything in English, he had no notion of what transpired.

Geoffrey. How could I have forgotten about him? "Geoffrey Scovill is here, Edmund, he was hired by John Cheke to find you. We were attacked and robbed and held captive in Heidelberg. Oh, Edmund, he is terribly sick."

For several hours after that, all attention went to Geoffrey. The bishop ordered him taken to his own palatial residence, with the crest of the Tudors over the door. The bishop said Geoffrey and I would stay there during our time in Regensburg. The bishop dispatched messengers, and soon physicians and apothecaries and barber-surgeons flocked to the bedside of the unconscious Geoffrey. All of their efforts were channeled through Edmund, who'd tossed off his formal diplomatic clothing and worked steadily at Geoffrey's bed, the sleeves of his high-necked linen shirt pushed up his elbows.

After nightfall, Edmund, in consultation with the physicians, pronounced that Geoffrey would survive the illness, although the recovery time could prove lengthy.

Edmund himself looked exhausted, and I had had only a few hours of sleep in the last two days. Still, there was no choice but to begin our conversation, for I was desperate for an explanation. It began that night and continued most of the next afternoon, as we walked the streets of Regensburg.

He said quietly, "After what happened in Dartford on our wedding day, my relapse into weakness and sin, I felt that I could not continue in this world, Joanna, unless I found some path to accepting my action years ago in signing the Oath of Supremacy."

I'd long known that that was the darkest moment of Edmund's life. Years ago, the king's commissioners stormed his Dominican friary demanding that everyone formally submit to Henry VIII as the head of the church. All of those friars and monks at other religious houses who'd refused to sign the oath were imprisoned and sometimes executed. Edmund loathed himself for lacking a martyr's courage. That was why he took his first dose, to dull the pain of his failure in submitting to the king as head of the church.

"Did you seek out Paracelsus because of his expertise with opium? I have learned that when you first told me about that evil substance in the priory and called it the 'stone of immortality,' you were quoting him."

Edmund said, without shame, "Yes, that was part of it. Paracelsus created laudanum, the tincture that was the safest method of administering opium. I thought that if anyone knew how to control it, he would. But I wasn't the only man to travel to Salzburg with that as my quest. And he had no patience with me at first. It took me weeks to earn his trust. He said he despised me as a taker of opium—which he believed should be used only to ease the physical pain of the dying—and as a former friar and as an apothecary. He said the apothecary shop was a 'foul scullery from which come nothing but foul broths.'"

To my amazement, Edmund laughed, those faint lines crinkling in the corner of his brown eyes.

"Once I'd won him over—no easy task—we had many fascinating conversations," Edmund continued. "I gained such insight from Paracelsus into the human mind, the possibilities of healing, and most of all the forces that connect us to the natural world. Some decry his theories as magic, and the work of sorcery, but they are not seeing everything, Joanna. Beliefs of all sorts are being questioned. Do you know there's a mathematician in Poland who believes he has proven that the earth revolves around the sun? The rumors are that this Nicolaus Copernicus is preparing to publish his book *On the Revolution of the Celestial Spheres*, and I expect it to change everything we believe. Everything."

Listening to him, I couldn't help but think that the greatest change of all was in Edmund. I should have been ecstatic to see him this way: laughing and full of enthusiasm. Perhaps it was because I had spent so long thinking of him as anguished and lost. But whatever the reason, I found it difficult to make the adjustment. It did not help that he seemed full of praise for someone who practiced a form of magic. Paracelsus.

After his time spent with the controversial physician, Edmund said that he realized he needed to find his faith again. He had heard of a Dominican order in Pforzheim, a town at the entrance to the Black Forest, and decided to see if he could be accepted. It was a great distance between Salzburg and Pforzheim, and the morning that he was to set out, he was seized with a conviction. He should travel the entire way in the spirit of Saint Dominic: without possessions, humble, walking barefoot from village to village, preaching the word of God. Edmund possessed a real talent for languages, and he soon learned enough German to make himself understood. The journey was a profound experience, full of lessons on the goodness of mankind, Edmund said, his eyes shining.

"But why didn't you write to John Cheke after you saw Paracelsus?" I asked. "That's when the letters stopped, and he began to worry."

"I was devoted to the word of God, and England seemed like another man's life." Edmund shook his head. "It must sound terrible to you, but it simply didn't occur to me that anyone would miss me or wonder at my absence. I know I can never make amends to you and Geoffrey and John Cheke for this mistake. All I can do, Joanna, is ask for your forgiveness."

Forgiveness was one matter. Understanding—and acceptance—was another.

"How did you come into the employ of Bishop Gardiner?" I

asked. "There was a time when you and I both despised him and feared him. Now you seem devoted to his service, and he seems to trust you utterly."

Edmund continued his saga: "I did reach the Black Forest, stopping first at Pforzheim. The prior and friars were good to me, but I couldn't formally enter their order. With the German friars pouring in from other parts that had turned Lutheran and closed their monasteries, there was no room for an Englishman. Winter approached, and although it was difficult, I traveled farther into the Black Forest. I spent time at another monastery near Freiburg, offering my skills as an apothecary. I was sent to a nearby village where illness struck some children, and I tended to them for many days. But after I returned to the monastery, the abbot took me aside and said that some men came looking for me, men that seemed to him to be capable of violence. They were sent away; the abbot told them he didn't know me. I couldn't understand who they were or what they might want with me. I still don't."

With growing horror, I realized that those must be the men sent by Jacquard Rolin. When the spymaster grew frustrated with my intransigence, he decided to seize Edmund to try to force me to cooperate. When Señor Hantaras learned that Edmund had left England, a search was launched for him and imperial operatives found a trail into the Black Forest. But there they lost him and gave up the quest.

Edmund said, "I did not want to draw the attention of evil men to the monastery at Freiburg, so I left. I missed the company of books and had heard admirable things about the university at Heidelberg, so that was my next destination."

"You were in Heidelberg?" I asked, shocked. The way our stories intertwined, whether Edmund was aware of it or not, left me shaken. I had sent Brother Theodoric back to Castle Heidelberg, with my profound thanks. I saw that the good monk who'd liberated me also took back to his monastery a gift of money from Bishop Gardiner. The abbot's gamble had paid off in many ways.

Edmund said, "I registered there as a visiting scholar, and I began

a translation that I'd long planned of Saint Augustine. I was very surprised to receive one day a letter from Bishop Gardiner. Somehow
he learned of my work there—he has a vast network of informants,
after all. The bishop wrote that he was sure that there would be
another Diet, and this one could settle the question of religion for
good. He intended to be there personally, and wanted me to prepare
for his attendance with detailed theological research. Once he arrived, he asked me to work as his principal secretary because of not
only my research but my facility with German."

I told Edmund I still found it hard to accept his agreeing to the
position, knowing our history with the bishop. Edmund once told
me that he had longed to be employed by Gardiner, to be trusted
by him. But the Bishop of Winchester only used his weakness for
opium to force him to do his bidding. Something had shifted.

Edmund said, "The objective is so much more important than
anything that transpired in the past. Don't you understand, Joanna,
that this is the time, this is the opportunity, for Catholic and Reformer to stop fighting, for compromises to be reached? The Holy Father recognizes the need for change, for greater purity in the Catholic
Church. We can find a new path to one Christian faith again—yes,
it is possible. King Henry asked Bishop Gardiner to serve as his ambassador to the Emperor Charles, to ask the emperor, when the time
comes, to arbitrate between the pope and the king. It is possible that
England will become faithful to the Catholic religion once more. I
feel that *this* is the reason God put me on this earth, to help in every
way I can to heal the breach and return us all to grace."

It was a perfect spring afternoon as he said that, and we'd come
to the end of a cobbled street overlooking the Danube. A long boat
loaded with boxes eased by.

After a long, tired silence, Edmund said, "Do you know that
Regensburg was a Roman outpost raised by Marcus Aurelius, and
ever since the Danube has served as a trade route? Once we were
Christian, the boats men of Regensburg brought crusaders to the
Black Sea."

This was familiar to me, Edmund's love of the past. Was this not what he labored on now, a return to one church? Although I was not ready to share Edmund's conviction that the two sides could be brought together, I did understand, finally, why he would have devoted himself to the cause. And I understood a man of God who cut himself off from everyone while he did it. But I couldn't help but feel there was a selfishness to what Edmund had done. His obliviousness to the feelings of his friends almost cost Geoffrey his life.

As for my life, Bishop Gardiner offered to write personally to King Henry and attempt to explain that I had chosen to take this journey to find a lost friend in the German lands. "His Majesty may be angry with you for neglecting your tapestry duties," the bishop warned. "You shall have to express great penitence for what he shall see as an insult and a mistake." Realizing I needed the support of the bishop as never before, I agreed.

It took a few more days, but finally Geoffrey recovered enough from his illness to be able to talk to me. A barber had shaved him, and I was happy to gaze at his beardless face again, though he was shockingly thin.

"I am so happy that you're recovering," I said, sitting on a stool by his bed. An apothecary assistant mixed potions by the windows.

"Yes, when he was not too occupied saving Christendom through his work for the Bishop of Winchester, it seems that Edmund Sommerville saved my life," Geoffrey said sourly.

And so we were returning to the dislike of our days in Dartford. My heart sank. Seeing my expression, Geoffrey muttered, "I'm sorry, Joanna."

As I sat by his bed, searching for something to say, an awkward silence settled over the room.

Geoffrey finally said, "Bishop Gardiner has offered to mediate with the prince elector of the Palatine, to try to get Cheke's stolen money back. We have to recoup our money. I don't see how else to get you home."

Home. At that moment I didn't know what I found more daunting: the prospect of traveling for weeks through Europe again or facing an angry king of England. And there was another problem, too.

"Do you have any reason to think I am out of danger in the king's court?" I asked.

"No," he said. "But once I am recovered, we can't stay here. Wouldn't you agree, Joanna? We can't stay here."

"No we can't," I said, not meeting his eyes. In a moment, I found an excuse to leave the room.

What was wrong with me? Why did I feel so full of regret and sadness? What had happened to my closeness with Geoffrey? Perhaps it was no more than that I felt uncomfortable in the bishop's residence day after day, the four of us under the same roof: Gardiner, Edmund, Geoffrey, and myself.

On a warm spring morning, I decided to go alone to visit Saint Peter's Cathedral.

Those who called this cathedral the jewel of Regensburg weren't wrong. It would have been cherished in any country. The cathedral was a marvel of stone and structure; inside, I gloried in the cool, damp air, the mingling smells of incense and candle wax and the softly echoing voices, my favorite sensations to be found within a soaring house of God.

More than the colorful stained glass, what captured my attention was a carved statue of an angel attached to a massive pillar. The curly-haired angel appeared to be broadly smiling, something I'd never seen in a stone statue.

As I stood there, a priest paused in his walk across the nave.

In Latin, I asked, "Can you tell me about this statue, Father?"

"It is the Angel Gabriel," he answered, "the visible expression of the Gospel of Christ. Sculpted three hundred years ago by the Master of Saint Erminold."

With a bow, he continued on his way.

I decided to sit in the cathedral and think and pray for a while, and I wanted to sit where I could look at the smiling Angel Gabriel.

Some time passed—I don't know how long—and the main door

boomed open. There was the flutter of a dozen voices, kept low from respect but emanating from a large group nonetheless. I guessed that they, too, had come to tour the famous cathedral.

In a few moments, the cluster of men made their way to the nave, near where I sat. I saw the red robes of a cardinal, surrounded by bishops, priests, friars, and secretaries—this must be attendees of the Diet.

A thin but stooped man said in Spanish, "Observe this angel, Your Eminence, have you ever seen such a happy countenance?"

Another spoke up, "Which angel is it, though? This is the Cathedral of Saint Peter's, so one must assume that this blessed fellow is Saint Peter."

A third chimed in: "I heard there was a well-loved statue of Gabriel in here."

A bishop said, "So which is it—Peter or Gabriel?"

Without thinking, I said, also in Spanish, "The statue is the Angel Gabriel."

As one, the group of a dozen men turned to stare at me.

"What's a Spanish woman doing in Regensburg?" exclaimed one.

"I'm English," I said, although I said it in Spanish.

"That is nonsense," said the stooped man. "Yours is the face of Spain, and no English woman can speak our language."

The only Spanish person I'd known my entire life was my mother. Not even Ambassador Chapuys was of Spain; his homeland was the Savoy. Señor Hantaras was from Portugal. Now, finally, I was among people whose blood ties I shared, and, blushing, I told them who I was: Joanna Stafford, the daughter of Sir Richard Stafford and Isabella Montagna, of a family of Castile.

"But I have heard of you, I know your family," said the stooped man, in wonder. He turned to the bishop and the cardinal. "She waited on Catherine of Aragon, as her mother did, and then took vows in a Dominican Order when the saintly queen died."

The cardinal gestured for me to approach and I knelt to kiss his ring. He blessed me, I rose, and he moved on with several attendants while the bishop and Spaniards lingered. The bishop said, "Stephen Gardiner uses a brilliant secretary who was once a Dominican friar. Are you also in service to the bishop?"

Not knowing how best to answer that, I nodded.

The bishop turned to two men and, beckoned, saying, "And what do you think of this?" The men moved toward me, and to my joy, I recognized the black capes and cowls over white robes of Dominican friars. All of the men seemed as delighted to learn of my existence as I was to learn of theirs. There was a volley of questions before, bowing, they took their leave. I felt regret to see them go. I couldn't remember the last time a group of strangers had made me feel that immediate sense of belonging.

As I sat there, reflecting on the experience, a shadow stretched before me. It must be another of the Spaniards, come to say a final word.

I looked up, a shy smile on my face, and, an instant later, I shrank back into the pew, convulsed with terror.

Standing before me was Jacquard Rolin.

36

Am I not to receive the same courteous treatment as the bishop's party?" asked Jacquard. "You enchanted all the others."

Jacquard hadn't changed one iota as he stood before me, a feather curling from his jaunty cap, smiling with those full red lips. At first glance, a man of slight build. But the tightly fitted finery he wore concealed a lethal strength and reflexes faster than any other man's or woman's. In our training, he'd tried to teach me how to move as quickly as he did, but he was impossible to match. The only time I'd done it was when, certain he was about to kill me, I seized a silver tray and smashed him on the head, leaving him senseless. And that was also the last time I had seen Jacquard.

"What are you doing here?" I said.

"I go where I am needed," he said, with that elegant half shrug. "The Diet of Regensburg is an important conference of delicate diplomacy. The Emperor Charles requires a wide variety of talents."

I remembered what Chapuys once said—Jacquard was the premier spy in the emperor's service. That is why the ambassador requested him for the delicate mission of my recruitment to fulfilling the prophecy. Like Agrippa, he infused his talent for spying with his expertise in dark magic.

Tilting his head, he said, "The more interesting question is, what are *you* doing here, Joanna Stafford?"

I said nothing.

"I suppose, once I spotted Edmund Sommerville scurrying after

Bishop Gardiner, I should have known there was a possibility of you turning up. You were always in love with that dreary friar."

"Stay away from him, Jacquard," I said.

"Of course I will stay away from him. He knows me as the clerk from the Low Countries who assisted with the building of the king's manor house in Dartford. I could not risk his seeing me here in Regensburg, although it has created inconvenience for me to avoid being in the same place as the English party."

Fear leaped even higher inside me. Jacquard did not take well to being inconvenienced.

His voice silky, he said, "And what about me? Do you want me to stay away from you?"

Summoning all of my courage, I said, "I believe that goes without saying."

He laughed, quietly, glancing around me to see who else was in this part of the cathedral. Thankfully, there were other people within sight, examining a shrine surrounded by votive candles.

"Just when I least expect it, Joanna Stafford, you can make me laugh. It's an important quality in a woman. Well, I will say good-bye and join the others. And I will attempt to get over my hurt that you were so much sweeter to them than to me, in particular the Inquisitors."

"Inquisitors?"

"Don't you remember what I taught you? In Spain, the friars of the Dominican Order control the Inquisition. The emperor never travels without at least two of them. In fact, it is just possible that those two who just bowed to you in a Bavarian cathedral would have tried you and burned you for heresy should you have remained with me in Ghent."

Don't show him your fear. Jacquard thrives on fear.

I blurted, "You never would have let me escape in Ghent, no matter what I did. That was your plan, Jacquard. To kill me, one way or another."

Jacquard blinked, twice, and then smiled again, but it was a tight one.

I rose to my feet and said, "Ambassador Chapuys told me that the emperor forbade anyone to harm me. I know that, too."

"Of course, Joanna Stafford," he said, and with this time a broader smile. "The emperor did issue a decree concerning you. I am most familiar with it."

It took all my strength, but I turned and walked toward the entrance of the cathedral. To turn your back on Jacquard Rolin was perhaps the most foolhardy thing anyone could do. But I had to drive home to him that I knew I was safe.

My arms trembling, I pushed open the heavy cathedral door and stepped back into the sun.

During the walk back to Bishop Gardiner's residence, I found I had lost all reluctance to set out for England. Being in the same city as Jacquard seemed an incredibly bad idea. I hurried to the room where Geoffrey convalesced, but he slept, a slight wheeze in his breathing. I looked down at him in his bed, curled up in his blanket, his arm thrown over his head. How vulnerable Geoffrey was. What would Jacquard do if Geoffrey saw him in Regensburg? He was forbidden to harm me, but that protection did not extend to Geoffrey—or to Edmund, for that matter.

Geoffrey's eyes suddenly opened, and I gasped.

"What is the matter?" he said, his voice scratchy.

"Nothing. I came to see how you fared."

He struggled to sit up, with the help of the apothecary. "You're frightened, Joanna. Why?"

"You're mistaken," I said. "I am merely anxious to discuss our plan for returning to England—which route we should choose, and how a ship's passage should be arranged. Those things."

Although I continued to deny being frightened, Geoffrey was not fooled. That evening, he insisted on coming downstairs for supper rather than eating in his room. The conversation at the table centered on the news of the Diet. Edmund said that the first four articles— the integrity of man before the fall, free will, the cause of sin, and original sin—had passed, with agreement between Catholic and

Reformer. There was much reason for optimism, Edmund insisted, and he did not seem wrong.

After I'd finished my meal and was about to climb the stairs to my small room, Bishop Gardiner materialized. I hadn't known he was in the house. He beckoned to me to follow him to the parlor.

"The Spanish bishop mentioned meeting you in the cathedral today, Joanna, and wishes to invite you—and myself and Edmund—to a banquet he is holding next week. The emperor himself will attend."

I took a step back. "Oh, I don't think I should attend. I am not important enough."

The bishop's mouth tightened in disappointment. How he hated it whenever I did not immediately comply with his wishes.

"Your humility is most becoming, but as we both know you are of noble blood, and if you were to decline the invitation, it would be seen as an insult—and injurious to me."

But I did not want to be presented to the Emperor Charles, the man who had allowed Ambassador Chapuys to recruit me into a secret and deadly conspiracy in England and who had issued a decree about my life just months ago. How would he react when told my name, particularly when he had Jacquard Rolin at his disposal—and the Inquisitors?

Bishop Gardiner continued: "I don't think you understand how important the Diet is, not just to the kingdoms concerned but to individual lives, including yours."

"Mine?"

"If the Church can be unified, King Henry is prepared to consider returning to obedience," said Gardiner, his voice quivering with emotion. "It is negotiable. Now that Cromwell is gone, we can be blessed again."

"I've prayed for this," I said, "over and over and over, but it seemed impossible."

"It *is* possible," said Gardiner. "And while a sweeping return of every monastery is unrealistic, I believe that a few abbeys and priories of England can be restored—such as the Dominican order of the Sisters of Christ."

I covered my face with my hands, I was so overcome. I hadn't allowed myself to hope that I could ever put on a habit again.

"And Edmund?" I choked. "Will he, too, be restored?"

"Edmund is a different matter," said Gardiner. "He could retake his vows as a friar, but I have other plans for him. With his superior mind, I believe he could have a future at court, serving the king's council. I can even see Edmund one day donning the miter of a bishop."

To my astonishment, Gardiner beamed with the pride of a father.

"This is so much to take in—I must, I must pray on it," I stammered.

"Of course, Joanna, or should I say 'Sister Joanna'?" said Gardiner with one of his rare smiles. "Do you like the sound of it?"

Without waiting for an answer, Gardiner left the parlor. Tears gathering in my eyes, I left, too, and nearly collided with a man just outside the door. It was Geoffrey.

"So you'd like to be a nun again, Joanna?"

"You were listening to us!" I was appalled that Geoffrey would do such a thing.

"Please answer my question."

"Bishop Gardiner is offering a future that does not exist," I said. "First the Diet must come to an agreement, and heal the deep divisions of more than twenty years. And then King Henry must be persuaded to agree to restore some of the monasteries, which, in spite of the bishop's enthusiasm, I doubt he will want to do."

Geoffrey stood there, his eyes burning into mine, and I knew that was not the answer he hoped for.

"You want too much from me, Geoffrey." It escaped from my lips before I could stop it. "I cannot deny my faith, my calling. I was the happiest I've been in my whole life when I was in the priory. I was a novice when I met you."

"But you weren't wearing your novice habit that day," he said, arms folded.

"No," I conceded. "I wasn't."

Suddenly Geoffrey looked exhausted. He was still far from well. "You're right, Joanna, I probably do want too much from you," he murmured. "We will not speak of this again, not until we return to England." He turned away, and paused on the stairs, saying in a stronger voice: "But I *will* find out what frightened you so much at the cathedral today."

As he made his way upstairs, it sank in that by eavesdropping on Bishop Gardiner, Geoffrey had managed to put together my eagerness to leave Regensburg with my visit to the cathedral, a link I had tried to conceal from him.

Try as I might, I could not think of a way out of attending the bishop's banquet. All that was left to me was to hope that I'd not be presented to the Emperor Charles, or, if I was, that a man whose empire stretched across most of the world would have forgotten about me.

"Bishop Gardiner, these are your two Dominicans?" purred the beautiful woman who received us at the banquet. She wore a violet dress, with diamonds shimmering on her exposed bosom. I had no idea who she was or why she would possess hostess status at the bishop's residence. But I knew enough not to ask.

"Ah, but they are both so attractive," she said, looking me up and down, and Edmund, too. I did not like this, it felt as if I were a piece of sculpture, or even a doll, wearing the Bavarian-style full-sleeved dress that Bishop Gardiner had obtained for me.

Looking sideways, I detected a blush on Edmund's cheeks. He, too, did not enjoy this inspection. It had always pained Edmund, the moral corruption of some of the church leaders.

The Emperor Charles was the last to arrive, with his large retinue. The room was already boiling over with conversation—all the dignitaries of the Catholic countries coming together and a trio from England, too. Reverent silence replaced the chatter when the emperor appeared. Discreetly looking over the room, I was thankful for not seeing Jacquard Rolin, although it struck me that he would blame Edmund and me for missing such a prestigious evening.

Charles V looked much older than his sister, the queen regent, but I saw a resemblance: plain features, sallow skin, and long chin. With Queen Mary, a restless energy and curious mind lent her a certain charisma. The emperor, not surprisingly, emanated a more somber dignity. He did not wear large jewels or a crown. Unsmiling, he took his seat at the head of the highest table, next to Cardinal Gasparo Contarini, the representative from Rome and the same prince of the church I had spoken to at the cathedral. I noticed the two Dominican friars—the emperor's Inquisitors—take seats much lower.

To my surprise, we were all served simple German fare. Bishop Gardiner explained in a low voice that the emperor requested grilled sausages and ragout of meat with bread dumplings and iced beer. He was forced to travel his dominions near constantly, often at the head of an army, and missed the Flemish and German meals of his youth. As I watched the Emperor Charles devour his ragout with abandon, making loud chewing noises, I couldn't help but contrast his table deportment with Henry VIII's exactitude when dining. What made it still more curious was that the Hapsburgs were a family of ancient royalty, and the Tudors recently elevated.

The meal finished quickly, and the moment arrived for our presentation, something that could not be avoided. I tried to quiet my nerves, hovering behind Bishop Gardiner.

"Your Imperial Majesty, this is Mistress Joanna Stafford," said Gardiner.

I curtsied as low as I possibly could.

The emperor's sad features brightened as he regarded me, and I had a sense that Charles V enjoyed the company of women.

The Spanish bishop leaned over and whispered in the emperor's ear.

"Ah, your mother was of Castile and served my aunt the queen of England, that is interesting," the emperor said. To my surprise, his Spanish was far from melodious. He sounded more Germanic than the men in his Spanish retinue.

"Yes, she had that honor, Sire," I said.

The Spanish bishop said something else. A line deepened in the forehead of the emperor. His blinked, twice, and sat back in his chair. In response, my heart beat faster, and I felt a drop of sweat trickle down the back of my Bavarian dress.

The emperor said, his features forming a scowl, "You were a novice of the Dominican sisters in a town near London?"

"Yes, Sire, the town is Dartford," I said and curtsied again. It was not protocol to dip a curtsy when answering a question—I was so frightened, I did not know what I was doing. Out of the corner of my eye, I saw Bishop Gardiner glaring at me.

"You should stay there," he said. "You should stay in Dartford."

Bishop Gardiner stepped forward, words were said of reassurance, and I moved back. It was Edmund's turn to be presented. All who were close enough to have heard the emperor stared at me, curious. I longed to run from the room, but to where? Bishop Gardiner's residence was hardly a safe place, even if Geoffrey was waiting for me there. He didn't know of my connection to the Emperor Charles, Ambassador Chapuys, and Jacquard Rolin. What did Geoffrey say in Antwerp? *It's like fighting with both arms tied behind my back.* Never did I want to confide in him more than now. But never was the truth more dangerous for him to learn than now.

Back in our seats, it was Edmund who said, "Joanna, don't be troubled."

"I'm not," I said, fingering my goblet of wine, poured from a bottle carried all the way from Portugal.

"I'm afraid I know you better than that," said Edmund gently. "I've been in the same room with the emperor for months now. He is beset by strange moods. You did nothing wrong—you were splendid, as you always are."

I turned to look at Edmund, to really look at him. These weeks under the same roof had been strange, and rather difficult. I'd spoken to him nearly every day but rarely had I looked at him like this, straight into his large brown eyes.

"Thank you for your kindness, Edmund."

He smiled at me, and for a moment, it was as if we were back at Dartford, engaged to be married.

I have so missed such kindness. I wanted to say it, but couldn't.

Gardiner was of course upset by my encounter with the emperor. Why did learning of the location of my priory displease Charles V? I professed myself just as confused.

But in the days to come, the bishop had more pressing matters to worry him. Conflict sprouted at the Diet; compromises that seemed secure wavered. June approached, and the conference threatened to stretch on for a good while longer.

Geoffrey, who had been eager to return to England and seemed recovered in health, kept generating excuses for both of us to linger in Regensburg. One day, I managed to speak to him alone about it. "This Diet could continue for the rest of the year," I said. "Why should you and I remain? We have no role in this. We need to return to Dartford."

Geoffrey admitted to me that the bishop had refused to allow me to travel with him, even accompanied by a fleet of servants, because of the impropriety.

"The bishop does not rule over me," I fumed.

"Perhaps not," Geoffrey said. "But you know I have not been able to recover John Cheke's money and I don't have the means to travel out of the German lands without Gardiner's help." The prince elector of the Palatine, while enraged by the actions of Arnulf and von Seckenburg, had not been able to extract the stolen money from them because the two had disappeared.

"We have no choice but to stay, although Bishop Gardiner has said I can leave alone at any time and he'd loan me some funds. King Henry gave him a vast sum to travel here with a retinue of servants. But even if I had the money for such a journey, I would not leave you behind. I have a bad feeling, Joanna. A very bad feeling."

37

I lost my position as tapestry mistress in a letter I was not allowed to read.

It arrived from England in June, bearing the seal of King Henry VIII. A long letter, from the looks of it, bearing instructions to Gardiner on all matter of things. One of the instructions was to tell me that I would not bear responsibility for the tapestries any longer.

"But why?" I asked, in equal measure hurt and relieved. This meant I would not have to go to court. My life was mine again, to pursue in Dartford, safe from harm and surrounded by friends. This gave me joy. Yet there remained an undeniable part of me enthralled by the king's exquisite tapestry collection and proud of my responsibilities.

"This is my correspondence, and I have shared with you the facts that pertain to you," Bishop Gardiner snapped, and left the room. As the Diet grew more charged with conflict, Gardiner's temper worsened.

Edmund was distraught. "Because of your journey to find me, you've lost a worthy position, and it revolved around your great talent for tapestries—oh, Joanna, I wish I could think of a way to correct this."

I assured Edmund that I would be fine. "The future of the Diet, that seems to be of graver concern."

He couldn't deny it. The fighting grew more heated, the opposing positions more fixed. And one day, Edmund told me that the

Diet had failed—the emperor personally implored the Protestants to accept the disputed articles, and they refused. Then the Catholics refused to consider any change in church treatment of transubstantiation, our belief that bread and wine becomes the body and blood of Christ.

"War shall surely follow," said Edmund, his voice tight with grief. "Here, in the German lands, in the Netherlands, in France. The wars of religion could annihilate all of Christendom. England shall continue its descent into heresy. And we were so close, I really thought we could do it—achieve unity."

I felt the familiar quake of worry over Edmund's distress. Would he now disintegrate spiritually and end with reaching for opium? That was his tragic pattern. But as I spoke to him more of the failure of the Diet, I realized that Edmund was a different person. Perhaps it was his long sojourn through the wilderness, emulating Saint Dominic, followed by his passionate efforts to heal the religious breach— Edmund had finally found inner strength.

Bishop Gardiner was another story. He locked himself in the study of his residence and refused food or water. Finally, Edmund and I persuaded him to let us in.

His eyes were red from weeping, I was shocked to see. I'd thought the Bishop of Winchester impervious to such storms of emotion.

"God's plan is hard for me to understand," he admitted. "I thought that at last we were to be forgiven—that I would be forgiven." His voice broke. I remembered when I first met Gardiner, in the Tower of London, and he told me that his was the legal mind that supplied King Henry with the strategy he needed to divorce Catherine of Aragon, which led to the break from Rome, thus unleashing forces he could not control.

"You have done all that you could, surely," I said.

"You are needed more than ever, Bishop, to safeguard the souls of those in England who are far from God's grace," said Edmund.

Gardiner was silent for a long time. I'd begun to think we

should leave the room when he stood up, nodding. "You have given me valuable support"—he turned to me—"both of you, which God in His wisdom knows that I did not deserve, after how I have treated you in the past. I shall make amends. That, at least, is in my power."

I should have rejoiced that relations between myself and the bishop were so harmonious after years of conflict and resentment, but instead I tensed inside. I wasn't sure that Gardiner's idea of amends would be to my liking.

After we left the parlor, Edmund said, "What shall you do when we return to England, Joanna?"

"Now that I am no longer expected to serve the king, I expect to live in Dartford once more, labor on my tapestries." I thought for a moment. "I shall renew my efforts to bring Arthur back down."

I glanced at Edmund, who was deep in thought.

"I suppose you will join the bishop's staff at Winchester House?" I asked. "He has said how highly he esteems you."

"Yes," said Edmund, "that seems to be the plan."

It felt strange to realize that when, weeks ago, I'd walked along the Danube with Edmund, I feared he was living in the past. Now he was the one pushing forward into the future and I was retreating to the life I'd led more than a year ago, when the summons arrived on my doorstep from Whitehall. It was like the children's game that forced the one who threw the marble the shortest distance to creep back to the line of the beginning.

The hour was late and the house quiet. I wasn't sure if Geoffrey was awake upstairs. It was past time to retire, but Edmund did not seem to want to say good night.

Clearing his throat, he said, "I know that I have lost your trust, Joanna, but if you could give me a chance to rebuild, if I knew that we could be friends . . ."

"We shall always be friends, Edmund," I said. Hope leaped in his eyes, which pleased me and yet saddened me, too. We could never be married, it was against the king's law. Did I still wish to be Edmund's wife? I wasn't sure. One thing I was quite sure of—Geoffrey wanted a future with me, and there was no legal impediment. But was it right to marry him if I still felt this wistfulness for Edmund? That didn't seem fair to either of them.

And so we returned to England, an uncomfortable journey, not because of physical deprivation but because of my confusion. Every day I saw the two of them, and every day I struggled to understand my feelings for these men: Geoffrey and Edmund. Did I love both of them? Neither of them? Was I even someone who was capable of love for a man and should be married? I simply did not know.

Moreover, I had two conversations along the way that troubled me deeply. The first was with Bishop Gardiner, and at my initiation. I wanted to know what was happening at the English court. My thoughts were much with Catherine Howard, whom I had neglected for so long. Although she must know I was in Germany these many months, she had written no letter to me through Gardiner. She was the queen of England, the first woman of the land, pampered and adored. It was ridiculous to think that the absence of my friendship had caused her any great hardship. But when I thought of her sharing the bed and board of Henry VIII, a strange fear clawed at me. I had to be sure she was safe.

"Queen Catherine has brought much happiness to the king," the bishop assured me.

"My cousin the Earl of Surrey said at the time of the wedding she restored his youth," I ventured.

The bishop frowned, and said, "Yes, undeniably so, in those first weeks. But His Majesty is no boy, it must be said. He's suffered serious health mishaps in the last year. During one of them, he sent the queen away. I think he could not bear for her to see him like that. It is not always easy for Queen Catherine. And I fear that her household is not of the best quality."

I pressed Bishop Gardiner for explanation. It seemed that Norfolk had planted every possible Howard relative in the queen's household, whether they held the proper qualifications or not, to take part in the spoils of the king's favor. And Lady Rochford over-saw them all.

"Does Catherine wield any influence on the king?" I asked.

"She has attempted it," Gardiner answered. "She spoke up for Margaret Pole, the king's elderly cousin still in the Tower."

I was impressed that Catherine would show such bravery—Margaret Pole, the countess of Salisbury, was the mother of Reginald Pole, the king's greatest enemy, and of Henry Pole, Lord Montagu, beheaded for treason.

But then I noticed Gardiner's pained expression. "Did it not go well—was the king angry with her?" I asked.

"The queen's concern was that the countess suffered from the cold in the Tower last winter, and she asked that blankets and warm clothes should be sent to her, and the king agreed to it." He paused. "Nonetheless, the king decided that Margaret Pole was a dangerous traitor and she was executed in May while I was away in Regensburg."

Horrified, I said, "But the countess was seventy years old. Did anyone find new evidence of her guilt?"

The bishop shook his head and closed his eyes. We both knew that the crime of Margaret Pole was to possess too pure a strain of royal blood. Yet how could a sick old woman pose any sort of threat? I worried anew for Catherine, married to a man who would do that.

"But I do believe all is calm now," said Gardiner, with the firm-ness of someone trying to convince himself. "The king and queen went on progress to the north of England this summer—we should return to London before they come back to the south. I have received word that it was a successful progress. The king's motto for Catherine is 'No Other Will But His.' He has found the perfect wife, he tells everyone."

So Catherine was definitely in high standing. Still, I wouldn't be at ease until I saw her. I'd just need a pretext for a visit. The only thing I could think of was to finish the tapestry of Niobe, with Cath-erine's face. It would be my gift to her, and a way to thaw the ice between us.

Just as disquieting, but on a different front, was a story Edmund told me about the Black Forest. There was a certain episode he'd omitted when we walked along the Danube, whether it was to spare me or because he was too unsettled to bring it up, I wasn't sure.

At Freiburg, the abbot asked Edmund to go to a village in the Black Forest where the people were tormented in spirit. Their terror was caused by a man with access to dark magic, to the secrets of necromancy, who had died in their midst and been buried, but his corpse did not rest in the ground. Because of the Dominican reputation for courage in the face of heresy, the abbot thought that Edmund could calm the village.

"When I reached the place, I learned that the dead man was no crossroads sorcerer but a German professor named Johann Georg Faust, who practiced astrology and alchemy."

"I've heard of this man," I exclaimed.

"Yes, he was infamous. The most appalling story was that he sold his soul to the devil for the secret of great knowledge."

I crossed myself, and Edmund joined me.

"Faust died in the middle of one of his alchemy experiments nearby. Some sort of horrific explosion. In the past, he had supposedly been in the presence of the nobility, of royalty, and even had an audience with the Emperor Charles."

My stomach tightening, I said, "The emperor?"

"The emperor and his inner circle have always been interested in seers and magicians, though Charles the Fifth is as likely to turn them over to the Inquisition for burning as to listen to their words and believe in their tricks. It is probably a rumor, but in the village I heard that the emperor told Faust, who presented himself as a conjurer, that the man from history he most wanted to see was Alexander the Great—and Faust was able to summon him."

I crossed myself again and said, "Edmund, do *you* believe that the dead can be conjured by these dark magicians?"

"I don't know. I only know that the villagers told me that Faust was buried in the ground facing up, but then when some troublemakers dug up the body, the body had turned itself facedown, for better entry to Hell."

Now I was churning with fear. Seeing my state, Edmund apologized profusely. "Joanna, to assuage the villagers' terror, I oversaw the disinterment of the man's body. The story was untrue. The dead man faced up. I said prayers over the reburial of Faust and sprinkled holy water on the ground."

I could not leave it at that. "Edmund, do you believe that there are ways to summon up forces, not through prayer to God but other sorts of forces, that can control what men do?"

Edmund frowned. "You mean, can magic be practiced such as the type of spells written about by Cornelius Agrippa?" he asked.

It was the name I most feared hearing, and there it was. I struggled to present a calm face as Edmund pondered my question.

"There is a danger in reaching into the deepest crevices of the past, of losing your soul to the writing of the ancient scribes—especially when they are mixed with pagan practices of the forest," he said. "Even Paracelsus was seduced by that elixir, and he drew close to heresy time and again. But, Joanna, I do not think that a man's mind can be unduly influenced or damaged if there was no weakness there to begin with. And in the end, only the gentle miracles of Christ can save any of us."

Was that the explanation? Sir Walter Hungerford was an immoral man, no question. But my cousin the Earl of Surrey was no worse than reckless and vain, and Thomas Culpepper—what was his weakness? What had changed him? I tried to make sense of all I had learned, in England and in Europe, but could not be sure of anything.

And so, in September of 1541, we returned to England. Bishop Gardiner hurried to the court of the king, taking Edmund with him, as I had expected. Geoffrey disappeared to his home in Dartford and then resurfaced as the constable of the town, to the joy of those who had missed him. I waited for Geoffrey to come to me, but he did not, which caused me both relief and regret. Every time I saw him, he was most cordial. But the closeness between us had vanished. It was as if I never laid my head on his shoulder in a cart rumbling to Heidelberg.

I tried to take up my life again. I wrote to my cousin Lord Henry Stafford, asking again that he send Arthur back to Dartford. I visited Agatha and John Gwinn, and learned that the farmers were blessed with the year's harvest. The nightmare of the previous year was not repeated. I went to see Sister Eleanor and the other nuns of the priory, too, and there I was presented with my tapestry of *The Sorrow of Niobe*, finished except that the face of the central figure, the tragic queen, was a blank. I thanked them profusely and, grateful for a task to occupy me, set about completing the weave. Hans Holbein's sketch of Catherine's lovely face would guide me.

I woke up quite early one morning, intent on finishing my work. It was the first week of November and cool, but no clouds obscured the sun. Enough light poured through the front window to work efficiently. The design of the tapestry was balanced between in the upper left an angry god of Olympus stretching down from a thunderous cloud with one hand and Niobe, in the lower right, her hands outstretched, as she was changed to stone. Her beautiful shimmering dress hardened to a gray slab where feet and legs should be. Because the agony of her children's deaths was so unbearable, the gods agreed to the transformation. I had worried all along that Catherine's cheerful face would be too hard to incorporate into the tragic tableaux. But I was able to capture her features and coloring without sacrificing the mood of despair.

I finished the tapestry by early afternoon and was preparing to remove it from the loom when a pounding sounded at the door.

"Joanna, Joanna—let me in!"

It was the Earl of Surrey, his voice rough with panic. He tumbled into my home, travel-stained and disheveled. He had ridden hard down from London. Two bewildered Howard retainers stood behind him.

"You have to help them," he said. "You are the only one who has the sense and the strength to help them."

"What is it—who should I help?" I beckoned him inside.

The minute the door slammed behind him, Surrey said, "The queen. Catherine. She is in great danger. The king has ordered her investigated."

As stunned as I felt in the first seconds, there was recognition, too, of the moment I had waited for, in dread, for months. Henry VIII turned against everyone eventually: his family, his ministers, his wives.

"Is she taken to the Tower?" I asked heavily.

"Not yet. She is kept close in her apartments at Hampton Court."

"What are the charges?"

"That she was lewd before marriage."

I said angrily, "Is this a joke of yours? Everyone knows she was the king's mistress before their marriage."

"Not with the king. With someone else. Such a corruption threatens the succession should the queen have a child." Surrey's eyes narrowed. "Wait. You knew, didn't you?"

I saw no point in keeping Catherine's secret now, when we must pool our knowledge to save her. "I knew such a man existed, but not his name. How could this be matter for investigation? It was long ago."

Surrey told me that the question was whether Catherine had relations with the man *after* marrying the king. "He is her private secretary, Francis Dereham. The king received a letter containing reports that she knew Dereham when very young, that she committed wanton acts with him in the house of the Dowager Duchess of Norfolk."

"No," I said emphatically. "I cannot believe Catherine would commit adultery with anyone after her marriage."

Surrey shouted, "She is innocent of adultery with Dereham. The man is a lout and a scoundrel. He blackmailed her into giving him a position."

"Won't your father defend her?" I said. "The Duke of Norfolk can explain everything to the king."

Surrey closed his eyes in anguish. "At the first moment of crisis, he abandoned her."

"Who is it that brings these charges to the king's attention?" I demanded. "Who pushes for her destruction?"

"Archbishop Cranmer gave the king a letter that detailed her past immorality."

So the mild-faced archbishop showed his true colors. I took a deep breath. "Then we must do all we can to bring the truth to the king. I will go to him, if that is why you've come. I will speak for Catherine."

"He has left Hampton Court and is in seclusion, emerging only to see his council," said Surrey. "The king will most definitely not see you. And the guards will admit no one to Catherine's chamber."

"Well, what can be done?" I demanded. "You must have a plan."

Surrey said, "I came to you, Joanna, for the plan."

I paced the floor, trying to think.

"When you came in the door, you said, 'Help them.' Whom do you mean by *them*? Catherine and King Henry?"

"No." The earl shook his head, as if he could not believe something himself.

"What is it, Cousin? Tell me."

"There could be another man whom she *has* committed adultery with. It's Thomas Culpepper."

I took a step back, stumbling on a table, and nearly fell.

He held up a hand. "I am not sure. No one is. But it is possible. There are rumors."

I remembered Catherine's confession in the garden park of Winchester House. She had fallen in love with Culpepper before she was forced to captivate the king. His rejection of her inflicted a deep wound—it was even part of the reason she was ready to become the king's mistress. She thought it would goad Culpepper, whom she longed for. He stayed clear of her the entire time I was in Whitehall, but after she became queen, did something happen?

"Is Culpepper arrested?"

"No." Surrey swallowed. "Not yet."

"Have you spoken to him?"

Surrey said that nothing had changed since he confided in me on the day of Cromwell's execution. Culpepper was profane, swaggering, and dangerous. He laughed at Surrey's efforts to rein him in.

"Where is Thomas now?" I asked.

"At Hampton Court—that's where everyone is," my cousin said. "I need to get you there as soon as possible. Bring some clothes. I honestly don't know how long this will take. I don't even know what we can do, but we must do something."

I rushed to gather clothes, and snatched a book of Scripture. As we prepared to leave, Surrey said, glancing at my book, "If only I'd been able to find the fourth book of Cornelius Agrippa, then there could have been a chance for Culpepper. There must be men who can interpret it—priests, perhaps. And then we could have reversed the hex, the incantation, whatever it is that corrupted him. I tried, Joanna, but I had no luck finding it."

I was two inches from the door when I froze.

"Of course," I said. The Queen Regent Mary had told me that Chapuys was godfather to one of Agrippa's sons, that they were close. Edmund said, *The emperor and his inner circle have always been interested in seers and magicians.*

I turned to tell Surrey, "I am fairly certain that Ambassador Chapuys has the books of Agrippa."

"Chapuys?" Surrey said in wonder. "Yes, yes, you must be right. He is a great scholar, I've heard, educated in the same part of the world as Agrippa. But why didn't you write to me of this at once?"

"I didn't realize it until this moment."

Surrey said, greatly excited, "I know where Chapuys resides in London."

"Then we must go there together before we attempt anything else and try to find it. There should be some way to see his library, whether the ambassador is there or not."

Determined, I pulled open the door—and there stood Geoffrey Scovill, the Howard retainers behind him.

"Where are you going, Joanna?" he asked.

"Constable, I am taking her to Hampton Court," said the Earl of Surrey, who'd met Geoffrey at the Rose Tavern and now pushed past him.

"That's unwise," Geoffrey said.

"This is not your concern," said my cousin, beckoning for his horse. He told one of the men to give his horse to me, and find some other way back to court.

"Joanna, listen to me, when I say—" Geoffrey began.

"We don't have time for this," interrupted Surrey. "I don't see why this man feels he has the right to offer an opinion on what you do, Joanna, or to follow you around any longer, especially in view of Bishop Gardiner's plan."

I whirled on Surrey, demanding, "What plan?"

"The bishop is working on an exception to be made for his secretary, Edmund Sommerville, to marry even though he was once a friar. You can be his wife after all."

38

"I know nothing of this exception, you must believe me," I said to Geoffrey, rendered silent by Surrey's news. He stared at me, his eyes full of ravaged pride.

Moments later, my cousin practically threw me onto the back of his servant's horse.

"If we don't leave now, we won't make London before nightfall," said Surrey.

"Give me a moment to speak to Geoffrey," I pleaded.

Surrey said, "This is Catherine's *life*." He jumped onto his horse, and with a swift kick he was off, my horse surging right behind. I turned around, frantic, trying to see Geoffrey without tumbling out of the saddle. He had not moved—he stood watching us go. He would not follow this time.

Surrey rode his horse so hard I had a difficult time keeping up. He was as a man possessed—fear and guilt made for a powerful combination. As for me, I felt torn in two. I wanted to do everything in my power to help Catherine Howard and Thomas Culpepper, whose lives were in danger. But I was sick with regret that Geoffrey had been told in such a brutal fashion that Edmund meant to marry me. And I was furious that I'd not been informed. How dare Edmund and Bishop Gardiner make these sorts of plans for me?

While waiting to cross London Bridge, our horses quivering with exhaustion, I asked my cousin if he thought Ambassador Chapuys would be at home. It might be easier to talk our way into the residence, ask to see the library and then make excuses, all before the ambassador returned. I wasn't sure how to best go about securing the book. We could ask to borrow it, of course. But I was not above stealing it for a cause as crucial as this.

Surrey said, "Chapuys is probably still at court, waiting to hear the news of the king's council. The council meets for days, investigating Catherine and preparing possible grounds for divorce—and other possibilities." Surrey winced. "Of course, the king himself is not there. As I told you, he is in seclusion. At this stage, he is always like Henry the Second: 'Will no one free me of this woman?'"

A strange feeling churned; I almost felt as if I would be sick. Another realization had sunk in.

Ever since Geoffrey told me that in London the play actors who enacted the tragedy of Henry II and Becket were part of the plan, I'd wondered why they picked that tableau from history. The most frightening scenario I'd grappled with was that it was a reference to the night that Edmund and I joined the monks on their mission to rescue the bones of the saint from Canterbury Cathedral. But now I was struck by another possibility. Just as the four knights who killed Becket wanted to please a powerful king who desired the death of the archbishop but dared not directly order it, what if my adversaries were trying to please someone who wanted to destroy me but could not give the order?

The men in charge of London Bridge gave the signal, and the Earl of Surrey and I rode through. The crowd was thin; it was near dark. We rode toward Chapuys's house.

That's when I felt it—that strange itch, something alighting on my shoulder and the back of my head. I swung around, but recognized no one.

"What is it, Joanna?" asked Surrey.

"Nothing," I said. Except that I was now convinced that the house of Ambassador Chapuys was the last place on earth I should be riding to.

But what about Culpepper and Catherine?

I took a long look at my cousin. He was heir to a dukedom and a celebrated courtier and poet. Also a soldier, a man trained to fight. No one would dare trifle with me while I was by his side. And it would take only a few moments to obtain the book. I'd simply never let Surrey out of my sight.

When we reached Chapuys's house, there was a candle burning inside, but just one. A good sign. The ambassador must not be home. We knocked on the door, and told the startled young man who answered that we were there to call upon Chapuys. Surrey instructed his own servant to remain outside with the horses.

"I will make inquiries," said the young man.

He led us to a small downstairs parlor without a single book in it and then disappeared. This was going to be more of a challenge than I thought. We couldn't rampage through the ambassador's house. What excuse could I give for going upstairs?

"Greetings, my lord Surrey—and Mistress Stafford," said a familiar voice. Señor Hantaras smiled in the doorway to the parlor. "I am most pleased to see you here. My master the ambassador is not at home. Would you like to wait?"

Smiling right back at him, we said we would like to do just that. Surrey's friendliness was more genuine than mine. The sight of Hantaras always made my flesh go cold.

"The ambassador has a superb wine collection—may I offer you refreshment?"

Surrey agreed with enthusiasm, as I feared he would. This was not a social occasion. We must not get distracted from our goal: finding the library.

"We can't ask to see the library at once," Surrey whispered. "It would be more natural after conversation and a drink."

Hantaras was gone for quite a while, but then reappeared with a bottle. He personally poured the wine. As he filled my goblet, bending down, I saw that his neck was damp. He must have greatly exerted himself to break out in a sweat on such a cool night.

I didn't touch the wine. Glancing out the mullioned windows, barely listening to the casual conversation between Surrey and Hantaras, I wondered when Chapuys would arrive.

"Considering how painfully and with what goodwill they have proved it, I find it interesting that—" My cousin broke off in the middle of a sentence, and loosened a button on his doublet.

"Forgive me," he muttered. "I'm feeling . . . rather warm . . . terribly warm . . . I regret that . . ." With that, Surrey blinked, and coughed twice, and slithered out of his chair and onto the floor in a faint.

I sprang to his side and cradled his head in my hands. My cousin was breathing but his eyes were shut, dead to the world. "What is wrong?" I cried. "You drank one glass of wine, how could this be?"

I looked up, at Señor Hantaras. He still stood on the other side of the room, his hand on one hip. He hadn't moved a single inch.

"The Earl of Surrey needs help—can't you see that?" I snapped, his head in my lap. "What are you waiting for?"

But that didn't send him across the room. Nor did he seem offended by my angry tone. He just kept studying me. Not the unconscious earl. Me. As we locked eyes, all of his hospitality drained away, replaced by unadulterated hatred.

I heard a creak on wood, like the sound of a step on stairs. And a second and third, steady steps on the stairs. Not a large man, to move like this. Someone light and graceful, but with purpose. Was Ambassador Chapuys at home after all? Had they practiced a deception? Rage flooded through me that they would trifle with me and my cousin in such a way.

Señor Hantaras turned his head toward the sound on the steps and nodded, once, to someone I couldn't see. And with that, I knew who would appear in the doorway a split second before he appeared.

Jacquard Rolin, smiling as he came into view, said, "After all that we've been through, all the waiting and watching and making our attempts, in the end she comes right to me, like a lover." He patted his chest. "It's just so incredibly touching."

The most important thing was to keep thinking. Jacquard taught me that. I must not lose my head. There was only one door to the room, and Hantaras stood just inside it. But there must be something else I could do.

"I couldn't believe it when their horses turned onto the Strand and then stopped here," said Señor Hantaras. "Once they were inside, I had to climb in through the back window to come through the house to receive them."

I looked down at Surrey's slack face. "You drugged him."

Hantaras said, "I would have drugged you, too, and then I wouldn't have to look at you one moment longer. But you didn't touch it, you troublesome bitch. I thank God I won't have to deal with you after today."

I knew now.

"It was you," I said to Hantaras. "You were the one who watched me. Every single time."

"Either me or someone directed by me, and I hated it, every minute," Hantaras snarled. "It was a lot of work, and enormous expense, to get hold of you."

I said, "In London, in the Whitehall gatehouse, at Tower Hill, it was you."

Without looking down, I began to ease the earl's head off my lap, using the smallest of movements. When I made my dash, it would have to be a surprise. Until then, I must keep them talking. "Have you been in England without my knowing it, Jacquard?" I asked.

"Not until last month," he said, coming around the table by the door to stand nearer to me, unfortunately. "I devised the plan with Hantaras in letters, and agreed on various scenarios for your abduction. He was to hire men to hold you in England, outside London, until I could find an excuse to book passage and deal with you, finally, myself."

"But Chapuys forbade it," I said. "I was not to be harmed."

Out of the corner of my eye, Hantaras scowled, shifting from foot to foot. He didn't like what I said. Which must mean one thing.

"The ambassador does not know anything about this," I said.

Jacquard shrugged. "He was the one who received the edict from the ambassador after you betrayed us and saved the life of your king. 'No harm shall come to the woman in Dartford.' How long we have analyzed that sentence! Did he mean no harm should come to you at all? Or that no harm should come to you but only as long as you remained in Dartford? In the end we decided the emperor must mean the latter. Every time you left Dartford, you were fair game."

You should stay there, the emperor said in grave reproof in Regensburg. He knew the sort of men who worked in his service, and so he knew that was the only place of safety for me.

I had to keep them talking while I continued to ease Surrey's head down onto the floor. "If you were confident with your interpretation, why not bring Eustace Chapuys into it?" I asked, turning to Hantaras.

But he responded by turning to Jacquard, "Get her out of here."

Jacquard took a step closer to me, his lips moist. "It's too early, there are people still on the street who will notice unusual movements outside the ambassador's residence. Chapuys won't be back for at least an hour. I can accomplish quite a bit in an hour."

Fighting down nausea, I said, "Chapuys must have said something about wishing to be rid of me, and you decided that was all you needed. 'Will no one rid me of this troublesome priest?' Wasn't it like that? It must have been, for you to stage that little play in London. You must have loved the thought of sending me a coded message."

Jacquard smiled, in delight. "You see how clever she is? That's the pity of it all. She was my finest pupil. But I just couldn't break her spirit. And if you can't break in an animal, you have to put it down."

He took another step toward me. He was no more than six steps away now.

I said rapidly, "You taught me always to think things through, Jacquard, to have contingencies for everything, and I don't think you've thought *this* through." I turned to Hantaras. "You shouldn't have let Jacquard talk you into drugging us here, you should have tried to take me when I was alone. What are you going to do when the Earl of Surrey wakes up? And what about his man outside? This will cause an incident, my going missing and the earl falling mysteriously ill in the ambassador's house. Señor Hantaras, you have failed your master tonight."

"Get her out of here!" shouted Hantaras in Spanish. "Get her out!"

I slid Surrey's head all the way to the floor and sprang to my feet. I dashed for the window. I'd scream my head off and pound on the glass. The window was close to the street—the attention they feared would surely come. At the least, Surrey's man would come running in.

I was inches from the window, and opening my mouth to scream, when a powerful hand seized me by the waist and hurled me back. I felt a sharp pain on the side of my neck, like the chop of a hand, and darkness spread.

When I regained consciousness, my wrists hurt and I could hardly breathe. Something filled my mouth. My legs were free, but my hands were tied to something and my arms were spread apart. The room was lit by candlelight, and I looked up at the canopy of a bed.

I smelled Jacquard before I saw him, that musky amber he doused himself with.

A rope tightened around my left wrist, stretched high and tight over my head. I strained to look up. Jacquard, a knife between his teeth, tightened the rope around my wrist. He was tying me to the backboard of a bed. I tried to cry out, but a rag was stuffed in my mouth.

Finishing the knot, Jacquard took the knife out of his mouth. "You see, Joanna Stafford, we learn from experience. I learned in Ghent that I have to tie you up before the fun begins. That was my mistake, one of the biggest mistakes I made in my entire career."

He tilted his head, regarding me.

"You shouldn't have taunted me in Regensburg, you realize that? That's what made me come here, to accomplish the task once and for all."

There was a terrible silence for a moment, and then Jacquard leaped on me. With one hand he pressed down on my thighs so I couldn't kick him, and with the other he pulled the rag out of my mouth.

"I am curious about one thing, and I'm afraid that after our interlude tonight you won't be able to answer questions. I have to know. What did you do with our man on the boat? Or should I say our woman—our wonderful blind woman."

I coughed for a moment and said, "When he tried to stab me on deck, I poked him in the eyes with my fingers. He threw himself overboard."

Jacquard laughed. He threw back his head and laughed and laughed. "I taught you too well," he said.

Hantaras appeared in the doorway, furious. "What are you doing with her on the ambassador's bed?"

"I'm not going to kill her on the bed," Jacquard said curtly, annoyed at being questioned. "Now get out, unless you want to watch. Which I never object to."

"I should not have permitted this—you have lost control of yourself, Jacquard. This was all a mistake," Hantaras said, glaring at Jacquard with even more hatred than he'd shown toward me.

Jacquard slammed the door and then returned to me. He sat next to me on the bed and patted my cheek, as solicitous as an adoring father. I shrank from his touch. I couldn't hold back my disgust.

"It is harder to do than I thought," he mused. "I've hated you for so long and dreamed of how I'd kill you. The thought of my vengeance has kept me warm at night for months—I have barely needed a woman. But at the same time, you are my masterpiece. The way you've stayed alive is remarkable—and choosing to go for the window, not the door? *Magnifique.*"

He ran his hand down my entire body, feeling every inch, until he reached my ankle. With his other hand, he took rope out of his pocket, and began to tie my left foot to the bedpost.

The end of my life was near, I knew it, and I fought through my revulsion to pray to God for deliverance to His kingdom.

"Forgive me, Father, and take me to Your mercy," I said. "And forgive this man for what he is about to do."

"Don't pray for me," he ordered. "I heard enough of that from you to last a hundred lifetimes."

"You cannot stop me," I said. "You can bind my mouth, you can violate me in the foulest manner, you can cut my throat. But the last thought I have will be of your salvation, Jacquard."

Jacquard wasn't smiling or laughing any longer. To rob him of his sadistic pleasure was the only defiance left to me. He took a step toward me, fingering his knife. I had less than a moment now.

We both heard raised voices downstairs. I recognized Ambassador Chapuys.

Jacquard sprang toward the head of the bed, groping for the rag, but before he could stuff it into my mouth I screamed so loudly my ears rang.

I heard the stamping of feet, and in less than a moment, in the doorway, stood Ambassador Chapuys. "Mother of God, what are you doing here, and what have you done to Joanna?" he roared.

"She defied us—she betrayed us, and for that she has to die," Jacquard said haughtily. "I shall take the responsibility with the emperor."

"You've gone mad," said Chapuys. "I always feared you had that potential."

"And you are a coward," said Jacquard. "You should have ordered her death last year. You wanted to do it, admit it."

"She isn't going to die."

Jacquard laughed. "She most certainly is! After what she knows now? You can't take the chance she won't tell all, and what are the implications for the emperor?"

The ambassador looked at me, shaking his head in horror and

dismay, but it was over what Jacquard was just about to do to me. He didn't share Jacquard's loathing. "She hasn't said a word thus far," he said. "Or I would know."

"I will not be prevented!" screamed Jacquard. He was losing control, and that was the moment it happened. Señor Hantaras burst in from a door to the side of the room. He must have been ordered to go around and wait his chance. He tackled Jacquard and threw him to the ground.

Hantaras punched him in the face, again and again, until the premier spy of the emperor was broken and senseless. I found I could not watch the final savage blow that knocked him unconscious.

Ambassador Chapuys freed me and helped me down the stairs. After Señor Hantaras had used that same rope to tie up Jacquard Rolin, he joined us as we worked together to revive the Earl of Surrey.

He vomited twice and looked wretched indeed, but the earl was not seriously damaged.

"Sorry, Joanna," he muttered. "I can't believe that a small amount of wine could do that to me."

Ambassador Chapuys insisted that the wine had gone bad and he promised to make amends. "May I know why you honored me with your presence today?" he asked, genuinely puzzled.

"We came here to see your library," groaned Surrey.

"My *library*?"

I turned to the ambassador. "I understand you were once friends with the man Cornelius Agrippa. Is it possible you have any of his books?"

To my astonishment, Ambassador Chapuys smiled. "Of course," he said, and sent the young servant who'd reappeared to fetch the book. Surrey and I exchanged glances. We would finally have it, the means to save Culpepper's soul.

A moment later, the servant handed Chapuys a book with these words on the cover: *Declamation on the Nobility and Preeminence of the Female Sex.*

Surrey said, "But is that all? Agrippa wrote other books, books of magic."

"Ah, yes, there were the three books he wrote," said Chapuys. "Interesting texts, though controversial. There aren't many copies that exist. Perhaps some other publisher will attempt it."

Surrey, unable to control himself, said, "And there was a fourth! A grimoire of hexes, chants, and conjurations."

The ambassador waved his hand at us dismissively. "Agrippa had nothing to do with that, I tell you. Nothing. Some charlatans assembled a book of nonsense and put his name to it. I can tell you this, for I knew him better than any other man, there is no fourth book written by Agrippa. I would swear my life on it."

39

After a distraught Surrey stormed off to find his servant waiting on the street, Chapuys took me aside and said, "You need never fear Jacquard Rolin again. He will be dealt with and the justice will be severe. Hantaras will pay as well. He redeemed himself to a certain degree by subduing Jacquard at my command, but I cannot trust a man who would work in secret on such a terrible cause."

He winced in pain, for the ambassador's gout was most severe. After gathering himself, Chapuys said, "Joanna, I must ask you, as difficult as it may be, to try to forgive me. Not just for what happened tonight but for entangling you in the conspiracy from the beginning. I was convinced that it was justified in the service of God and emperor, but now I know that what we did, what I did . . . I was wrong."

"I understand," I said.

"If there is any other service I can render you, you need only ask," he said.

Soon enough, there was.

Just a week later, the king's men arrested Culpepper on suspicion of improper relations with the queen. He had not confessed—nor had Catherine—but those who served the queen told the king's investigators of notes passed and secret meetings. The attendants were anxious to save themselves and did not hesitate to betray Catherine and Culpepper and could even have embellished their stories. Lady Rochford was the guiltiest of arranging the queen's supposed assignations—and the most anxious to betray her. But to curry favor, she told so many stories in which she played a principal part that she implicated herself in treason, too. She then denied some of it, but too late to extricate herself. Lady Rochford was arrested.

It was Thomas Culpepper whom I vowed to see. Chapuys was able to arrange it through a series of enormous bribes. I had no book of magic to aid me, just prayer. And friendship. Those were the only things I brought with me to the Tower of London.

"You should not be alone in the same cell as this prisoner," said Sir John Gage, who had replaced the failing Sir William Kingston as constable of the Tower. "He is a despicable man."

"That is the arrangement," I said. "No matter what occurs, I give you my word that you will not be blamed."

At last the door swung open and I was admitted to the dark, foul cell of my friend Thomas Culpepper.

"I don't want you here," said a hoarse voice from the corner.

I picked up the sole lit candle from a table in the corner and made my way to him. Culpepper was sitting in straw, slumped over, in the opposite corner. By the candlelight, I could see his face was bruised and swollen, his eyes mere slits. His wrists were swollen as well, and stained with dried blood. This was what had become of handsome Thomas Culpepper.

"You have been tortured," I said, struggling to keep my voice steady. "Of course."

I knelt on the floor, I opened my book of Scripture.

"Joanna, don't do this to me," he said.

I began to pray:

"Hide not thy face from me; put not thy servant away in anger.
Thou has been my help; leave me not, neither forsake me,
God of my salvation.
When my father and my mother forsake me,
then the Lord will take me up.
Teach me, my Lord, and lead me in a plain path,
because of mine enemies.

I must believe to see the Lord in the land of goodness.
Wait on the Lord, be of good courage, and he shall strengthen thine heart.
Wait, I say, on the Lord."

I kept praying aloud and sharing psalms and words of courage. It took a long time for Culpepper to break his silence. An hour. Perhaps two. But when I paused between prayers, I heard a strange guttural moaning from the straw. He covered his face with his hands while he sobbed for a long time.

I knelt by his side. "I know about the covenant," I said. "I know everything."

"Surrey told you?"

"Some of it, he did," I said. "Some of it I pieced together myself."

Culpepper laughed, but it sounded more like choking. "Always so clever, that's my Joanna Stafford." He turned quiet. "I had thought that if anyone would visit me, it would be the Earl of Surrey."

"He has gone back to East Anglia with his father," I said heavily. "He did not wish to go—he fought against the duke harder than I've ever seen him do. But in the end, he always sides with his father, and his father has abandoned Catherine and anyone associated with her. He is trying to ride this out in his Norfolk stronghold."

Culpepper was silent.

"Tell me what happened to you," I said. "Please, I want to help you in any way I can."

Culpepper swallowed, and then told his story.

"After Hungerford was arrested, I was undone," he said. "I thought that any moment, while I was attending the king, I'd be taken. Arrested, tortured, and killed. It does things to a man, suffering that for weeks. I started to drink wine, more and more, and to spend my time with those of poor conduct who've sought me out every day since I was appointed to the king's chamber—my brother chief among them. I lost myself to their company. When Hungerford was beheaded with Cromwell, I thought I was safe. I told myself, 'That is the sacrifice he made, what we all made, to kill

Cromwell.' But then—the king did not change! He was no more
merciful after Cromwell was removed. He killed more people than
ever, from Protestant preachers to old Catholics and a seventy-year-
old woman who'd committed no crime at all. I began to see that it
had all been for nothing. And I hated him. While I was dressing
him, and gambling with him, and running his errands and laughing
at his jokes, I hated him. I thought I would go mad from it."

Culpepper looked down at the straw-covered floor of his cell,
unwilling to meet my gaze. "One day, I had to take a message to the
queen and I could see that she still loved me. I decided this was how
I would take my revenge on him for turning my life into hell."

"Do you think it was the covenant that changed you?" I asked.

Culpepper was silent for a while. "I don't know what happened
that night—I can't be sure of anything. Did Orobas's spells and
magic turn the king away from Cromwell? Or was it just in his nature to kill those he tires of, and I was too blind to see it?"

It was hard to do, but I told Culpepper what I'd learned, that
Agrippa most likely did not write the fourth book. The grimoire was
filled with meaningless gibberish; its blasphemous incantations did
not come from the magus.

Culpepper began to weep again. "Fools, all of us. Surrey and
Hungerford, they recruited me to their covenant, but I was eager to
do it, to commit any sin for what I thought was glory. Even if we did
not use the black arts that night, did not summon the powers of the
devil, I am damned. There are so many things, but among the worst
is what I did to Catherine. She would never have betrayed the king
with anyone else but me."

"Did you love her?" I asked.

"I have never loved anyone," he said simply. "I do not believe it is
in my nature. I think the kind of man drawn to the court of Henry
the Eighth is at heart a weak man, and I am the weakest of all."

"I don't believe that," I said. "You helped me when there was
nothing to be gained by it. There is goodness in you. You are not beyond God's love, of that I am certain."

He took a deep breath and said, "Nonetheless, I deserve death. But Catherine doesn't. Is there anything you can do—any way you can help her? The last thing I heard was that the king might send her to a nunnery."

There are no more nunneries in England. But this gave me another thought, and then a plan.

I said, "I promise you I will try to help her."

And with a final prayer and a good-bye, I left.

On December 10, Thomas Culpepper was executed at Tyburn. The king had condemned him to the full penalty of being hanged, drawn, and quartered. At the last moment, it was commuted to a swift beheading.

I did not bear witness.

There was only one hope now for Catherine Howard, and it would put me in more danger than I'd ever faced before in the court of Henry VIII.

40

Although Catherine had never been a woman of much religious conviction, truth be told, and her crimes were of a moral nature, her husband the king commanded, after he was certain of her guilt of adultery, that she be taken to Syon Abbey, once a prestigious nunnery, rather than to the Tower of London. No one was sure what would happen to her next, although most assumed she would follow the example of her cousin Anne Boleyn and be sent to the block. Still, Queen Anne was dispatched swiftly, with just seventeen days between her arrest and her decapitation. It was not the same with Queen Catherine. Some said the king was indecisive with grief, others that he had sworn to torture Catherine personally. Still others said he mulled over who should be his sixth wife.

King Henry returned to Hampton Court after his wife had been removed to Syon. I sent two letters to Sir Thomas Heanage, chief gentleman of the privy chamber and groom of the stool, asking to see the king. I had no clear idea who was in power now. Norfolk had fled and his ally Bishop Gardiner was weakened. Some said the Seymour brothers were in ascendance. Others were betting on Wriothesley. No matter who fought their deadly game for a seat at the council table, I suspected that Heanage still held sway with the king. Just a few days after Culpepper's execution, a message came back granting my request. That month at Whitehall had taught me enough.

The first snowfall of the season was settling on the grand red-brick walls and towers of Hampton Court when I was ushered inside. A smooth-faced page escorted me to the presence chamber, as graceful as Thomas Culpepper must have been when he eagerly began serving the king of England.

Along the way, tapestries shivered and dazzled along the walls—different ones, ones I had not studied and catalogued in Whitehall. As Heanage moved inside the innermost chamber to announce me, I was struck by the one hanging on the opposite landing, the Hercules tapestry I'd seen and approved purchase of in Brussels. Here was the half man half god committing his acts of strength, conquest, and lechery.

Henry VIII sat under his cloth of state, his leg propped up, completely alone except for Heanage. I had not seen the king for eighteen months. He looked to have aged by at least a decade. The ruddiness was gone from his skin. Although he wore a purple robe lined with fur and his fingers were laden with diamonds, the overwhelming color was gray: wrinkled pasty gray skin and hair now more gray than red.

As I sank into a curtsy, I felt an emotion I never expected and did not welcome: pity.

"I thank Your Majesty for granting this audience when I know that I have offended you," I said. "I did not carry out my duties as tapestry mistress to your satisfaction."

"You did prove a disappointment," he said indifferently.

"I propose to remedy that with offering myself in a new position of service," I said.

He said nothing and did nothing but raise an eyebrow.

I took a deep breath and said, "I have experience in a nunnery. Install Queen Catherine in a nunnery of your creation and I will run it for you and see that all is done the way you would wish. You can be merciful, knowing that I, your kinswoman, will ensure she is kept away from the world."

Henry VIII's gray face mottled with red. His voice shrill, he said, "Do you not realize there are laws in our kingdom and she broke the law? She is guilty of high treason."

I took a step closer and then knelt, bowing my head.

"You are the law," I said. "You are our anointed king and supreme head of the Church of England."

This was the moment. He would either move toward considering my idea or punish me savagely for suggesting it.

But Henry VIII did neither.

"Do you think I do not realize how they laugh at me?" he said, his voice now rough with pain and grief. "How forsaken I appear to every man in England. If I let Catherine live, I am no longer a ruler of this land." He had dropped the royal "we," I realized with a start.

I could think of nothing else to say but, "She is nineteen. Can you not find it in your heart to show mercy?"

There was silence as I stared at the polished floor, still on my knees. I prayed to God to move the king's heart. Through my prayers, the stench of the king made me feel like choking. There was no more musk or floral waters. There was only the rotting of his leg. Like the stench of death.

"If I spare her, I could lose my throne."

I understood now. For so many years I'd feared him, we'd all of us feared him. But beneath the jewels, crowns, satins, and furs, behind the heroic tapestries and posturing murals, was the truly terrified man. So much of the violence, both of the flesh and the soul, was committed from his fear, not his strength. Culpepper said weak men were drawn to the center of the court. But at the center was the weakest of all.

"You may see her, to say farewell," said Henry. "That is all I can do."

I rose and curtsied a last time, my eyes filling with tears, as I managed to choke out, "I thank Your Majesty."

Sir Thomas Heanage gently guided me from the chamber and made the arrangement for me to go to Syon.

As I walked across the room once used by sisters and novices and abbey servants and now devoted solely to Catherine, I saw a woman changed as much as her husband. She had lost all her plump, dimpled, girlish prettiness. The fallen queen who sat rigid in her chair was a haunted beauty of high cheekbones and solemn eyes.

"Joanna," she said simply, her hands in her lap.

"I'm told I can only have a moment or two," I said.

"Shall we pray together?" she asked.

"If you wish," I said, "but I think I should tell you about what happened when I saw Thomas Culpepper."

Her face blazed with life. "You saw him?" she said. "I thought no one saw him."

I told her that I had prayed with and spoken to Culpepper. "I know that you loved Thomas very much."

She bowed her head. "I tried my best to be a good wife, to be the queen that Henry wanted me to be, what my uncle the Duke of Norfolk needed me to be." She paused. "In some ways, my husband is not as terrible a man as you think he is, Joanna. In other ways, he is very much worse." Her face hardened at some difficult memory. "But I betrayed him, and now no one speaks for me or attempts to see me. Except for you."

"I am so sorry," I said.

"Some days I have courage, like today, but others I am so afraid, Joanna." Her voice trembled. "Is there anything you can tell me that Thomas said, anything that could help me through what we both know is still to come?"

"He said his chief regret was hurting you, for committing this sin," I said.

She took that in. At first it comforted her, but then her face fell again. "Nothing else, Joanna?" she asked, desperate. "Nothing to help me?"

I took a deep breath, asking God for forgiveness. I would pray for her, by her side, now, and before the altar of every church I entered for the rest of my life. But there was something I could do for her today to ease her suffering, even though to do so was a sin.

I said, "Thomas told me that you were the only person in his life he had ever loved."

Catherine collapsed into my arms, saying, "Thank you," again and again. The last words she spoke to me rang in my ears for days and weeks afterward: *You were always my dearest friend.*

41

A nd so, the week before Christmas, I returned to Dartford for good. I planned never to set foot in the court of Henry VIII again. And I would never sell *The Sorrow of Niobe*. I would keep it with me, always. Before leaving London, I'd heard the king ordered the destruction of every painting of Catherine Howard, the works created by Master Hans Holbein and every other artist. My tapestry could be the only image of her that survived.

I ordered another drawing from Brussels. I would not have royal commissions, but there were other people in England who would pay good money for a beautiful tapestry.

By the time the new drawing arrived, I would be busy indeed. I'd received word from Stafford Castle—my cousin Henry had finally agreed to send Arthur back to Dartford. His mind had been changed by the Earl of Surrey, who apparently materialized at Stafford Castle and made a passionate case for me. Being half Stafford, he was listened to. What a passionate, reckless person my cousin was. So he had been listening in Whitehall when I told him how much I wanted to get Arthur back. All these months later, he decided to do something about it. He careened through life, damaging some people's fortunes, repairing others. I suspected there was guilt in his actions, but if it brought Arthur to me, I didn't care.

Tapestries to weave, Arthur to raise, friends to cherish. It was what I wished for. Yet soon there was more.

The day before Christmas, Edmund reappeared. I saw his familiar gait as he made his way up the High Street, his white-gold hair gleaming in the winter sun. I went back to my house, considering what to do. After an hour of pacing around my house, I followed in the direction I had seen him walk.

My heart pounded as I made my way up the street, passing the townsfolk I had come to know. Gregory, our onetime porter, waved to me, his baby daughter in his arms, and I forced myself to smile in return.

Yes, Edmund returned to the infirmary he once ran. It had stood empty, the simple furniture remaining but the medicines and herbs sold off. He had a box of fresh potions with him, and was restocking the shelves.

"Oh, Joanna, you're here," he said, smiling as I slipped in the door.

"Are you no longer in the employ of Bishop Gardiner?" I asked.

"No," said Edmund. "It was impossible."

He explained that he had resigned as secretary for the bishop. The reason was the work he had been compelled to do to substantiate the bill to be put through Parliament to justify the execution of Catherine Howard. "It was clear to me that an annulment was more just because her intimacy with Francis Dereham constituted a marital precontract," said Edmund. "And I believe the king could have been persuaded, but Bishop Gardiner would not risk attempting it."

"No, of course he wouldn't," I said bitterly.

Edmund said, "I think it came down to a question of how much was I willing to sacrifice of my soul, my conscience, for what Bishop Gardiner called a higher purpose. He would do anything if it meant bringing him—and this kingdom—close to God."

"He has always been that way."

"The bishop felt that to fight to spare Queen Catherine's life would weaken him too greatly and that the spiritual cause in England was more important." He shuddered. "I could not live with myself, though, the sins of omission when it came to the queen. I could not do it."

"He must have been angry with you," I said.

Edmund said quietly, "The bishop was disappointed."

Glancing at the half-stocked apothecary shelves, I said, "So now you will use all of those skills in diplomacy and negotiation, your study of theology, here, in Dartford?"

Edmund, placing his hand on a box of dried, greenish-brown herbs, said, "Paracelsus taught me that the meaning of creation, of the life God gives, can be understood in the properties of the humblest plant." His brown eyes saddened. "Paracelsus died at the end of September. I just had a letter telling me of it."

I told Edmund how sorry I was for his loss.

"It is time for me to step forward—I have too long sought out mentors to guide me: my priors when I was a friar, Bishop Gardiner, even Paracelsus." He looked out the window and then back at me. "The bishop said that he would still sponsor the exception allowing me to marry. I shall be an apothecary for the rest of my days. My vows as a Dominican friar can be permanently set aside."

I sat down at his apothecary bench, fingered the familiar grooves in the wood.

"Is that what you really want, Edmund?" I asked.

"Yes," he said.

I looked at Edmund for a long moment. I had to be certain. When I knew that I was, I took out the letter I'd brought with me when I saw his return. John Cheke sent it to me, with an accompanying note: "Once I showed you a letter to bring about a result. Now I share with you another letter, and I think you will see why."

I put the letter on the table. "You wrote this to John Cheke in Regensburg, before I came," I said. "In it you expressed excitement because you'd met someone at the Diet who spoke of forming a new order and you were considering joining."

Edmund stared at the page of his own writing. "Yes," he said. "The pope last year gave permission to Ignatius of Loyola to form a Society of Jesus, to strengthen and purify the Catholic Church." He looked up at me. "But the order is based in Rome. And the men who join it must be ordained priests."

"I know that," I said.

Edmund's sensitive face quivered with warring emotions. "But, Joanna," he said so softly I could barely hear him, "I don't want to leave you again."

"You can't go back, neither of us can," I said. "What we must do is seek ways to go forward. There is an artist in the king's court, his name is Hans Holbein. He became my friend. He spoke to me of the need for transformation. I was never certain of what he meant until today."

Edmund nodded, closing his eyes.

"It is a most confusing world, full of danger and sorrow," I said. "But there are possibilities, too. I know that your hope for our church is what gave you strength. You have to follow that hope."

He opened his eyes and said, "You are the only woman I ever loved, and the only woman I shall ever love."

I pushed myself up from the apothecary table and I said good-bye to Edmund Sommerville.

I needed to ask three different people where the house of Geoffrey Scovill was. The tanner knew, and I set out, the winter sun creating a bit of a muck on the narrow road leading out of town. By the time I'd reached his small farmhouse, my skirts were drenched and dirty.

Geoffrey was chopping wood behind his house. I called out to him when the ax was down. I knew that he would be surprised by my arrival and I certainly didn't want the ax to fly out of his hand.

"May I speak with you?" I asked.

He took a long look at me, a smile curled and was gone, and he said, "I suppose so, but Christmas is tomorrow, and I have many matters to attend to."

In his kitchen, he poured me some sweet wine to sip while he lit a fire. Then, sitting down across from me, he said, "What's wrong, Joanna?"

"Quite a few things," I said. "I hope you can help."

He nodded, resigned. "Please relay the list."

I said, "What's wrong is that I don't have you to talk to. Or to walk with, to laugh with, to quarrel with. I don't have you to make plans with."

Geoffrey showed no reaction.

This was a mistake.

My heart beginning a fast, painful beat, I went on. "I suppose you are right—we don't get on well."

"No, we don't," Geoffrey said. He was coming around, pulling me to my feet and kissing me, cupping my face in his hands, pulling off my cap so he could run his hands through my hair.

"You came," he said, kissing my throat. "You finally came."

"I wasn't sure you wanted me to," I said. "We've been here, in Dartford, for three months, and you didn't say a word."

"I made a new covenant with myself, Joanna. I vowed that I would not harry you or work to persuade you or anything else. If we are to marry, then it must be what you really want. Not many women would come to a man to tell him how they feel. But you're not a typical woman, Joanna. I just had to wait."

I kissed Geoffrey, the sort of kiss that I knew would banish any doubts that he could have about me ever again. The fire crackled and snapped, and finally burned down, before we let go of each other.

"Geoffrey," I whispered, "Merry Christmas."

And we laughed, together, and I kissed him again, and told Geoffrey Scovill to rebuild the fire.

LIST OF CHARACTERS

THE STAFFORDS

Joanna Stafford, former Dominican novice

Sir Richard Stafford, Joanna's father and younger brother to the Duke of Buckingham

Lady Isabella Stafford, Joanna's mother and maid of honor to Catherine of Aragon

Henry Stafford, third Duke of Buckingham, executed 1521

Margaret Bulmer, illegitimate daughter of Buckingham, executed 1537

Arthur Bulmer, Margaret's son

Lord Henry Stafford, Buckingham's oldest son

Lady Ursula Stafford, Lord Henry's wife and daughter of Margaret Pole

THE TUDORS

Henry VIII, crowned king of England in 1509

Anne of Cleves, fourth queen of Henry VIII

Mary Tudor, Henry VIII's daughter by his first wife, Catherine of Aragon

Elizabeth Tudor, Henry VIII's daughter by his second wife, Anne Boleyn

Edward Tudor, Henry VIII's son by his third wife, Jane Seymour

THE HOWARDS

Thomas Howard, third Duke of Norfolk

Henry Howard, Earl of Surrey, the duke's heir

Catherine Howard, daughter of Edmund Howard, the duke's younger brother

Charles Howard, Catherine's brother

Elizabeth Howard, Duchess of Norfolk and daughter of the Duke of Buckingham

Agnes Howard, the Dowager Duchess of Norfolk, the duke's step-mother

THE KING'S COURT

Thomas Cromwell, Earl of Essex and Lord Privy Seal

Stephen Gardiner, Bishop of Winchester

Thomas Culpepper, gentleman of the privy chamber

Sir Walter Hungerford, lord of Farleigh Hungerford Castle

Hans Holbein, court painter

Jane Boleyn, Lady Rochford, widow of George Boleyn

Sir Andrew Windsor, keeper of the king's wardrobe

Sir Anthony Denny, gentleman of the privy chamber

Sir Thomas Heneage, chief gentleman of the privy chamber

Doctor William Butts, court physician

Samuel Clocksworth, barber-surgeon

Father Francis, priest and confessor in Chapel Royal

John Cheke, instructor at Cambridge University

PEOPLE OF DARTFORD

Geoffrey Scovill, constable

Edmund Sommerville, former friar of Dartford Priory

Oliver Gwinn, farmer

Agatha Gwinn, second wife of Oliver Gwinn and former novice mistress

Sister Eleanor Watson, a former nun of the priory

Father William Mote, priest of Holy Trinity Church

Gregory, clerk and former porter of the priory

IMPERIAL COURT

Charles V, Holy Roman Emperor and King of Spain

Queen Mary of Hungary, sister to Charles V and regent of the Netherlands

Eustace Chapuys, ambassador in England representing Charles V

Jacquard Rolin, spy in the service of Charles V

Pedro Hantaras, aide to Chapuys

ACKNOWLEDGMENTS

The Tapestry was written and researched, in part, in the New York Public Library, Stephen A. Schwarzman Building. Within that grand and historic building, I worked at my allotted space in the Wertheim Study, endowed for future authors and scholars by Barbara Tuchman. I am grateful to Jay Barksdale for renewing my status in the Wertheim so that I could once again take advantage of the NYPL's world-renowned collection and be inspired by the building's beauty.

The other exquisite New York City institutions I drew inspiration from were the Cloisters Museum and Gardens of the Metropolitan Museum of Art and the Cathedral of Saint John the Divine. Both of them display spectacular tapestries from the fifteenth, sixteenth, and seventeenth centuries and are sources of information on tapestry design and production.

Touchstone Books published my trilogy of novels in North America, and I am fortunate to have such a team. *The Tapestry* was acquired by the wonderful senior editor Heather Lazare, who oversaw the publication of *The Crown* and edited *The Chalice*. Lauren Spiegel edited *The Tapestry* and I am grateful for her talent and insights and her sense of humor, too, which helps in all situations. On these three books, I've been fortunate indeed to work with senior publicist Jessica Roth and marketing manager Meredith Vilarello. I thank art director Cherlynne Li, production editor Martha Schwartz and copyeditor Anne Cherry, and editorial assistant Etinosa Agbonlahor.

The Tapestry would not exist without my literary agent, Heide

Lange of Sanford J. Greenburger, and her topnotch assistants Rachel Mosner and Stephanie Delman. Without such guidance, I would be lost. I am also grateful to the agents at HSG in New York City and Abner Stein in London.

When an author sets out to dive deep into sixteenth-century history, there is no chance of success without help. I am grateful to Mike Still, assistant museum manager of the Dartford Museum, for his store of knowledge of life in Dartford in centuries past. Hans van Felius and Jochen Schenck helped me with the task of re-creating sixteenth-century Antwerp, Brussels, and Germany. Sister Mary Catharine Perry, OP, Dominican nuns of Our Lady of the Rosary, kindly read my book for accuracy. I enjoyed my theological discussions with my sister, Amy Bilyeau.

As with my first two novels, author and teacher Russell Rowland steered me in the right storytelling directions. I humbly thank my readers and send my apologies for e-mailing them chapter after chapter for reaction. I know that at times they read my manuscript at some inconvenience to themselves. I will always be grateful to Emilya Naymark and Harriet Sharrard for reading *The Tapestry*, and also for the contributions of Kris Waldherr and Judith Starkston.

I must thank my magazine family at *DuJour*: Jason and Haley Binn, editor in chief Nicole Vecchiarelli, Stephanie Jones, and the rest of our supertalented staff. A special word of thanks to James Cohen, president and CEO of Hudson Media Inc.

Other people who've helped me on my journey: Rosemarie Santini, Max Adams, M. J. Rose, Bret Watson, Bruce Fretts, Max McDonnell, Ellen Levine, Donna Bulseco, Megan Deem, Lorraine Glennon, Jessica Branch, Daryl Chen, Christie LeBlanc, Sophie Perinot and the authors of Book Pregnant, Christopher Gortner, Amy Bruno, Debra Brown, and the like-minded friends on Twitter. A special thanks to Sue Trowbridge, website designer.

Finally, my most profound gratitude to my husband and two children, for their patience with me while my head was lost in the sixteenth century. I love you with all of my heart.

BIBLIOGRAPHY

Agrippa, Henry Cornelius. *The Philosophy of Natural Magic.* Chicago: De Laurence, Scott, 1913.

Ankele, Daniel, and Denise Ankele. *Hans Holbein the Younger, 120 Renaissance Reproductions.* Grover Beach, CA: Ankele Publishing, 2011.

Aquinas, Thomas. *On Evil.* Translated by Richard Regan. New York: Oxford University Press, 2003.

Arblaster, Paul. *A History of the Low Countries.* New York: Palgrave Macmillan, 2006.

Ball, Philip. *The Devil's Doctor: Paracelsus and the World of Renaissance Magic and Science.* New York: Farrar, Straus and Giroux, 2006.

Bernard, G. W. *The King's Reformation: Henry VIII and the Remaking of the English Church.* New Haven: Yale University Press, 2005.

Boreham, Peter W. *Dartford's Royal Manor House Re-Discovered.* Dartford, Kent: Dartford Borough Council, 1991.

Bradley, Simon, and Pevsner, Nikolaus. *London 1: The City of London.* The Buildings of England. New York: Penguin, 1997.

Byrne, Muriel St. Clare, ed. *The Lisle Letters: An Abridgement.* Chicago: University of Chicago Press, 1981.

Campbell, Thomas P. *Henry VIII and the Art of Majesty: Tapestries at the Tudor Court.* New Haven: Yale University Press, 2007.

Coby, J. Patrick. *Thomas Cromwell: Machiavellian Statecraft and the English Reformation.* Plymouth, UK: Lexington Books, 2009.

Collinson, Patrick. *The Reformation: A History.* New York: Modern Library, 2004.

Corrozet, Giles. *The Dance of Death by Hans Holbein*. New York: Scott-Thaw, 1903.

Duffy, Eamon. *Saints, Sacrilege, Sedition: Religion and Conflict in the Tudor Reformation*. London: Bloomsbury, 2012.

———. *The Stripping of the Altars: Traditional Religion in England, 1400–1580*. New Haven: Yale University Press, 1992.

Dunham, S. A. *History of the Germanic Empire*. 3 volumes. London: Longman, Rees, Orme, Brown, Green, & Longman, and John Taylor, 1834–1835. The Pergamum Collections.

Fraser, Antonia. *The Wives of Henry VIII*. New York: Knopf, 1992.

Gasquet, F. A. *English Monastic Life*. London: Metheun, 1904.

Gidlow, Christopher. *Life in a Tudor Palace*. New York: The History Press, 2011.

Godwin, William. *Lives of the Necromancers*. London, 1834.

Grimm, Taylor. *The Complete Brothers Grimm Fairy Tales*. New York: Gramercy Books, 1981.

Hunter, George Leland. *Tapestries: Their Origin, History and Renaissance*. New York: John Lane Company, 1912.

Hutchinson, Robert. *Thomas Cromwell: The Rise and Fall of Henry VIII's Most Notorious Minister*. New York: St. Martin's Press, 2009.

Lee, Paul. *Nunneries, Learning and Spirituality in Late Medieval English Society: The Dominican Priory of Dartford*. York, UK: University of York: York Medieval Press in association with the Boydell Press, 2001.

Loades, David. *Catherine Howard: The Adulterous Wife of Henry VIII*. Stroud, Gloucestershire: Amberly, 2012.

Mackay, Lauren. *Inside the Tudor Court: Henry VIII and His Six Wives through the Writings of the Spanish Ambassador Eustace Chapuys*. Stroud, UK: Amberly, 2014.

Maltby, William. *The Reign of Charles V*. New York: Palgrave, 2002.

Muller, James Arthur. *Stephen Gardiner and the Tudor Reaction*. New York: Macmillan, 1926.

Norman, Gertrude. *A Brief History of Bavaria*. Munich: Heinrich Jaffe, 1906.

Norton, Elizabeth. *Anne of Cleves: Henry VIII's Discarded Bride*. Stroud, UK: Amberly Publishing, 2009.

Redworth, Glyn. *In Defence of the Church Catholic: The Life of Stephen Gardiner.* Cambridge, MA: Blackwell Publishing, 1990.

Ridley, Jasper. Henry. *VIII: The Politics of Tyranny.* New York: Viking, 1985.

Rofocale, Lucien. *Necromancy the Forbidden Art.* Create Space, 2011.

Shepherd, Robert. *Westminster: A Biography: From Earliest Times to the Present.* London: Bloomsbury, 2012.

Smith, Lacey Baldwin. *Catherine Howard.* Stroud, UK: Amberly Publishing, 2010.

Starkey, David. *The Reign of Henry VIII: Personalities and Politics.* 1985. Reprint, London: Vintage, 2002.

Stow, John. *A Survey of London: Written in the Year 1598.* Introduction by Antonia Fraser. Phoenix Mill, UK: Sutton Publishing, 1994.

Thomas, Keith. *Religion and the Decline of Magic: Studies in Popular Beliefs in Sixteenth and Seventeenth Century England.* New York: Penguin, 2003.

Thurley, Simon. *Whitehall Palace: An Architectural History of the Royal Apartments, 1240–1690.* New Haven: Yale University Press: 1999.

Warnicke, Retha M. *The Marrying of Anne of Cleves: Royal Protocol in Early Modern England.* Cambridge: Cambridge University Press, 2000.

Way, Twigs. *The Tudor Garden: 1485–1603.* Oxford: Shire Library, 2013.

Weir, Alison. *Henry VIII: The King and His Court.* New York: Ballantine Books, 2001.

Wolf, Norbert. *Hans Holbein the Younger, 1497/98–1543: The German Raphael.* Los Angeles: Taschen, 2004.

Woolley, Benjamin. *The Queen's Conjurer: The Science and Magic of Dr. John Dee.* New York: Henry Holt, 2001.